The Purse

Julie A. Burns

Copyright © 2016 Julie A. Burns

All rights reserved.

No part of this book may be reproduced in any form, including photocopying, recording, or other electronic or mechanical methods—except in the case of brief quotations embodied in articles or reviews—without written permission by the publisher.

ISBN: 978-0-578-17703-8

First Edition February 2016

Rambunctious Ramblings Publishing Inc.
Norristown, Pennsylvania 19401, USA

www.ramrampublishing.com

For Dawn.

Without you, this book would have never been written. It was you who showed me the original "purse" and taught me to find joy when things were at their worst. You were a force of nature in my life that will always be with me. I will see you again.

Acknowledgements

I would like to thank RRPI, and especially Aaron Hughes, for taking a chance.

A huge thank you to Kathrin Hutson, the best editor ever. Without her, I would be lost in editing.

Cindy, you are my world.

Carey Burke Roberts, for your unwavering belief and support.

My daughter, Brittany Burns, thank you for making me NANA to Sophie Ann. Best job ever.

Chapter One

LYDIA QUICKLY PUT DOWN the phone, grabbed her keys, and raced outside to her car. She'd expected the news, but still the feeling was strange. William Blackwell was near the end of his life. Lydia climbed into her new Jeep Cherokee she had just bought the month before and sat at the steering wheel, lost in thought. For a brief moment, she hugged the steering wheel, put her head down, and cried. Finally, she sat back and dried her eyes. As the autumn leaves danced around her windshield, she saw her father's face as she'd seen it so many autumns before. How he loved this time of year. Her father used to say it made him feel so alive, witnessing the changing of the seasons. If only he could feel that now. Lydia took a deep breath, put her car in reverse, and backed out of her driveway.

During the drive to Kenilworth, Lydia reflected on her father's life, wondering what it all meant to him. She knew he would never tell her, but there had to be something missing. Rarely was there anyone of importance in the house, especially women. Lydia could only assume that her mother had been the real love of his life and he was just too devastated to ever marry again. Lydia had no memories of the woman. After all, she had only been three years old at the time of her mother's fatal car accident. The void left by Cassandra Lexington Blackwell's absence, however, was one that Lydia felt every day of her life.

At thirty-eight, Lydia Blackwell was a striking woman, taller than most, but not quite six-foot, with long, flowing black hair and hazel eyes in which many men could lose themselves. Many men, however, would not. It took several years for Lydia to realize that men didn't make her heart beat faster. It wasn't until college that she discovered her real self, thanks to a beautiful, blonde study-partner. Something in her had captured Lydia's heart and she was never the same again. To many of her friends, it had just been "experimenting". But this was Lydia's life, her soul, and her very being. Still, it wasn't everything.

For years, Lydia kept her innermost thoughts and her secret life to herself. Her father would never have understood her way of thinking—of being. It was possible he could have made the assumption. After all, there were no men around and no children. There were so many things she couldn't discuss with her father, nothing resembling emotions, or even people about whom she'd felt emotional. No, nothing like that. Certainly not even Danielle. *Oh Danielle.* Lydia's mind drifted away as she traveled the open road closer to her father's house.

Danielle Baldwin certainly had issues, but issues were Lydia's specialty. Lydia was a psychotherapist and ran her own practice in a posh suburb of Chicago. Five years had passed since she first saw Danielle smile, and now Lydia held therapy groups out of her home. So much had changed, yet somehow the feelings remained the same. Lydia still remembered it like a scene from a movie. Though Danielle wasn't a client, she could have been and probably should have been. She had only been there to accompany her friend, Susan, who had been so distraught over her last lover that she'd felt she needed professional help. How could Lydia have known what was to come?

Danielle smiled at Lydia when she called Susan into her office. Though it was just a courteous smile, Lydia noticed it. Danielle Baldwin was not what one would call beautiful, or even striking, but there was something about her and Lydia couldn't help but be fascinated. Danielle, unlike Susan, was not overtly feminine, but there was an inner magnificence in the woman that couldn't be denied. Dark curls surrounded her olive skin and she was about average height, but Lydia suspected there was nothing average about Danielle Baldwin. Lydia was intrigued by her story, whatever it might have been, and during Susan's session she Lydia learned a few things about Danielle.

Susan and Danielle were a couple years before, but had settled on friendship when things didn't work out. Danielle, Lydia discovered, was not too comfortable with her sexuality and didn't want to discuss herself, or anyone else, being gay. Apparently, it was...another issue.

So, for the next three months Danielle would accompany Susan to her sessions and Lydia got used to seeing her in the office. Then, one rainy afternoon, Susan needed to rush off to another appointment directly after her session, and since they had taken separate cars that day, Danielle and Lydia were left to themselves.

"You have a gorgeous office, Dr. Blackwell," Danielle complimented.

The office had a cozy feel to it with pastel colors on the walls and no dark paneling or hanging diplomas. Lydia felt that dark themes and displaying her degrees made her appear better than her patients, and that wasn't the message she wanted to convey because it wasn't true. Instead of a couch she had several lounging chairs and three big recliners, all positioned in a semi-circle around an oak coffee table. Lydia's desk sat in the corner, where she usually kept her laptop. Lydia answered the phones herself, making appointments and doing her own filing. It saved her money, and consequently she didn't have to charge astronomical fees like her colleagues. She didn't really care about the money or material things; she just wanted to help people make it through their hard times.

Lydia smiled. "Thank you, but really, I'm not a doctor. Just a therapist. And please, call me Lydia."

Embarrassed, Danielle gave a nervous smile. "Okay then, Lydia. It's nice to officially meet you."

"Likewise. Would you like to have a seat and chat for a minute? I promise not to charge you," Lydia offered before she could stop herself.

Danielle laughed. "Well, as long as you promise, I'd love to." Danielle sat down on one of the lounging chairs and Lydia took the other. "Susan thinks you are a wonderful therapist and easy to talk to."

"I'm pleased to hear that. It's what I strive for with my patients."

"What else do you strive for, Lydia?" Danielle asked, getting right to the point.

Lydia blushed slightly. "What do you mean?"

Danielle looked her in the eye. "You know...life, love, and the pursuit of happiness...if I may be so bold as to ask."

A nervous smile came across Lydia's face. "I strive for what everyone else strives for. I'm no different. You know, love...someone to count on and be there for when the going gets tough. And passion is always good."

Danielle glanced quickly at Lydia's hand. "I don't see a wedding ring. You mean no man has been smart enough to snatch you up?"

Lydia laughed at the question and answered her distinctly, "No, no man has."

Danielle's brown eyes lit up suddenly. "Oh really? How fascinating. So you are—"

"A lesbian," Lydia interjected with a smile. She never knew why it had taken so long to utter the word and not care what the world thought about it. "Just like you," she added.

Danielle fidgeted in her seat. "Well, I don't like to label myself. I'm just me. I'm not gay or straight or anything."

Lydia rolled her eyes. "Isn't that a cop out, Danielle?"

"I don't think so. I just choose not to label myself, that's all. There's more to me than my sexuality," she stated.

"I quite agree."

Danielle glanced at her watch. "Would you like to go for a drink? I'm enjoying this conversation too much to have it end."

"Of course. I'd love to," Lydia agreed.

And that had been the beginning of it all.

As Lydia pulled up to her father's mansion, she had to stop the memories from flooding her mind or they would overwhelm her. It was time to concentrate on life in the present, and now her father needed her. Lost in her own memories, Lydia didn't hear the knock on the window. Startled, she jumped in her seat and rolled down the window when she noticed Jackson standing on the other side.

"I'm sorry, Miss Lydia. I didn't mean to frighten you. Apparently, you were far away," he told her.

"Oh, hello, Jackson...yes, far away in another place and another time. How is he?"

Jackson Taylor had been employed with the Blackwells for thirty-five years and had been there to watch Lydia grow into a beautiful young woman. "He's not well, honey, not well at all. I think the end is near," he stated in a faint whisper.

"I see you have his favorite vest on today, Jackson. He would love that." Lydia gave Jackson a knowing smile because she knew how Jackson adored her father, and the feeling was mutual. Jackson's distinguished looks made him appear like he was born to be a butler, but William Blackwell didn't like the formalities of uniforms. Jackson was six-foot-two and in great shape for all of his sixty years. He had salt-and-pepper hair with more salt than pepper, a neatly trimmed mustache, and a deep, raspy voice. He always wore black dress pants, a button down white shirt, and a different vest every day. That was his trademark. The gold vest he wore today was William's favorite, and Jackson wanted to honor him in a small way.

"Thank you, Miss Lydia. I hope so."

Lydia sighed as she got out of the car and walked into the big brick building with Jackson. As she ventured up the long spiral staircase that led to her father's room, her heart weighed heavy with memories of her father and his spectacular, yet somewhat mystic, life. When Lydia reached the top of the stairs, a tall man with dark hair came out of her father's room with tears in his eyes. She'd never seen this man before, but assumed he must have been a business associate of her father's; it was nice that he cared enough to come by.

The man stopped for a split second, stared into Lydia's eyes with a look of compassion, and walked by her without saying a word. Down the long hallway, she saw Rosita, the housekeeper and Lydia's nanny for many years. Rosita was the mother Lydia never knew, and the woman stepped up to Lydia and embraced her tightly.

"He's been asking for you, child," she said softly into Lydia's ear. Rosita Sanchez, now sixty-eight, had been hired all of forty-eight years before by Annabelle Blackwell, the matriarch of the Blackwell family. After a few years, Rosita worked her way up through the ranks to be the one housekeeper upon whom Annabelle depended.

Lydia nodded and walked slowly to her father's room. As she opened the pasty white door, the smell of sickness overwhelmed her senses.

"Is that you, Lydia?" the weakened voice called out.

"Yes, father, it's me," Lydia answered softly, walking to his bedside.

His gaunt appearance shocked her. He was so thin, she barely recognized him. This was not the strong, virile, handsome man she remembered. William Blackwell in his youth had been quite dashing—tall, with thick black hair and a muscular physique. He had bright blue eyes that sparkled when he smiled. Now, the chemo had made him lose all his hair and his cheekbones had sunken in. Hardly the same man.

He quietly motioned for Lydia to sit beside him on the bed. She did as instructed, then gently kissed his forehead and took his hand.

"My darling Lydia, the sweetest girl ever born. So many regrets, my girl. Most of all, I wish I had been a better father to you. You deserved better," he whispered.

Lydia shushed him. "Father, you did the best you could. I know that and I love you for it," she reassured him.

William Blackwell shook his head at his daughter and in a hoarse voice

Continued. "No, no, darling. I must say all I have to say. I realize now that the choices I've made for you probably weren't the best ones. I see your life as it is now, and I want you to make me a promise."

With tears in her eyes, Lydia nodded and solemnly whispered, "Anything, father. Anything."

"My angel, I know what you've been through, and I know the kind of life you must lead. I love you with all of my heart, and the only thing that matters is your happiness. Promise me...never, never be ashamed of who you are or even..." William Blackwell paused to take his oxygen tube off, then looked Lydia deep in her eyes. "Or even who it is that you love. Trust me, child, I know."

Taken aback by her father's words, Lydia briefly wondered if he did know. After the many years of being secretive about her life and who she was...could he have possibly known all along? Lydia searched for words, but there were none.

"Lydia," he began, but was interrupted by a violent fit of coughing. Lydia placed his oxygen tube back on her father's face and gave him a few sips of water before he continued. "Lydia, there are so many things I should say...about your mother." His breathing suddenly became erratic, puffing out in short bursts. "Your mother...she's alive."

In one instant, William's breathing stopped and his hand slipped from Lydia's grasp. His eyes closed and there was nothing but silence in the room. William Blackwell was gone.

Chapter Two

LYDIA STARED IN DISBELIEF. He couldn't be gone. She thought she'd prepared for this moment, but somehow her readiness for her father's death was non-existent now. She nestled her head on his chest while the tears flowed from her eyes in a never-ending stream.

Finally, after what seemed to be an eternity, Lydia took a deep breath and wiped her eyes. She kissed his forehead and whispered, "Goodbye, father. I'm sorry I didn't tell you how much I loved you...not nearly enough."

Lydia walked out of her father's room and down the spiral staircase toward the library, but with every step she saw the wall to her left covered in memories. She stopped at the landing and sat on the wooden steps, mesmerized by each photograph. Some were of people she knew, but most were of those she didn't know. Her father had traveled with friends Lydia didn't even know he had, and she realized then how little she'd really known her father. Now it was too late. Lydia stood up, dried her eyes, and took in a tortured breath. It was time to begin making the arrangements.

The funeral would not be lavish, nor would it be some big, social gathering one might expect from William Blackwell, a prominent force on Michigan Avenue as a financial broker and lawyer for many years. He'd made an enormous amount of money early on in his career and chose to retire at fifty-five. Now, ten years later, he was gone. And in true William Blackwell fashion, his Will specifically stated his intentions. The funeral was to be simple and private, with only family and friends in attendance. The actual service and burial were to be in the back lot by the gazebo, just a few yards from the rose bushes he loved and toiled over for thirty years.

Lydia thought it odd that a man like her father, so strong and the epitome of masculinity, could nurture anything as delicate as roses. But no one could deny how extraordinary they were, which said much for the man who grew them.

Lydia's mind was so occupied with making arrangements for her father's burial that she hadn't given one moment's thought to his last words. Such a devastatingly powerful disease cancer was to make someone so delirious. Hypnotized by the fragments of thought running through her brain, Lydia did not hear Jackson and Rosita enter the library.

"Miss Lydia?" Jackson's voice was soft.

Lydia turned around, startled for a second. "Oh, Jackson...Rosita...I'm sorry, I didn't even hear you come in. I'm so...so...lost." Lydia stood and walked over to embrace them both. They'd been her surrogate parents and, sometimes, better than the real thing.

"Sweetie, we are so sorry about your father. We loved him..." Jackson's voice trailed off before he could finish.

"I know, I know. I don't know what he would have done...what I would have done, without you two all these years."

Rosita put her hand on Lydia's shoulder. "At least he is not suffering any longer."

Lydia smiled faintly and nodded. She then stopped and suddenly recalled her father's last words, shaking her head in amazement and disbelief. "It's really bizarre how irrational people become at the end, isn't it?"

"How so, Miss Lydia?" Jackson pressed.

Lydia half-smiled and said, "My father's last words were 'Your mother is still alive.' Isn't that strange? After all these years, never discussing her at all or even allowing the mere mention of her name, and yet she was his last thought."

The room suddenly went silent. Rosita gave Jackson a frenzied glance, then cleared her throat. "That is strange."

As if awakened from a trance, Lydia noticed the apprehension between Jackson and Rosita. "What's wrong with you two? You look like you've seen a ghost."

"Oh, it's nothing, dear. It's just so shocking, that's all." Rosita looked at Jackson. "Jackson, there's something in the kitchen I need to show you right away," she hinted.

"What?" Jackson appeared not to sense Rosita's hurried tone. "I just came from the kitchen, and believe me, there's nothing to see." Rosita suddenly pinched Jackson's behind. "Ouch, woman! What has gotten into you? Are you mad?" Jackson shrieked.

"No, but I'm going to be if you don't come with me now!" Rosita exclaimed.

Rubbing his back end, Jackson finally followed Rosita as she pushed open the swinging door to the kitchen. "Now what in bloody hell is so damned important that you—" Jackson began, but was soon interrupted.

***

The kitchen was Rosita's realm. William had let Rosita take over the kitchen and make it her own after his mother died. The cabinets stayed the same; the deep, rich mahogany that went along with the rest of the house was too beautiful to part with, but the walls, appliances, and furnishings were all Rosita. The walls had been painted in bright yellows and reds with a Mexican flare that reminded Rosita of her birthplace. Above the long center island hung pots and pans, and the small kitchen nook served as the place where Rosita, Jackson, and any other hired help coming in usually ate. William had always told both Rosita and Jackson that they were family, and not just hired help. And they'd grown to act like it.

"Christ! Are you that stupid or are you trying to impress me?" Rosita howled. "Don't you get it?" She thought she'd give the man a minute to compose all the parts of his brain.

"Get what? What the hell is going on?"

"Oh, God. You really don't get it, do you? Did you hear what Lydia said? Mr. Blackwell told her that her mother is still alive! My God, how could he tell her that now, after all these years?" Rosita paced around the room and then stopped. "He said he would take it to the grave. He almost made it."

"What are we supposed to do, Rosie? We made that idiotic promise all those years ago never to talk about it." Jackson gently touched Rosita's arm. "I know you're big on loyalty, but this is a secret that never should have been. She's a grown woman, now. Don't you think it's time she knew the truth?"

Rosita could not say a word.

"And even now," Jackson added, "all she thinks is that he was delirious and out of his ever-lovin' mind."

"Jackson, we cannot tell her. We simply cannot. Yes, she's bound to find out sooner or later, but it cannot be from us. Do you understand me?" Rosita glared at her counterpart.

Jackson Taylor shook his head in disagreement. "Rosita, I will not volunteer the information, but if she asks, I won't lie to her. Let's just pray she finds out on her own, because one day she's going to hate us for keeping the truth from her."

Rosita stared Jackson down with determination. "That's a chance we'll have to take."

Chapter Three

SEPTEMBER IN ILLINOIS WAS indeed beautiful, especially at the Blackwell Estates. The autumn leaves were beginning to turn and, if the breeze was right, the fresh aroma of the creek water would capture the senses. It was a beautiful day for a funeral, the weather seemingly a telling sign of William Blackwell. Lydia knew her father must be looking down upon the day to be sure things were picture-perfect.

Lydia dressed in her old room for the funeral. It was a day she had dreaded for the past year. She wore a respectable black dress—short sleeves with delicate black lace down the front—and a matching jacket. Lydia Blackwell abhorred high heels. She could never understand being uncomfortable for fashion, even though women had done it for eons. Not Lydia. She wasn't the make-up and nails type, but she could be breathtaking, given the chance.

She took stock of herself in the mirror and decided she was presentable. Taking a deep breath, she gazed all around her. Her room was gorgeous, though she hadn't spent much time in it as an adult. There were a number of family heirlooms strung about, from the old cedar chest to the cherry wood dresser and mirror, down to the comb and brush set and little delicate doilies for her night tables. They were things she'd been told belonged to her mother before she died. Lydia cherished them, though she didn't exactly know why.

Lydia sat on the edge of her king sized canopy bed and thought of her mother. Had she lived, Cassandra Blackwell would be with her now and Lydia herself wouldn't be the one carrying the load. She let out a heavy sigh. There was no sense in thinking those thoughts. Just as she rose from the bed, attempting to shake out the cobwebs, she caught a glimpse of something extremely familiar—*someone* familiar, three stories down, right there in the garden.

"Oh, my God. What the hell is she—" Lydia interrupted herself to race down to the gazebo, her heart pounding out of her chest along the way. Right when she was about to step outside, she slowed down to a casual stroll, not wanting to appear anxious.

"Danielle...what a fascinating surprise. I wouldn't have expected you to be here...especially considering the fact that we haven't spoken since—" Lydia stopped in mid-sentence when Danielle finished her thought.

"Since you left me," she stated somberly.

Lydia nodded and whispered, "Yes…since then."

Danielle nodded back. She took a deep breath and spoke nervously. "Lydia, I read about your father in the paper and I want you to know how sorry I am. I know how much he meant to you." She reached out and touched Lydia's hand.

Lydia nervously looked around at the people gathering in the back lot and skillfully pulled her hand away from Danielle's grasp. She paused for a moment, searching for the words to say to this woman. "Thank you, Danielle. It says a lot to me that you're here, though it's quite unexpected."

"Many things have been unexpected, love. Not all good and not all bad." Danielle had not even noticed the term of endearment she'd used. But Lydia did.

"Love." Lydia sighed, her memory taking her back in time.

Suddenly, Danielle realized what word she'd let pass her lips. Instantly, it had felt natural, but it didn't sound that way. "I'm sorry, I didn't mean to... I mean… Oh, dammit, Lydia. I don't know what I mean or don't mean anymore. Do you have a few minutes for me right now? I know the timing is awful, but I really need to talk to you." Danielle searched Lydia's eyes. "I don't deserve your time, but I need it."

"You surprise me, wanting to talk after all this time. Why now?"

Lydia was intrigued, but still didn't want to appear eager. She wanted Danielle to work for it.

"I just needed to see you, talk to you. Please, just give me a few moments...for everything we've shared together," Danielle pleaded.

Lydia finally agreed. "Okay. I have a few minutes before the service begins. Let's go inside."

Danielle followed Lydia inside the beautiful mansion, through the dark wooden hallways, and around corners until finally they reached their destination. The library was Lydia's favorite room. Once Danielle entered the massive book-filled space, Lydia gently closed the door behind her. Danielle seemed so awestruck by the elegance of the bookshelves and the extreme detail in the woodwork that Lydia wondered if perhaps she'd forgotten why she was there. The bookshelves were built ten-high on all walls, surrounding a cozy fireplace, soft, overstuffed chairs, two sofas, and a coffee table. "Wow," Danielle voiced aloud. "I never knew—"

"So what was it you wanted to discuss?" Lydia interrupted.

"Lydia...I...damn, I don't know where to begin." Danielle stumbled over the words.

Lydia found it interesting that Danielle was so nervous. "How about at the beginning?"

"Ah, a very good place to start," Danielle quipped with a faint laugh.

"Funny." Lydia smiled, but only for a split second.

"I guess I'll start by telling you...how right you were to leave me when you did," she admitted.

The confession shocked Lydia. "Really? That sounds strange coming from you, Dani." She was even more intrigued by whatever it could possibly be her former lover really wanted.

"I know, Lydia, but I've been through a lot since you left. You leaving hurt me in ways I've never known before. I didn't see the problem for what it was."

"What was it, Danielle?" Lydia wanted her to say it.

"I know what you want me to say...the problem was my

drinking." Danielle sighed and looked off in the distance. "That wasn't all of it, Dani...and I'm not saying that you were responsible for it all. I never have. I completely shut down and avoided things I really shouldn't have," Lydia admitted.

"I think we both did," Danielle replied. "I did more of that after you left. I never realized the effect my drinking had on you. My opinion was that if someone didn't like it, that was their problem, not mine. But I was wrong. It was always my problem." Danielle walked around the room, looking nervous and worried about something. "It's amazing that I remember anything from that time. I was in such a drunken fog those last few months we were together. I can't imagine the hell you went through. God knows I wouldn't listen to you."

Lydia still wasn't sure what Danielle wanted. "I see," she said, still not trusting her. "So, you've escaped the fog now, is that what you're telling me?" The tone of her own voice even startled herself.

"No, not escaped," Danielle corrected. "I walked out freely with nothing holding me back. But not before I hit bottom, of course." She looked at Lydia with wide eyes, blinking back what, for a moment, looked like forming tears. "I felt so damned angry when you left, blaming you for everything." Danielle then half-smiled. "I remember what you said to me the day you left. Do you?"

"Of course." Lydia was not about to play into her hands just yet. "But go ahead and tell me."

"You said it was easier for me to blame you than admit the truth. You were right...so right. It was easier. I thought I was tough, so tough that I didn't need anyone, that I was better off and nothing could get to me. You always saw through me...even when I didn't want you to."

Lydia fought back the tears herself. God, she couldn't let Danielle see her cry. She turned away from the woman's glance and walked over to the window. She didn't dare look in her direction. "You said you hit bottom. What happened?"

"You mean besides you leaving me?" Danielle asked, watching her intently.

Lydia let out a half-hearted laugh. "I'm sure that wasn't it,

Danielle. You barely knew I was around towards the end."

"I guess that's true," Danielle stated quietly. "I think it was a culmination of things, really. When you left, I felt betrayed, and then you were just one more reason for me to keep drinking."

Lydia could not find the words. This was not the Danielle she knew…and had loved for so long. When she didn't respond, Danielle continued.

"The alcohol was making me paranoid and it took me months to come to grips with the fact that I couldn't blame you anymore. You were the one good and true thing in my life." Danielle started to walk closer to Lydia, but Lydia felt her approaching and abruptly moved away from the window in the opposite direction.

She sighed. "I'm glad you've had these revelations, now. What else happened to cause this turnaround?"

"Well, no one came around anymore and I was alone. Then, early one morning as the sun came up, after a night of submerging myself in alcohol, I had a moment of clarity. But then I walked around the house and it just seemed so empty. I'd been alone before...for years, but somehow this was different. You were everywhere, and for as many things as you took with you, even more of you stayed there. I started remembering you in a way I hadn't allowed myself for so long. I just wish you could understand, Lydia."

Lydia's back was turned toward Danielle, but there was no denying the quiver in her voice, the wet sound of crying through her words. Danielle stepped closer to Lydia and this time did not let her escape. She touched Lydia's shoulder and turned her around to face her.

"Dammit, Lydia, I realized no one has ever loved me like that. You took care of me, even when I stepped all over you. I know that you loved me, and I also know that it took everything you had in you to leave me." She reached out to wipe the tears from Lydia's face.

Lydia's defenses were all but down, now. There was nothing left with which to fight, and there was no point. Danielle pulled Lydia closer and held her for what seemed like an eternity, and Lydia finally let herself sink into the familiar arms of the woman she'd left over a year ago. It lasted only a few moments, and then Danielle broke away from their embrace and held Lydia's face in her hands. She kissed Lydia with all the passion she'd felt for her since the beginning. Lydia returned the kiss, knowing it was what she'd wanted all along. Then, breathlessly, she pulled herself away.

"Dani...I. . .I really shouldn't be doing this. Oh, God, it would be so easy to fall into your arms...but I can't. As much as I want to."

Danielle appeared shocked by Lydia's reluctance. "Why can't you?"

"I don't think I could go back to that life...I'd be scared to," Lydia told her softly. "I can't tell you what it means to me that you're here, not just for my father's funeral, but coming to me like this. Knowing you've gotten your life together...it makes me feel so much."

"Thank you. But, you know, there's still one thing missing," Danielle whispered as she moved closer.

"What is that?" Lydia asked. She already knew the answer.

"You. I was so wrong to let you go." Danielle's voice quivered again.

"You didn't let me go," Lydia said, looking her in the eye. "There was no choice but for me to leave. You don't know how long I've waited, hoping one day you'd say these things to me, that you would understand why I left. I never thought it would come...you were so hell bent on hating me, Dani. It's difficult to imagine you this way."

Danielle followed Lydia around the room until she faced her. "I love you too much to not say these things to you. Things I should have said so long ago." Lydia couldn't say a word. She was frozen. Danielle grabbed her arm. "Did you hear me? I said I love you, Lydia!"

Tears streamed down Lydia's face. "I love you, Danielle...I've always loved you. Even now, I—"

Suddenly, the massive, wooden double doors opened. "Miss Lydia? I'm sorry dear, but it's time," Rosita said softly. She gazed at Lydia for a few seconds, then smiled at her guest and left the room, closing the doors behind her. Lydia started for the door.

"Wait. Tell me, Lydia," Danielle said, hurrying after her.

Lydia opened the right side of the door slightly and turned to look at Danielle. She knew the moment had passed and it was time to have some closure. "Dani, we all travel down the road that was meant for us. Once you get to the end of the road, all you can do is appreciate the scenery you've passed along the way, because you can never go back exactly the way you came." Lydia gave her one last glance and walked out.

Chapter Four

THE SERVICE WAS BEAUTIFUL. Lydia placed a single white rose on her father's casket as William's friends looked on. She smiled slightly, realizing William Blackwell knew exactly what he was doing. This was the most exquisite spot for her father's final resting place. The burial would not be until later in the day, since William had specified it was to be a private affair.

After she hugged the last person and they drove away, Lydia made her way back into the big mansion, the only home she'd ever known as a child. Walking into the study, just off to the right from the back entrance, she gave out a sigh of relief now that the formalities were over. Still, she couldn't shake the odd feeling left over from Danielle's visit. Danielle stayed for the funeral, out of respect for Lydia. She knew she'd been right to end things with Danielle right then, instead of making a new beginning that would only lead to more heartache. But God, it was tempting.

Lydia Blackwell opened the French doors in the study to a balcony overlooking her father's precious rose garden. She closed her eyes to soak in all the beauty. When she opened them, she looked out as far as she could see, then back down below her. She could see her father's plot from there. Her eyes stopped when she saw a dark figure by her father's casket. Looking closer, she made out the form of a man sitting on the ground with his arms wrapped around his legs.

Curious, Lydia walked outside again to the garden. Not wanting to give herself away just yet, she hid behind the gazebo. The man was elegantly dressed in a black three-piece suit, white shirt, and black tie.

Though she couldn't see his face, she heard him sobbing hysterically. The man suddenly reached over and picked up the dozen red roses on the ground next to him, then stood up. Slowly, he dropped each rose, one by one, around the shape of the burial plot. As he made his way back to where he'd started, he noticed Lydia and almost jumped.

"I'm sorry. I didn't know anyone was there," the man apologized.

Lydia smiled for a moment, but then recalled his face. This was the man who had come out of her father's bedroom the day he died. "That's all right. I didn't want to interrupt your...time." After pausing for a moment, Lydia added, "I remember seeing you the day my father died, but forgive me if I don't recall meeting you."

The man shook his head. "No, Lydia, we've never met face to face. My name is Derek Meade. Your father was truly...an extraordinary man. I was...quite close to him. I'm sorry if I intruded."

"No, really, it's all right, Mr. Meade. I know there were plenty of others who loved him. Everyone deserves their time." She eyed the man carefully, not sure she understood the connection to her father. The whole idea of a man bringing another man roses and crying his heart out seemed a bit odd. Unless…no, that couldn't be. How absurd. Lydia shook the thought from her mind quickly.

"Thank you, but please call me Derek." He smiled and turned to look back at the casket. "You know, your father was quite proud of you and loved you so."

"I always hoped so. He was a complicated man." In an instant, it occurred to Lydia that this man knew who she was right away. "My father talked about me with you?"

"Oh, yes, quite often," he said without offering more information.

"If you don't mind me asking, just how were you associated with my father?" Lydia couldn't push aside her curiosity any longer.

"We met almost forty years ago. Your father saved my life," Derek admitted, still looking down at the casket.

"How strange," Lydia remarked.

"What do you mean by that?"

"Strange that you've known my father all these years, and yet the only time I've seen you was the day he died. He never mentioned you to me, at least not that I recall." She'd grown up with most of her father's friends and acquaintances, and even though her father undoubtedly knew more people than that, it struck her that she'd never heard of this man in particular.

Derek nodded. "Yes, it does seem strange, but there are reasons." He seemed perfectly comfortable to hear she didn't have a clue who he really was.

"Derek, I find you intriguing. If you have a few minutes, would you like to come into the house for some cappuccino? I'd like to learn about those reasons."

"Well, I don't…" Derek hesitated.

Lydia wasn't going to give him a chance to refuse. "Please, Derek. I believe there were many things I didn't know about my father. It's important to me."

"All right." Derek gave her a nervous smile and followed Lydia into the mansion.

Lydia stopped abruptly just before they reached the kitchen. "You've been here before, haven't you?" She watched him closely, noticing that he seemed familiar with the layout of the rooms.

"Many times. It's a beautiful home. I've always admired it," he told her, gazing at the decor.

"I see," Lydia acknowledged softly as she pushed open the swinging door to the kitchen. They entered, and she watched the man visibly relax as he glanced around. "It must be something quite pleasant to make you smile like that, Derek."

"Why, yes, actually. It is...especially warming to be here once again."

As Lydia ground the beans to make their cappuccinos, it astounded her that this man had been virtually kept a secret from her. Quite possibly, her assumptions were correct, but she had to be sure. "So tell me, Derek...you mentioned earlier that my father saved your life. How did that happen? Do you mean figuratively or literally?"

Derek looked up at the exquisite woman who definitely held the essence of her father, only in a different package. "Actually, it's both. He saved my life in many ways. One day, maybe you will come to understand."

"With all due respect, Derek, I'm thirty-eight years old and hardly a child. I understand more than you think. I realize you want to be loyal to my father's memory, but you must be honest with me. I've encountered a number of mysteries since his death, and you are one of them."

Derek looked at her with a mixture of confusion and amusement. "I apologize. I will tell you whatever you want to know, if I can." He took a deep breath as Lydia set a cup of cappuccino in front of him with a chocolate-dipped biscotti on the side. "Thank you."

"You're welcome. Please tell me the story, Derek." Lydia sat across the table from his and made sure to look at nothing but his eyes.

He took a short taste of the drink before he began. "It was 1964, I believe, and I was walking out of a downtown Chicago bar after having a few drinks with some friends when I was jumped by three men. Your father happened to be walking from another bar and stumbled onto the scene. He rushed in to help me. Two of the men ran off, but the one kept punching me and was about to stab me. Your father hit him in the head with the butt end of his pistol he'd had strapped to his leg. We got out of there as fast as we could, and your father took me back to his guesthouse and nursed my wounds. We found we had much in common and formed a strong bond. His friendship to me all these years has never wavered."

"Wait a minute." Lydia had to stop him. "My father, William Blackwell, owned a pistol *and* a holster?" It seemed so unlike the man she knew. "Fascinating. Though I must admit, it's hard to imagine my father jumping into a fight that way," Lydia commented while picking the chocolate off her biscotti.

Derek smiled. "Your father used to do that."

Lydia returned the smile. "You seem to know a lot about him. Why is that?"

"We were close friends for many years. There's a lot I know about him." He sipped his drink again, but Lydia didn't miss the strange look when his eyes flicked up to meet hers.

"I hope you'll forgive me, Derek, but I don't buy that," she told him. It was hard for her not to let another smile slip.

"What do you mean by that?" Derek's sudden surprise seemed an act.

"Well, I'm not sure, but it's just the way you talk about him. There's something in the tone of your voice. I can't put my finger on it." Lydia paused for a moment, trying to find a better way to explain. "Don't try to fool me. I'm a therapist," she added, thinking it might make a difference.

Derek closed his eyes and sighed. "Okay. I'm going to be honest here, Lydia. It's hard to talk about...but your father and I were lovers."

Lydia's naked cookie fell from her hands. "Oh my God..."

"I understand how shocking it must be for you, and I'm sorry to have to tell you like this. But you must see that it's nothing shameful. We were just two people in the world that loved each other." Derek stared boldly at her, sitting rigidly as though he expected some other response from her.

"No, Derek, it's not shameful, but it explains many things. You have no idea." Lydia chuckled and then fell silent for a moment, trying to comprehend the notion of her father being in love with a man. "No one understands more than I do. I'm gay." Her eyes suddenly glossed over. "I wish he would have confided in me." Her voice trailed off into thin air.

"I know, Lydia...I know. And your father...he knew. Though, I don't know why he didn't tell you he knew. I begged him to, but he seemed remarkably against it," Derek added.

"That's just it, Derek. He did let on, but not until the end. He didn't come right out and say it, but...I got this amazing feeling he was giving me his blessing."

Derek touched Lydia's hand gently. "I'm glad, dear."

Lydia smiled softly and held Derek's hand. "I'm glad you had each other."

"So am I." Derek smiled. When his smile faded, he continued. "His reasons for not telling you or anyone, I believe, have to do with your grandmother. She was quite a harsh woman, if you don't mind my saying so."

"Not at all," Lydia said. "Your instincts were correct about her. She was a horrid, horrid woman. Annabelle Blackwell would never have allowed such a travesty in her son...or even her granddaughter."

"Lydia," Derek began, seemingly hoping to change the subject, "there's something I want to show you." He reached inside his jacket pocket.

"Really, Derek. I'm flattered, but not interested," Lydia joked. She felt suddenly comfortable with him now, like a part of her father was still around in someone much different.

Derek let out a hearty laugh. "Don't worry, I'm not offering. I love your sense of humor. Don't ever lose it." He then pulled out of his pocket a stunning, silver-beaded coin purse.

"Oh, Derek, it's beautiful. It reminds me of something my grandmother might have had when she was a girl. In the roaring twenties, perhaps. Where did it come from?" The elegance of the bag hypnotized her.

"Actually, it came from that very night I met your father. The man who attacked me dropped it out of his jacket when he fell to the ground. Your father picked it up and kept it, until he fell ill, when he gave it to me. It was sort of a keepsake for that moment, the day we met. Lydia, I want you to have it. Keep it with you always, to remind you of a love that can survive everything working against it." He handed the purse to her, and a single tear rolled down his face.

"Derek...I...I couldn't take this. This is a symbol of everything you and my father shared together," she told him, gently caressing the purse.

"Symbols are only good if they share a commonality. Please take it, and remember...be true to your heart, and you will never go wrong." Derek stood from the kitchen nook, kissed Lydia's cheek, and then

Lydia walked him back the way they'd come.

She heard him utter one more goodbye to William as he passed the grave site, and he waved to her as he walked to his car by the back lot.

As Lydia watched him disappear from her sight, she tearfully whispered, "No wonder my father loved you, Derek Meade."

Chapter Five

AS DEREK DROVE AWAY from the mansion in his blue '69 Mustang convertible, he smiled, thinking of Lydia and what a beautiful soul she was. She was much like her father—a subtle beauty just beyond the surface. He was glad he gave Lydia the purse. It would give her some tangible piece of a love she knew nothing about.

For years, Derek had wondered about the purse's true ownership and why William himself didn't give it to Lydia. He let out a sigh of relief and exhaustion as he pulled into his driveway in Highland Park. Kenilworth was just a mere twenty-minute drive, and he was glad to be home. It was a charming, red brick house with redwood shutters. Not quite the white picket fence, but he adored the place. Derek was never disillusioned enough to think William would ever leave the sanctity of his mansion, or even ask Derek to move in with him. The life they could have had together… Then Derek smiled. Then he remembered the life they *did* have together. It was one in a million, and Derek was so grateful.

He shut off the engine and sat quietly in the car. Everything was just a memory now. How could William really be gone? God, he missed him. His smile, the way he lit up a room, and especially the way he loved him. William Blackwell had loved Derek Meade, silently but fervently. The world couldn't take that away.

Before he could get out of the car, his cell-phone rang beside him. He recognized the number. "Hello?" Derek stared at the front door of his house as he listened to the voice on the other end. "Yes. As it turns out, I have just enough free time for a quick visit. I'll be there tonight."

Once he placed his cell phone back in the passenger seat, Derek Meade started up his car again and backed out of the driveway. He could delay coming home to relax in his living for one minor detour—one he always enjoyed taking.

***

Later that night, Mr. Meade stepped out of his car and strolled up to the front door of the house. As he slipped the key into the lock, the door suddenly opened. "We've been waiting for you, old man," the voice beckoned. A hand reached out and grabbed Mr. Meade's arm to pull him inside quickly.

"What the hell is go—" he started to say, only to be silenced by a powerful blow to the stomach. He fell to the floor, gasping for air.

"I will ask the questions here, old man," the voice demanded. The figure stepped into the light. "Where are my manners? I've neglected to properly introduce myself. The name is Joel." He knelt down on the floor to look Mr. Meade in the eye. "I'm here to settle an old score."

The man on the floor moved slightly. "I don't even know you. How could there be a score to settle?"

Joel gave a nod to the two men standing by the door. They walked over to the man and kicked him in the stomach several times. When blood finally oozed from Mr. Meade's lips, Joel gave the nod to stop. "Well, you see, Mr. Meade, that's where our opinions differ. I know you through my father…you and your little boyfriend, William Blackwell. He took something that belonged to my father, and since he's no longer with us, God rest his soul, it has come down to me to retrieve what rightfully belongs to my family. So…where is he?" Joel lit up his Cuban cigar and blew smoke rings in the man's face while waiting for the answer.

The man's head spun from the pain in his abdomen and could barely focus on the conversation. Out of breath, he gasped, "Where is who?"

"You know, Mr. Meade, I am a busy man these days. Just tell me where your boyfriend's hiding," Joel said between drags on his expensive cigar.

"He's dead," Mr. Meade reported through painful breaths.

"Oh, what a terrible shame that is, Mr. Meade. But it does save me some time. You do realize what this means. It's all on you, little lady," Joel told him. He circled around his prey like a vulture, watching and taking pleasure in the torture. Taking another long puff of his cigar, he bent down and brought his face only inches away from his victim's. "I want the purse."

"I don't have it." The man grunted, the pain worsening.

"Do you have a death wish, Mr. Meade, or do you just enjoy pain? Tell me where it is!"

Knowing he only had a small chance of surviving this break-in, the man couldn't come up with any plan even remotely successful enough to save himself. "I told you, I don't have it." His breathing came fast and labored now, and he couldn't even try to slow it down. It was difficult to believe some little trinket William had kept for so long was so important...important enough to kill for its possession.

"You really expect me to believe that, don't you? I'm supposed to believe that, after all these years, your little boyfriend never gave you the purse or told you where it is?"

"I don't care what you believe, it's the truth." The man could do no more than whisper.

Joel grinned. "Oh, is that so?" He signaled to his men again.

In an instant, the man felt more blows to his face and stomach as the men overpowered him. Blood poured from his nose and mouth. "I told you, I don't have it and I don't know where it is."

"It's interesting that you would rather die than tell me the truth. Well, so be it." Joel walked towards the door, turned back, and signaled his men one last time.

Two hours later, Mr. Meade was dead.

THE PURSE

Chapter Six

"JACKSON! JACKSON! COME HERE!" Rosita yelled from the kitchen.

Running from the den, Jackson appeared before Rosita with rapid breaths. "Woman, what in the blue blazes is wrong with you? You know, we do have a real intercom system. I've heard the old-fashioned way is out."

"That might be amusing, Jackson, if I weren't the only one worried about Lydia," Rosita told him in a huff.

Jackson had grown weary of Rosita's incessant babbling. "What's the point in worrying, Rosie? You know damn well she's bound to find out sooner or later, and when she does, then we'll deal with it," he told her calmly.

Rosita paced around the kitchen. If she were a smoker, she'd be a chain smoker. There was no keeping Rosita Sanchez still for long. "It's bad enough that her own father lied to her, but even worse that we agreed to be a part of this mad scheme."

"Yes," Jackson nodded in agreement, "but you know as well as I do that, at the time, we would have lost our jobs if we didn't play along."

"And all because of Annabelle Blackwell. My God, she was a nasty woman.

Mr. William just didn't know how to fight her. I don't think anyone could. How can we ever tell her that her mother is alive and well and—"

Just then, both Jackson and Rosita heard the ever-familiar squeak of the swinging door to the kitchen opening. "And what, Rosita? Alive and well and taking a vacation at Club Med? Were you ever going to tell me?" Lydia had apparently heard the entire conversation. She looked livid, shocked, and curious all in one instant. "This is unbelievable!"

"Oh, God, Miss Lydia. I…I don't know what...I am so sorry...I..." Rosita nervously stumbled over her words, not knowing what to say.

Lydia's eyes burned. She held her hand up in the air. "Save it. What I don't understand is how you could sleep at night knowing what you know. Apparently, it's what you've always known. It was you, Rosita. You were the one who held me at night when I cried myself to sleep, missing a mother I never knew, a mother I believed to be dead. You were the one who talked about the angels taking her to Heaven, and she would always be looking down on me to keep me safe. You don't know how I held onto that. And now, to think she's alive somewhere and you've known all along." Lydia shook her head in disbelief. "My life has become one lie after another."

Rosita moved toward Lydia to embrace her, but Lydia pushed her away, seemingly not wanting any part of the woman who'd raised her. She didn't say a word to Jackson, who could not express anything but silence. Instead, Lydia walked right past him and out the door.

***

When the door closed, Lydia took a deep, cleansing breath. "Oh my God, my mother is alive," she whispered aloud without even realizing it. The dream she'd had so often as a child now surfaced in the light of day. Lydia was suddenly awakened by the notion that it had always been true. Her mother had always been alive. The only difference now was that she knew it.

That night, Lydia couldn't sleep. With all the recent discoveries about her life thrust upon her, it was impossible to keep her mind clear. She rolled over on her side and glanced at the clock on her bedside table. Midnight. The moon was out in full force, lighting the darkened sky. Lydia wondered briefly if Derek knew about her mother. She sat on the edge of her bed, opened the drawer in her table, and found the piece of paper with Derek's number written on it. She reached for her phone and, even though it was late, quickly dialed the number. No answer. She hoped Derek was somewhere peaceful, able to deal with his grief.

She rose from her bed and walked to the sliding glass door leading to her balcony. She slowly slid the door open to reveal the crisp night air. Stepping onto the balcony and gazing out at the night, it seemed strange to realize that, in some other place, some other life, her mother actually existed. The one who had given her life. What was the woman's reason for leaving? Was her mother so spineless that she let Lydia's grandmother run her out of town and out of her own daughter's life? Lydia shook her head once again in an attempt to rid herself of the clutter. She turned to go back into her bedroom when she noticed Rosita standing on the other side of the door.

"For God's sake, Rosita, what are you still doing up? It's after mid—"

"I know very well what time it is, child. I won't be able to sleep until I have my say. You will sit now and listen to me, and when I'm through, feel free to hate me all you wish. You must hear the whole truth before you judge," Rosita told her firmly.

"Fair enough," Lydia said as she walked into the bedroom and sat on the edge of her bed. She motioned for Rosita to sit next to her on the plush mattress, and as the woman did so, she let out a sigh.

Then Rosita took a deep breath and began the sordid tale. "I remember when your father brought Cassandra home. She was so lovely, quite a delicate woman. She had long, flowing blonde hair and piercing blue eyes. They had secretly married the month before and journeyed home to tell your grandmother the news. As you can guess, your grandmother was less than pleased. She didn't have any control over the situation, which was what bothered her the most.

"That next month, your father announced that Cassandra was pregnant. After you were born, it was a happy time. That is, whenever your grandmother wasn't around. She attempted to spoil any happy moment she could. Your parents did not seem like a normal, happy couple who'd just had a baby. I believe your parents truly adored each other, just not romantically. Later on, we learned of your father's...umm...other life. I think you know what I mean, dear."

Lydia smiled slightly and nodded. "Yes, I know what you mean."

"I thought you did. Anyway, I think your mother felt trapped. She was young and had not seen the world."

"Enter grandmother," Lydia stated with a huge sigh.

"Yes. I believe your grandmother made her an offer for her silence. Your grandmother knew of your father's preferences, or at least suspected, but didn't want to acknowledge it. Annabelle was a hateful woman. She gave specific instructions to us to say only that Cassandra was dead. We were not to mention her name or even discuss her with you except in the past tense. It was an awful thing to keep from you, and you have every right to be angry with us. It was wrong...job or no job. There is no excuse. But I want you to know something. I love you, Lydia, just as if you were born to me."

Lydia was silent for what seemed like hours. Suddenly, tears formed in her hazel eyes. "Thank you, Rosita. I do love you. You're the only mother I've known. It's just hard for me to comprehend such madness. Tell me, don't you think my grandmother would have wanted her there, even if just to ward off any rumors of my father's lifestyle? I mean, people marry every day just for the appearance of normality."

"Well, one would think so, but your grandmother wanted complete control over every aspect of your father's life, and with your mother in the picture, I guess there was less chance of that happening." Rosita shook her head, clearly not understanding it herself.

"I just recently found out about my father. Obviously, I was shocked," Lydia offered.

"Who told you, dear?"

"Derek told me. Do you know him?" Lydia was curious to see just how much the women really knew.

"Derek…Derek Meade?"

"Yes," Lydia answered quietly.

"Oh, yes, I recall seeing him at the funeral. He's a sweet man, and someone I believe truly loved your father. Your father was so happy, content, when Derek was here." Rosita smiled at the thought. Then a puzzled look washed over her face. "I wasn't aware that you knew Derek, sweetie."

"I didn't before today. Rosita, did you know *I'm* gay?" Lydia thought it was time the woman knew, here, for this conversation.

"Yes, child, I suspected it long ago. If you are truly happy within your soul, that is all that matters. Not what anyone else thinks about it."

Lydia's eyes brimmed with tears. "Rosita?"

"Yes, dear?"

"Do you think my mother would be proud of how my life has turned out?"

Rosita blinked a few times as she held Lydia in her arms. When they parted, she wiped the tears from Lydia's eyes. "Oh, my beautiful child, how could a mother not be proud to have you for a daughter? You've always been true to your heart no matter where it leads you. No one could ask for more than that."

Lydia smiled through her tears. There were no more words to say. The two women embraced each other tightly, and Lydia *did* feel better after the conversation. When Rosita bid her goodnight and left her room, the questions still filled her mind. She decided, as she crawled into bed, that maybe she would never understand. She gently closed her eyes and let sleep overtake her.

When she awoke some eight hours later, she tried once again to call Derek. Still no answer. There were so many things she wanted to discuss with him. She decided that, on her way out for various errands later that day, she would just drive by the address in Highland Park he'd given her the day before. She felt unusually close to this man she'd barely known twenty-four hours. She glanced at the silver purse on her dresser. How stunning it was. Walking to her dresser, she picked up the purse and let her fingers graze over the exterior.

Suddenly, her eyes caught a glimpse of something she hadn't noticed before. Lydia opened one of the top drawers of her dresser to find the magnifying glass her father had given her many years ago. Upon closer examination, the letters *CLB* were imprinted just beneath a detailed wreath design below the clasp. "Hmm...CLB," she heard herself whisper. Her eyes widened with the sudden realization. Cassandra Lexington Blackwell.

Chapter Seven

THE DRIVE TO DEREK'S house was just as scenic as it was relaxing. She passed by plush green yards of normal, regular people, and she loved it. That was one of the reasons she didn't live in her father's mansion. It just didn't suit her. After moving out of the condo she'd purchased with Danielle, she'd bought a modest three-bedroom home in the quiet suburb of Glencoe. She converted her den into a large therapy room and brought her practice home. It seemed more relaxing for her patients, which led to more progress in their recoveries.

As Lydia pulled in front of Derek's house, there appeared to be no movement around the house, no windows or curtains open to bring in the sunshine. Lydia looked down on the piece of paper she held in her hand. Yes, this was the place...9456 Stoakely Street.

Lydia parked her car behind Derek's in the driveway and stepped out, thinking she remembered seeing him drive away in a Mustang. She must have been mistaken. As she ventured up the sidewalk, she noticed a quaint little rose bush in front of the picture window. It made her smile; that had to be the work of her father. She rang the doorbell and waited for a response. Nothing. She rang it again. Still nothing.

A strange, dark feeling came over her without warning. Slowly, she turned the brass doorknob and opened the door, but a bit too easily, as if it were barely latched. Cautiously entering Derek's house, she smelled a faint odor she couldn't name. "Derek? It's Lydia. I'm sorry for just walking in, but I was worried and needed to talk to you." There was an eerie stillness in the air. All she could hear was the echo of her own voice.

She walked around the living room and then through a hallway leading to the kitchen area. "Derek? Where are you?" Every step made her more nervous and frightened by the second. The kitchen was empty; everything appeared untouched. *Maybe Derek just went on a trip*, she rationalized. Lydia walked through yet another hallway and came to a staircase. Holding on tight to the railing, she climbed quietly up the dark, carpeted stairs. Her heart beat out of control and was the only sound she could hear. She perused all the rooms—all except for one. Derek's bedroom. For some unknown reason, Lydia didn't want to know what was on the other side. She was sure she was overreacting, but the feeling wouldn't let go. Taking a deep breath, she pushed open the slightly ajar door. "Derek?"

He lay in the bed beneath the blankets, seemingly asleep. Lydia knew something was not right. She made her way over to the king-sized bed. His body lay there, perfectly straight with his arms by his sides on the outside of the blankets which covered him. Dried blood and bruises colored his face, and his lips were swollen. Lydia bent down and touched his arm to shake him awake. "Derek?" As she touched his arm, she felt the coldness of his skin and knew it was bad. Lydia's heart pounded nearly out of her throat, yet she tried to keep her emotions in check. She also knew she was failing miserably. Taking a deep breath, she moved the blankets to reveal several gunshots to his chest. She shrieked and put a hand to her mouth, taking in the sight but unable, for a moment, to comprehend what had happened. But it was real. "My God, no." Her eyes suddenly overflowed with tears as she managed to breathe again.

After composing herself as best she could, she placed two fingers on the side of Derek's neck to check for a pulse. Finding none, she covered him again completely with the blankets, noting how her hands shook, and left the room. She walked downstairs to the kitchen and sat at the table. Reaching into her bag, she found her cell phone and called the police. Then slowly, in a daze, she walked to the front of the house, opened the door, and sat down on the front steps to wait. She hung her head and sobbed for the friend she'd made and lost in less than a day.

The police arrived within ten minutes. Lydia didn't notice the shadow standing in front of her, but when she looked up, a white handkerchief dangled in front of her eyes. She looked up further to see a woman with short blonde hair, dressed in blue jeans, a white t-shirt, and a maroon sweater that covered her five-foot-three frame. Though she appeared small, she had a solid, muscular physique that had the potential to be intimidating.

"Thank you," were the only words Lydia could utter.

"You're welcome. Lydia Blackwell?" the woman inquired.

"Yes. And you are?" Lydia tried to be polite through the tautness of her face where her tears had dried.

"Lieutenant Sonja MacIntosh, Highland Park Police Department. Sorry to meet you under such circumstances. Could you tell me more about what happened here?" The Lieutenant got out her notepad and pen, then gave her crew the clearance to go inside, secure the area, and retrieve the body.

"Certainly, Lieutenant," Lydia stated and relayed the story as best she could.

"How well were you acquainted with the deceased, Ms. Blackwell?"

"Well," Lydia explained, "Derek was a close friend of my father's. I only met him yesterday at my father's funeral."

"I see. I'm sorry for your loss," the Lieutenant said softly.

"Thank you."

"I'm sure this doesn't make things any easier, but would you be willing to retrace your steps for me, from the time you entered the residence to the time you phoned the police?" the Lieutenant asked.

"Of course, Lieutenant MacIntosh."

"Please, call me Sonja," she said with a thin smile.

Lydia nodded and stood. "Only if you never call me Ms. Blackwell again. It's Lydia."

Sonja MacIntosh grinned. "It's a deal, Lydia."

She led the Lieutenant through the entire house, retracing her steps from the beginning. Once they made their way upstairs, Lydia felt suddenly anxious about viewing Derek's mangled body again. Once was enough. She heard the snapping of cameras and the rustle of people moving around in the bedroom, thinking the whole thing was like a bad dream.

As if sensing her mood, Sonja touched her shoulder gently. "You don't have to go in, Lydia. I know it's gruesome."

"Thank you," Lydia whispered. "Gruesome doesn't begin to cover it."

"I know. Do you know if Mr. Meade had family here, or anyone we can call to identify the body?"

Lydia shook her head. "No…well, the truth is, I don't really know. There's so much I didn't know about Derek. Now, I never will."

Sonja slid her hand from Lydia's shoulder to her arm. "I know. It's an awful thing. Listen Lydia, thank you for all of your help. Here's my card if you can think of anything else that might help the case."

"Thank you for being so understanding. Will you call me if you have any breakthroughs in the case? Nothing makes sense anymore," Lydia told her.

"Of course. I'd be glad to keep you informed as much as I can," Sonja agreed, looking at her with pity in her eyes.

Lydia reached into her bag and grabbed her wallet with her business cards in it, pulled one out, and flipped it over. "May I borrow your pen?"

"Certainly."

Quickly, Lydia wrote a number on the back of her card. "This is the number at my father's house where I'm currently staying." She handed Sonja the pen back and their fingers slightly touched.

Sonja turned the card over and her eyes widened. "Oh, so you're a therapist?"

Lydia nodded. "Yes, I am, though now I may have to give myself therapy," she joked.

"I understand what you mean. If there's anything I can do to help, please let me know."

Lydia nodded. "Thank you, Sonja. I appreciate it. I just may take you up on that." She shook Sonja's hand and walked out of Derek's house with the weight of his death and the world on her shoulders.

***

"Lieutenant?" One of the officers broke Sonja's attention as she watched Lydia drive away. "Forensics wants to go over a few things with you upstairs," he informed her.

"Of course. I'll be right there," she told him, pulling out the notes from her discussion with Lydia to review them. Robbins left to continue his work fingerprinting the living room.

Sonja walked back through the kitchen and stared out the glass sliding door overlooking the backyard. There she saw her partner, Hank Kovacs, scouting the yard and taking samples. Hank was a stout, burly man of thirty-five with dark brown hair and a matching goatee. He had been with the department for ten years and worked his way up the ranks, finally making detective two years ago. He always wore his signature Wrangler jeans and a button-down shirt beneath a western-style jacket.

After a moment of contemplation, Sonja slid open the door. "Hey, Kovacs, anything here?"

"Nah, a whole lot of nothing so far. Did anything turn up with the woman?" Hank asked.

"Not much to go on. Apparently, they just met yesterday at her father's funeral."

"Yeah, I read about him in the paper. William Blackwell," Hank added.

Sonja shook her head and then looked suddenly startled. "Oh my God, I don't believe it!"

"What? Is it weird her father was William Blackwell?" Hank looked up at her with wide, expectant eyes.

"No, that you actually read a newspaper." She laughed at her own joke.

"Ha, ha. You oughta take that act out on the road. Real funny."

Hank couldn't help but snicker just a little.

"Seriously, though, who was William Blackwell?" Sonja asked matter-of-factly.

"You oughta read a paper yourself once and awhile. He was a famous lawyer downtown. A real high-end lawyer, too. It's a shame his daughter has to deal with this so soon after her father," Hank explained as they both stepped back into the house. "Say, Sonja, I'm going to take another look around." Hank walked around the kitchen and then made his way into the den.

Within another twenty minutes, they met again outside on the front step. "Sonja?"

"Yeah," Sonja answered half-heartedly. She was still lost in thought, remembering the look on Lydia's face, the way she'd smiled when she handed Sonja her card. She looked up and saw Hank staring at her with a crooked smile. Hank was one of the few on the force who knew about Sonja's personal life. Of course, there were those who suspected, but she never told anyone she didn't trust with her life. It just wasn't safe for a cop, male or female.

"I knew it!" Hank yelled.

"What?" Sonja asked, not paying much attention.

"Don't give me that innocent act. I can see it on your face." Hank moved closer and whispered, "You're interested in her, aren't you?"

"Hank, really. I don't know what—"

"Don't bother denying it, MacIntosh!" Hank was relentless.

"Why would I be interested in her? I just met the woman." Sonja tried to be convincing, but had to admit that Hank knew her better than that.

"Never stopped you before," he said with a grin.

Finally realizing it was time to give it up, she relented. "Damn, I hate how well you know me. And I wouldn't say 'interested', anyway. I just wonder what her story is, that's all."

"Right," Hank said sarcastically. "Nice try. I don't buy it."

"All right, already. She's fascinating. Happy now?" Sonja tried to glare at him, but she couldn't help but laugh.

"Ecstatic."

She went back in the house and went over a few items with forensics, including taking another glance at the body. Someone had to answer for this. This was brutal.

An hour later, Sonja watched the medical examiner take away Derek Meade's body. Too many questions. No leads. No clues. For the first time in her career, Sonja MacIntosh wasn't sure where to go. Except that something was leading her to Lydia Blackwell.

Chapter Eight

"MAY I PLEASE SPEAK with Lieutenant Sonja MacIntosh?" Lydia decided it was time to speak with a professional, and the woman had offered, so what the hell? It had been three days since she'd found Derek's body. The funeral services were pending because of the autopsy and subsequent investigation. As far as she knew, no one was coming forward to claim Derek's body. She decided that, when it was time, she would hold a service herself for the man she barely knew. Maybe someone could tell her she wasn't insane.

***

The phone rang on Sonja's desk. "Lieutenant MacIntosh speaking. May I help you?"

"Lieutenant—I mean, Sonja, this is Lydia Blackwell. I'm sorry for interrupting your work, but I was wondering if I could meet with you. I've decided to take you up on your generous offer to help. I could really use some right now."

"Certainly. I would be glad to if I can. Where would you like to meet?" She attempted not to sound too excited about seeing the woman again.

"Do you know Allie's Coffee House?" Lydia suggested.

"Do I know it? I practically live there," Sonja joked. She also knew that Allie's was known as a lesbian hangout, and now thought it possible that she and Lydia had a few more things in common.

"Great! When are you free?" Lydia asked.

"How about two this afternoon?"

"Sounds good, Sonja. Thank you so much for meeting me. I'm not sure who else to talk to at this point," the woman said softly.

"I'm so glad you called, Lydia. I'll see you at two."

Now, Sonja was even more intrigued by Lydia Blackwell. She couldn't help but stare at the phone and smile. Her sudden surge of excitement did not go unnoticed by her doughnut-eating partner.

"Wanna doughnut, little lady?" Hank asked with a mouthful.

Sonja had to laugh. "Geez, Hank, you're a pig...and I don't mean cop-wise, either."

Hank grinned and slithered up next to her. "I don't know why you try to hide it. I know you want me."

"In the worst way." Sonja chuckled. He always made her laugh, managed to keep her grounded when the job seemed more of a burden than anything else.

"I get that a lot." Hank grinned and winked at her. He'd married his college sweetheart when they were in their twenties, but the stress of being married to a cop who was married to the job had been too much for his wife, and they'd divorced after eight years. It had been a difficult time for Hank, but his form of therapy was to dive into work. He adored Sonja and counted on their partnership—a partnership that had made them good friends. He was like a big brother who looked out for her when she didn't look out for herself. He also felt comfortable enough to tease Sonja about her personal life, and she returned the favor in kind.

"Seriously," he added. "What's up with the phone call?"

"Could be a lead on the Meade case," she reported in a professional tone.

"Funny, I've never seen you smile quite like that about a possible lead. Could it be a certain Lydia Blackwell?

"Maybe."

"Be careful, MacIntosh," he told her, the smile fading as he looked at her beneath a raised eyebrow.

Sonja put her hand on his shoulder. "Relax, Hank. She just wants my professional opinion."

"Oh, really? Well I have an opinion." Hank nudged her with a closed fist.

"I bet you do," she said, looking back down at the paperwork on her desk.

"So, you think there's a connection somewhere?" Hank asked.

"Could be. I don't know, but I'm not leaving anything to chance." Sonja glanced at her watch; it was nearing noon. "I'm going to check on some things before I meet with her. I'll be back later."

"That's cool. I have to finish this damn paperwork. Have fun."

Sonja grabbed her jacket and left the office. She made a trip to see the medical examiner for the status on Derek Meade's autopsy. They weren't quite finished, and since toxicology and ballistics could take some time, the final results would take even longer.

Some two hours later, Sonja arrived at Allie's Coffee House, wondering what this meeting would bring. A familiar face greeted her when she walked in the door.

"Sonja! Where have you been all my life?" Bertie was co-owner of the coffee shop and a good friend of Sonja's for years. She'd met the woman when Bertie was a waitress and so shy she could barely speak. No one would ever imagine that, now.

"Same place I've always been, Bert. Out of your league," Sonja joked. Bertie was as straight as they came, but they both enjoyed ribbing each other every chance they got.

Allie's was a place where Sonja could just spend time having some good coffee and meeting with people. It wasn't a bar, so it promoted a quieter atmosphere where people could have intimate conversations and good food. It was a warm and welcoming place, with brown and orange walls, bookshelves filled with books donated by customers, antique coffee grinders, and old coffee makers, some of which were for sale. A long coffee bar extended from the front to the back, and they even had a small stage to the right for the occasional acoustic performance.

"Ooh, good one, Sonja! You've been practicing, haven't you?" Bertie grinned.

"Well, I have to keep up with you, don't I? Don't want you showin' me up." Then Sonja spotted Lydia from across the room. It would be difficult not to. She was breathtaking, but not just outwardly; there was something about her that Sonja couldn't name, but she it felt it drawing her toward the woman.

Bertie eyed Sonja and motioned her over to the coffee bar. Bertie leaned in and whispered, "I didn't know you knew Lydia. Coulda knocked me over with a feather when she said she was meeting you."

"We just met, actually. This is purely a professional meeting, Bert."

"All right, sure. So you say," Bert teased with a raised eyebrow. Bert was momentarily interrupted with another order, then returned her attention to Sonja, who still watched Lydia. "So, you want your usual?"

"Yes. Mocha with a double shot, please. And cookies. Lots of cookies." Then she walked briskly to the back table where Lydia sipped on her drink. "Hey, Lydia. Good to see you again. Thanks for calling me. I needed the break." She reached out to shake Lydia's hand.

Lydia stood as their hands met. "I'm glad you could meet with me." They sat across from each other, and Bertie quickly brought their drinks and cookies. Lydia grinned. "I love biscotti."

"Well, then, you have excellent taste. These are my favorite. Orange-almond," Sonja said, taking a sip of her coffee and loving the way Lydia smiled at a simple thing like cookies. "So, tell me what's on your mind."

"So many things have happened. It's hard to know where to start." After pausing for a sip of cappuccino, Lydia added, "I guess it began when my father died and I met Derek." Then she laughed.

"What's funny?" Sonja asked.

"Oh, I was hearing myself, a practicing therapist, start to spill my guts to someone else. I'm sorry if this seems strange. I don't even know you, and I'm telling you my family secrets."

"You haven't told me any secrets yet. It doesn't seem strange to me. Maybe it's time the tables were turned…or couches, or whatever you use."

"No couches. At least, not yet. Thank you, Sonja." She took another nervous sip of her drink. "Anyway, ever since my father passed, it feels like things are just spinning out of control. I don't understand what happened to Derek."

"So senseless," Sonja answered, feeling the smile fade from her face as she remembered the crime scene. "Didn't you tell me Derek was a close friend of your father's?"

"That's correct." Lydia let out a long sigh. "I had a long conversation with him the day before he died, and that's when these…these revelations came out."

"What sort of revelations?" Sonja wanted desperately not to sound like she was interrogating the woman. She studied her as she talked, the way her mouth moved as she formed words, and suddenly realized she was lost in everything the woman said.

"The sort that knock you off your feet. Derek told me he and my father had been lovers for many years," Lydia said. She sounded almost indifferent, but Sonja had seen this kind of reaction before and chalked it up to residual shock over the whole situation.

"Wow. Had you ever suspected?" Sonja asked before she could stop herself.

"Not at all. I'd never seen Derek until the night my father died. My father would be the last person I'd suspect of having a relationship with a man. After Derek confided in me, he gave me this." She took the silver purse from her bag.

Sonja was speechless for a moment. "That is quite the piece. Can I ask what the significance of it is?"

"Of course," Lydia noted, "but I haven't a clue."

Sonja grinned at the woman sitting across from her and silently gave herself the pep talk. The one about not falling in love ever again.

"All I know is what I've been told…and I'm not sure what I trust anymore," Lydia told her solemnly.

"Understandable." Sonja took another long sip of her

cappuccino. "What is it, exactly, that you've been told?"

"Well, Derek confided to me that, back in 1964, some men attacked him after leaving a bar, and that was when my father came along and jumped into the fight. Apparently, one of the men dropped the purse out of his coat, and my father picked it up and kept it all these years."

"Fascinating," Sonja admitted. "Your father never told you or mentioned this purse?"

"My father didn't tell me a lot of things." Lydia's eyes wavered with tears.

Sonja wanted to reach out to her; she could feel her sadness. "I understand. What other things didn't he tell you? I'm sorry for prying, but I'm just curious," Sonja said, reaching out to touch the back of Lydia's hand.

"You're not prying, Sonja. I'm the one who called you." Lydia awkwardly fidgeted with her watch and took another sip of her drink. "It's about my mother. All my life, I was told she had died in a terrible car accident when I was three. Just a few days ago, I found out she's still alive."

Not being able to contain her shock, Sonja's jaw dropped. "Oh, God."

"That was basically my reaction. I think it had to do with my grandmother running her out of town...I don't know. Then Derek was attacked, and now..." Lydia's voice trailed off into a whisper.

"Now? What happened, Lydia?" Sonja was dumbfounded. What else could possibly happen to this woman?

"It's about the purse. I believe it belonged to my mother. It has the initials CLB engraved on it…her initials. But there's more. When I looked at the purse more closely, I found this inside." Lydia pulled a tattered piece of paper from her bag and handed it to Sonja.

"It looks like a birth certificate. Yours, I presume?"

"Apparently, though the writing's faded." Lydia let out a frustrated sigh and took a nibble from her cookie while she studied Sonja's face.

"Strange that your father isn't listed," Sonja muttered, reading the paper over and searching for anything else she might find odd. It was what she did every day.

"I agree. I can't begin to tell you how confused I am. It seems to get worse by the minute. I'm becoming my own soap opera," Lydia quipped. "Sonja, how do I get answers? Where would I start?"

Sonja stared at the seal on the paper once again. "It says Nevada, so I guess you could start there. I can do some checking for you, if you like."

"That would mean the world to me. Do I have to stay in town for the investigation, or am I free to come and go?"

"You can do as you like, Lydia. Of course. But if you leave town, make sure you give me the number where you'll be...just in case." Sonja's Police voice had returned, and she couldn't decide whether or not that was a good thing here.

"Of course. If my mother is still alive, I've got to find her. She holds so many answers to life's questions. My life's questions."

They finished their coffee and had refills twice over while they talked for two more hours, revealing what they already sensed about each other. Sonja found herself spellbound by this woman, who seemed to know nothing but tragedy and betrayal. She hung onto every word, every incomprehensible outcome. Sonja knew she'd been right. There was so much more to Lydia Blackwell.

Chapter Nine

"LYDIA? IT'S SONJA MACINTOSH."

"Hi there, Sonja. How's police work?" Lydia asked.

"Riveting." Sonja chuckled. "Listen, I did some checking, and the only thing I could come up with is that a Cassandra Lexington lived in Reno, Nevada back in 1969. Everything goes cold after that." There was a long silence through the phone line. "Lydia, are you there?"

"Yes, I'm sorry. This all seems so...surreal to me. I can't really be listening to you tell me my mother is alive and living in Reno."

Sonja couldn't imagine the things going on in this woman's head. "I know, Lydia, but it's possible she's not in Reno, and it's even more possible this woman is not your mother. Most people aren't in the same place after ten years, let alone over thirty."

"I guess you're right. Thanks for all your help with this, and I apologize if I bored you with my soap opera life yesterday," Lydia told her.

Sonja laughed into the phone. "Are you kidding? It's more riveting than police work!"

"It *is* police work!" Lydia chuckled. "Thank you. I don't remember when I've laughed so much...especially lately."

"Then you should make it a point to laugh more often." The echo of Lydia's voice rang in her ear. Something about this woman made it too easy. Sonja's own laughter came too easily to share with someone she'd just met. "What will you do now?"

"Look for my mother. I guess Reno's as good a place to start as any, and I need a vacation anyway."

"Please keep in touch with me. If you need anything, let me know." She gave Lydia her cell phone number. "Call me night or day." Sonja knew she was getting in way over her head with this one, but she couldn't resist the temptation.

"Thank you again, Sonja, and I will definitely be calling you. I appreciate your help and just listening." And with that, their conversation ended.

***

Just as Lydia placed the cordless phone on the desk, Rosita stumbled into the den.

"Miss Lydia, what's going on? You look troubled, child." She moved closer to her and gently touched her shoulder.

"Of course, I'm troubled. You made a chocolate cheesecake and didn't even have the fortitude to come and get me," Lydia teased. "You just can't find good help these days."

Rosita pointed her finger at Lydia. "Don't change the subject on me, young lady."

"I wasn't aware we even had a subject." Lydia couldn't help but egg her on.

"Have it your way. I will just sit here until you tell ol' Rosita everything." Rosita sat down in the overstuffed chair close to the desk where Lydia had taken up residence.

Unable to tolerate Rosita's constant glaring, Lydia relented. "All right! All right. The phone call was from a Police Lieutenant. She did some checking for me about my...my mother."

"She? Who is this person?" Rosita insisted.

"I told you, a Police Lieutenant. Her name is Sonja MacIntosh. She's one of the investigating officers looking into Derek's death."

Rosita's eyes grew wide. "What in the world are you doing hanging around with the police?"

"Oh, for God's sake, Rosita. I'm not 'hanging around with the police.'" Lydia sighed and then laughed. It sounded so absurd the way

Rosita put it. "I should tell you about the other thing, but you'd better promise not to overreact."

Rosita waved her hand, dismissing the notion. "Me? Overreact? Don't be crazy, Lydia."

"Yes, you. You're the queen of overreacting."

"Does it have to do with Mr. Derek's death?"

"Sort of. Before Derek left the day of father's funeral, he gave me this purse," Lydia explained, retrieving the purse from her leather bag on the floor by her feet.

"Oh, my," Rosita gasped, staring at the sparkle of the piece even in the dimly lit room. "Where did it come from?"

After Lydia recited the story of her father's and Derek's meeting, Rosita only sat in stunned silence for a moment. "I didn't know they met so long ago. Isn't it strange that he gave you that purse, and then he was murdered?"

"I'm not sure what to think." Lydia stared intently at Rosita. "So, I take it you've never seen this purse before?"

"I would have remembered something so breathtaking." Rosita gave the purse back to Lydia. "What does your mother have to do with this?"

Lydia rose from the desk. "I don't know, but I'm sure going to find out."

"What does that mean, Lydia? You certainly aren't thinking of going to—"

"Yes," Lydia informed her, "I'm going to find my mother. She holds the answers to so many questions. Not only about this purse and where she's been all this time, but answers about me. She's the only one. My father is gone, and as much as I love you and Jackson, you can't give me what I need. I need my mother." Lydia hugged Rosita and left to go upstairs.

She headed down the familiar hallway to her room, then suddenly changed her path and moved toward her father's bedroom instead. Quite possibly, she could find some clues to this mystery she called her life. She stood in front of the door before opening it, recalling the last time she'd seen her father. That had also been the first time she saw Derek. How ironic that now they were both gone.

As she walked into the bedroom, the smell of her father's cologne lingered even through all the sickness that had been in the air. Stepping over to the deep walk-in closet, Lydia opened the double doors to reveal her father's suits, ties, and shoes. She made a mental note to have Rosita donate her father's clothes so they didn't hang like a shrine. She stared at every inch of the closet until her eyes fell on a small shoebox buried on the top shelf. Lydia retrieved the step-ladder from within a hidden compartment in the closet's wall and stood on it to pull down the shoebox. Without thinking, she strolled over to her father's bed, sat down, and went through all the memories kept in the cardboard box.

Many were just baby pictures of Lydia, and then she discovered a picture of her mother when she was pregnant. How beautiful she was; she looked so happy and carefree. What in the world could have happened? More questions, no answers. Lydia decided to keep the picture with her. Digging deeper yet into the box, she also found pictures of her father and Derek together. They made a handsome couple, though it was still difficult to believe her father had been involved with a man. At least true love hadn't escaped him as she'd previously thought.

She shifted her feet beneath her, and the movement made the box of pictures slide off the bed. Lydia knelt to gather them from the floor, then noticed a torn piece of paper sticking out from beneath the pile. Picking it up, she carefully opened it to find her parents' marriage license. Lydia had to stop momentarily to think. The date of their marriage did not coincide with Lydia's birthday. That meant her mother had been pregnant possibly two or three months before she married William Blackwell. Lydia sighed with a deep sense of torment under her skin. She grabbed the marriage license and the picture of her mother, then put the box back in the shadows of her father's closet. A closet of secrets. She left her father's room, more distraught now than when she'd entered it.

Lydia walked slowly to her bedroom. She wondered why she'd stayed in her father's mansion since his death. Perhaps it was for comfort, perhaps it was something else. In the mansion, at least, she felt like she belonged somewhere. But maybe that, too, was an illusion. And if William Blackwell wasn't really her father, her whole life was an illusion.

Chapter Ten

IT HAD BEEN TWO months since Lydia's father passed away. The November chill filled the air and the frost had already covered her father's precious rose bushes. Winter announced its arrival without hesitation.

Just over a month before, Lydia had put together a small service for Derek back by the gazebo near her father's plot. It was only right for them to finally be together. There were a few people, but no family ever came forward to say goodbye. It all seemed so strange, and Lydia had an odd feeling there was more to Derek's story than she knew. Sonja told her the medical examiner reported that Derek was shot nine times in the chest. She called it "overkill".

Once Lydia made the decision to search for her mother, she realized quickly that she couldn't just leave in a whirlwind. She did have responsibilities and people who depended on her. She put her search on hold until everything was in order with her patients. After all, it had been thirty-five years; a few more weeks probably wouldn't make a difference. Her patients needed their own reassurance that she would be back, and Lydia made arrangements with a few of her colleagues to take on her patients in case of emergency.

Finally, with all the last-minute preparations complete, Lydia was ready. She had already gone to her house in Glencoe, spoken with her neighbor about looking after her house while she was gone, and grabbed some extra clothes and comforts to take with her. She felt oddly comfortable being at the Estates now after not having lived there since she was in college. But once back at her own home, she realized how much she'd missed it.

There was also someone else she missed—Sonja. In the past two months, Lydia and Sonja had enjoyed many meals, countless cappuccinos, and what seemed to be endless conversations about nothing and everything. Lydia knew she was falling for the woman, and in record speed. Now that she prepared to leave, she felt her heart sink just a little. Lydia promised she would call Sonja along the way and keep her updated, and the Lieutenant promised to do the same. With one last hug goodbye to Rosita, who made sure to put on record that she opposed this journey from the start, and Jackson, who was his usual strong and stoic self, Lydia drove away from the mansion in her Jeep Cherokee, leaving Blackwell Estates in her rearview mirror.

Lydia loved being on the open road. With no time restraints, no schedules to keep, or meetings to get to, she could almost make herself believe she was on vacation—at least, if it weren't for the dead and the undead. Still, she needed the diversion and was glad for the opportunity.

She drove until she was tired, which ended up to be in Omaha, Nebraska. She'd only been there once, many years before, for some training. For once, she just went where the road led her, and hopefully her mother would be at the end of that road.

Lydia stopped at a fairly decent-looking motel off Interstate 80 just for the night. Once in her room, Lydia put her things on the floor and fell into bed. She turned on the television, made a call to Rosita, and fell asleep before her head hit the pillow.

The next morning, Lydia rose promptly at seven. Four hours out of Omaha, she stopped in North Platte, Nebraska to stretch and have some lunch at a local sandwich shop. Then she headed into Wyoming, a state she'd never been through before. It was a shame, because Lydia couldn't believe how different the air was.

She made it to Cheyenne by four in the afternoon and decided to stop for the night. After all, there was no hurry. She fell asleep to the television and then awoke to daylight at eight. She packed up her car and inhaled a deep breath, filling her lungs with the mountain air.

Rejuvenated, she felt ready to take on the world.

Driving on for hours, there seemed to be no signs of life, at least not modern life—just mountains and hills. She kept going, cruising along with the radio and, on occasion, books on tape and music she'd recorded. Then without warning, the hood of her car popped up. Trying not to panic, Lydia pulled over to the shoulder. "Dammit!" She didn't even know where the hell she was. Sitting at her steering wheel and watching the white smoke billowing from beneath the hood, she tried not to scream in frustration.

Getting out of the car, she checked under the hood once the smoke had cleared. She knew enough about cars to realize it was her radiator hose. Checking her cell phone, she found she was out in the middle of nowhere, and surprise—no service. Looking up across the highway, she noticed a highway patrol officer and flagged him down. He drove to a crossing to turn around and pulled up to Lydia's steaming car.

"Howdy, Ma'am," the officer greeted her and tipped his hat. "Radiator hose, eh?" He was average-looking, older, and stout with a slight belly and silver, thinning hair. He not only wore the beige and brown uniform—he *was* the uniform.

"Apparently so." Lydia was thrilled by the officer's knowledge of car mechanics.

"I can take you into town and you can get that fixed in no time," he offered.

"I'd appreciate that. Where is town, by the way? I'm not sure I know where I am."

"Rock Springs, Wyoming, Ma'am," he informed her.

"I see." She didn't remember seeing it on the map.

"Come along with me, Ma'am, and I'll call the tow truck for you." Lydia gathered up her personal belongings and stepped into the patrol car, then waited for the officer to make the call. While they waited on the arrival of the tow truck, the officer started some conversation. "So, where are you from...uh...I'm sorry. I didn't get your name, Ma'am."

"My name is Lydia, and I'm from Chicago, or thereabouts."

"Well, hello, Lydia from Chicago. Martin Stoddard, at your service. It's a pleasure to meet you. Ah...a city girl. My word, you are a long way from home."

"Yes, and I love it. Although, this part I could do without." Lydia glanced at her watch a few times, feeling like she was late for something.

"Don't worry. It'll all work out," Martin Stoddard assured her as he motioned toward the approaching tow truck. "See, here he is."

"Oh, good," Lydia said, and opened the door to step out of the patrol car.

In a matter of twenty minutes, everyone was on their way to the service station just down the road, according to Officer Stoddard.

"The service station is a good one," he informed her on the drive, "and the restaurant next door is the best in town. My wife is a waitress there."

"That sounds good. I'll consider myself lucky to have crossed your path, Martin Stoddard." She watched the scenery go by and wondered where this little incident fell into the grand scheme of things.

The drive only took a few minutes. Lydia noticed the wonderful aromas coming from Jack's, the restaurant Officer Stoddard had mentioned. After talking with the mechanic and thanking Martin, Lydia stepped into the rustic-looking restaurant. She checked her watch. It was after four in the afternoon, and she doubted anyone would be working on her car at this late hour.

Just inside the front door, she stopped and took in the sight of animal heads—bears, cougars, moose, and antelope—mounted on the walls of the restaurant. "Good thing I'm not a vegetarian," she whispered, not expecting anyone would hear her.

"Not in Wyoming, dear," a voice answered.

Embarrassed, Lydia's face flushed a bright shade of red. She turned to face a woman wearing an apron and a warm smile. "I've just never seen so many dead animals in one place before," Lydia added.

"Oh, a newcomer! I love it! Hi, there. I'm Emily. Follow me," the woman instructed, leading the way to a booth towards the back of the restaurant. It also happened to rest directly beneath a mounted bear's head. Emily grinned at her customer. "Don't worry, he's up there to stay."

"Thank goodness. I'd hate for that to be on my epitaph," Lydia joked. "What's good here?"

"Well, darlin', just about anything. Personally, I like the chicken-fried steak and eggs." Emily leaned in to whisper as she pulled out her notepad and pen.

"Sounds awfully unhealthy...I'll take it."

"Guess what?" Emily asked her.

"What?"

"It comes with fried potatoes and a biscuit with sausage gravy." Emily twirled her pen around her finger, acting like a performer only too eager for the next trick.

"Oh, even better! Might as well throw in some strong coffee and do it up good."

"You got it," Emily said, writing on her pad before she scurried off to put in the order.

Looking around the restaurant, Lydia recognized the signs of the rugged lifestyle for which Wyoming was famous. Old cowboy pictures hung on the wall, reminding her how privileged she was. Maybe it was just the mountain air, but something about being there excited her, though she wasn't sure exactly what it was just yet.

She wondered if her waitress was Martin's wife. The restaurant's atmosphere felt much like Emily's demeanor—friendly, outgoing, and familiar. It was the small-town ambiance that most attracted Lydia. And she didn't have to wait very long for her food.

"One heart attack special, just for you, darlin'," Emily teased. "Hope you enjoy every sinful bite."

Lydia clapped her hands together once, so excited to eat. "I know I will. Thank you." She paused for a few seconds, looking Emily up and down. "Are you by chance Martin Stoddard's wife? He helped me get here when my car broke down."

"Oh, no. Not a chance, dear. That would be Christie. She's right over there." Emily pointed across the room. "Why do you ask?"

"He drove me into town after we called a tow truck for my car, and he said his wife worked here. I was just curious," Lydia explained.

Emily nodded and left to take care of her other customers. When Lydia looked over her shoulder to see the woman Emily had pointed out, she was even more curious. Quickly, she reached into her handbag and pulled out the picture of her mother. She looked again at the woman across the room. The resemblance was striking, to say the least, but it couldn't possibly be her. What were the odds of that happening? No. It just couldn't be. Emily had said the woman's name was Christie.

Lydia tried to work it out in her head. Christie...Cassandra. She could have changed her name, but why wouldn't she? Lydia shook it from her mind. It would be far too easy to suddenly find her mother here. It was impossible. She glanced at the woman again only to see Emily talking to her and pointing to Lydia's table.

No! Lydia didn't want to talk to her *now*. What if it wasn't Cassandra Lexington? Then an even worse possibility played out in Lydia's mind—what if it was?

Chapter Eleven

"HEY THERE, HONEY. I'M Christie. Emily said you ran into my hubby on the interstate," the raspy voice rang out.

Taken aback for a moment, Lydia was unsure how to react to this woman. "Hi. Yes, that's right. It's nice to meet you. My name's Lydia. Your husband rescued me and said his wife worked here, so I thought I would say hello. Tell him I said thank you."

Christie smiled. "Of course. I'm lucky to have him, but if you tell him I said so, I will deny everything!" Then Christie looked Lydia up and down for a moment. "You must not be from around here."

Lydia grinned. "Am I that obvious?"

"In a word...yes, but we're tired of regulars and enjoy anyone new who comes along. So, what planet are you from?"

"Another world called Chicago."

"Really? How refreshing."

"Refreshing?" Lydia asked. "That's a word I would use to describe Wyoming, not Chicago." She had to laugh at the hustle and bustle of Chicago being referred to as 'refreshing'.

"Well, it is around here, let me tell you." Christie studied her customer.

Lydia noticed Christie's eyes briefly making their way across the table. The woman's face drained white as a sheet, like she'd seen a ghost.

"Listen," Christie said, her voice suddenly shaky. "I'd better get back to work before my boss thinks I've gone off the deep end. It was wonderful meeting you, and I hope you enjoy your meal."

"Thank you, Christie." And then, just like a summer breeze, she was gone. Lydia hoped the woman was okay. She'd looked a bit sick at the last second.

She wondered if it was even remotely possible the woman was actually Cassandra Lexington. Could she be her mother? Christie wasn't at all like Lydia would have expected her mother to be, certainly not working as a waitress in some truck stop. If Annabelle Blackwell had paid her mother to leave town, it had to have been a hefty sum, enough to keep her quite comfortable for years without having to work. Lydia reminded herself that it had been over thirty-five years and anything could have happened. No, Lydia told herself. It was just a coincidence that she looked like the woman in the picture. What would the odds be of coming across her by accident? A million to one. Impossible.

Lydia shook it from her mind once again and reached out to grab her napkin. Instantly, her hand grazed across the picture she'd forgotten to put back in her purse. All at once, she remembered how fast Christie's face had paled. She must have seen the picture.

Now, Lydia couldn't help but think it remarkably more possible that Christie Stoddard was indeed Cassandra Lexington. How bizarre that she'd traveled toward Reno to look for her mother, only to be stranded in Rock Springs, Wyoming and find what she wanted. She couldn't be entirely sure, but she couldn't just let this go. Lydia had to find out who Christie really was.

She left a twenty-dollar tip for Emily, then went to check on her car. Stepping into the small Texaco station, she felt uneasy as she took stock of her surroundings. It was dirty and dull and but yet strangely reassuring. A mechanic stepped out and told Lydia there hadn't been time to see her car, let alone fix it. He left quickly, telling her to come back the next day by noon.

Lydia found a phone book on a table next to the dirty popcorn machine, which looked as if it needed an overhaul itself. First, she found a hotel and the number. After digging out her cell phone, she discovered she now had service, so she called and made a reservation, telling the clerk where she was. The hotel turned out to be just down the road. Lydia wondered if that was a common expression or if everything was "just down the road." The clerk also called a cab for her and within a few minutes, a bright yellow car pulled up to the station.

It was now past six. She settled into her room and turned on the television, reflecting on the day's events. Somehow, she just couldn't concentrate on the latest news coming out of the speakers. Looking out her balcony, she saw the splendid outline of the mountains. But even looking at their beauty, she couldn't get the thoughts about Christie out of her head. It was just too eerie a coincidence for the woman to look so much like her mother. It had to be her, especially when she remembered the look on Christie's face. Lydia didn't know how, or even if, she should confront her. What if Christie denied it? What if her husband didn't even know about her past? Too much had happened, and Lydia needed a drink.

She left her room and walked to the restaurant, heading for the bar. Upon finding the perfect stool, she climbed up, had a seat, and ordered a double rum and coke.

Going over it in her mind, Lydia couldn't decide what her next step would be. One way or the other, though, she had to find out if Christie was her mother. Grabbing her cell, Lydia found Sonja's number. She needed to hear that voice, the one she'd become accustomed to for the past two months. Her heart raced as she pressed the call button. With every ring, Lydia felt more ridiculous for giving in, but there was an inner struggle she couldn't fight.

"Sonja, here. Who's calling?"

"Sonja? It's Lydia. I'm sorry to bother you, but I just felt like calling," she said, feeling nervous as she fidgeted with her napkin at the bar.

"Lydia! I've been thinking—wondering about you. Where are you, anyway?"

"You won't believe it, but I didn't make it to Reno. I'm in Wyoming—a town called Rock Springs."

"Ha! How in the world did you end up there?"

"Well, my car broke down on the interstate, though nothing serious. It should be fixed tomorrow. But you know what? I don't think I'm driving on to Reno after all. I may have found what I've been looking for." As she said the words aloud to Sonja, she couldn't believe that she'd just let everything out to a woman she barely knew. A battle brewed between her head and her heart. Not long ago, life was the same as it always was, but now her mother existed somewhere, as did a woman on the other end of the phone about whom she couldn't stop daydreaming.

"Your mother? You found your mother in Rock Springs?" Sonja's curiosity came thick through the phone.

"I think so," Lydia said, "but I'm not one hundred percent sure yet. I want to investigate some more. Gee, maybe you're rubbing off on me!" she teased.

Sonja laughed into the phone. "This is a good thing! Where did you find her?"

"She's a waitress at a restaurant called Jack's. Sonja, she looks just like the picture I have of my mother, just an older version. She accidentally saw the picture on the table and had an obvious reaction to it," Lydia explained.

"What will you do now?"

"I don't know, but I may have to confront her. If she turns me away, so be it, but not before I find the answers I'm seeking." Lydia's sounded bold and determined even to her own ears.

"That's awfully courageous of you. How are you, really? I have to admit, I've been thinking about you," Sonja confessed

"I've thought about you, too. I've missed hearing your voice, and now that I have, it makes me feel better."

"Me too. I only wish I could be there to help you. I'm still working on Derek's case. There's just been nothing to go on. I can't really leave...but I want to."

"I understand completely," Lydia said. "I want to get this figured out, and then I'll be back. Maybe we can get to know each other even more once I get to know myself." Her mind was filled with thoughts of

Sonja's smile, her eyes, and even the way she used expressions like 'y'all' when she spoke, even though she wasn't southern. Even as she listened now, Lydia noticed that the roughness of being a cop seemed a little less jagged. Mostly, Sonja was beginning to feel like home. But she couldn't tell her that—not just yet.

"I'd really like that, Lydia. I've liked what I've seen so far," Sonja said softly.

The women chatted on for a few more minutes, and they reluctantly ended their conversation. As Lydia put her phone down on the bar, she felt a little tug at her heart. And she liked it.

After a night of sound sleep, Lydia took a cab back out to the truck stop. It was about ten in the morning, and she couldn't resist the temptation to have breakfast at Jack's. Christie wasn't on duty, and it was just as well, since Lydia hadn't made a decision on which path to take. At least, not yet. But she did see someone else—Martin Stoddard by himself, having coffee. That made her paranoia kicked in. Her heart raced just like the first time as she wondered if Christie had spoken with her husband about the picture. Lydia wanted to know, but then part of her didn't.

After making eye contact, Martin strolled over to Lydia's table. "Ah...biscuits and gravy. My favorite. Mind if I join you, Lydia?"

"Not at all. Please, have a seat." As Martin sat down across from her, she was wracked with whirling thoughts about how the conversation would go. Lydia wanted to run away from this man. Maybe she was wrong about Christie. Maybe the woman wasn't her mother.

"I hear you spoke with my wife yesterday," he acknowledged.

Lydia nodded, keeping the conversation light. "Yes, she's a lovely woman."

"I have to agree with you, there. I'm a lucky man." After a short pause, Martin looked right at Lydia. "She seemed a bit upset when she came home yesterday, though I couldn't get out of her exactly why."

Lydia took a sip of her coffee for some added strength and placed the cup down slowly. She watched Martin's eyes searching hers for a response. She let out a sigh and said, "I'm sorry to hear that, Martin. I hope she's okay." She took in more coffee and another bite of her breakfast to avoid saying too much.

"Lydia, I need to ask you if you know why she's upset. She just shut me down. I noticed it when she talked about meeting you. She just seemed. . . different."

Lydia wasn't ready for this conversation. "Well...I don't think that I—"

"This is important. I've never seen her so shaken. Please, Lydia,"

Maybe this was the perfect time to talk about it. Lydia could sense his frustration and knew she had to start somewhere. She finished her coffee and sighed. "If I told you, I doubt you would believe me, and it might cause a lot of hurt. And besides, I'm not sure I believe it myself."

"Lydia, I'm an officer of the law. I've heard and seen it all. Try me,"

"All right." She needed just a second longer to steel herself. "I think Christie is my mother."

Chapter Twelve

"SHE'S WHAT? WHAT IN the world would make you say such a thing?"

Lydia reached into her coat pocket and pulled out the picture of her mother.

"Oh my God, it's remarkable. But...this can't be her. The woman in this picture looks, what? At least eight months pregnant. Christie told me she's never been pregnant...she couldn't have children," Martin told her quietly.

"Really?" Lydia's heart dropped a million miles downward. A thousand knives couldn't have hurt her more. The woman didn't even admit to her very existence. She knew she had to hold it together and, minute by minute, the task only became more difficult. "I don't know, Martin. Nothing is what it seems."

Martin Stoddard glanced at his watch. "I've got time. Suppose you tell me about it?"

"I've probably said too much as it is." Lydia didn't feel right having this conversation.

"You haven't said anything, Lydia...except that my wife is your mother." Martin paused and took a breath. "Do you have any proof?"

"No, I don't, at least not physical proof. All my life I was told my mother died in a terrible car accident. My father just passed away recently, and through a series of events I've discovered she's still alive somewhere. It's only a twist of irony that I'm here right now," she explained.

"Where were you headed before your car broke down?"

"Reno. A police friend of mine did some checking and found that my mother had lived in Reno. I was going to start looking there, but ended up here in Wyoming." Lydia wasn't so sure she was doing the right thing by confiding in Martin.

"Reno..."

"What is it?" Lydia noticed his eyes looking off into the distance, leaving an awkward silence.

"Oh, nothing. I—" Martin's beeper broke the atmosphere of the restaurant and their conversation. "Damn. I'm sorry, Lydia, I've got to go. Are you staying in town?"

"Yes. There's no way I can leave until I solve the mystery," Lydia told him.

"I understand. I'm sorry if I sounded pushy, Lydia. I'm just trying to get to the heart of the matter."

Lydia looked deep into Martin's eyes. "So am I, Martin. So am I." Martin nodded and left the restaurant. Lydia finished her biscuits and gravy and her second cup of coffee. Then she, too, walked out of the restaurant, more determined than ever.

Making her way next door to the garage, she could see her car in the parking lot. After paying her bill and seeing everything was in order, Lydia drove back to the hotel. She asked the clerk if there were any messages for her—there were none. Lydia was exhausted, and it wasn't even noon yet. She thought she'd rest for a while, then maybe go for a swim later. Riding up in the elevator, she wondered when it would all be over and she could go on with her life. But she also knew her life could never again be the same. Lost in thought, the ring of the elevator awakened her from her silent musings.

She entered her room and immediately sensed something was different. The lingering scent of perfume filled her senses—a perfume that wasn't hers. Lydia closed the door behind her, and when she turned around, Sonja stood in front of her, smiling from ear to ear. Without waiting for any words, Sonja pulled Lydia close to her, wrapped her arms around her, and kissed her full on the mouth.

Lydia couldn't resist such passion and didn't remember the fact that maybe she should have tried. She returned the kiss with everything in her. Sonja led her to the bed and undressed her, covering her with breathless kisses all the while. They made love without words or inhibition, letting their desires override everything else. No promises, no talk of love, just a physical ache which had been building since the day they'd met.

***

Sonja lay in Lydia's arms, watching her tenaciously. "So, how've you been?"

Lydia said, "Now that you ask, I'm great. I have to say, you know how to welcome someone home."

"Well, I do what I can."

"Yes, you most certainly do. By the way, I thought you couldn't leave work." Lydia remembered their phone conversation.

"I convinced my boss I needed a short vacation," Sonja replied. "Some of my best work, I must admit."

"I'm really glad you're here, Sonja. I've thought a lot about you and…didn't know if I should."

Sonja pulled Lydia's hair from her eyes gently. "I can't believe you fit me in with everything you're going through, but I'm glad."

Lydia bent down and softly kissed Sonja's lips. "I don't know how it's possible, but I feel drawn to you."

"Really?" Sonja nibbled on Lydia's ear and whispered, "I'm drawn to you...right now." They made love again in the late afternoon, with not a care in the world. Except each other.

Two hours later, when hunger interfered with their physical desire, they ventured downstairs to the hotel restaurant. When the waiter seated them, Sonja ordered two glasses of Chablis to relax them both after the long day, even as wonderful as it had ended. When the waiter brought the wine, Sonja picked up her glass, raised it in the air, and looked at Lydia with her soft brown eyes. "Lydia, I hope you find what you're looking for and that it's everything you've dreamed it would be."

"That is the sweetest thing anyone has said to me. Thank you." Lydia raised her own glass and clinked it gently with Sonja's. "This is wonderful. I actually feel relaxed for the first time in…forever."

"Good. That was the intention." The waiter returned to take their orders, but Sonja could only stare at the woman across from her.

"Ma'am? Are you ready to order?"

"Oh, I'm sorry. I'd like the smothered chicken, baked potato, and broccoli...butter and lemon, too, please," Sonja told him.

"Okay, me too," Lydia added.

"So," Sonja asked, "what's your next move?"

"Well," Lydia said, "I thought we'd eat dinner and then I'd try to charm you back to the hotel room."

"Sounds good. Very good." Sonja took another sip of her wine and then spoke more softly. "Lydia, you know what I mean. What about this Christie Stoddard?"

Lydia sighed heavily. "I don't know. I believe my only real choice is to confront her. Deep down, I really feel she *is* my mother."

"And if she's not?"

"If she's not, then she's not, and I go to Reno. But I'm not giving up until I know for sure. Until I have proof one way or the other."

"Good for you, darlin'. You shouldn't give up. I want to do some more checking on this woman and see if there are any connections. I have a friend in the records department out of Salt Lake City."

"Sonja, I really appreciate all your help, but I don't want you to feel obligated."

"I'm not obligated. I wouldn't be doing this if I didn't want to. Not only that, but since you told me this whole story, I want to help unravel the mystery," Sonja told her.

Finally, their dinner arrived and the two shared wonderful conversation, learning more about each other than ever before. They talked of relationships, careers, and who should pay for dinner. Lydia won that argument.

Sonja eyed Lydia while they waited for her change. "I think I'm ready now to see those moves of yours."

"Really? I think I can rustle something up."

Chapter Thirteen

IT WAS SIX PM and Martin Stoddard was still at odds with the information Lydia had reluctantly discussed with him. It seemed so far-fetched, it couldn't possibly be true. And if it were true, that meant the woman he cherished most in the world had lied to him. He knew he had to get to the bottom of it before it exploded. Lydia was sure to confront his wife soon.

"Darlin', how was your day off?" He made simple conversation, though Christie seemed not to hear. "Honey?"

As if shaken out of her trance, she finally answered, "Oh, yes, dear. Dinner will be ready in a few minutes."

Obviously, she hadn't heard a word he'd said. "Honey, I asked you how your day off was. Didn't you hear?"

"Marty, I'm so sorry. I guess my mind is somewhere else."

"I can tell. I think I know where your mind has been," he admitted.

"Really?" Christie shook her head. "It's nothing, Marty. I'm just overworked, that's all. Really tired," she told him, attempting not to look at him.

"I saw Lydia Blackwell today," Martin told her, looking for her reaction to the name. "It turns out her father is, or was, William Blackwell. Someone told me he was a famous lawyer in Chicago."

"I see."

Martin Stoddard observed his wife and chose his words carefully. "It's strange, the people you meet on a whim. Isn't it?"

"I guess so. I never really thought about it."

Martin could sense his wife avoided getting too involved in the conversation. With her short, unattached answers, he knew she was hiding something. "Take Lydia, for example. She seems like a lovely person, don't you think so?"

"Sure, I guess so. I didn't really get much of a chance to speak with her." Christie kept moving around the kitchen, busying herself around the stove and with dishes, but couldn't seem to stand still.

"That's too bad," Martin said. Then he took a deep breath and, without testing the waters first, just dove right in. "She told me something quite fascinating. Crazy, but fascinating."

"Really? What was that?" She cut the vegetables for their salad at a rapid pace.

"Well...she thinks you're her mother."

Christie dropped the knife on the floor. "Dammit!" she shrieked, then bent down to pick the utensil off the floor.

Martin rose from his seat and put his arms around his wife. "Christie, stop. You've got to talk to me. What is this all about?"

"It's nothing, Martin. Absolutely nothing. The girl's mistaken. Leave it alone." Her tone didn't leave much room for argument as she got a clean knife from the drawer.

"I won't leave it alone." Martin let out a long sigh and eyed his wife for an instant. "You saw that picture, didn't you? That woman in the picture...that's you, isn't it?"

"Martin, I told you—" she protested before her husband firmly grasped her shoulders and turned her around to face him.

"Isn't she?" His voice rose in volume with the repeated question.

The tears slid down Christie's cheek. She obviously couldn't hold back her anguish any longer. The many years of torment and lies had finally come to a head. "Yes."

"Are you telling me it's true...all of it?" Martin wasn't entirely sure how to react now that she'd admitted what he'd feared and suspected all at once.

"The picture is me, yes. But, God help me, I don't know if I'm this poor girl's mother. How do I know where in the hell she got that picture?"

"How can you deny it, darlin'? She has your eyes." Martin hesitated for a moment to catch his breath. He couldn't comprehend this was even happening. "How in the world could you lie to me all these years?"

"You don't understand. In all of God's green earth, there's no way you could possibly understand," Christie told him, then looked away.

"All right," he said, reaching out again to embrace his wife of twenty-six years. "Then make me understand."

Finally, Christie nodded, leaving her husband's arms to pour them both a fresh cup of coffee and put dinner on hold. They sat at the small kitchen table, face to face so as not to miss a single emotion. "My God, it was so long ago. But as long as I live, the pain will always be a part of me."

"Everything we bury must somehow rise again, my love," Martin whispered as he touched her hand from across the table. Inside, he was screaming. What could she really say that would justify the lies?

"Apparently so. She *is* beautiful, isn't she, Marty?" She sighed again and shook her head as if doing battle with her inner self. "No. No, I can't allow myself to even remotely believe it's her."

"You can, Christie. And yes, she is beautiful. Tell me more."

"Many years ago, I met a man. I thought he was everything—Brenton Pritchard. Just the name oozed sophistication. He was twenty years older, and of course the relationship made my parents unhappy, and they disapproved. I was nineteen and ran away from home to be with him. He promised me everything under the moon, and for a while he was wonderful, and everything was so good. I lived with him for about a year before things turned ugly. He became controlling, and our home turned into my prison. Brenton wouldn't let me leave, threatening me several times, and so I was scared to do anything. Just when I felt there was no hope, I met William Blackwell. He was so dashing and charming."

Martin was confused, but kept his silence, taking a sip of his coffee.

"Honey, the truth has been hidden by many people for many years. I'm sure even Lydia doesn't know the truth...the whole truth. Life was so miserable with Brenton. William worked for Brenton in an investment firm. I think he could see how miserable I was. We became close friends."

"Did you have an affair?" Martin surprised himself by suddenly pushing out of his own silence.

"No, we didn't. It didn't take me long to find out that William was...you know...gay."

"But you must have…" Martin's mind spun out of control. How could she be with a homosexual?

"No, it wasn't like that. William saved me. I found out I was pregnant with Brenton's child and I was about to get an abortion. I didn't want to have the baby; it was a horrible thought in and of itself. William stopped me and offered to marry me and help raise the baby as his own. He'd always wanted children and said it didn't matter if Brenton was the father, that if we raised her with love and respect, that was all that mattered. It was an out for William, too. He didn't want to be found out by anyone, least of all Brenton. But William never understood what living that lie would cost him."

"Sounds like you both paid a high price for that lie." Then Martin couldn't find anything else to say for a moment as he tried to take it all in. "So, Lydia is not William's daughter, after all. She's Brenton's."

"That's correct. But that's only part of the story. William was an intelligent man. He devised a plan to sneak me out of Brenton's house, where I could have fallen off the face of the earth and not be found. To this day, I don't know what he ever told Brenton about my whereabouts. William always said it was better if I didn't know," Christie recounted.

"So, you married William and then had Lydia, I take it," Martin said, still trying to understand this strange series of events.

"Yes. Though, obviously, it wasn't smooth sailing. The rest of this story belongs to William's mother, Annabelle Blackwell. Of course, he led his mother to believe Lydia was his daughter, another reason he wanted an out. The inevitable happened, and she discovered the kind of life he led. Annabelle Blackwell was the one person I can honestly say I despised."

"What happened when she found out?" Martin was entranced by the story, momentarily forgetting about the lies in hearing the tangled web of tales.

"As you might suspect, she blamed me for everything and was horrified by my presence. This went on until Lydia was three. It was difficult to live at that mansion. In a sense, it was yet another prison for me. I got really discouraged and frustrated that William would not defend me against his mother. He just couldn't stand up to her. I was so young, and I realized I couldn't make it on my own with a child to care for. Annabelle offered me a lot of money to leave town, but on the condition that I abandon my child. The one stipulation was that I was never to contact William or Lydia. Lydia had a home there and all the advantages I would never be able to provide for her. It was the price I had to pay for my child to have a good life." Christie began to weep quietly, and soon she could barely speak.

"But, sweetheart," Martin said as he held her hand, "that was your child...how could you accept money, no matter how much, in place of your flesh and blood? Not only that, but—" Martin had to stop his thoughts before he got too carried away.

"Marty…" She looked him in the eyes with the saddest face he'd ever seen.

Then it hit him. "You didn't take the money, did you?"

"How could I? I still felt it was best to leave. I've regretted it ever since the day I watched Lydia in the rearview mirror of the cab."

"Honey, Lydia said she'd always been told her mother died in a car accident, and that she only just found out her mother—you—are actually still alive," Martin told her.

"My God. My poor baby…"

"You couldn't have known." Martin held her hands in his, hoping to ease her pain. He watched her and remembered her lies. "But you should have told me. What did you think I would do if you'd told me sooner?" He got up from the table and looked out the kitchen window, trying to calm his own nerves.

"I know I should have, Marty. I guess I thought if I didn't talk about it with *anyone*, then it couldn't be real."

"Christie, I still can't believe you lied to me all these years!" Martin's anger got the better of him, and he slammed his hand down on the counter. "Now I wonder if I know you at all!" He glared at her and realized he couldn't hear any more. "I'm going out for some air."

He left the kitchen and went out the front door to sit on the front porch swing, which was cold to the touch. It was November in Wyoming, and winter was still sporadic. As he swung slowly back and forth, he took the cold, crisp air into his lungs. Tears formed in his eyes just to think about the betrayal. She hadn't cheated on him, but the hurt was still there. "Dammit," he said aloud, though no one was there to hear. Finally, he let out a long sigh and went back inside to face her.

Christie stood from the table when he entered the kitchen. "Martin, I don't know what to say except I'm *so* sorry."

He could not look her in the eye, but said, "I believe you truly are." He grabbed the coffee pot and poured himself another cup. "I want you to tell me the rest. Everything. Don't leave anything out," he told her as he sat back at the table.

Christie nodded but was silent for a few minutes. "I knew Annabelle was mean and hateful, but I never dreamed she would go to these lengths. I left my child there with her, never to be heard from again. I don't know how to face her after so many years."

"You will, because it's what has to be done. She's convinced it's you." He remembered Lydia's smile. "You know, no matter how angry I am now, it seems this was meant to happen. Her car broke down on her way here so she could find you, I have to believe that. It has forced you into facing some truths, and for that I'm grateful." Martin rose from the table and approached the counter, setting his cup down carefully. He turned around to leave the kitchen, and Christie rose from her seat, reaching out to touch his arm.

The emotions, positive and negative, filled her eyes. “Marty, will you ever forgive me?”

He shook his head slightly. “I don’t know.”

Chapter Fourteen

LYDIA HAD JUST FINISHED getting dressed for the day when she heard the phone ring. Sonja was there, still asleep, so Lydia couldn't imagine who was calling her. She strolled over to the phone quickly so it wouldn't wake Sonja. "Hello?"

"Yes, may I speak with Lydia Blackwell, please?"

"This is Lydia Blackwell. Can I help you?"

"Lydia...um...hello. My name is Christie Stoddard. I know you might find it strange that I'm calling you, but I—"

"Oh my God." It was all Lydia could say. She froze and literally could not move or speak for a few seconds.

"I'm sorry for calling. Well, actually, no. I'm not sorry. I was wondering, if...well...if you wanted to get together and…talk."

Lydia swallowed the lump that seemed to find a permanent home in her throat. She still couldn't believe what she was hearing.

"Lydia? Are you there?"

"Oh, yes. I'm sorry, Christie. I'm just really…surprised," Lydia said, finally finding her voice.

"Yes, I know. I was too when Martin came home and mentioned you had spoken," Christie said softly.

"I'd love a chance to talk with you, Christie. Where would you like to meet?"

"How about for lunch right there in your hotel?"

Lydia wondered if Christie had chosen the place specifically because it was public. It seemed like something she would have suggested herself. "That sounds wonderful. How about eleven-thirty?"

she offered.

"Great. I will see you then, Lydia."

Lydia was amazed. She wondered what Martin had said to his wife to cause this phone call. Lost in thought, she didn't hear Sonja stirring in the bed they'd shared the night before.

"Lydia? Who was on the phone?" Sonja's sleepy voice inquired.

"You won't believe it," Lydia said, turning to her.

"Christie?" Sonja guessed.

Lydia smiled and nodded. "She wants to have lunch and talk. I was not expecting that."

"Come here, you," Sonja said, inviting her back to the bed where she still lay naked beneath the covers. "It's going to work out great. If she really is your mother, she'd be a fool to let you go and not want some sort of relationship with you. You're a beautiful person."

Lydia gently touched Sonja's face. "Where did you come from? You're sweet, and I'm so happy you're here with me right now." Lydia bent down and kissed her softly, just barely touching her lips. Sonja smiled and wrapped her arms around Lydia's neck, pulling her closer in one passionate gesture. She kissed her deeply, as if she'd never kissed her before.

Lydia's body responded to the tune of the woman's passion, and it wasn't long before the clothes she had so carefully put on just an hour before were in a pile on the floor.

At eleven, Lydia once again made the finishing touches to her appearance. She wanted to have the perfect look; she wasn't sure why. Her gut instinct told her Christie Stoddard was indeed her mother, but now the apprehensiveness set in. Was she crazy? This woman had seemed to fall from the sky and into her lap. *How could this be happening?* she thought. But it was and Lydia had to go with it, right or wrong.

At precisely eleven fifteen, Sonja said goodbye and left for the day to run some errands. She'd offered to accompany Lydia to this meeting, but Lydia had declined because she knew she needed to do this on her own.

She walked to the elevator and nervously pushed the button. As she waited for it to arrive, she fidgeted with her attire, knowing it still wasn't perfect. Then she stopped. Christie Stoddard—or Cassandra Blackwell—would have to accept her for who she was, and no one else. She heard the ring of the elevator, and when the doors opened, she took a deep breath as her heart raced out of control. This was it. Lydia stepped into the elevator that would take her to meet the woman who had given her life.

The hostess in the restaurant was getting used to seeing Lydia on a daily basis, and smiled when she saw her enter. "Lydia, how nice to see you again. Are you alone for lunch today?" She was also used to seeing Lydia with Sonja.

"No, actually, I won't be alone. I'm meeting someone here. She's a tall, blonde woman, somewhat older." Suddenly, Lydia didn't even know how to describe Christie, though she'd memorized the picture she'd carried with her for days. She knew every line, every strand of hair, every piece of clothing worn in that picture.

"Wonderful. How about your favorite booth?" the hostess asked.

"Wow. I've only been in town for three days and I already have a favorite booth. Am I your only customer?"

The hostess said with a wink, "Nope. It's you and that guy over in the corner."

"Well, at least he has good taste. That booth will be fine, thanks." Lydia followed the hostess to the table. After the hostess left, she anxiously checked her watch. Eleven twenty-five.

"Hello, Lydia." The voice was close.

Lydia turned around to see Christie standing in front of her, and she stood from her seat. "Hello, Christie." She reached out to shake the woman's hand, then motioned for her to join her at the booth. "I thought I'd wait for you before I ordered."

"Great," Christie said, quickly glancing at the menu. The waitress arrived to take their drink orders.

"Cappuccino." The voices blended together in unison, and the waitress left the women staring up at each other in amazement.

"You like cappuccino?" Christie asked.

"I'm an addict. Father never could understand it. He had to leave his bl—"

"Black. It sure has been a long time since I've thought about...any of that," Christie whispered, glancing down at the table with a blank expression.

"I understand. I'm sorry if I've in any way been disruptive. It's just that I've needed some answers...not only for myself, but also for someone else," Lydia explained. Christie met her gaze, and Lydia noticed the woman seemed to relax just a little.

"I completely understand," Christie said "I just don't know where to begin. Look, I don't mean to sound untrusting, but I need to know one hundred percent that you are who you say you are. Do you have any identification or anything that could tell me for certain?"

"Of course." Lydia nodded and pulled out her driver's license, then suddenly thought of the purse.

Christie examined the license carefully, making note of the address. "I've never seen a good driver's license picture until now. How did that happen?"

"You've got to be kidding! My patients have also told me I couldn't take a bad picture, but some of them are not of sound mind."

Christie raised an eyebrow. "Patients? Are you a doctor?"

"Oh, no, I'm a therapist. I have my own practice now, which I run from my home. I really enjoy it," Lydia said.

"That's wonderful. What got you interested in that line of work?" Christie asked.

"I think I've always been fascinated with people's problems and what's under the surface. Or maybe it's due to the sense of mystery I feel surrounding my own life." Lydia paused for a moment, wondering whether or not now was the right time to bring up the most important part of this meeting. "Christie, speaking of mysteries, I have something I'm hoping you might recognize." She pulled out the silver purse.

"My God. I thought that was gone forever. I assumed it was stolen." Christie's eyes were wide, glistening with tears that didn't spill.

"I take it the initials engraved on it belong to you. Cassandra Lexington Blackwell." Lydia chose the words carefully, scrutinizing the woman's reaction.

"Not Blackwell. It's Burnham. I had the purse before I ever knew William. It was an old family heirloom and was given to me by my grandmother. She was given it when she was just a girl, coming out."

Lydia's mind wandered thinking about the words. There was so much more to 'coming out'. Secrets and mysteries were everywhere, and she knew Christie must have had as many of each as she did herself. "I think people would be thrilled to get a purse nowadays when they come out."

"I think you're right," Christie said. "How funny that would be." There was a brief silence. "How in the world did you come across this purse, Lydia?"

"It was given to me by a friend. Maybe you knew him. Derek Meade?" It was a shot in the dark, but she couldn't let any of the pieces of this puzzle slip by her.

"Oh my God, Derek. What a sweet, sweet soul." The light in Christie's eyes faded, and just a little of the color left her cheeks. "What do you mean, 'knew'?"

"Christie...he was murdered. The first time I ever saw him was right before my father died, and then I met him at the funeral. It was so odd," Lydia told her guardedly, not wanting to rehash the chilling scene. She felt bad for bringing the news up like this, but she didn't want to lie.

Christie put her hand over her mouth. "How? Why would anyone... Derek?" The woman seemed unable to put her words together.

"I don't know."

"Lydia, you know about your father, right?" Christie asked in a wary tone.

"I know he was gay, if that's what you mean. But I only found out when Derek told me. The whole thing had eluded me, and if anyone should have known, it was me."

The waitress finally came to the table for their order. Lydia ordered the lemon chicken salad with dressing on the side and Christie couldn't decide, so she ordered the same.

"Lydia, I have to say I'm a bit overwhelmed by all the information you've shared with me. But it does tell me one thing." Christie stopped before she could utter the words.

"What's that?"

"That you really are my little Lydia...my daughter. I didn't want to believe it at first, but now as we sit here, face to face, I know you're my baby girl," she said, and the tears rolled down her cheeks.

For a moment, Lydia refused to meet the woman's gaze, fearful of the consequences. But when she did, she felt her eyes water and she reached out to hold Christie's hand. "I have one question," she said, looking back and forth from one of Christie's eyes to the next, studying her.

"You want to know why I left you, don't you?" Christie's grip on Lydia's hand was strong.

"Yes," Lydia acknowledged. "I have a feeling it had to do with my grandmother. Am I right?"

"Yes, it did. Oh, it's so complicated, or seemed so at the time. Annabelle offered me money to leave town. More money than anyone I know has ever seen before."

"You needed the money," Lydia said slowly. "It's okay, I understand. Not many people could turn that down." She gazed down at the table, more disappointed than she'd expected to be.

Christie reached out to take Lydia's other hand. "No, Lydia. I left, but I did not take the money. I just couldn't. I was young and naïve, and Annabelle did a good job convincing me I was no good for either you or William. You had a home there, and you had your father. I'm sure it's no comfort to you now after all these years, but you should know, if I had it to do over again, I'd do things much differently."

"I never knew any of this." Lydia found herself staring at their clasped hands. "I only just discovered you were alive. I was told you'd died in a car accident. And I only found out this wasn't true because I happened to overhear a conversation I wasn't supposed to hear."

"Let me guess. Jackson and Rosita?"

"Yes. But I don't blame you. I've learned we all make choices to the best of our ability at the time." Lydia took a deep breath. "I do, however, blame my grandmother. She was the reason I wanted to leave that house from an early age."

"Annabelle did a lot of tasteless things to a lot of people. But I've never stopped thinking of you, Lydia. I hated not being a part of your life, knowing I had nothing to do with the person—the woman you've grown to become. I don't know what brought you here, what forces of nature or fate caused you to break down on that interstate, but I am so glad." Christie's voice shook in her throat as she obviously held back most of her threatening emotions.

Lydia couldn't stand it any longer. She stood from the table, somehow still surprised when Christie did the same, and they embraced there at the table, all the years past seeming to fade away. They hugged and shared tears just as if they were all alone. But they weren't.

Chapter Fifteen

LYDIA COULD SENSE SOMEONE watching her every move. When she turned away from Christie's conversation, there was no one in sight. Christie picked up on Lydia's preoccupation.

"Lydia? Are you okay?"

"Hm?" she half-heartedly answered. "Oh...no, I'm not sure. I'm just getting this strange feeling. I'm probably just paranoid. It's nothing."

"Well, it's no wonder with all you've been through. Your father's death, meeting Derek and discovering his body, and then finding your crazy mother after all these years. I think you're allowed," Christie said as she worked on finishing her salad.

"I guess you're right. It sounds so awful when you spell it out like that." Lydia paused and took a deep breath. "I have another question."

"Ask away. I'll try to answer as honestly as I can. There's been enough deception

"Thank you. It means a lot that we're able to sit here and have this conversation. So many times I've dreamed of it, and for years, I've lived for this day." Nervously, Lydia took another sip of her second cup of cappuccino. "Something was hidden in the purse."

"Really? I wasn't aware of anything inside it. Of course, anything could have happened while it was out of my possession."

"I found what appears to be a birth certificate. I'm curious to know why there's no father listed. It says 'Unknown'." Lydia handed the weathered piece of paper to Christie.

"That's strange. This isn't the original certificate," Christie said after looking it over carefully.

"What do you mean?" Lydia was more baffled than ever.

"I'm saying this is a forgery. Your original birth certificate named your father as your biological father, and you weren't born in Reno."

Lydia couldn't even think what may have happened to her birth certificate. But something else nagged even more intently in the back of her mind. She had to know. "That leads to my next question." Lydia dug in her handbag once again.

"My God, girl, what all have you got in there?"

"My whole life," Lydia said solemnly. "I found this in an old shoebox buried deep in my father's closet. No pun intended." She handed the paper over to Christie.

The woman examined it and put it down on the table. "I do recognize this. It's a marriage license...mine and your father's."

"Yes, I know. I've done the math and it just doesn't add up."

"What doesn't?" Christie asked, but she bit her lip and it seemed she already knew.

"I need to know who my father is." Lydia decided to be blunt. It was now or never.

Christie's head hung low. "You're right, Lydia. It doesn't add up...and there's a reason for that. Your father's name was Brenton Pritchard. I was involved with him when I was quite young. He came from a powerful family and was quite controlling, to say the least. I lived with him for a while, but soon I felt trapped by his power over me. I met your father—I mean, William, around that time. He was a young lawyer in Brenton's business at the time. It didn't matter to me about William's preferences. He was my one, true friend, and I took solace in that friendship. It meant the world to me. I then discovered I was pregnant, and that was when I knew I had to leave. A child of Brenton's would be a dangerous thing if he knew. William knew this, too, and offered to marry me. And so—"

"He saved you," Lydia finished for her.

"He did. He really did."

"And then he took your life away," Lydia said, suddenly feeling angry with the only man she'd ever known as her father.

"Honey, don't blame your father. He was a good man, a decent man. He just couldn't stand up to his mother. That's all. I made my peace with it long ago."

"How?" Lydia couldn't understand. "How could you make peace with having your life, your identity, not to mention your daughter taken away from you? You must be a saint, because God knows I couldn't do that, and I can't make peace with it. Even now."

"I understand," Christie said softly. "You've had so much taken away from you, much like myself. I'm so glad you found me, Lydia. Thank God you found me."

"Thank God," Lydia said, knowing there had to be a reason for it all.

They finished their lunch and a third round of cappuccino before they left the restaurant. After glancing at her watch, Lydia realized they'd been talking for over three hours. "My, how time flies when you meet your mother," she teased.

"Lydia, I adore your sense of humor. I look forward to getting to know more about you. A piece of my heart has been missing since the day I left. I realize we have far to go, but I'm still so proud that we've come together this way." Christie embraced Lydia in the lobby of the hotel and promised to call her in the morning.

In the elevator, Lydia still couldn't resolve the feeling she'd had in the restaurant. It hadn't occurred to her to be frightened, even after Derek's murder. There was no reason to be, she told herself, but inside she was shaken. She made a mental note to talk with Sonja about it when she saw her. Lydia assumed Sonja would still be running errands or visiting the relatives she'd talked about who lived just a few minutes away. She was anxious for her to return so she could tell her all she'd learned at lunch.

Lydia stepped off the elevator with her room card in hand, ready to relax for the rest of the afternoon and evening. When she opened the door, she saw a single red rose on the table by the bed. She dropped her things and walked toward the table. She didn't notice anyone standing behind her, and by the time she did, it was too late. A sharp pain shot through the back of her head, and everything went black.

Chapter Sixteen

"NICE WORK, MACINTOSH. LOOKS like she's out cold," the voice rang out.

"Was that absolutely necessary?" Sonja couldn't believe what she'd just done. She was actually starting to care about this one.

"You've played your part well—an award-winning performance. Now, get the purse and that birth certificate," the voice ordered.

"What are your plans? How do you expect to get away with this?" Sonja knew she was playing with fire.

"I'm sure you will see that I do...or you know the consequences."

"Joel, I know what the price is. It's not necessary to remind me every second," Sonja snapped.

"I suggest you watch your tone with me, sweetheart. Besides, how do you think your little lesbian lover here would react to you working against her, hmm?"

Sonja reluctantly dug through Lydia's handbag to retrieve the purse and birth certificate. "Here it is." She handed it to him, not even looking up. All she could see was Lydia passed out on the floor. "I'll expect you to keep your word."

Joel winked. "But of course. I *am* a gentleman, not that you would know anything about that."

"Neither would you." Sonja just wanted him out of her life for good. If she was ever found out, there would be bigger problems than Joel informing the entire police department about her sexual orientation. She'd helped commit a crime. Sonja MacIntosh had turned dirty.

Within seconds after Joel and his entourage departed the hotel room, Lydia regained consciousness. "What happened?" she whispered, holding her head.

"I don't know, honey. Are you all right?" Sonja asked, feeling strange to be acting like she didn't know a thing.

Lydia started to get up off the floor and stopped, steadying herself. "Whoa. I've got a massive headache." She stopped and looked at Sonja. "How long have you been here?"

"I just came in and saw you lying on the floor. Looks like a robbery of sorts. You must have been knocked out. I'm sorry I wasn't here sooner," Sonja said, attempting to cover her lies with sentiment.

"I'd call the police, but you're already here. It sure is handy, sleeping with a cop."

Sonja attempted a smile. *Some cop*, she told herself. "Of course I'm here. I wouldn't be anywhere else. But we do need to call the police and make a report. Let's look around and see if anything was taken, okay?" Sonja helped Lydia off the floor and waited for her to get her wits about her. She then went to the phone and called the Rock Springs Police Department. "They're on their way," she told Lydia a few minutes later.

"Okay, thanks," Lydia said while looking through her handbag.

Sonja watched nervously, knowing full well what Lydia's reaction would be. Her mind kept going back to just a few minutes before, when she herself had been the one ransacking Lydia's purse. She was glad she'd remembered to wear gloves. Leaving fingerprints was the last thing she wanted.

"No!" Lydia screeched.

"What is it?" Sonja asked, hating herself more every minute.

"The purse! It's gone. The birth certificate, too." Lydia exploded into hysterical weeping.

Sonja sat down on the bed and held her, trying to keep her calm, as though it were even possible. Then there was a knock at the door. "Yes?" she answered.

"Rock Springs Police Department," the voice called from the

other side of the door.

Sonja opened it slowly and stepped back to let them inside. “Hello, officers. I’m Lieutenant Sonja MacIntosh from the Highland Park Police Department.” Sonja flashed her badge to the two men.

“Nice to meet you. I’m Officer Phelps and this is my partner, Officer Davis. Is that Highland Park, Illinois?”

“Yes, it is,” Sonja answered. Every minute ticking by chipped away at her conscience.

“You’re far from home, Lieutenant. What’s the story here?” the officer inquired, getting out his notepad.

“Well, this is a friend of mine, Lydia Blackwell. I’m not here officially, just visiting. It looks like she was robbed. I had just walked in, because the door was open, and I saw her lying on the floor.” Sonja was careful not to give out too much information.

“I’m missing some valuable articles, officers,” Lydia interrupted.

“What’s missing, Ms. Blackwell?” Officer Davis asked.

“A silver antique purse and the birth certificate inside of it,” Lydia explained. “I had quite a lot of money in my purse, but they didn’t touch that.”

Officer Davis spent the next fifteen minutes with Lydia, getting a specific description of the missing items. “We’ll take down a report, Ma’am, and do some fingerprinting of your handbag and its contents. Would you like us to escort you to the hospital for a checkup?”

“No. I’m fine, really. I just need a really big aspirin.” Lydia stepped into the bathroom to find something for her headache.

Officer Phelps went to the squad car to retrieve his kit for pulling fingerprints from Lydia’s purse. Officer Davis stayed and reassured Lydia they would do what they could to find her things.

***

Finally, after almost two hours, the officers left and Sonja turned around to look at Lydia. “I know you’re upset, Lydia, but we’ll figure this out. I promise. Not to change the subject, but how did the meeting with Christie go?" She wanted to do anything to distract her from the war waging inside her own head.

"Really well," Lydia said slowly It took her a minute to shift gears from her apparent robbery to the surprisingly pleasant conversation she'd had over lunch. "Quite informative. Sonja, I think this is somehow related to my mother. Why else would somebody take only the two most personally important things to me right now instead of the money? I don't see any other explanation."

"I'm not sure," was all Sonja could say.

"If that's the case, my mother could be in danger."

"I suppose it's a possibility. Listen, Lydia, I need to go for a bit. Are you going to be all right?"

Lydia shrugged, still not quite convinced this wasn't a dream. "Sure. Don't worry, I'm fine. I think I'll just relax here and watch some TV. Don't be too long."

"I'll be back soon." Sonja leaned over and gave Lydia a quick kiss on the cheek.

***

Sonja couldn't open the door fast enough. It was pure torture, but she knew she deserved it for what she'd done. As soon as she was out the door, she grabbed her cell phone from her back pocket and called to make reservations to leave Rock Springs that night. Taking a deep breath, she looked back at Lydia's door, thinking about the person on the other side. Not long ago, she would have walked away from a situation like this and not felt a thing. But now—now things were different. Lydia would never forgive her for what she'd done, blackmail or not. When the elevator doors opened, she stepped inside, wondering what was to become of her life now. Then she made her way to the hotel bar.

"What'll you have?" the bartender asked.

"Two Valium and a Prozac," Sonja quipped.

"Wouldn't you know? That shipment never arrived today. Any

substitutes?" the bartender asked, shining wine glasses with his bar rag.

Sonja closed her eyes, as if to transport herself into another time and place. She read the name tag on the bartender's vest and grabbed some money out of her coat, placing it on the counter. "Issac, I would love a long island ice tea, heavy on the island."

"You got it. One heavy island, comin' up."

"Thanks." It didn't take him very long at all, thankfully. Taking a sip, Sonja grinned and raised her glass to the bartender. A few of these, and she could forget her name. God only knew she wanted to. After drinking half of it, she once again pulled out her cell phone and dialed the only other number she could think to call.

"Kovacs, here. What can I do ya for?"

"In your dreams."

"Sonja! I've missed your face!"

"You too, Hank." She always felt a comfort from her partner, like going home. And that's where she wanted to be right now.

"What's up? You're never sentimental," Hank acknowledged in a soft whisper.

"I'm in trouble. Big trouble." It was an understatement, and she knew it.

"What kind of trouble? Talk to me."

Sonja wasn't sure where to begin, but she definitely wasn't going to relay the whole thing over the phone. "It's a long story, and I can't go over it now. I'm coming back tonight after I figure out a few things. I just needed to hear a friendly voice instead of my conscience."

"What time does your plane arrive? I'll come fetch ya. Then you can fill me in," he offered.

"Midnight. Thanks, Hank, it means a lot. I'll tell you everything when I see you."

"No problem. See you then."

Sonja ended the call and set her phone down on the bar. After ordering another drink, there was one more call she needed to make. She quickly dialed the number before she lost her nerve.

"Joel Pritchard, please."

"Speaking. Who the hell is this?"

"MacIntosh. I'd like to have a meeting with you. It's important." Sonja knew she was taking a chance, but there was no going back now.

A deep laugh came through the phone. "You want a meeting with me? How cute. Sure, why not? You have me curious, little girl. You realize nothing matters now, since I have what I've been after. Thanks to you. Meet me at seven."

Exasperated by his tone, Sonja tried to maintain some level of dignity, even if it was artificial. "Fine." She quickly hung up. The less time she spent with the man, the better. If only she'd picked up on being followed from the airport. Being a cop, she should have known, or at the very least felt it. But when Joel Pritchard's men grabbed her and knocked her out cold in the hotel parking lot, there was no doubt. She still hadn't managed to escape the memory of being gagged and tied to a chair.

After she'd come to, she was in a cold, dark room with three men.

"Lieutenant Macintosh, what are you doing in Wyoming?" the voice had boomed around her.

Sonja hadn't been able to see who asked the question. "Visiting a friend. How do I know you?"

"You're the detective here. Maybe you can figure it out. I'm looking for something that belonged to my father many years ago. On his deathbed, he asked that I find it. I believe you can help me."

"And what if I don't?" Sonja had asked bluntly.

"I think it would be in your best interest to help me, if we understand each other."

"This is crazy. I am an officer of the law. You can't just—" A hand came out of nowhere and made contact with her face.

"You've underestimated me, Lieutenant. That is not good. You are in no position to defy me. I understand there's a secret you'd like hidden from your police force, one that could destroy a career in no time flat. I'm sure you wouldn't want to halt your promising rise within the department. You've come so far for a woman in a man's world. It would be a pity," the voice in the shadows taunted.

Damn! Sonja couldn't fathom where he could have found out about her. Hank certainly wouldn't have told anyone, and she'd been so sure she'd covered her tracks. "Where did you get your information?"

"Oh, don't you worry your pretty little lesbian head about it, sugar. It wasn't that difficult. Now, let's carry on with the business at hand." A tall, dark shadow stepped into the light.

"Pritchard." Sonja knew about Joel Pritchard and his mobster family. They had eluded police in the Chicago area for years.

"You know me. Good. Now, this Lydia Blackwell person, she has what I want. She has the purse and its contents. You will get it for me. I don't care how, but you will."

"Forget it," Sonja had replied stoically. "She's been through enough as it is." Once again, a hand slapped her across the face, the blow so intense it practically knocked her off her seat.

"My dear Lieutenant, I'm afraid we have a miscommunication here. I said you *will* get it for me. It's not up for negotiation," Pritchard reiterated. "If not, you know what will happen."

"Okay, okay." She had worked too hard, spending years taking the jokes, the needling from lazy, sloppy men on the job. Sonja was better than that and she knew it. She'd had to make sacrifices, and this was no different. "Give me a few days, please. I don't want her hurt, do you understand me?" She'd forgotten to be scared of the man the minute she'd thought of Lydia.

Joel Pritchard moved closer—so close she had felt his breath on her skin. "Just so there's no further miscommunications, I don't take orders from a lesbian...unless there's something in it for me," he whispered, running a finger down the side of her neck.

Remembering it now sent a chill down her spine. Shaking it out of her head, she took one last sip of her drink. Sitting for a moment, not moving and barely breathing, Sonja found herself suddenly lost in her own despair. She knew what she had to do and why.

Chapter Seventeen

SONJA GLANCED AT HER watch again. Two minutes before seven. She was glad she'd suggested Soldier Park for their meeting. Nestled in an older part of town, it was secluded and suited her purposes. The trees surrounding the small park almost acted as a circular wall, blocking the outside world. Sonja stepped out of the black Toyota Corolla she'd rented at the airport and walked over to the pavilion in the middle of the park. She took notice of the only other people around—a young couple, holding hands and walking through the pathway built around the park.

It was five minutes after seven when the black limousine pulled up on the side street across from the park. Sonja watched carefully as Joel's entourage assisted him out of the long black car. She thought it amusing that people with money could no longer do things for themselves. Dressed in a dashing beige Armani suit with a long tan overcoat, Joel Pritchard was the picture of perfection. Even if it was Wyoming.

He walked slowly with his two best men toward her. He carefully sat on the bench directly across from her, staring her down intently, watching her every move. "So, MacIntosh, to what do I owe the distinct pleasure of this meeting?"

"I'm calling your bluff, Pritchard. You blackmailed me into doing something that was completely wrong. The irony is that whether or not you tell the entire world my personal business doesn't really matter to me anymore. I could lose more than my career. I could lose my freedom. I want out of this mess." Sonja spoke emphatically and without a single doubt in her mind. Even if she lost everything, it was worth standing up to the bastard.

"I see. You think I won't make good on my promise, is that it? Hell, I don't even need you anymore. I got what I wanted. The purse and that document are all I was after. So what if we had to knock the dame out to do it? Live with it," Joel told her, looking hard into her eyes. After pausing, he leaned in closer. "Don't misunderstand me. You were just dirt on my shoe, sweetheart. I'd just as soon kill you as look at you, but let me offer you one piece of advice. Don't ever cross me. I can and will make life pure hell for you."

"You already have. I've got nothing left to lose, Joel. I just want it ended, that's all. I'm not out to cross you. I want out, and that's where I plan to be. Goodbye." And with that, Sonja got up from the bench without taking her eyes off of him. She turned and walked back to her car, knowing full well he could shoot her in the back and be done with her once and for all.

***

Once in her car and driving, Sonja let out all the fear pent up inside her with a scream. Strange, that he didn't have his men follow her—or worse, kill her. Talking to Joel Pritchard was not the hard part. Confessing everything to Lydia would be. Sonja didn't know how to face her; she could barely face herself. But it was time to bite the bullet, even if it meant she never saw Lydia again.

Sonja pulled into the hotel parking lot around eight. Her heart beat in rapid succession because it, too, knew this wasn't going to be easy. She'd gotten herself into this mess and, somehow, someway, she was going to get out. After a few reflective minutes sitting in the car, she stepped out and walked into the lobby. The ride in the elevator seemed endless as she went over the conversation in her mind—how it would start and how on earth she could possibly defend her actions. She stood in front of the door, nervous about going inside. She really wanted to make a run for it and never look back. Finally, she knocked on the door before opening it, just in case Lydia might be edgy since the break in.

"Sonja?" Lydia called out.

"Yeah, hon, it's me. I didn't want to startle you."

Lydia strolled briskly up to Sonja and threw her arms around her, holding her as tight as she could. "God, I've missed you."

Sonja held Lydia tight, knowing it might be the last time after what she was about to do. Pulling away suddenly, Sonja looked longingly into Lydia's eyes. "Lydia, I need to talk to you...desperately."

"Well, I kinda like desperate women, especially when they're desperate for me."

Sonja let a faint smile cross her lips for a split second. "After you hear what I have to say, your thoughts might change."

Lydia took stock of Sonja's demeanor, but her smile didn't quite fade. "I don't see how."

"Just hear me out, Lydia. Here, we'll need to sit. Please." Sonja motioned for her to sit on the edge of the bed, then joined her.

Lydia nodded. "Sure. I'm all yours."

Sonja let out a deep breath to cleanse her entire body before uttering one word. "First of all, something happened yesterday when I was leaving the hotel. I was kidnapped on the way to my car and thrown into the back of a limousine. I don't remember much else except that when I awoke, I was in a dark room, gagged, and bound to a chair."

"*What?*" Lydia yelled. "Why the hell didn't you say anything to me, for God's sake? Are you all right?" Lydia reached out to embrace Sonja, worry instantly dominating her features.

"Yes, I'm fine," Sonja told her, breaking away from Lydia's embrace. "Lydia, please hear me out," she said, suddenly afraid she'd never get through this nightmare.

Lydia let out a heavy sigh and nodded. "Okay, go on. I'm sorry."

"That's okay. The man responsible...well, his name is Joel Pritchard. Do you know him?"

"Holy shit," Lydia declared in amazement.

"I'll take that for a yes," Sonja acknowledged.

"It's just that, if I'm right...my God."

Sonja watched as Lydia's eyes rolled around and she stood up, walking back and forth in one spot, appearing somewhat manic. "Slow down. What are you trying to say?"

"In my conversation with my mother today, she told me who my father is—or was. Brenton Pritchard." Lydia sat back on the bed next to Sonja.

"Oh boy. That's Joel's father and the head of this crime family. Joel may not even know your story but, either way, that purse and birth certificate are quite important to him," Sonja told her.

"What are you saying, that Joel stole them out of my handbag?"

"It's more than that," Sonja said as she rose from the bed to pace around the room. Her hands were sweating as she planned the next words before they left her lips. "God, I don't know how to explain this. Joel blackmailed me into helping him get what he wanted. He told me that if I didn't help him, he would make a phone call to the Chief of Police in Highland Park and every department in the area and inform them of my so-called 'lifestyle'. He must have had to do some real digging in the first place."

"What?" Lydia said, staring at Sonja with wide, unblinking eyes. The color left her face in a flash. She got up from the bed where she'd been so calmly sitting, taking in what Sonja told her. "It was *you*? I don't understand...I thought we were—I mean, we've shared so much. How could you?" Lydia openly sobbed without even looking at Sonja.

Sonja felt she could hardly meet Lydia's gaze, even if it was offered. She had little to say to defend her actions. What could she say? "I know. I felt like I had no choice. And, oh Jesus...I was the one who knocked you out. Lydia, there was a gun at my back. I could have been dead at any minute."

"Apparently, I could have been, too!" Lydia turned from the window in one quick movement to glare at her.

"Baby, don't you think I know how and where to hit someone on the back of the head without giving a serious injury?" Sonja realized suddenly how ridiculous that sounded.

Lydia looked carefully into her eyes. "Oh, how comforting." After pausing for a moment, she added, "And don't 'baby' me." Lydia walked around the room, pacing and choking back tears, going through the impossible array of emotions. Then she screamed. "I don't believe this. I trusted you!" She returned to stand inches from Sonja's face, wordless for a few seconds as she glared. She seemed to have problems breathing, huffing out in short bursts. "Those things are all I have of my identity. And now they're gone." She sat down again on the bed and hung her head in her hands, weeping.

"I'm so sorry, Lydia. Don't you think I know what I've done? That's why I met with Pritchard tonight and told him I was out. Done. Let him tell the whole goddamn force. I don't care anymore. I know that saying I'm sorry doesn't even remotely begin to make up for anything. I wish I were stronger, because after it happened, I realized...it just hit me that—"

"That what? What did you realize?" Lydia sneered at her, and the look of hatred burning behind her eyes made Sonja think the woman didn't really see her in that moment.

"I realized I had to confess everything, because…" Sonja was suddenly afraid to say the words out loud.

"Because what, Sonja?" Lydia's voice came soft and quivering, a sudden contrast to her anger.

Sonja turned to face her, the tears streaming down her face. "Because I love you. I fought it so much. You have no idea. Then tonight, the thought of losing you for good was something I just couldn't face. So, there it is. I love you,

Lydia," Sonja's sobbing voice rang out.

Finally, after what seemed like hours of silence, Lydia whispered under her breath, "I love you, too."

Sonja's tears subsided long enough to make out the words. But she wanted to be sure. "What?"

"I'm saying I love you." Lydia stared at her, and though she didn't smile, Sonja knew she really meant the words. Unbelievably, after everything, Lydia still cared for her—loved her. "But I am *so* angry I can barely stand the sight of you. I don't know what emotion I'm feeling right now."

Sonja averted her eyes from Lydia's glare. "I know. I'm angry with myself for letting him use me that way over something I didn't want to get out. I'm afraid of my own truth, my own life." She inhaled and let out a troubled sigh. "But no more." She stood up and faced Lydia, then grabbed her hands. "Please give me a chance to earn your trust again. I want to help you get that purse back," she said softly.

"That's a tall order right now," Lydia said. "People have lied to me nearly my entire life, and I don't know how I can look at you without seeing the betrayal. But I love you." Lydia touched her face with a gentle hand, then turned away. "I have to have that purse *and* the birth certificate."

Sonja let out a deep breath and slowly shook her head. "You don't need the birth certificate."

Lydia frowned, wiping the tears from her eyes. "What do you mean? I need it and Joel Pritchard has it."

"Joel has a fake," Sonja said, feeling the weight of her actions lifting a little. She'd manage to at least do something right, even if it was a small thing.

Lydia's breathing had slowed. "Go ahead and explain that part to me, too," she said.

"I made a fake copy of the birth certificate and switched them in your handbag. I was sweating it for a few seconds, hoping to hell I didn't get caught. Here's yours," she said and handed Lydia the piece of paper. "I may have managed to do something right in all this mess."

Tears immediately returned to Lydia's eyes. "How did you do that in such a hurry?"

"Well, it was a struggle, but I took the certificate yesterday and made a fake while you were with Christie. I'm sorry for taking it, but I had to." Sonja really didn't know if Lydia would understand, but it felt like their chances were better now.

Lydia gave a very small smile, even through all this madness. "It's all right, Sonja. I can hardly be mad at you for that." But the other thing was another story and they both knew it. Lydia put her face back into her hands, and in seconds her shoulders shook again with another wave of weeping.

Slowly, Sonja went to her and put an arm gently around Lydia's shoulders. She didn't think there was anything else she could possibly say in the moment.

"Do you think Derek had a reason for giving me that purse?" Lydia asked, turning her head slowly to meet Sonja's gaze.

"What kind of reason?" The thought had occurred to Sonja, too, but she'd never mentioned it.

"Like maybe he knew something would happen to him." Lydia stared blankly at her hands, like she couldn't quite believe her own thoughts.

"It's possible. From what you've told me about Derek, though, I don't believe he would have knowingly put you in that kind of danger."

"I guess you're right. Do you think Joel…" Lydia stopped.

"What?" Sonja raised an eyebrow, wondering what was going through Lydia's mind, though her own thoughts were a jumbled mess.

"I just realized... According to what my mother told me, Joel is my half-brother. What if he's responsible for Derek's death? That's how it looks, doesn't it?"

Sonja nodded. "Yes, that's what I'd think, too. I want to get that purse back and figure this whole thing out, Lydia." She strolled over to the phone and dialed a number.

"Who are you calling?"

"I'm canceling my plane reservations. We have a lot to do, and I've decided I'm not going anywhere, unless it's with you." Sonja was glad she'd chosen not to board that plane, and more grateful than anything for Lydia's affections.

Lydia, by any stretch of the imagination, had not given her trust back to Sonja and would never forget the betrayal. Sonja saw this all too clearly on the woman's face. But she had, in a sense, forgiven her, even when Sonja couldn't forgive herself for what she'd done.

Sonja finished her business on the phone and turned to see Lydia sitting on the edge of the bed, lost in thought. She knew she would have to work harder than ever to earn back the trust she'd so foolishly thrown away. Sonja MacIntosh, for the first time in almost a decade, was now willing to be that brave. She sat next to Lydia on the bed, put her arms around her, and kissed her on the cheek.

"So," she said, "tell me about your mother."

Chapter Eighteen

THE THOUGHTS IN LYDIA'S head took over completely. Why did Joel Pritchard want the birth certificate and the purse so badly? What were they to him? The whole thing was complete madness. She was curious about the Pritchard family, now that she knew she was a part of it. What were they hiding? If this was her heritage, she wanted nothing to do with it. The only heritage Lydia cared about was the one the silver purse held for her.

It seemed to take hours for Lydia to tell the tale of her meeting with Christie. Sonja stared at her through all of it, her eyes widening with everything Lydia told her.

"Unbelievable. I'm still puzzled about the birth certificate and what Joel wants with it."

Lydia shook her head in disbelief. "I don't know, but Christie did say the one I showed her was a forgery." As if to find something she might have missed, Lydia rummaged through her infamous bag to find the faded paper which somehow held her fate.

"What are you looking for? You've seen it a million times."

Lydia sighed in frustration. "I don't know. I thought a million and one wouldn't hurt, I guess." She walked over to the bathroom and held it up to the bright light. "Wait a minute. Sonja, look at this. Am I seeing things, or has this been altered?"

Sonja examined the paper scrupulously. "I think you're right, but I can't make out the letters beneath. I say we get it closely examined."

"Fine by me. This whole thing gets more mysterious every day. I wonder if I'll ever know the truth of where I come from." Lydia shook her head.

Sonja reached out and held Lydia, whispering softly, "You will. I promise, you will." She stroked her hair gently and then kissed her cheek. "How about we go get some dinner? There's a great Chinese place down the street."

"That sounds perfect." Lydia grabbed her coat and the women left the hotel for dinner. She wasn't sure how to feel about Sonja's actions. If there was one thing she did know, it was that she loved her. She just prayed it was enough.

After dinner, they went for a drive around town, talking about anything they could and avoiding the subject on both their minds. Finally, Sonja pulled over in the community college parking lot. It was a spot she knew well since she'd been a young girl visiting her parents. It overlooked the entire city and was quite beautiful at night. "Lydia," she said, turning off the engine, "I need to tell you something."

Lydia turned toward her, reached out, and softly touched her face. "Sure. Tell me."

"I don't know where things will end up with us, especially now, but I need you to know just how very much I love you. I haven't said that to anyone in over eight years and I swore I never would. But you…you make me feel things I never knew I could feel," Sonja confessed, her eyes suddenly misty.

Lydia didn't have the words to react. Instead, she reached out and held Sonja as close as she could. Then she whispered in her ear, "I love you, Sonja." After pulling away from their embrace, she looked her in the eye and held herself there, as if seeing the woman for the first time. "I don't know, either. I just know I can't walk away right now."

Sonja started the engine again and they ventured back to the hotel. Once in the security of Lydia's room, the events of the past few hours were momentarily forgotten. They spent the night talking, laughing, and loving as if the outside world simply did not exist.

***

As morning appeared, Sonja and Lydia still lay in each other's arms. Sonja was the first to wake, but she couldn't make herself move. All she wanted to do was watch the woman she loved dreaming in peaceful splendor. Within a few moments, Lydia's hazel eyes opened to see Sonja staring at her. "How long have you been watching me?"

"Not long. Just all my life." Then, after a long silence, she asked, "What do you say we go home?"

Lydia let out a deep sigh. "I…I don't know. I just found my mother. I'm not sure I'm ready to leave her just yet."

"I understand that, babe, I really do. Why don't you give her a call and ask if she's up for a vacation?"

"I wonder if she would. It would give us a chance to get to know each other." Lydia nodded when she made up her mind. "I'll give her a call after breakfast."

"Wonderful." Sonja studied Lydia with a close eye. She began to realize just what an amazing person Lydia really was. Sonja knew she should have been on a plane by now, kissing this whole mess goodbye, but Lydia had changed that future, and she was grateful for it. They got dressed for the day and made their way downstairs to the restaurant for croissants, juice, and coffee.

"I love sharing breakfast and this daily stuff with you," Lydia said, taking her last sip of coffee. "I'd forgotten, or maybe I've never even known, how nice it is."

"It's amazing, isn't it? By the way, I love you," Sonja whispered. They stood from their table to leave.

"I love you, too, Sonja," Lydia told her as they got on the elevator to go back to the room. Once inside, she kissed Sonja on the cheek and said, "Now it's time to call my mother."

"What a lucky woman she is." She watched Lydia and felt her heart jump when she saw her press the speaker button.

Lydia's face flushed when Christie's voice rang out. "Hello?"

"Hello, Christie. It's Lydia."

"Lydia! It's wonderful to hear from you. I wanted to tell you how much I enjoyed our lunch yesterday. I'm just about ready to head out to work," Christie said, her voice coming out a little rushed over the speaker.

"How would you like to skip work for a while?" Lydia asked, her voice shaking a bit with nerves.

"I would love it, but I really can't."

"What if you didn't have to worry about money for a change? Christie, I wanted to ask you if you'd consider coming home with me to Chicago for a while. Or, to be more specific, back to Kenilworth. I know you have a life here, and I don't want to interfere with that, but I think we could work together and solve this mystery called my life...and your life, too."

"Oh...I just don't know. Going back would be both wonderful and heart-wrenching. It's so kind of you, really, but financially, I—"

"Christie, please. Let me take care of it. I've never had a mother to dote on and take care of, or even spend time with. Please come with me. I'd like this chance to get to know one another," Lydia pleaded.

"You make it so tempting, I have to say. Let me talk to Martin. The thought of it is exciting, and Lord knows I could use a vacation. Thank you, Lydia."

After Lydia hung up, she straightened her shoulders and let out a huge sigh of relief.

Sonja watched her reaction and walked toward her. "I'd like to think it was me who put that glow on your face, but since it's your mother, I can live with that."

Lydia pulled Sonja close to her and they embraced as tightly as they could. When Lydia finally pulled away, she looked right into Sonja's eyes. "You give me another kind of glow." She gave Sonja such a passionate, fevered kiss, it rendered Sonja speechless for a moment.

"Lydia, I love you. I really do."

Lydia pulled away. "I know you do. I can feel it."

They spent the night just holding each other. Sonja knew, and accepted, the fact that Lydia wasn't ready to give all her trust back just yet. She knew she would eventually, but for now, Sonja had to be content with the way things were. Even with the tension hanging over them, it felt better than anything she could ever remember.

***

Just a few miles away from her daughter, Christie Stoddard awaited her husband's arrival. She wasn't sure how he would feel about her going away with the daughter she'd just reclaimed after thirty-five years.

"Martin?" She'd waited until he was settled with his after-work beer.

"Yes, honey, what is it?" He was actually paying more attention to the paper he read, but she had to bring this up now.

"I received a surprising phone call today."

"Really? Who was it?" he asked half-heartedly.

"It was Lydia." The name felt oddly natural passing her lips.

"That's great. What did she have to say? It must have been something wonderful to make your eyes sparkle like that."

So he *had* noticed. "Well, as a matter of fact, it is. She's going back home soon, and—"

"And she wants you to go with her?" He seemed remarkably unsurprised.

"Yes. She did ask me, Martin, and I was apprehensive at first, but I think it's a wonderful opportunity to get to know my daughter."

"I do too, darlin'. What about money? Expenses?"

She was thrilled that he seemed to support the idea, and his next questions didn't take her too off guard. Martin always made decisions based off money. "I know," she said, "and that's why I was a bit hesitant. But Lydia offered to cover everything, saying she wants to be able to dote on her mother."

"You've already decided, haven't you?" He tried to frown, but the joy shone through the attempt and Christie knew she already had him on her side. He let out a hearty laugh. "Well, honey, send me a postcard."

Christie jumped up and down like she was twelve and hugged Martin so tight she only barely realized it might have made it difficult for him to breathe. "Thank you. Thank you, Martin! I love you so much! I better get packing!" She kissed him several times before rushing off to get ready.

While she packed in their bedroom, she called the restaurant to let them know she'd be taking an indefinite vacation, and if she didn't have her job when she returned, that was okay. Her boss reassured her it didn't matter. There weren't many waitresses as good as Christie, so her job would be waiting for her. She hung up and couldn't wait to make the next call.

"Lydia? It's Christie."

"Hi, there!" Lydia exclaimed.

"I talked with Martin, and I guess you have a travel companion!" Christie squealed into the phone.

"Wonderful! I was planning on leaving tomorrow morning around eight, if that's all right. We can take our time getting there and find a hotel room for a few nights. I thought that would give us a chance to get better acquainted."

"That's a great idea. Thank you again, Lydia. It means the world to me." Christie knew this was a chance to really know the woman her daughter had become, but beneath that remained the knowledge that it would open old wounds. At least now, she had Lydia.

***

For their last day in Wyoming, Sonja played tour guide and drove Lydia up into the mountains where she used to camp. Along the way, they dropped in on a cousin of Sonja's just a few miles north of Rock Springs. The rest of the day rapidly succeeded into evening. After enjoying watching the sun go down together, they went out for dinner before heading back to the hotel.

Once the door to the hotel room closed behind her, Sonja smiled as she watched Lydia from across the room, then walked toward her, touched her shoulder, and turned her around so they could be face to face. She took Lydia's face in her hands. "You know, you are my favorite scenery." She held Lydia in her arms, not saying a word, just feeling a closeness that needed no expression.

After pulling away, she asked the poignant question burning in her mind. "Lydia? Have you told Christie that you're gay...or about us?"

"What? I'm gay?" Lydia made a face.

"Well, if you're not, you're a damn good actress!"

"Why, thank you." Lydia took a bow as if taking her curtain call. "But no, I haven't. We talked about my father, William, and then Derek, but nothing overtly personal. I have a feeling I'll be telling her in the next few hours. I don't think she'll have a problem with it, but there's always that fear. I've come too far, now. It seems so trivial compared to everything else."

"True enough. I'm anxious to meet the woman." Sonja's detective instinct took over. Secretly, she was skeptical about this sudden relationship between mother and daughter. It seemed too fast to suit her. Thirty-five years gone, and now they were taking a road trip. She wanted to know just what secrets Christie Stoddard still held; what did she have that would put together the missing pieces of Lydia's puzzle? And just where did the purse fit into that puzzle? Lost in thought, Sonja hadn't noticed Lydia flipping pages in the phone book. "What are you doing?"

"I wanted to order some special food for our trip. I want her to have the best, if only for once in her life."

"Babe, she has the best. She has you for a daughter."

Chapter Nineteen

LYDIA ARRIVED IN FRONT of Christie's house at precisely eight the next morning. It was a quaint little house, faded yellow with brown shutters and a white, painted front porch. A single-car garage sat to the right and appeared to be newly sided. The front yard was small with a sidewalk leading up to the screened-in porch. It was not what Lydia had expected, but she loved the coziness of it and it seemed to suit her mother—or what she knew of her so far.

Sonja had driven her rental car back, because it was just easier than dealing with life at the airport. Sonja and Lydia said their goodbyes at the hotel and planned to meet up in Nebraska to spend the night. Lydia gave her the name and address of the place she'd stayed on the way out.

Lydia walked up to the screen door and knocked. Christie smiled when she answered the door. "Hello, there."

"Hi. I'm so excited about this trip, Christie. I think it's going to be great." As Lydia grabbed Christie's bags, Martin walked toward the sound of the commotion to give Christie one last hug.

"Hi, Lydia. So, you're the one taking my gorgeous wife away from me, eh?" He smiled, and that smile alone told Lydia she had his blessing.

"That would be me. Whenever you get some time, Martin, feel free to join us. Let me know, and I'll send you a plane ticket."

"I just might take you up on that if I get too lonely," he said. "Listen, you better take good care of her, or I'll be there to grab her faster than you can say radiator hose."

Oh, don't worry, I plan to take very good care of her." She gave Martin a warm hug and thanked him for picking her up that fateful day when her car had broken down.

Martin grabbed the bags from Lydia's hands and carried them out to the car as mother and daughter strolled behind him. After loading all the bags, he hugged his wife tightly, as if he would never let her go.

"It's okay, Marty. Thank you for giving me this chance—especially after everything. I'm not sure I deserve you," Christie said.

Martin stroked his wife's face gently. "Sure, you do. You know I can't deny a mother spending time with her daughter. Just know how much I'll miss you. And even more than that, I love you."

"I love you, Martin. I'll call you when we get in." Christie gave him one last kiss before getting inside Lydia's Jeep. They both waved as Lydia pulled the car away from the curb.

Pulling onto the interstate, Lydia glanced over at her passenger. "I'm so glad you're coming home with me. I feel like we have so much to catch up on."

"Only a lifetime, dear." Christie watched her carefully as she drove.

Lydia felt her eyes upon her, but it wasn't uncomfortable. Still, the car fell silent, and her mind wandered over the past few days.

Christie noticed the silence. "What's on your mind?"

"What do you mean?" Lydia felt her heart race, finding it a bit eerie that Christie easily recognized her conflicting thoughts.

"You just seem to be worrying about something, like there's something you want to say. Don't be afraid. You can't lose me. Not now."

Lydia wanted so much to spill her secrets and intimate thoughts, but decided against it. "I don't know how you can know me so well without really knowing me," she said, pausing for a moment to take a deep breath. "I want to wait until we stop for the night to talk to you about this. It could take a while."

"I look forward to our first heart-to-heart," Christie said, then turned her attention to the landscape passing them by.

As they drove, they munched on specially prepared salami, fresh fruit, cheese and crackers, and ginger ale. They stopped at a rest area to have lunch just outside of Cheyenne. Lydia told Christie about her patients, her practice, and philosophies on life. Christie talked about her life with Martin in Wyoming and, oddly enough, discovered that she and her long-lost daughter were more alike than not.

"I have to commend Rosita. She did a marvelous job raising you. I'm so proud, though I don't know if I have the right to be," Christie stated solemnly.

"Of course you have the right. And thank you. As exasperated as I get with Rosita sometimes, she's been like a rock. She thinks she did a good job, too." Lydia wanted to pinch herself. It couldn't be real. The innermost part of her knew the woman in her Jeep was her mother. She had to be. The bond was immediate, and Lydia didn't question how right it felt.

Soon, curiosity got the better of her. "I have to ask you something." She'd decided posing the question once they got back in the car was the best idea, so she wouldn't be able to run away from the question.

"Sure," Christie said. "You can ask me anything." She studied her daughter with guarded eyes as if waiting for a bomb to drop.

Lydia took in a deep breath. "Why didn't Martin know about me and your past? I have to confess, it hurt, and I'm sure Martin was upset learning about it from a complete stranger."

"Oh," Christie said. She stared out the window and didn't turn to look at Lydia. "I don't know if I can ever explain the depths of what Annabelle did to me. Leaving you ripped my heart out, but she had me convinced I was a danger to myself and, really, I believed the lies. Until I saw you."

Lydia nodded as if she understood the torment her grandmother had caused. She knew all the years could not be wiped away in a single meeting, but it was a start. "You know, I think it was meant to be." She reached out to hold her mother's hand. "It's a brand new day."

It didn't take long for them to reach the hotel in North Platte, Nebraska, just a few miles south of the interstate. It was nice to be able to relax and stretch before finishing the trip. Sonja, of course, was already waiting for them there. She had been checked in for over an hour and had called Hank to go over some work details. She'd also managed to find adjoining rooms for the three of them the day before.

Lydia checked in, grabbed their room key, and parked right in front of the room. When they brought their bags up, Lydia was impressed by the modest room, clean and well-equipped with two queen-sized beds. After getting settled, Christie sat down on one of the beds, Lydia sat on the other, and they just looked at each other for a moment.

"I think we need champagne!" Lydia exclaimed, suddenly remembering she had some in the cooler.

"Is there anything you haven't thought of to make this trip wonderful?"

"Ah-ha, found it!" Lydia said, pulling the champagne from the bottom of the cooler and suddenly realizing how much food she'd brought. She twisted the bottle open.

"You look like you've done that before. I'm not even sure how that all works. Any time we've been able to splurge on Champagne, Martin takes care of that twisting stuff."

"My father taught me a lot of things. I could be stranded in the middle of nowhere and not have a clue, but, by God, I will know how to open a champagne bottle." Finally hearing the pop, Christie retrieved two glasses and held them for Lydia to pour the sparkling liquid. "I think a toast is in order, here."

"I agree completely," Christie said, raising her glass in the air.

"To a new beginning," Lydia stated, and their glasses clinked together.

"And here's to fate bringing mother and daughter together at long last," Christie added.

"Especially that," Lydia agreed, her eyes shining like the Champagne in her glass.

After taking a few sips, Christie watched Lydia persistently. "So, why don't you tell me what was on your mind earlier?"

Lydia took a large gulp of champagne to get up her nerve for this conversation. Taking a deep breath, she sat down next to Christie. "Okay, here it is. Remember how we talked about my father and Derek and the nature of their relationship?"

"Of course." Christie's eyes widened as she anticipated her daughter's next words.

"Well, I was able to relate so well to that information, when I found out, because I…because I'm gay myself." Lydia was so relieved to finally have the words out of her mouth.

Christie threw her hands in the air. "Oh! Is that all? My goodness, here I thought it was something awful." Christie touched Lydia's face. "I think it's great, honey, I really do. You know, after being around William and Derek, I understand it more than many people, I suspect. You have to live to be happy—happy within yourself, not for others."

"I don't recall feeling any other way. Thank you, mom." The word seemed to spill out of her mouth before she could stop it. She pulled away from Christie. "I…I'm sorry. I wanted to hear how it sounded."

Christie's eyes widened. In one fantastic gesture, she wrapped her arms around Lydia. "It sounds like a symphony. I've wanted to hear that word for so long…you have no idea." They embraced again, knowing how far they'd both come to be together and feeling neither one had to voice any more of it.

They spent the rest of the night talking about everything. Lydia shared details of her first memories, her coming-out story, and, of course, Danielle.

"It seems like fate has had a hand in your life before," Christie noted.

Lydia nodded. "I think it's all about fate."

"What about Danielle? Was she fate?" Christie asked.

Lydia sighed. "I think so. I believe a part of me will always love

Danielle. She did so much for me. I felt like I was a part of something...of someone, like never before." Lydia's brought up the long-forgotten image of Danielle, remembering their life together.

"Life is funny, isn't it?" Christie acknowledged.

"How do you mean?"

"Oh, the choices we make and the people we fall in love with. You just never know what the outcome will be," she said, then turned her attention back to her daughter. "I'm sorry you went through those times alone. It just hurts my heart."

Lydia touched her mother's hand. "It's not your fault." But internally, a part of her felt it was her mother's fault. But now, there seemed little point in blaming her. "There were a lot of forces against you. It's unbelievable that we have a second chance."

"Yes, definitely." Christie took another sip of champagne. "So tell me, is there someone new in your life?"

Lydia's face instantly flushed several shades of red, and she couldn't speak.

"I'll take that as a yes. Tell me all about her." Christie poured them both another glass of sparkling courage.

Lydia told her of how she'd met Sonja and caught her up on the latest Joel fiasco. She heard herself say the words, but she still had trouble believing it actually happened.

"What?" Christie exclaimed. "For God's sake, why didn't you call me?"

"Everything happened so quickly. I just found out a lot of things yesterday," Lydia explained carefully.

"How on earth could Sonja do that to you?" Christie asked, but then she answered her own question. "Well, the man *is* a Pritchard, which, I guess, explains a lot. There are quite a few mysteries surrounding us all, aren't there?"

"Don't get me wrong, I was angry and hurt when Sonja confessed it all to me. And I still am."

"I admire her courage in telling you the truth," Christie said with a nod. "She must be quite a woman to stand up to Joel like that...if he's anything like his father."

"She is." Then Lydia remembered Sonja's room was just next door. "Gosh, I forgot. The man at the front desk told me we have an adjoining room with her."

"Well, I'd love to meet her," Christie said, laying a hand on Lydia's shoulder.

"Let me go get her and see where she's been all this time." She decided to go to the front door instead of the adjoining door to surprise Sonja. She tapped on the door lightly and soon Sonja opened it wide, barely able to hold back her excitement.

"Baby, you better get in here," Sonja said, grabbing Lydia's hand to pull her into the room. She gathered Lydia in her arms and held her tight. "I've missed you!" She kissed Lydia deeply and they held each other for a moment in the doorway.

"Wow! I guess you did," Lydia said, getting her breath back. "I've missed you too. I couldn't wait to see you."

Sonja kissed her on the cheek. "So, did you have that certain talk with Christie?"

"I did, actually, just a few minutes ago. I decided it wasn't a good idea to come out to her in a moving vehicle, just in case."

"How did she take the news?" Sonja's eyes sparkled in a combination of excitement and anxiety.

"She was wonderful about it. I can't imagine a better reaction. I told her all about you, about us, and she wants to meet you."

"Well, by all means, let's meet mother," Sonja said, obviously not realizing the door was still open.

"Mother is honored," Christie chimed in from the doorway as she watched the lovers. "Christie Stoddard. It's a pleasure to finally meet the woman I've heard so much about."

"The pleasure is all mine, Mrs. Stoddard. I hope Lydia hasn't told you everything. Some things are better left to the imagination."

"I quite agree. But please, if I'm going to hang around you young people, the least you can do is call me Christie."

"You've got a deal, Christie."

Lydia could only laugh at the exchange between her lover and her mother. Lucky didn't even begin to describe how she felt. Though she had a handful of things to work out with both Sonja and Christie, it seemed life was finally looking better by the minute.

After chatting for a while, the women decided to explore the town and look for a good restaurant. They let the aroma of steak-grilling lead them. The restaurant was just a few miles down the street from their hotel, and after having a good steak dinner with all the trimmings, they ventured back to call it a night.

Before going into their rooms, Christie watched her daughter and Sonja. "Why don't you two stay together in Sonja's room tonight? It will give you a chance to have some time together. I just couldn't stand to be the reason you two were apart."

"I like the way you think. Thank you," Sonja said with a nod.

Lydia was thrilled. "Thanks, mom." She hugged Christie tightly, excited by the way things already seemed to fall into place.

"You kids get outta here," Christie said, and returned to her room for the night.

Lydia stepped in briefly to grab some clothes and overnight things. She thanked Christie again and hugged her one last time before retiring to Sonja's room. They snuggled down to watch TV together, and that night, everything seemed perfect.

Chapter Twenty

AFTER A PEACEFUL NIGHT'S rest, the women packed their clothes once again and loaded them in their perspective cars. When the bill was all settled, they got an early breakfast together at a small café inside the hotel, said their goodbyes, and ventured off on the next leg of the journey.

Though she genuinely liked Christie, Sonja still attempted to be objective. She was still skeptical of the woman who called herself Lydia's mother. They were even calling each other mother and daughter now. It seemed too fast of a bonding session to suit Sonja. Now that she knew she was deeply involved with Lydia, she found her protective side taking over, and she wouldn't allow anything to happen.

***

They stopped early that day in Lincoln, Nebraska, taking their time to relax, talk, and get to know one another more. Christie made a call to Martin, assuring him she enjoyed herself very much, and Lydia called home to Rosita. She explained the whole scenario and gave the woman the time they'd be arriving back at the estates. Rosita's joy for Lydia's discovery still sounded tinged with caution, but Lydia knew how the housekeeper loved to spoil and fuss over houseguests. Christie insisted she and Sonja share a room again that night as well, and Lydia thought the last few days couldn't have been any better.

After making the necessary pit stops the next day, they arrived in the Chicago area in the late afternoon.

"Are you sure you're all right with staying at the estates?" Lydia asked as she made her way through Chicago traffic.

"Don't worry, Lydia, I'll be fine. It's time to make amends. I have many wonderful memories of the estates. The beauty of it always astounded me," Christie told her. "And besides, I don't want to deal with the wrath of Rosita if I don't stay." That made them both laugh, as they each knew it wasn't far from the truth.

"Rosita said she's looking forward to seeing you and, as usual, preparing a feast. You realize what you've done now, don't you?"

"What would that be?"

"Rosita won't be fit company with people to spoil," Lydia joked.

"Aw, hell, there are fates worse than Rosita forcing me into her hospitality."

"Don't be so sure." Lydia joked about Rosita, but she was always thankful for her hawk-like watch over Lydia's life.

"And there's something else even more important," Christie added, grasping Lydia's hand. "I want to thank her for doing such a magnificent job raising my little girl."

Lydia's heart raced with happiness. There were no words to say.

Pulling up to the Estates, Lydia saw Sonja already standing beside her own car, gazing at the large building in front of her. As Lydia drove up the long road, Christie fell strangely silent. She glanced over at her mother, suddenly realizing how difficult this experience might be for her even though she had chosen to come. She gently placed her hand on Christie's arm. "Mom, are you okay?"

Shaken from her deep reverie, Christie looked at her daughter. "It's just more difficult than I imagined. The last time I was here, I saw your little three-year-old face in the window, waving me good-bye."

Lydia didn't bother to ask her if she was sure, because she knew her mother was determined to visit her past and bid it farewell at long last. After Lydia stopped the car, she gave her mother a moment to compose herself, then asked, "Well, is it time?"

Christie dried her face with a tissue from her purse. "Yes, my dear, sweet child. It's time."

Lydia smiled back at her mother and they stepped out of the car. There stood Rosita and Jackson to greet them. Lydia embraced each of them warmly, and a bit tighter and longer than usual. They had always been the foundation upon which she depended.

"My Lord, it *is* you. Miss Cassandra," Rosita acknowledged, her brown eyes widening with disbelief.

"In the flesh, Miss Rosita. You look *so* good," Christie said as she hugged the woman tightly. Then she turned her attention to Jackson. "Jackson, so wonderful to see you."

"Miss Cassie, you're looking quite beautiful. I'm so happy you've returned." She embraced him, and time seemed to stand still, if only for a moment.

Rosita stared intently at the new face standing next to Lydia. "Lydia, shame on you for not introducing me to your friend."

"You can give me a hundred lashes with a wet tortilla. I'm sorry. Rosita and Jackson, this is Lieutenant Sonja MacIntosh. Sonja, welcome to the Hispanic Inquisition," Lydia joked.

"Very funny. Hello, it's a pleasure to meet you. Thank you for looking after Lydia," Rosita stated with a smile, shaking Sonja's hand.

"It's been my pleasure, believe me. She's a wonderful woman."

Rosita winked at Lydia. "I know." The housekeeper looked at all three women and pointed them inside. "Dinner will be served in twenty minutes, so feel free to relax in the parlor with a drink or three. And don't look at me like you didn't think I'd make a big dinner," Rosita said as she went inside. Jackson left them to grab the luggage from the back of Lydia's car.

After they stepped inside, Christie spent a moment staring up at the walls around her. "Such wonderful memories of this place."

"Well, at least Grandmother's gone now," Lydia quipped.

"Lydia, you shouldn't speak ill of her. I'm sure she only wanted what was best for you and your father…in her own way," Christie stated, trying to be diplomatic.

"Still, this house has a much different air to it now that she's gone, I can tell you that." Lydia felt little remorse for the woman who had been the instigator of her torment. She cleansed herself with a deep sigh. "Let's step into the parlor for a drink." Sonja and Christie followed her into the big room. "What sounds good to you two?"

"Gosh, I don't know," Christie said. "Any suggestions?"

"Well, what do you like?" Sonja asked her.

"I seem to recall Miss Cassandra always enjoyed amaretto and coke," Jackson offered as he entered the parlor.

"Jackson, that's it! How sweet of you to remember after all these years."

"Okay, then. What about you two?" Jackson asked, glancing at Lydia and Sonja.

Sonja requested beer and Lydia said, "As long as you've got the Coke out, throw some rum in there and call it good."

"I'll be right back," Jackson said and left to restock the ice bucket. There was a small bar in the parlor, but it hadn't been often used since the day William had become ill.

"Lydia," Sonja interjected, "I need to call Hank and let him know I'm back in town. I'll be back in a minute." And, as if she didn't care who was in the room, she stood up, walked over to Lydia, and kissed her on the cheek. Lydia blushed and sat on the couch next to her mother.

"It's quite apparent, you know."

"What is?" Lydia asked, though her eyes followed Sonja out of the room.

"How much she loves you," Christie observed.

Lydia nodded. "I hope so, because she's everything to me."

Jackson appeared with more ice for the bucket, then grabbed Sonja's beer from the small refrigerator behind the granite-topped bar. He mixed the other two drinks while they waited for Sonja to rejoin them. Handing one to Christie, he said, "If you'll forgive me, I will always know you as Miss Cassandra, ma'am."

"It's nice to hear that name again, Jackson." She took a sip of the drink so meticulously mixed by Jackson and moaned in delight. "You remembered just how I like it. You may call me whatever you like. Thank you so much."

Lydia thanked Jackson for her drink as well and then he left the room. "Mom, have you thought about changing your name back?"

Christie shook her head. "Not really. I've become accustomed to it now. It started out as a new identity, but it's been so long since I've been Cassandra, it would seem strange."

Lydia nodded. "I can understand that." She paused for a moment, then said, "I'm going to check on Sonja. I'll be right back."

"Of course."

Lydia stepped out into the hallway but didn't see Sonja. She strolled slowly past the library, where she heard Sonja's voice. Smiling at the sound, she stopped to wait for her. In an instant, the smile faded when she heard the conversation.

"Hank, I don't know. I just want to be sure of this woman. It seems a little too wonderful and, for Lydia's sake, I want to be sure she is who she says she is. I don't want Lydia hurt. She's been through enough. Do what you have to. I want that background check by tomorrow." Sonja hung up, then turned quickly to find Lydia standing there, her face flushed red.

"What are you doing?" Lydia asked point-blank.

Sonja stammered, "Look, Lydia, I just—"

Lydia didn't wait for an explanation. "You just what? You just go behind my back and do a check on my mother? What is that about? I don't understand..."

Sonja tried to comfort her, but she backed away. "Lydia, I love you. I love you more than anyone I've ever loved in my life. I'm just worried. This whole thing seems a bit too fast, that's all."

Lydia sighed, realizing that maybe Sonja had a point. "I know it does. I wish you could understand. I feel in my heart she's the one person I've wondered about my whole life. And besides, if you had any doubts, you saw that Rosita and Jackson knew her right away."

Sonja reached out to her again, and this time Lydia didn't resist. "Sweets, I believe she's your mother. I want to know her history, that's all. I'm just playing cop. I'm sorry."

Lydia knew she couldn't stay mad at Sonja when the woman had only been looking out for her, but it still bothered her. She wanted Sonja to be as excited as she was and not so suspicious. "I want to know, too," she admitted. "That's why I wanted her back here in Kenilworth, at the Estates, so I can know the things I need to know. I feel so connected to her."

Sonja held Lydia's face in her hands and kissed her softly. "Let's go back in. I bet it's about time for dinner. If you like, I'll tell Christie my plans, so no one thinks I'm being underhanded."

"Okay." They stared at each other for a moment. "Sonja?"

"Yes?"

"Thank you for loving me that much." No one else had given that much of themselves to her before.

Sonja shook her head, obviously trying to hold back her emotions. "Don't thank me. It's what I was born to do."

Chapter Twenty-One

AFTER A DINNER OF Rosita's pot roast with the works, followed by Lydia's favorite cheesecake with fresh strawberries and whipped cream for dessert, the three women journeyed back into the parlor for coffee. Sonja felt it the prime opportunity to question Christie on the happenings of her past. The detective inside Sonja MacIntosh knew they had not heard the end of Joel Pritchard—especially once he found out the birth certificate he held in his hands was a fraud.

Christie asked if they could go out to William's grave by the gazebo, where the house lights still illuminated the grounds enough to see. Lydia said it would be a good place to take their coffee. The air was cool and brisk, but not bad for November. Sonja, Lydia, and Christie gathered up their coats and made their way outside.

Sonja glanced briefly in Lydia's direction. Something within her police training and gut instinct told her there was more to Christie's story than the woman let on. Determined to get to the bottom of it, she walked with Lydia and Christie outside to the gazebo. Kenilworth had seen its first snow, though it barely covered the ground, and even in winter, the view from the gazebo was breathtaking. Acres and acres of land stretched as far as the eye could see. "Lydia, this is the most magnificent scenery I've ever seen."

"Well, I don't think it compares to the mountains of the west, but it is beautiful."

Sonja quietly nuzzled close to Lydia and whispered in her ear, "Not as beautiful as you."

"You don't have to say that. I'll sleep with you anyway."

Sonja put her arm around Lydia as they walked toward the gazebo. Christie knelt among the finely cultivated, snow-covered roses, and Lydia and Sonja sat inside the gazebo, sipping their coffees so Christie could have some privacy.

The former Mrs. William Blackwell sobbed openly for a man she was never in love with, a man she'd never made love to, but a man, nonetheless, she adored. Christie dried her eyes and face, and after a minute of catching her breath, stepped over to join Lydia and Sonja.

"Are you all right, mom?" Lydia asked.

"Just fine. I needed this, as hard as it is. I really needed it." Christie took a sip of her coffee she'd left sitting on the gazebo bench.

"Christie? I was wondering if you were up to some questions," Sonja asked quietly.

After another deep breath, Christie answered, "Of course. I've got nothing to hide. Not anymore."

"First of all, why *did* you think you needed to hide?" Sonja asked.

Christie's face lost some of its color. "Is this on the record or off, Lieutenant?"

"It's not really police business, if that's what you're asking. I'm just curious because of my dealings with Joel Pritchard. I want to know the whole story and why you might think Joel is so insistent on getting the purse and birth certificate."

"Sonja, I don't think that—" Lydia attempted to stop Sonja from her interrogation.

Christie held her hand up toward her daughter. "It's all right, Lydia. I don't mind at all." Then, Christie began the sordid tale of how everything started, so long ago.

After half an hour, Rosita came out to the gazebo. "There's more coffee, everyone, but we need to take this party indoors. Too cold for old Mexican women." She promptly went back inside to work on the coffee, and the others followed her inside. Finally, once inside the parlor and settled, Christie finished telling of the life that had brought her so much pain and now such mystery.

Sonja was astounded. "So, it's true that Brenton Pritchard is

Lydia's father, not William. That's amazing. Do you have proof of that?" Sonja asked, without realizing she wasn't on duty.

"Actually, no, I don't. I just know."

"So, you never had any paternity tests performed? I have a valid reason for asking, I assure you," Sonja reassured Christie.

"Which is?"

"The birth certificate in the silver purse. I'm going to take it to some experts and have it analyzed because Lydia and I scanned it closely and noticed a name, once there, appears to have been covered up," Sonja informed her.

"I see," Christie said as she fidgeted in her seat. "Sonja, I know you believe I have the answers to these questions, but truly, I'm as puzzled by the events of the past as you."

"What's the significance of the purse?" Sonja had been curious about it from the beginning, and she couldn't help but ask this question as well.

Christie was already shaking her head. "I don't know, Sonja. It's a family heirloom I believe Brenton took from me. He knew it meant the world to me. It was just one more thing to hold over my head to keep me from leaving."

"So tell me again when you met William Blackwell." Christie appeared disgusted with the interrogation. Sensing her apprehension, Sonja attempted to justify her questions and curiosity. "Look, Christie, I'm here for Lydia, and if we're going to get the purse back from Joel, I want to make sure we have all the information."

"I understand. It's just that I didn't expect all this when Lydia found me that day. I'm a little overwhelmed." Christie let out a deep, cleansing sigh that seemed to finally relax her entire body. She then started the story again, this time from the very beginning.

Sonja was unusually quiet after Christie finished. She walked around the parlor, scratching her head in true Sherlock Holmes fashion. Without even looking at Christie, Sonja broke her own silence. "So, William offered you marriage, even knowing it was Pritchard's child?"

"Yes, that's correct. He was an amazing man," Christie

acknowledged.

"What about the birth certificate?" Sonja was even more intrigued.

"What do you mean?"

Sonja silently contemplated her words in an attempt to further the conversation before Christie quit talking. "I mean, whose name did you have inscribed on the birth certificate as the father?" Sonja asked bluntly.

Christie wouldn't stop fidgeting. "William's, of course. The whole point of my marrying William was, in essence, to hide from Brenton, so I certainly wouldn't leave anything to chance."

"I see." Sonja then shot a glance at Lydia. "Lydia, could you get that birth certificate out of your bag for me?"

"Sure," Lydia said as she got up from her seat on the couch and walked over to the table where she'd thrown her bag. After handing the document to Sonja, she sat back down on the couch.

"Thanks," Sonja said with a smile.

"Look, Sonja, I've told you everything I know to be true."

"I'm sorry if it sounds like I'm giving you the third degree," she said to Christie. "I'm just trying to figure this thing out. We really are on the same side." After taking a deep breath, Sonja handed the birth certificate over to Christie. "Take a look at this...closely."

Christie examined the document she held in her hands. "Like I told Lydia, this has got to be a forgery. I saw the original with William's name on it."

"Where is it now?" Sonja asked.

"I don't know. I remember, years ago, when I packed my things to leave, I went through my papers and couldn't find it. It was gone. It wasn't where it was supposed to be."

Sonja's eyes widened in disbelief, feeling the mystery surrounding Christie growing deeper. "Any ideas where it might be or who might have it?"

"I'm not sure." Christie scrutinized the paper yet again. "Wait a minute, here." She held the entire paper up to the light. "I can make out some different letters...letters that don't make any sense to me."

"We did too, mom," Lydia interjected. She'd kept her silence throughout this questioning session.

"I find that quite odd," Christie stated in a puzzled tone. "This thing keeps getting more and more mysterious."

"That's why I'm determined to get to the bottom of it," Sonja interjected. The conversation had not erased the doubt in her mind about the woman Lydia so easily called "mom".

Lydia took a deep breath and then looked at Christie. "It's getting late. What do you say we call it a night?"

Christie nodded. "Great idea. I'm exhausted. Are you two staying here tonight?" Rosita had insisted Christie stay, so much so that she really had no choice in the matter.

"Of course we are, mom. I wouldn't just bring you here and leave," Lydia stated.

"Wonderful. I guess I'll see you both in the morning." Christie walked toward Lydia and Sonja, hugged them both goodnight, and made her way up to the room Rosita had prepared for her so eloquently.

Sonja gathered Lydia into her arms. "Oh, I've been waiting to do that all night."

"I'm sorry if I assumed you'd stay here, Sonja. I hope you don't mind."

Sonja broke away from their embrace and looked her lovingly in the eyes. "I couldn't go to my apartment now after being with you all this time. I've gotten used to having you next to me. I wouldn't be anywhere else."

"I was hoping you'd say that. How about we turn in for the night?" Lydia asked her with a wink.

"I thought you'd never ask." They walked up the massive staircase, hand in hand, and Sonja was more than grateful.

***

When the sun rose in Christie's room, she was already awake to witness it. Not only awake, but up and dressed. She'd forgotten how beautiful the view was from the mansion—from anywhere on the Blackwell property, actually. Christie looked around her room. It was a smaller guest room, but overlooked the back patio area off the kitchen. The view of the Blackwell land seemed to stretch for miles and miles. The bed was a solid oak, king-sized bed with bright white linens and a dark, burgundy bedspread with curtains to match. There was a bathroom and sitting area, though Christie stayed by the window, engulfed in her thoughts. The knock at the door didn't stir her right away. "Yes?" she finally answered after several taps at the door had sounded.

"Miss Cassandra...oh. I'm sorry, Christie. Forgive me. I just heard you up and about and wondered if you'd like some coffee and scones here in your room before everyone else is up," Rosita offered as she entered the room.

"That sounds spectacular, but only if you'll join me. That is, if Lydia doesn't have you doing other things this morning."

Rosita threw her hand in the air. "Oh, who cares if she does? I'd really enjoy that, Cassa—Christie. By the way, what should I call you?" she asked.

"Whatever you're more comfortable with, though I warn you, it's been so long since I've been Cassandra, I may not answer right away," Christie told her. The thought of her life as Cassandra sent a sudden shiver down her spine. So many ghosts.

"Fine by me. I shall return with coffee and scones for two, then." And with that, Rosita left the spacious room, where the smile that had appeared on Christie's face a moment ago systematically faded into worry.

She let out a deep, troubled sigh. This trip had turned into more than getting to know her daughter. There was danger ahead; she could feel it in her soul. If Joel Pritchard was anything like his father, he wouldn't let it rest until someone was hurt or dead. Derek had seen the wrath of the Pritchard legacy, she was sure of that.

And Cassandra Blackwell Stoddard knew there was more to come.

Chapter Twenty-Two

WHILE CHRISTIE AND ROSITA enjoyed their breakfast by the vast picture window in Christie's room, Lydia and Sonja were just waking up to a new day. Lydia had to admit, it was nice being back home, though she'd grown to love the mountains in Wyoming. She turned to notice the pillow next to hers was empty. Her eyes scanned the room to see Sonja fixing her hair in the bathroom mirror. "Leaving me?" Lydia asked with a grin, though the question always scared her.

"Define leaving you," Sonja said as she continued getting her things together for the day.

Lydia rose from the bed and stepped up behind Sonja, wrapping her arms around her. "I think it means, 'you no here no more'."

"How eloquent. I'm not leaving you, so to speak. Maybe just temporarily. Duty calls. A lot of things to catch up on." Sonja checked her hair in the mirror.

"Now comes the hard part." Lydia suddenly didn't know how to be without her.

Raising her eyebrows, Sonja seemed puzzled. "How do you mean?"

"I have to share you with the rest of the world," Lydia said somberly, meeting Sonja's gaze.

"Only some of me." Then Sonja sighed a deep, heavy sigh, her apparent attempt to contain it failing. "Lydia, no matter what happens now, I want you to know that the time we've spent together has been the best I've ever known, and I wouldn't trade it for anything. You have no idea how much I love you."

"There's a 'but' in there somewhere. Are you just letting me down easy because I'm weak and vulnerable right now?" It was meant as a joke, but suddenly, Lydia wondered if maybe she had taken too much for granted. How could they even have a future when Lydia was so at odds with the past?

"Oh, sweetie, not at all. I'm telling you because...well, because I'm a cop and I don't want things left unsaid, should anything happen. Life can turn on a dime. After all, it was only because of Derek's death that we met in the first place."

A tear slid down Lydia's cheek as she nodded. "That's true." Sonja kissed away her tear, then kissed her goodbye for the day, promising to call her later. Sonja said she was taking the birth certificate into the forensics department so they could analyze it and possibly give them all some answers.

***

Before Sonja could make her way out of the mansion, Jackson followed her to the door. He placed his hand on her arm. "Take care of her, will you? She needs some happiness in her life."

Sonja smiled, though somewhat shocked by Jackson's words. He'd never said much more than a hello or a goodbye. "That's my plan. We could all use some of that." With one last wave, she drove down the long, blacktop road and headed out into real life.

Forty-five minutes later, she arrived at her apartment. There were several messages on her machine, including an urgent-sounding call from her Police Captain. She was to be in his office as soon as possible and, by the tone of his voice, nothing good could come of it. Sonja gathered herself and her thoughts together to make the jaunt into town. It was time to face the music.

Inside the familiar brick building, she strolled quickly down the long hallway, turning twice into yet another hallway toward forensics. There, she handed over the birth certificate, giving strict instructions on the tests to be run. Just as she stepped out of the door, a tall, swanky man confronted her.

"MacIntosh, I need to see you in my office. Immediately," the man barked.

Dark-haired Bradley Pennington was not always popular within the department and thought of generally as a power-hungry tyrant. He dressed the part, always wearing three-piece Armani suits. Sonja often wondered how he could afford such extravagances on a Captain's salary. He was not one to deal with any petty nonsense or interoffice friendships...except when it suited his purpose. Bradley Pennington did not approve of Sonja's promotion to Lieutenant, but he could not argue with her natural instincts as a cop.

"Yes, sir," Sonja answered and followed him to his office. She knew what the meeting was about, and her nerves seemed to wriggle up out of her throat.

"Have a seat," Bradley offered, pointing to the leather chair in front of his desk. Sonja nervously sat down in the plush chair, as if awaiting her execution. "Welcome back from your vacation. I trust everything went well for you. What I want to discuss with you is somewhat personal."

Sonja fidgeted around in her seat, and then with a raspy breath said, "I see. What is it, Captain?"

"Things have surfaced regarding events which took place on your vacation...things which I find hard to believe."

A deep, uneasy sigh found its way out of Sonja's lungs.

The sigh did not go unnoticed. "I see you know what I'm talking about, MacIntosh. Would you care to enlighten me?"

"That depends, sir. I'd much rather you tell me what you know first. With all due respect, I don't want to incriminate myself unnecessarily." Sonja was no fool and trusted no one.

"Very well, MacIntosh. It has come to my attention that you've been involved with a known mob boss."

"Not by choice, sir. It was a matter of life and death." Sonja wasn't about to just give away any information. She was nervous and angry, only aware of her foot tapping against the carpeted floor.

Blurting out everything and defending herself was not her call of action. At least, not yet. The less said, the better.

Bradley Pennington apparently couldn't help but let the smile form on his lips. "Let's, just for a moment, talk about choices. A few things have become clearer to me as of late."

"Such as?" Sonja knew the next part so well, she could sing it like a canary.

"Such as the reason you ended up in Wyoming. Christ, no one goes to Wyoming."

"If you'll excuse me, Captain, what difference does it make where I went? Just go ahead and say what you need to say." Sonja knew, but she wanted him to say the words.

"A certain Lydia Blackwell. Does the name ring a bell?"

"Don't bring Lydia into this. She's innocent of this whole mess. It was because of her, and I think it's tied in with the Meade murder."

"Interesting. Well, I know the truth about you now. Although, I've never understood about you girls, how you could be without a man." Pennington paused momentarily and then got back to business. "A true officer of the law wouldn't have even considered doing business with a mobster."

"It wasn't business. It was blackmail. Evidently, Pritchard made good on his threat. Now, I have no alternative but to accept the consequences of my actions."

"I'm afraid I have to suspend you without pay for thirty days." Bradley Pennington sat behind his desk, intently staring down the woman across from him while gnawing on his pencil, the wheels spinning. "MacIntosh, there *is* a way out of this, you know."

"Really," Sonja said in a sarcastic tone.

"It's simple, really. Let's say you show up at my house tonight to discuss things over a few drinks and—"

"Are you insane? How dare you talk to me about being an officer of the law and in the next breath hit on me?" Sonja was livid. The sight of the man made her nauseous.

Bradley Pennington laughed. "I'm sure a real man could change you around, MacIntosh."

Sonja had heard enough, and without a word or a glance she got up from her chair and headed toward the door. She turned back to Pennington and, with a leer, said, "You know, a real man might do the same for you, Captain." And with that, the door slammed shut, along with the opportunity for Captain Bradley Pennington to put one more notch on his bedpost.

When the door closed behind her, Sonja was astonished that even Pennington was capable of such stupidity. God, how she wanted to report him to Internal Affairs, but it would mean opening up the whole can of worms. She wasn't sure she was prepared for those repercussions. Instead of making more trouble, she resigned herself to the fact that she would at least have a month off, and though money would be tight, she could still discreetly play detective. Sonja MacIntosh had no intentions of backing off.

She walked quietly to the office she shared with Hank, who worked diligently on some paperwork he'd neglected at the desk across from Sonja's. He turned to face her.

"Hey there, blondie. It's great to have you back in the trenches."

A smile came to Sonja's face, but then quickly faded. "Thanks, but it's not the big homecoming you think." She grabbed a box from a nearby shelf and rummaged through her desk, throwing things into the box.

Hank stared at her. "What's going on?"

"Suspended without pay." Sonja didn't even look up from her desk when the words came out of her mouth.

"Bastards. How long?"

"Thirty days." She looked up into Hank's eyes and could see the hurt he felt. He was a true friend. "Hey, you big lug, it's all right. I expected something. Besides, it gives me more time for stuff." Sonja winked and playfully punched Hank's arm.

"Still, it's bullshit and you know it."

"Yeah, well, bullshit happens, Hank. I'll deal. I look at it as a blessing in disguise. This will give me time to sit around in my underwear and eat bologna sandwiches," Sonja joked, trying to make Hank more comfortable about the whole thing. She was careful about what she said, just in case the office or her desk was bugged.

Hank laughed. "You do that already." After looking her in the eye, he asked her, "Just where will you be staying?"

"At my apartment, of course. Where else would I be?" She knew what he was getting at and couldn't help but tease him.

"You know perfectly well, you little brat." They knew each other so well, some people out on the street assumed they were married. "How's that going, by the way?"

"Fantastic." Sonja didn't want to give out too much information. It wasn't that she didn't trust Hank, it was just her nature not to divulge too much so she didn't jinx anything.

Hank nodded in easy acceptance. Without saying much, Sonja told him everything he needed to know. She was in love with this woman.

She informed him about the forensics tests on the birth certificate. She wanted to make sure the certificate was in the right hands, because anything could happen. By now, Joel had to have discovered his copy was a fake. Time was becoming a luxury she couldn't afford.

Sonja bid Hank farewell but knew she would be in contact with him. She stopped one more time by forensics to get an update on the status of the tests. There was nothing yet, but she was anxious. She left three different phone numbers, one being Lydia's private line. There could be no room for missed phone calls. With heavy regret, she closed the door behind her and walked into the cold November air.

Chapter Twenty-Three

BRADLEY PENNINGTON STARED OUT his office window, lost in thought as he watched Sonja MacIntosh leave the building and make her way through the crowd. Somehow, he had misjudged her. With a slight smile, he searched his jacket pocket for his cell phone. Carefully, he dialed the familiar number. "Pennington, here," he stated softly, so his voice wouldn't carry outside to his secretary.

"Pritchard. Talk to me," the voice ordered.

"It's done. Mission accomplished," Pennington reported.

Laughter came from the other end of the phone. "Hardly, Pennington. I won't be satisfied until that woman is permanently removed from my memory. What exactly did you do?"

"Nothing permanent right now. I don't want to arouse any suspicion. I suspended her for thirty days without pay."

"That's it?" Pritchard sounded disgusted. After a moment's pause, he added, "I suppose that will do for now. I'll let you know what your next move is. Be prepared."

"Of course," Pennington stated. Pritchard ended the phone call without notice and Pennington found himself on the receiving end of a dial tone. He was paid well for his loyalty and covered his tracks thoroughly. He also knew that Sonja wouldn't talk, at least for the time being. She had too much to lose. But Bradley Pennington was definitely no idiot. He had to keep a sharp eye on that one. Sonja MacIntosh was smarter than he anticipated.

***

Joel Pritchard sat in his imported, black leather executive chair and stared at his cell phone, lost in thought. His surroundings were plush; no one expected anything less from a Pritchard. His desk was custom made, a dark wooden table with fierce lions carved on the legs, meant to intimidate all those who sat before him. Joel loved that kind of power. His penthouse sat in the right block of the heart of downtown Chicago, but only because Pritchard had bribed many judges and zoning officials into allowing him to construct the five-story building. He'd made certain his accommodations were the picture of elegance.

The room was circular with wooden bookcases all around and a small bar and kitchenette for his every whim. It had to be something Brenton Pritchard would be proud of, and that was a feat in itself. Making his father proud was the very core of Joel's existence. It was the reason he would stop at nothing to honor his father's dying wish. Joel remembered the day well; it would be etched in his mind forever. All his hard living, smoking, and drinking had finally caught up with Brenton Pritchard. Even when he learned about the tumor, he drank and smoked more than ever before. There was no room in him to admit defeat, no matter the cause.

There were only two people in Brenton's life who dared act against him. That was the ultimate sin. Cassandra Lexington had made a fool of him and, dead or alive, there would be a price to pay. She was one. The other was blood.

Michael Pritchard, the eldest Pritchard son, had been quite the disappointment to Brenton. At twenty-five, he'd made the unfortunate mistake of wanting out of the family business. Michael had seen too much of the violence and could not comprehend the ease with which it was carried out. After Michael made his announcement, Brenton was mortified. He had groomed Michael all his life to take over the business, and now he'd been betrayed by his own flesh and blood. Compassion and understanding had not gotten Brenton Pritchard where he was. Loyalty. That was the seed from which everything bloomed.

Joel sat, silently remembering the argument between his brother and father. At twenty-two, Joel had vowed to himself not to be his brother. Michael had left that very night, never to look back again. But then, neither did Brenton. He held a meeting with his associates the next morning to announce that a terrible tragedy had occurred. Michael's car had veered off a ravine, instantly killing the eldest Pritchard son. And Brenton Pritchard took great pains to ensure the appearance of such a tragic event, right down to the way the car crashed into the ravine. Only Joel knew the truth. He knew that he was the one on whom his father depended to carry on the business.

Although it wasn't quite in the way he expected, Joel was ready and primed. He would not let the family down, no matter what the cost. He was awakened from his reverie by his right-hand man, Jonny Hammond, who currently played bartender.

"What can I get ya, boss?"

Without making eye contact, Joel uttered, "Scotch and soda. And hold the soda."

"Sure thing, boss." Jonny carefully rummaged behind the bar, looking for the scotch. The bar was built on the right side of the room, with mirrors behind it, a black stone countertop, and four barstools on the other side. Elegance and sophistication.

"Bottom shelf, third bottle from the left," Joel directed. Everything about Joel Pritchard was painstakingly perfect. Neat and tidy, nothing out of place. Just like his father had taught him.

"Thanks," Jonny whispered, embarrassed by his inattentiveness. Not paying attention in this job could get a person killed, and Jonny knew it.

"Don't mention it." Joel took the glass from Jonny's hand and quickly took a sip. "Excellent, Jonny." After taking another long sip, Joel stared ahead for a moment. "Jonny, I have something to discuss with you."

"Of course, boss."

Joel motioned him into one of the chairs opposite his exquisite desk. "How long have you been in the family, John?"

"Five years, sir. It's been great. You've been gr—"

Joel held up his hand, shook his head, and chuckled. "Jonny, don't try to bullshit me. Save that for a time when it will do you some good. Are we clear?" Sheepishly, Jonny nodded, not saying a word. "I believe the time has come to show your loyalty to the family. I have a job for you." Joel knew the man was eager to please and would do just about anything.

"Sure, boss. Thank you for the opportunity. What's the job?" Jonny inquired.

"Consider it a personal favor to me. I need you to stake out the Blackwell Estates out in Kenilworth. The deal is no questions. You will be paid handsomely, I assure you. That translates to enough money to ensure your loyalty. I don't believe I need to explain to you how I feel about disloyal family members. Understand, Jonny boy?"

"Yes, sir. I won't let you down, boss."

"You will receive strict instructions, Jonny, and I expect them followed to the letter. No one is to be harmed at this point. Consider yourself an information gatherer."

Jonny nodded and stood once Joel had given the signal that the conversation was over. Joel shook the man's hand and watched him leave the room. He stared at the empty chair in front of his desk and recalled the many men who had groveled at his father's feet, and the many who had perished due to stupid mistakes and disloyal acts. It was a learning experience he'd never forgotten. Joel knew his father was no saint.

Briefly, he thought of his mother...or what he knew of her. Anna Maitland Pritchard had heard enough and seen too much to go on being the wife of a mobster. When she attempted to take Joel and Michael with her, her husband had stopped her cold. There was no way out but death. It would be scandalous, he had told her. Seeing no other option, Anna kissed her boys goodbye, told them she loved them, and left them in the hands of her husband. She had walked out of the Pritchard Estate with nothing but the clothes on her back.

The next day, Anna's body had been found in a dark alley behind a bar in the downtown district—a place someone as classy as Anna Pritchard would never frequent. Lying next to her on the ground was an empty bottle of tranquilizers and a half-empty bottle of Jack Daniels.

Joel had been only five then, and Michael eight. They were too young to be told the truth about their mother. Brenton Pritchard felt no remorse for the mother of his children. It was just as well that she was dead; that way, he didn't have to do it himself. Brenton had told the boys that their mother had decided she didn't have the maternal instinct after all and wanted her freedom. Only Michael appeared distraught over the loss of his mother. His eight-year-old mind had not been able to comprehend his mother not wanting him. Joel had been so young, and it was his father who he looked up to, his father who he wanted to emulate.

Then the day came when Brenton decided to send the boys to a prestigious boarding school in England. It would harden them to life and get them into the proper social circles. This would also provide the necessary connections for Brenton. Of course, the boys were not thrilled about going, though Joel thought of it as a big adventure planned by his father. For Michael, it had been just one more thing...one more person who didn't want him around. Brenton Pritchard couldn't even be bothered to see them off on the plane. His hired men had taken care of that. They took care of everything; they always had.

Joel remembered those years in England, now. And he remembered his brother. It had been much harder for Michael to fit in; he'd kept to himself, didn't talk to many people. Joel didn't understand what was wrong with his brother. He did understand, however, that there was a hidden reason for everything his father did, and their education had been no different. Joel and Michael stayed for ten years and were allowed one visit home per year, usually at Christmas.

When Joel was fifteen and Michael eighteen, it was time to come home. Joel wanted desperately to learn the family business, but it was Michael Brenton wanted to groom and nurture into the top spot. For three years, Michael stood side by side with his father, mentally taking notes and looking to please him in any way. Then, when he was twenty-one, it was Michael's turn to pass his father's test of strength and loyalty. Brenton had informed Michael it was time for him to take over a portion of the business and report back to his father. Brenton's philosophy had always been 'do unto others *before* they do unto you'. Michael felt the pressure from his father to be like him, so he tried to please him, though he never quite felt comfortable in Brenton Pritchard's shoes.

Michael was supposed to give the order to kill a man for missing a meeting. Instead, he'd helped the man and his family leave town. He took great pains to make sure his father never found out. Disloyalty was rewarded with death. It hadn't been easy for Michael, and he avoided giving the "kill" order whenever possible. He did everything in his power to work things out without violence, but many times Brenton would force the issue. By twenty-five, Michael had aged ten years. The cars, the women, and the fast life did nothing for him anymore, but seeing his father give the order to kill a childhood friend was more than Michael could take. The next day, he made an appointment for a meeting with his father.

Joel remembered that day vividly, as he'd been allowed to stand at the back of the room and listen in on the conversation. Michael nervously entered his father's office early that morning. Brenton Pritchard sat behind his large desk as if he were God, ready to pass judgment on those below him.

"Hello, son. How good to see you first thing in the morning. What can I do for you?" Brenton asked, as if Michael were a business associate.

"Father, I've made an important decision of which I know you won't approve, but just the same, I must make it."

Brenton's attention focused intensely on his eldest son. "All right, son. You've peaked my curiosity, but I must tell you that whomever you've decided needs taken care of is fine. I trust your judgment."

Michael shook his head. "No, sir, it's nothing like that at all. I've decided I want to leave the family business."

"What? How exactly do you mean?" Brenton's face bloomed a scarlet red.

"Father, I can no longer condone this business, or even this family. Everything you've done is...well...it's just wrong. I can no longer be a part of it."

Brenton's stare was stony and cold. "Sorry, son, but this is not the time to decide you have morals. Christ—just like your mother. How dare you talk to me this way? You have no right. This is your heritage. You can't just walk away. You *will not* walk away. You've seen what happens to people who try. Don't think the same won't happen to you just because you're a Pritchard."

Listening, Joel hadn't quite known what to expect. He knew their father was ruthless, and he really wondered whether or not he would kill his own flesh and blood.

"If being a Pritchard means I have to live this kind of lifestyle," Michael began, "I don't want it." He rose from his seat, looked his father in the eye, and said "Goodbye, sir."

Enraged, Brenton stood from behind his desk and shouted, "Michael, if you walk out that door, you are dead to me! Do you understand?"

Michael never looked back and shut the door behind him.

As soon as the door had closed, Brenton was on the phone to his people. "Mario. Brenton. Michael's gone. You know what to do." No questions. No excuses. He would be dealt with appropriately. Son or not.

Forty-five-year-old Joel took another gulp from his glass of scotch and let out a long sigh. Michael and their mother had been weak. A Pritchard could not be weak. As for his mother, she should have turned her head to the business, not asked any questions, and did what his father asked. It was what Joel expected of any woman in his life. They were to look exquisite, please him, and make themselves scarce. Anyone who didn't follow those rules got hurt.

Sonja MacIntosh was asking too many questions. The purse

belonged to his father, and both Sonja and Lydia Blackwell had made things messier. Joel didn't like messes.

Chapter Twenty-Four

SONJA DROVE FRANTICALLY THROUGH traffic to get onto the freeway toward the Blackwell Estates. The background check on Christie had turned up empty. Hank said it was one of the cleanest records he'd seen. There was nothing tangible, but Sonja knew there was something off-center in the story Christie had given both her and Lydia. She just felt it. Driving up to the black, cast-iron gate which just read "B" in large gold print was indeed intimidating, but Sonja held steadfastly in her determination. Behind those gates was the truth and, somehow, Sonja would uncover it.

After she announced who she was, the gates promptly opened to reveal the familiar road up to the main house. Sonja could see Lydia in the distance waiting for her. Just in the few hours she'd been away, Sonja had missed her desperately, and it seemed insane. They hadn't known each other long enough for her to feel so reckless and passionate, and yet all the feelings were there. Lydia was so unlike anyone she'd ever met, and she wanted this one to last. Her heart brimmed with joy when she stepped out of the car and Lydia rushed to her, embracing her with just as much excitement.

"Wow, what a welcome. You just saw me this morning." Sonja tried to play it cool, though she was failing miserably.

"I know, I know. I just missed you, and it felt strange with you gone," Lydia confessed.

"You're so cute. I thought about you all day. My God, you're a distracting woman."

They broke away from each other and entered the mansion, arm in arm. Christie was there in the entryway, chatting with Rosita about her life the past thirty-odd years.

"Sonja, it's good to see you. How are things at the office?" Christie asked.

"Pretty dull compared to the past week, I have to say," Sonja replied.

"Oh, I don't know, dull sounds damn good right now," Lydia mentioned as she looked at Sonja.

"I know what you mean." Sonja glanced back and forth between Christie and Lydia, then she focused on her lover. "Lydia, can I talk to you?"

"Sure. Let's go into the library," Lydia offered with a tone of concern. She led Sonja down the hallway and through a series of twists and turns, and they finally reached the library. After closing the door behind them, Lydia took a deep breath. "What is it you couldn't say in front of anyone else?"

"Sweets, I feel like something's not right here. Something happened down at the precinct."

"What...what happened?" Lydia asked, sitting on the brown leather couch and motioning for Sonja to do the same.

"My worst fears, only a bit different. I've been suspended without pay for thirty days," she explained, curling up next to Lydia.

"Shit. Is it because of what happened in Wyoming?"

"Yes. Apparently, our friend Joel has been quite the little talker. That's not even the worst of it," Sonja said.

"What else?"

"My boss, Captain Pennington, politely informed me that I could get out of the deal if I performed sexual favors for him. It was disgusting." The thought of it repulsed her all over again.

"What? Did you report him?"

"Uh...no, I didn't." Sonja knew that, for now, she'd made the right decision.

"Why the hell not?" Lydia asked immediately.

"It would just be pouring salt on an open wound, Lydia. I'm not ready for that, and I don't think you are, either."

After a long sigh, Lydia shook her head. "I still don't like it. You shouldn't have to put up with that. It's all kinds of wrong."

"I know, but for now, I have to deal with it. I just wanted to tell you, that's all."

"I'm glad you did. What did you tell the poor bastard, anyway?"

Sonja made a face. "Well, he told me that the right man could bring me around." Lydia's face folded in disgust. "I politely declined his offer and told him the right man could turn him around, too."

They shared a good laugh over that, and Lydia wrapped her arms around Sonja's shoulders. "I just love you." She kissed her warmly. Sonja returned the kiss, but then pulled away suddenly. With a puzzled expression, Lydia stared her down. "What's wrong?"

"I love you, too, babe. That's why I'm so worried about this whole thing," Sonja confided.

"You said that before—that something wasn't right. What do you mean?" Lydia prodded.

Sonja rose from the couch and paced around the gigantic room, not knowing how to explain her uneasiness. "I don't know where to begin, or if I can even find the right words. It's just a gut feeling I have."

As if reading her mind, Lydia asked, "Is it about my mother?" She stood from the couch and walked toward her.

Sonja nodded. "Yes. It is."

Lydia's mood changed in an instant. "I wish you wouldn't do this."

"Look, it's not like I think she's out to get you. I just think there's more to her story than she's telling you...and me. Whatever her reasons are, I believe she's only told you half-truths, and in this situation, that's dangerous." Sonja felt like her attempt to explain fell incredibly short.

"You're one to talk about half-truths," Lydia blurted.

That hurt, but Sonja knew she deserved it after everything she'd done. She really couldn't blame Lydia for the comment. "You're right. I don't blame you for not trusting me, but I'm trying to earn that trust back." She fought back the tears, and she was not one to cry at the drop of a hat. It just wasn't her. "I think you're being a bit naïve, and I understand why, babe, but my instincts are telling me lots of pieces to this puzzle are missing."

Lydia turned away from her, then whirled back around and glared at her angrily. "In this case, your instincts are wrong. Dead wrong." Then Lydia stormed out of the library, down the hallway, and ran out of the house.

Sonja was surprised by the outburst, and it bothered her terribly. Still, she made the choice not to run after Lydia. Maybe she needed some time by herself. Lost in her own thoughts, she didn't hear Christie step into the room.

"What did you do to her?" Obviously, she'd overheard the argument and acted surprisingly overprotective of her newfound daughter.

Sonja was in no mood for a verbal lashing. "Lydia and I just had a disagreement, that's all. Nothing to worry about."

"I think there's something to worry about," Christie told her. "This disagreement...was it about me?"

"Christie," Sonja told her, "I really don't want to discuss it right now."

"I think we need to. That's my daughter," Christie informed her.

Sonja felt her blood churning. "Yes, I know." She walked to the window to see if she could spot Lydia.

"I'm getting the feeling you don't trust me, Sonja," Christie stated honestly.

Sonja still peered out the window, hoping for any trace of Lydia, but there was none. "Do we really have to talk about this now? I'm worried about Lydia. I'm going to go find her." She made her way towards the door.

Christie followed her and grabbed her arm. "Wait. I've got to know why you don't trust me."

Shocked that Christie would take such a strong initiative, Sonja froze for a moment. Not only that, but it was more than annoying that

Christie kept holding her back from going after Lydia. Finally, she turned back away from the door and exploded. "All right, Christie. You want to know? Fine, I'll tell you. I just think this whole mother-daughter thing is just too damn neatly put together. Don't get me wrong, I believe you're Lydia's mother, but because Lydia wants to believe it so intently. There's more to your story than you're telling, and one of these days I'm going to know what the hell it is. Let me tell you one thing, Christie. There's a woman outside who has been through hell and back because of people she trusted to tell her the truth. I love that woman, and I intend on finding out what that truth is. It's been almost forty years. Don't you think it's time?" She turned away from Christie, not giving her a chance to answer before she walked out of the library to find Lydia.

***

Stunned, Christie took a deep breath. Now she knew the extent of their relationship. It proved that Sonja really did love her daughter. She stepped over to the window as she had done so many years before to take in the view. This had been one of her favorite rooms of the house. Lydia was right. There was a different air to the mansion without Annabelle Blackwell.

In an instant, the conversation came flooding back to her. That conversation. The words still pierced her memory.

"You are no good here, Cassandra, and you know William can never love you in that way."

"Just what do you mean by that, Mrs. Blackwell?" Cassandra hadn't liked the way the dialogue had turned out.

"Dear Cassandra, you know exactly what I'm talking about. I'm not sure what you did to make him marry you, but I've let this go on longer than I should have. I am prepared to make you an offer to leave William's life forever, quietly." Annabelle's face was stone cold. She had been a sixty-two-year-old, white-haired woman at the time with a strong, masculine build that often scared people.

Christie's eyes filled with tears as she recalled that painful day. How could the many years have just passed her by? But they had, and now Annabelle was gone. But then, so was William. She'd wondered every day since then why she hadn't been strong enough to fight. She was now guilty of the very thing she'd accused William of doing. Nothing should have stopped her from staying, certainly not Annabelle Blackwell.

A shout echoed from the grounds outside. Christie ran out of the library and down the hallway to see what the commotion was. Opening the door, she saw Sonja running towards her in a panic. "What is it?"

"Lydia's gone."

Chapter Twenty-Five

"WHAT DO YOU MEAN she's gone?" Christie asked, catching her breath.

"I've checked the grounds as much as I can, and her car is still here. Something isn't right." Sonja was more worried than she let Christie know, but she didn't want to let her suspicions cloud her judgment. She could be wrong. It could happen. With all of her being, she hoped this was her time to be wrong.

The sky had already started to grow dark, and Sonja's heart felt heavier by the second. "Dammit! I knew I should have gone after her."

Rosita and Jackson appeared besides them. Rosita held a panicked look on her face. "What's wrong?"

"I can't find Lydia. We had a disagreement, and when I came out here, she was gone."

Rosita shook her head. "I don't understand. She was here just a few minutes ago."

"Where?" Sonja inquired.

"Over there by the gazebo, next to her father's grave. I saw her through the upstairs window. I called down to see if she was all right, and she said she was fine."

Sonja took a deep breath and let it out slowly. "Okay, let's not panic. I think we should split up to cover every area, and if we don't find her..." Her voice trailed off into thin air. She couldn't even think of that. Not now.

"Then what, Sonja?"

"We will find her. We have to, that's all there is to it." She left no room for doubt.

***

Rosita and Jackson went back into the house, checking each room, hoping for some sign of Lydia. There were no answers to their calls. It took about an hour for them to scour the large mansion, and they used the intercom system, but still there was nothing. Rosita thought of calling the security people, but she wasn't sure she wanted to cause a stir if all Lydia wanted was to be left alone. Then she realized that, if that were the case, Lydia would have told someone.

She turned to Jackson after they'd covered every area. "Jackson, I'm worried. Something's wrong."

"I'm sure she's just off by herself somewhere, Rosie." Jackson's composure remained positive and calm.

"You don't believe that any more than I do. Face it, you're worried, too," Rosita whispered.

"Yes, I am, but panicking won't do any of us any good. Let's go see if Sonja found anything." Jackson put his arm around her and they went back outside to check in with Sonja and Christie.

Sonja jogged toward them, her eyes wide with more worry than hope when she spotted them. "Did you find her?" Sonja asked, almost breathless.

"No," Jackson answered, "we didn't find any trace of her. We're not sure where to go from here. Rosita and I went through the entire house, every nook and cranny. I don't understand it."

A worried look passed over Sonja's face. "Dammit."

Rosita noticed the wheels in Sonja's mind spinning. "What are you thinking, Sonja?"

"A lot of things. I'm trying not to jump to conclusions, but it's difficult. This just doesn't fit together at all," Sonja said, a puzzled look in her eyes.

"It isn't like Lydia to just disappear. She might be upset, but she doesn't run off without a trace." Rosita paused for a moment and then something occurred to her. "Sonja, you don't think she..." Her voice trailed off into a tearful whisper. She couldn't even finish her words.

"That she what, Rosita?" Sonja prodded.

Rosita pulled herself together in order to let the words pass from her lips. "That she was taken?"

Christie joined them then, having obviously just heard the last part of the conversation. "What? You think she was kidnapped?"

"Settle down. Did you find anything?" Sonja asked her, though it was obvious to all of them she hadn't.

"Nothing." Christie's eyes filled with tears.

"Is that what you think, Sonja?" Rosita repeated.

Sonja turned away from Rosita for a moment, then stood straight and faced them again. "Yes, the thought crossed my mind. I have a feeling Joel Pritchard is behind this, and added to my suspension today, I think it's all part of his plan."

"What? You were suspended? Why, for God's sake?" Christie demanded.

"Look," Sonja began, "it's not important right now. We all need to concentrate on finding Lydia."

"But what do we do now?" Christie asked, clearly upset by the whole situation.

"If Joel did take her, then all we can do is wait. I haven't figured all this out yet. If you all will excuse me, I'm going to make some phone calls." Christie, Jackson and Rosita all nodded as they watched Sonja slowly enter the house.

"It's strange, isn't it?" Christie commented, gazing up into the sky, lost in thought.

"What's strange, Miss Cassandra?" Rosita asked. There was something different about Cassandra now. She seemed to have an edge, something Rosita never noticed when she was young.

"Oh, just how our past never seems to escape us, no matter how hard we try," Christie said, sounding very far away in her own memories.

"Dear girl, it's only when we try to escape our past that it comes back to haunt us," Rosita acknowledged, then glanced at Jackson before she went inside the house. She made her way to the kitchen but stopped outside the swinging door when she overheard Sonja's conversation on her cell phone.

"Hank, I don't know what's going on here. Too many unanswered questions and now Lydia's vanished into thin air. I need your help, at least officially unofficial, if you know what I mean."

"Sonja?" Rosita called to her softly

Sonja nearly jumped out of her seat at the kitchen table. "Jesus!"

Rosita laughed. "Not quite, dear. I'm sorry if I scared you." She reached out and patted Sonja's hand gently.

Sonja gave a half-hearted smile. "It's all right. I probably needed the jumpstart to my heart."

"Are you okay, dear?" Rosita asked as she handed Sonja a tissue. She sat down at the table next to the woman.

"Besides the obvious, you mean?"

"Of course." Rosita nodded.

"I don't know what to do. I can't even do anything officially because of my suspension. I feel responsible." Sonja stood, walked to the coffee pot, and poured herself another cup, staring out the kitchen window.

Rosita stood from her seat and approached the woman. "I don't know about any of that, but I do know one thing."

Sonja turned toward her. "What's that?"

"I know people. And I feel in my heart that you will move Heaven and Earth to find Lydia. You will, because you love her. It's that simple."

The tearful eyes which had dried suddenly glossed over once again. "I do love her, and I will find her, I promise you that." Then she asked, "Did Lydia ever tell you what happened in Wyoming?"

"Yes, she did, and I admit it was not the most comforting news," Rosita stated.

"I know, and I wouldn't blame you if you held it against me," Sonja admitted with a somber look.

Rosita reached out and embraced Sonja. "I understand about powerful people, Sonja. Lydia's grandmother was such a person. I regret deeply not having stood up to her at the time. That regret will live inside me until the day I die. Lydia has such a noble heart, and if she's forgiven you, it's not for me to judge."

"Thank you, Rosita. You're such a rarity. I understand now why Lydia loves you so much," Sonja said, then kissed her cheek.

With a smile, Rosita whispered, "I believe I can say the same of you." They embraced again and Sonja left the house to go home and get a fresh set of clothes and personal items. Rosita, with her power of persuasion, had talked Sonja into staying at the house, and after only a moment's hesitation, Sonja decided it was a good idea so she could get started bright and early on the search for Lydia. There was no more any of them could do in the dark.

***

As Sonja made her way through the nighttime traffic to get to her apartment in Highland Park, her cell phone rang inside her jacket. "MacIntosh, here. Speak to me."

"So--nj-a," the tiny, far-away voice croaked.

"Lydia! Are you okay, baby?" Sonja pulled over on a side street because, otherwise, she knew she'd have an accident.

"Aw, ain't that touchin'?" The new voice on the line definitely wasn't Lydia's.

"Joel. I knew you were behind this," Sonja said in disgust.

"Very good, MacIntosh. I assume you know why this had to happen," Joel stated.

"What the hell do you want? Lydia has nothing to do with this. Take me in exchange," Sonja pleaded.

Joel laughed into the phone. "Oh, I do enjoy a good chuckle, MacIntosh. What would I want with a washed-up dyke cop, hmm? Remember that conversation we had back in Wyoming? I seem to recall mentioning how I feel about being crossed. Maybe your little lover here remembers it."

Sonja heard the blood-curdling scream through the phone. "Don't you hurt her, Pritchard!" she screamed.

Joel laughed again. "My, how forceful of you, MacIntosh. Tell me, who wears the pants in this relationship? Or do you take turns? Please educate me."

The whole routine disgusted her, and she wanted to know what his deal was...and fast. "What do you want?"

"I want the real birth certificate, not a facsimile. You have until noon tomorrow, or your pretty little lover won't be so pretty anymore. Are we in agreement?" Joel would think nothing of killing Lydia, Sonja knew. It didn't matter that she was a woman.

"I have no choice but to agree, Pritchard, you know that. Will you let me talk to her?" Sonja felt like a child asking her mother's permission.

"You can talk to her tomorrow. Maybe. Be here at noon." Joel gave Sonja the location. "Ciao." Click. That was the end of her contact with Lydia.

She let out a scream inside the car, venting her anger at the man who held everything over her head. Sonja didn't even know if the location he'd given her was where he held Lydia or just a drop-off point. Panicked, she tried to reach Hank. He understood very well that his career could be in danger if anyone discovered him, but he would do anything to help clear his partner's name. Hank's voice came on the line after only one ring.

"Sonja?" he asked, making sure it was her.

"Yeah, it's me. He's got her."

"*Damnit!*" Hank yelled into the phone.

"I should have gone after her and this wouldn't have happened," Sonja said, realizing her hands shook.

"You know he would have gotten to her anyway. What are you going to do?"

"I'm working up a plan," she told him. There was no point in beating around the bush. She still didn't know what that plan was, but it had to be fool-proof and ready by noon tomorrow. Her instincts told her Christie still held back information about her past and, in this case, not knowing could really hurt someone. Lydia.

Sonja pulled back out into traffic, her mind spinning out of control, thinking only of Lydia and what the hell she was going to do now.

Chapter Twenty-Six

"WELL," JOEL BEGAN, SPEAKING after his phone call with Sonja ended. "It looks like your little girlfriend is smart after all. Sounds like she'd do anything for you." He paused for a moment, gathering his thoughts carefully. "Now for our business at hand, Lydia."

"What business could we possibly have, Joel? I don't even know you." Lydia's eyes searched the warehouse, then returned to the man in front of her.

"Maybe not directly, but you've had things in your possession that belong to my family. You see, family is the most important thing to me." Joel kept the gloves off for the moment.

"I quite agree. Speaking of family...did you know about me?"

"Okay, I'll bite. What do you mean?" This might be amusing, after all.

"I mean, about my real heritage. Do you know anything about it?" Lydia asked him point-blank.

"Of course. I know William Blackwell was your father, and that little tramp Cassandra Lexington was your mother," Joel stated, wondering where this dialogue would lead.

Lydia was already shaking her head when he finished speaking. "You're right on one account. My mother is Cassandra Lexington, but William Blackwell was not my natural father. It appears you and I are related."

Joel had to laugh at the idea. "That's the most absurd thing I've heard for quite some time. Okay, tell me, Lydia. Just how are we related? I'm fascinated."

"Apparently, we have the same father," Lydia told him.

Joel was speechless. Maybe the woman was trying anything so he would let her go. Crazier things had happened, and Joel knew desperate people would try desperate measures. "And who gave you this preposterous information?"

"My mother," Lydia answered.

Joel waved his hands in the air, dismissing her. "My dear girl, of course your mother is lying." But secretly, there lurked a worried Pritchard. What if it was true? What if this woman was indeed his half-sister?

"Is that your only answer? That my mother is lying? It's interesting that you can so quickly come to that conclusion."

"I see no other logical explanation." But Joel was troubled. Perhaps this was the whole reason behind his father's insistence on getting the birth certificate. Lydia was obviously the child it involved. Joel wanted to get Lydia off this subject, but it was already part of the problem. Joel shook his head. "I don't really want to discuss this any longer, Lydia. You're here for different reasons."

"Which are?"

"You're here to tell me what I want to know," Joel replied.

"What you want to know or what you want to hear?" Lydia asked, looking him square in the eye.

Joel Pritchard scoffed at the woman he'd ordered to be abducted. "Oh, Lydia, you are a brave soul, I have to admit. You and MacIntosh deserve each other."

"Why, thank you. I'll take that as a compliment. What is it," she continued, "that you think I can tell you?"

Joel rose from his chair slowly to exhibit his six-foot-four frame. He was a handsome man, and he used that feature constantly with women. He had thick, jet-black hair, kept it short, and worked out obsessively, so he was always in shape and looking better than anyone else. He wore a dark, olive-green Italian suit, black dress shoes, crisp white shirt with extra starch, black suspenders, but no tie today. He could have been an advertisement for GQ, if not for being the head of a crime family.

Joel walked over to Lydia, whose hands were still tied behind her to the chair. Kneeling down close, he whispered, "So many things," in a soft voice, almost seductively. He found Lydia appealing and momentarily forgot she was a lesbian...or that she might possibly be his sister. Joel wanted to scare her into telling him everything, but for some reason, he was unsure of how to do it. Lydia Blackwell appeared to be fiercely independent and courageous beyond all rationalization. He finally looked her in the eye. "Lydia, I don't think I need to remind you of the kind of man I am."

"No, you don't. I know very well the kind of man you are."

"That's good." Joel's cell phone let out its familiar ring. After a disgruntled sigh, he said, "Excuse me," then walked into a hidden area behind boxes and wooden pallets to take the call.

"Yeah? This better be good," Joel barked into the phone.

"Joey, it's Antonio," the voice stated.

Joel was shocked to hear such a voice from the past. Antonio Delgado was the man who had helped Brenton Pritchard get started in the business years ago. Antonio had kept a silent vigil over Brenton—and the Pritchard name since Brenton's death—and had made sure Joel still did the family good. He was the only one who could get away with calling him Joey. No one else dared.

"Antonio. I'm surprised to hear from you after all this time. To tell you the truth, now is not a good ti—"

The powerful voice on the other end came through. "Joey, don't put me off. I have some information you might be interested in. Things you don't know."

"Look, I appreciate you calling, but I'm in the middle of something right now," Joel told him as politely as he could. He certainly didn't want to make the man mad. That could be dangerous, not to mention disrespectful.

"I know what you're in the middle of, and that's why I'm calling. I know everything about the purse and the birth certificate. Just trust me," Antonio said.

Joel kept a close eye on Lydia, making sure she didn't attempt an escape. He motioned his two men to watch her while he talked to Antonio. "Of course I trust you, Antonio. Please, go on."

"I have it on good authority that you have Blackwell's daughter there with you. Am I right?"

"Yes," Joel acknowledged.

"When you question her, you need to ask about a cassette tape," Antonio suggested.

"What cassette tape?" Joel was perplexed. It was the first he'd heard of it.

"Ah, I didn't think you knew. That's why I thought it imperative to call. I'll tell you the details later, but essentially, it has a recording of a meeting between your father and some associates in the family, myself included. It's a dangerous thing to have floating around. Originally, it was in the infamous silver purse," Antonio informed him.

"Who made the tape?" Joel asked.

"I can only assume we were double-crossed by one of our enemies. All these years, and I haven't quite narrowed it down."

"Okay, I'll take care of this and end it." Joel paused, then decided to ask the question which had plagued him for the past hour.

"Antonio, do you know anything about my father having another child?"

The phone line went quiet for a moment. "That's a strange question coming from you, Joey. What gives?"

"I'll explain later. I assume you don't know anything about it, then?"

"No, I don't know anything about it, Joey. Of course, your father did get around a lot, so I guess it's possible."

They ended the conversation and Joel sat quietly in amazement. This situation was taking on a life of its own. One thing was clear. He had to find that tape. It could mean life and death for the family business.

Joel stepped from the shadows of the warehouse and back into the light, where his two men played cards at the table across from where Lydia sat. "Please untie the lady," he told them.

"Thank you, Joel." Lydia said.

"Certainly. There are some questions I must ask you. Being as you know what kind of man I am, I assume you have an idea of what could happen if you try to lie to me," Joel told her bluntly.

Lydia nodded. "Of course."

"First of all, where is the tape?" Joel thought of his conversation with Antonio and briefly wondered where it would get him.

Lydia's face held a puzzled look. "What tape?"

"A cassette tape inside the purse," Joel told her. He knew by her reaction that she hadn't known it existed, either.

"There was no tape inside the purse, as you well know," she told him with a hint of anger. "At least, not when it was given to me."

"Where did you get the purse?"

"From Derek. Derek Meade."

"Really," Joel said. "Fascinating." Pretty damn smart of the old man to get rid of it. Just in the nick of time, though in the end, it didn't help him any. "Did he ever tell you how it came to be in his hands?"

"Something about a fight outside a bar in downtown Chicago many years ago. It fell out of the attacker's pocket during the fight," Lydia reported casually. "Apparently, my father picked it up and kept it all these years. He gave it to Derek shortly before he died."

It surprised Joel that Lydia gave out this kind of information. Maybe it was because she really believed he was her brother. Whatever it was, he was grateful. "Your father never spoke of the purse all these years? I find that hard to believe."

"My father left many secrets behind. I didn't even know my mother was alive until he died. That should give you some idea of what my life has been like these past few weeks."

"I see." Joel sat pensively in his seat across from Lydia, not really knowing what to think or do.

"You do realize that purse belongs to my mother, don't you?"

Joel snapped out of his deep thoughts and glared at her. "I realize no such thing."

"It was stolen from my mother. Her initials are engraved right on it. It's part of my heritage, my family. I'd think you of all people would understand that."

Joel stood in one sudden movement and glared at Lydia. "Don't try that on me, Lydia. My father asked me to carry out this mission, and the wishes of a dying man must be honored."

Lydia nodded. "I understand that."

"Don't be understanding, Lydia. I'm not a nice man."

Lydia looked straight into his eyes. "You haven't killed me yet."

A smile came to Joel's face. "That's true enough, but it's not out of pure benevolence. You know as well as I do that I need you right now."

Lydia nodded. "Yes, I realize that, but what if I can't tell you what you need to know?"

"In my business, there are no 'what ifs'. It's black and white." Suddenly irritated and losing his patience, he added, "You sure ask a lot of questions for a kidnapped woman." Joel would never say it out loud, but he could not kill her.

"Well, in my business, Joel, it's all about 'what ifs'," Lydia told him. "What's a good therapist if she can't ask questions?"

"Oh, I see. That explains it." Joel laughed and then realized he was being too casual. The smile faded from his face. "Now, Lydia, tell me why you think the silver purse belongs to your mother, the tramp."

Chapter Twenty-Seven

AFTER GATHERING A SUITCASE full of clothes and some other personal items from her apartment, Sonja made the journey back to the Blackwell Estates. She could barely breathe, knowing Lydia was in the presence of a madman. And Lydia's entire future depended on Sonja's next action.

As she passed the security gate and her car rolled down the winding driveway, she knew the answers to many of her questions rested with Christie. Nothing would stop her from finding out the truth. Only the truth could save Lydia. At least, that's what she told herself as she stepped inside the mansion doors.

Rosita ran to the door to greet her. "Well?"

"Let's go into the library, Rosita. I want Christie and Jackson there, too." Sonja wanted everyone there as witnesses and, just in case, she had her mini cassette recorder in her jacket pocket, ready to go.

"Christie's already in the library," Rosita informed her. "I'll get Jackson." She scurried off to find Jackson, and within seconds they had all gathered in the library.

"All right, what's this all about, Sonja?" Christie urgently asked.

"It's about Lydia. On the way to my apartment across town, I received a phone call from her," Sonja reported. In an instant, three voices blended together, all talking at once, and Sonja could barely handle it. Finally, she shouted, "Hey! We need to be calm and rational, for Lydia's sake. Everyone agreed?"

Rosita spoke first. "She's right. We're all here because we love her. We agree, Sonja. Please, continue."

"Thank you. Like I said, she called, but I only heard her voice for a moment. Lydia's with Joel."

"Just as you suspected," Jackson noted.

"Yes, unfortunately. I offered myself in exchange, but Joel was against it. I can only guess he's keeping her because he wants information and believes she can deliver." Sonja kept a close eye on Christie's reactions.

"What did Joel say to you?" Christie demanded.

"He wants the birth certificate by noon tomorrow. He's going to call tomorrow with a location."

"That's easy. Just give it to him," Christie suggested.

Rosita glanced at Sonja and shook her head. Sonja walked to where Christie sat in an armchair. "Christie, it's just not that easy."

"Sure it is. This is my daughter we're talking about. It *is* that easy, dammit!" Christie shouted.

"Yes, you've made that abundantly clear, when it's convenient for you." Sonja was tired of hearing a reminder every five minutes.

"What the hell is that supposed to mean?"

Rosita finally stepped in. "Cassandra—Christie—remember, calm and rational? Let's not get into a fist fight."

"Listen," Sonja said, "the only thing that matters now is getting Lydia back home where she belongs and the Pritchards out of our lives. Christie, you have the answers, and you know what I mean." Sonja stared her down intently.

"Well, I don't—" Christie's objection was caught short when she met Sonja's gaze. Then she added, "I've lived with this for so long. I'm sorry, Sonja."

Sonja told her softly, "It's okay. I'm sorry, too. Are you ready?"

"Yes, I am." Christie took a deep breath.

"Okay." Sonja took the tape recorder out of her jacket pocket. "I'm going to record this, for all our sakes. Is that all right with you?" Quietly, Christie nodded. Sonja pressed the record button, and they all listened to the woman's hesitant tale.

"As you all know, I was with Brenton Pritchard when I was quite young. I had inside knowledge of certain business practices, and I used to keep a detailed journal of things I heard and saw."

"Why would you do such a thing?" Sonja inquired.

"I wanted out desperately, and Brenton made it difficult, if not impossible. I needed an edge," Christie answered solemnly.

"Something to hold over his head," Sonja stated.

"Yes. You don't know how desperate I was. Brenton beat and raped me several times and forced me to perform sexual favors for members of the 'family'. It was disgusting, and I hated myself. I got to the point where I didn't care if I was sleeping out on the street. I had to get out."

Sonja noticed Christie's body begin to tremble and she reached out to touch her shoulder. "It's okay, Christie. Remember, it's for Lydia. Everything is."

Christie nodded. "For Lydia. Okay, I'm fine." She took another deep breath and continued. "One day, after a severe beating from Brenton, I was cleaning myself up in the bathroom and I heard a meeting being held in the other room. I assumed it was with his business associates, and they spoke about who was on their way out of the 'family'."

"What do you mean?" Sonja asked. Details were vital, and she had to get them all.

"They discussed who was next on the 'kill list', as I used to call it. This was more than talking, mind you. This was actual planning—where, when, and how it would take place. I found myself wondering how on earth I could have ended up with a man like that. I'd heard the story of Anna Pritchard, Joel and Michael's mother. She'd tried to leave and take the boys with her. Brenton physically stopped her. I suppose he thought she would stay. She apparently went crazy. They found her body the next day in a back alley somewhere. I didn't want that to be me. It couldn't be me."

"What did you do?" Sonja pushed.

"I was so angry about my situation. I wanted revenge and was determined to get it. I found my tape recorder and made a tape of this meeting, at least what I could get of it. I knew it was my only way out."

Sonja stopped the tape, her eyes wide. "What? There was a tape recording? Why the hell didn't you tell me this before?"

"I'm sorry, Sonja. I don't know why I didn't. I guess I was scared of what could happen and I just didn't want to get involved with the Pritchards again," Christie told her as she hung her head, not even looking Sonja in the eye.

"Guess that plan backfired, because now we're all involved with the Pritchards...dead and alive," Sonja said and walked away. She threw her hands up in frustration and found herself pacing. She knew the woman was still hiding a lot. Knowing she had to keep moving, she took a deep breath. "Okay, let's get back to it." Sonja turned the recorder back on. "What happened to the tape, Christie?"

"I'm not sure. I put it in my silver purse and then locked it up in a safe deposit box at my bank. I thought it was secure there, but someone got to it."

"Any idea who that someone is?" Sonja said almost sarcastically as she ran her fingers through her hair and rubbed her eyes. Her frustration mounted as the wheels spun in her mind, trying to reconstruct Christie's life in her head. Christie was not giving up her past easily.

"Brenton. I have no doubt. He owned bankers everywhere, even outside of Chicago, so he had easy access. After all this time, I'd forgotten about it."

"All right. I want to get back to how you managed to escape Brenton's grasp, if you'll continue." Sonja pulled up a chair and sat across from Christie, hoping to at least be a little mentally intimidating.

"Well, I guess this is where William Blackwell comes into the story. He worked in an investment firm indirectly managed by Brenton. I met him at a dinner party Brenton had forced me to put together. I think William noticed the way Brenton talked to me in front of his associates and felt sorry for me. We talked the entire night and became fast friends. He'd take me for dinner, movies, and sometimes dancing. I was shocked that Brenton didn't even take notice of a man paying that kind of attention to me.

"William confided in me one night that he was gay. I felt instantly at ease with him, probably because of that fact. I didn't have to worry, you know? It wasn't long after I met William that I found out I was pregnant, and then my world really fell apart. I didn't know what to do. The thought of bringing another Pritchard into the world devastated me. I decided an abortion was the best way. Besides, I kept picturing Anna in the back of my mind. Brenton would never let me raise his baby on my own."

"You said before that William stopped you from getting that abortion. Is that right?" Sonja asked, wanting to make sure her facts were correct.

"Yes. He showed up at the clinic while I was there and begged me not to go through with it. He said I would regret it for the rest of my life, and he was right."

"What else did he tell you?" Sonja secretly thanked William Blackwell for saving Lydia.

"He offered to marry me and take me away from Brenton."

"Did he tell you why he was willing to make that offer?" Sonja asked, though she could understand a sacrifice like that, even in a friendship. She thought of Hank and knew they would do anything for each other in the face of danger.

"Remember, this was in the early sixties, when people just didn't talk about things like that. Being found out could be a matter of life and death. He was afraid of Brenton discovering his lifestyle, and it would put his career in jeopardy—among other things. William was quite persuasive and he made life sound so wonderful. I couldn't refuse."

"Did you know Derek Meade?" Sonja questioned, knowing there were no simple answers.

"Yes, he was a good friend to me, almost as close as William." Christie smiled at the memory.

"When did you meet him?"

"I actually met Derek briefly before I met William. Derek worked the summer as sort of an errand boy, doing odd jobs around the house or really whatever Brenton wanted him to do. Brenton actually made him take me out for lunch a few times to keep me busy and out of his hair. That was when I really got to know him."

"When did the fight happen?"

"I believe it was the fall of 1964. I'm sure Brenton was behind the attack," Christie remembered. "Do you mind if we take a little break?"

Sonja changed the tape in her recorder. "No, that's fine. I'm sorry if I've been pushing you. It's just that I—"

Christie put up her hand to stop her. "No apologies. I know how much you love her," Christie said. "I think I'm going to give Martin a call. Maybe I can coax him into joining me."

"I think that's a good idea," Sonja said, putting a reassuring hand on Christie's arm. She watched the woman quietly leave the room, then sat down on the couch, letting her entire body collapse. Rosita and Jackson left to get some coffee and cookies for everyone, since it was likely to be a long night. Sonja closed her eyes and let her aching head fall back to rest on the back of the couch. She enjoyed the peace and quiet, feeling there may not be a chance for much more in her immediate future.

Suddenly, she felt a presence in the room. When she opened her eyes, a tall, blonde-haired man dressed in khakis and a blue polo shirt stood across from her. As if she were on fire, Sonja jumped to her feet, her heart pounding out of control. "Who the hell are you and how did you get in here?"

The man stepped back and held his hand up to stop her.

"Answer the question."

"I'm sorry I frightened you. Your housekeeper let me in." The man dug inside his jacket pocket, then stopped. "Don't worry. I'm not going to shoot. It's my badge." He retrieved the black leather wallet and showed off the shiny metal FBI badge.

"FBI?" Sonja asked, not believing just a badge. Her eyes rolled back in her head with the realization that if he truly was an FBI agent, this was bigger than she thought.

"Excuse me. My name is Jacob Ashton, but you can call me Jake." The man extended his hand out to Sonja, who politely shook his hand with a leery gaze. "I'm sorry for stumbling in here clearly unannounced. Lieutenant Sonja MacIntosh?"

"Yes, apparently you know who *I* am. How do I know for sure you are who you say you are? You could have made a badge yourself, for all I know."

"True enough, Lieutenant. I can give you the name of my supervisor, if you wish. Currently, I would prefer we not waste valuable time."

"I can give you the benefit of the doubt…for now. Have a seat," she said motioning to the chair beside her. She studied him carefully, but his presence did nothing to alleviate her concerns.

"Thank you. I wanted to talk to you about Joel Pritchard."

"Oh, I see," Sonja said, shaking her head.

"I sense some hesitation in your voice, Lieutenant."

"Why are you here, Ashton?" Sonja had made sure no one else knew where she'd be, and the fact that this man had found her here only heightened her skepticism.

"What can you tell me?" he asked, taking out his notebook.

"Not so fast. What can *you* tell me?" She raised her eyebrows, staring him down.

"Fair enough. I can tell you that we think we have Joel's location narrowed down. We've been watching Pritchard for a while, now."

"Great." Sonja glanced at her watch several times in nervous anticipation, hoping that if she kept looking at it, she would know what to say. "So, what do you want from me?"

"We know about your troubles with Pritchard in Wyoming and what it cost you. I've seen your record, Sonja, and it's damn good. I have to believe Pritchard left you no choice."

Sonja was quiet, but then took several swigs of the coffee Rosita had brought in a few minutes earlier. As she drank, she realized the man had to be FBI. "That's true. So, am I to understand that you also know about the kidnapping?"

"Of course." He glanced over his notes. "A Lydia Blackwell. Time is running out, and this is why I need to know how we can work together on this to bring her home and take down the Pritchards."

A long sigh came from Sonja's lungs as she sat back on the couch with her coffee in hand. "Since you know all of these things, Ashton, you must know that I am unable to work with you, officially, on anything."

"Yes, I am aware of your suspension. I will take care of that, as it's all a part of our ongoing investigation. Will you allow me to do that for you, and help me in return?"

Sonja didn't take her eyes off of the man. "All I care about right now is getting Lydia back home. If that's what it takes, then fine."

"Good. Now, I know what your boss, Captain Bradley Pennington, told me. What's your side of the story?"

"It was blackmail." Sonja hated even remembering the blasted event.

"Sounds like Pritchard," Jacob stated without missing a beat.

"Apparently. He was on a mission to fulfill his dying father's wishes and didn't care who he stepped on in the process," Sonja informed him. She stopped for a short moment and then stared at him intensely. "Just what are you after, Jake?"

"We've been waiting to take down the Pritchard family for years. I'm sure you know as well as I do he's quite good at eluding the law. Pritchard knows the system."

"Joel gave me a location for a meeting with him tomorrow, but I don't know if it's where they're holding Lydia."

"We believe it's an old warehouse off the interstate near Wheeling. We've been following cell phone tower activity and narrowing it down. This confirms it, now."

Sonja took a deep, agonizing breath. She felt her foot tapping out of control. Inside, she was boiling over. "Close doesn't count, Jake. Not where Lydia's concerned. The clock is ticking. Hell, she could be dead now, for all we know."

"Lieutenant, I realize your concern for Lydia, but I don't believe Joel will kill her. He has too much to lose," Jake said.

Sonja got up from the couch in a sudden movement, ran her

hand through her hair in frustration, and paced again.

"I know you're worried," Jake said softly, "and I don't mean to make light of the situation. I want to bring them all down. Please, tell me everything."

Sonja stared at the floor, then nodded. "All right, but I want some insurance."

A smile slowly passed over Jake's face. "Of course, Lieutenant. I wouldn't have it any other way." He reached for the tape recorder inside his jacket.

"I'm afraid that's not good enough," Sonja told him firmly.

"It's the best I can do. Look, Lieutenant, I know it's difficult to trust people in our line of work, and sometimes it's deadly. If you stop trusting, you will never know if you've actually missed out on something good. I came here because I know what a good cop you are, and that sometimes bad things happen to good cops. I need your help."

Quietly, Sonja nodded and motioned for Jake to start recording. She was already suspended, and Lydia's life was on the line. There wasn't much left to lose. She grabbed her coffee, sat back, and began the sordid tale of how the Pritchards, past and present, wrought havoc in the lives of the Blackwells and, subsequently, her own.

Chapter Twenty-Eight

"WHAT?" MARTIN EXCLAIMED THROUGH the phone. "You're coming home, Christie. It's too dangerous there."

"Martin, please listen to me," Christie said. "Lydia is the one in danger, and I'm not leaving her. Not again."

"Don't you see what's happening?" Martin added. "You're getting sucked into this game, and the players are out for blood. You could get hurt...or worse."

"This whole mystery is because of my past. I'm already involved." Christie took a deep breath. She didn't want to argue with him, she just wanted him there with her. "I'm not coming home, but you could come here. Lydia has a ticket for you. Please, Marty. I need you."

Martin groaned into the phone. "I guess there's no choice if you're not coming home. Send the ticket."

"Thank you, Martin. I'll meet you at the airport. I've missed you so much. And I love you." She hung up the phone in the kitchen, and when she turned around she bumped straight into Rosita. "Rosita, you scared me! You shouldn't sneak up on people like that."

"I'm sorry, Miss Cassandra. I didn't mean to frighten you. How's your husband?"

"Martin's flying here tomorrow. He wanted me to come home, but I refused. I just can't leave Lydia," Christie said, still feeling the guilt time had failed to bury.

Rosita nodded. "That's good. Lydia needs you now more than ever."

Christie stared into Rosita's eyes, sensing something different.

"You're still not entirely sure about me, are you?"

"Not entirely, no." Rosita was not one to mince words, and they both knew it. There was no point.

"Why?" Christie stood with her arms crossed, watching Rosita's reaction. There were times when Rosita was her only friend in the big, lonely mansion, but now she wondered if the woman was now more of an enemy.

"Does it really matter?" Rosita said before turning around to walk away.

"Of course it matters. We were so close, once. I owe you everything for taking such good care of Lydia all these years," Christie said, reaching out to warmly touch Rosita's arm.

"I don't think you realize all that girl has been through, not just in the past few weeks, but her entire life. Lydia opened her heart to you, forgiving you for everything. You don't owe me a thing. You owe Lydia. Don't let her down," Rosita said, looking her straight in the eye. She quickly left the kitchen through the swinging door.

Christie had to admit Rosita was right. She couldn't let Lydia down, and unraveling this mystery of the past was the most important thing she could do. Lydia was the innocent one, and Christie realized there was more to her past than even she knew.

She heard voices in the hallway and the sound of the front door shutting. She recognized Sonja's voice, but not the other, and she walked briskly toward them. Nervously, she peered into the library to see Sonja sitting on the sofa, sipping her coffee. "Sonja? Who was just here? I thought I heard a man's voice."

"Jake Ashton," Sonja said without offering any other information.

"Who the hell is Jake Ashton?"

"He's the man who just left."

"You know what I mean. Who is he?" Christie was less than amused.

"He's an FBI agent."

"FBI? Did they find Lydia? Why are they involved?" The

questions whirled through Christie's mind. She couldn't comprehend how a simple trip to get away with her long-lost daughter had turned into an FBI investigation.

"Hold it, Christie. One at a time," Sonja said, holding her hand in the air. She poured herself another cup of coffee with some Irish crème "Jake Ashton was here to ask me some questions about the Pritchard family. And yes, he confirmed they think Joel is hidden at the location he gave me on the phone. We still don't know for sure if that's where Lydia is. I didn't even know the FBI was involved. Apparently, this case is bigger than we thought."

"So, what do we do now?" Christie didn't know what to do with herself. She felt so out of place and strange.

"I'm not sure. I want to charge right in there, get Lydia, and kick Joel square in the b—"

Rosita and Jackson entered the room. "Boots?" Rosita finished with a hint of mischief.

A red-faced Sonja blinked. "Um, yeah. Boots."

Rosita asked, "Any ideas of what to do, Sonja? Time is running out."

"I know, and that's what worries me. The bottom line is that Joel believes he's carrying out his father's wishes. I don't even think he knows the whole story." Sonja then looked straight at Christie. "Lydia doesn't even know the whole story." Christie turned away from Sonja's glances and walked toward the window, lost in a deep, dark place, longing for it all to be over. "Christie?" Sonja asked. "When was the last time you saw the purse?"

"The last time was in Wyoming, when Lydia showed it to me. Before that, I hadn't seen it since I put it away in the safe deposit box," Christie stated, still gazing out the window.

"Do you have any idea why the birth certificate is so important to the Pritchards?"

"I'm not sure. When Lydia was born, I named William as the father. There was no father listed on the document Lydia showed me." Christie shook her head in disbelief. "I just don't know."

"Did you ever tell Brenton you were pregnant?"

"Are you kidding?" Christie said, whirling around to face her. "I couldn't tell him that. He would never have given up until that child was his and only his."

"Christie." Sonja joined her at the window. "Pritchard was a powerful man. Don't you think he would have found out somehow?"

"I suppose so, but if he did, I never knew about it. Once I left, I never heard from him again." Christie tugged at her sleeve. Sonja's interrogation made her far more than uneasy.

"Wait a minute," Sonja said. "I just thought of something. Brenton wouldn't have had any use for that birth certificate."

"What are you talking about?" Christie tilted her head, watching Sonja in confusion.

"If the purse was stolen before Lydia was born and Brenton didn't even know you were pregnant, the birth certificate wouldn't matter. Two possibilities here—either Brenton did find out you were pregnant, or the birth certificate had been placed into the purse's lining by someone else later on. Joel probably doesn't even realize the purse really didn't belong to his father."

"Do you think he even cares?" Christie asked.

"I doubt it, but I'm going to risk it."

Chapter Twenty-Nine

AFTER FINALLY DRIFTING OFF to sleep around three in the morning, Sonja was awakened by the buzzing of her cell phone on the nightstand. "Yeah, MacIntosh here."

"Sonja. Jake Ashton. Sorry if I woke you."

Sonja glanced at her watch next to the lamp and attempted to focus enough to read the numbers. "It's after six. Don't be ridiculous, I've had plenty of sleep. What's going on? Have you found Lydia or Joel?"

"Slow down. I was wondering if you were up for breakfast. There's something I want to discuss with you."

"I'm up now. We have a deadline to meet today, as I'm sure you're aware. Just a little matter of life and death, remember?" Sonja could think of nothing else.

"Of course. That's what I want to discuss with you. Can you meet me in an hour?"

"All right. Just come to the Blackwell Estates. I'm sure Rosita's already up and making something," Sonja offered, suddenly feeling strangely used to Rosita's cooking schedule. The woman knew her way around a kitchen.

"Sounds good."

Sonja had been right; Rosita was already up and halfway through making a large breakfast. She supposed it was Rosita's way of dealing with the tension, and the woman had no issues with feeding people.

The doorbell rang, and when Rosita moved to answer it, Sonja stopped her. "It's okay, Rosita, I'll get it." She left the kitchen and walked briskly to the front door. Expecting Jake, she pulled it open and said, "It's about time you got—" But the figure in front of her took her breath away for a fleeting moment.

"Lieutenant Sonja MacIntosh?" the man inquired.

Sonja swallowed and whispered, "Um, yes. That's me. I'm sorry."

"If you invite me in, I'll explain everything," the man offered.

"Oh, of course. Please come in," Sonja said, her heart beating as if it would explode. "Let's go into the library." As she walked with him, her mind was in turmoil. The man looked just like the late Derek Meade—but that just couldn't be. She'd studied the body herself, watched the Coroner take it out of the house. The blood, the gunshots—she'd seen it all with her own eyes. No way.

"Excellent," the man said. He walked down the hallway with her as if he knew where he was going.

As they neared the library, an eerie feeling overwhelmed her and wouldn't go away. She closed the library door behind her. "You've been here before."

"Yes, many times. This is my favorite room," he acknowledged, gazing around.

Sonja battled with her mind in an attempt to rationalize what her eyes told her. She wanted to trust that everything would be explained—she just didn't know how.

"Allow me to introduce myself, Lieutenant. My name is Derek Meade."

"Derek Meade is dead," she said, finding her voice again. "I was there. I saw the body. Not just once, but several times, and I made sure it got to the coroner."

The door to the library opened. "Is this a private party, or can anyone join?" Jake asked and stepped into the room. "Hello, Derek. Good to see you." The men shook hands as if they were old friends.

Sonja's jaw dropped to the floor. "You know this man?"

"Yes, I do, but I think I'll let Derek fill you in," Jake said as he nodded toward the other man.

"I'm sorry, Lieutenant, for putting you through all of this, but it was necessary at the time," Derek began. "The man who was murdered in my house was..." His voice trailed off into a sad whisper, and he swallowed, blinking rapidly. "It was my brother, Dillon. My twin brother. He impersonated me without my knowledge, and in the process got himself killed. After that, I knew I couldn't return right away. At least, not until things settled down some."

"My God," was all Sonja could say. "So Lydia found your brother's body?"

"I didn't know it had been Lydia. That poor girl," Derek said, placing his hand over his mouth in disbelief. "And she thought it was me."

A knock sounded at the door and it opened again. "Breakfast is ready. Where would you—" Rosita stopped abruptly when she saw Derek's face. "Mr. Derek? How can you—what's going on here?"

"Rosita, love. So good to see you again, though I'm sorry it's under these circumstances," Derek said as he reached out to kiss Rosita's hand. "It's a long story."

"Suppose you tell it to me some time," Rosita said, eyeing him up and down. She obviously had less trouble accepting the shock than Sonja had.

"I certainly will, once Lydia is back home where she belongs," Derek agreed.

Rosita turned her attention to Sonja and gave her a knowing look. "Where would you like breakfast served?"

"The dining room is fine, Rosita. Thank you. We'll be right there." Sonja glanced at Derek. "Care to stay for breakfast?"

"Of course."

The dining room had been built beside the kitchen in all practicality, but once William had fallen ill, it hadn't been used often, if at all. Jake and Derek devoured their eggs, but Sonja couldn't bring herself to take a bite. She looked back and forth between the two of them as if she were watching a tennis match. Finally, the stress of it got to her. "Are you two insane or what?"

They stopped eating and looked at each other, not saying a word for several seconds. Finally, Jake glanced at her. "What do you mean by that?"

"How on earth can you sit here and eat when we have no plan for getting Lydia the hell away from Joel? What are you thinking?" Sonja's eyes were wide with fear. Time was running out.

"Relax, Lieutenant. We're all working together, now," Jake said as he buttered the biscuit on his plate.

"I can't work with you, at least not officially."

"I took care of that. No worries," Jake said without even looking at her.

"What the hell does that mean?" Sonja was not going to let up until she knew what was going on, and she sure wasn't going to have a nice, peaceful breakfast with these men while she fumbled around in the dark.

Laughter erupted from Jake, so much so that it took him a few moments to regain his composure.

"I'm glad you find this amusing." Sonja felt her blood pressure rising. She wanted to shake him and get moving.

"I'm sorry, Sonja, it's just that you look like a ball of fire when you get all worked up. Never fear, though, I think you'll be happy to hear what I've done."

"I'll be the judge of that. Spill it." She was so tired of playing these games. It wouldn't be long before there would be no time left for games.

"It seems that your Captain Pennington has been on Joel's payroll for quite some time. What's more, I believe your suspension was part of a sordid plan to get rid of you," Jake informed her.

"I can't say that surprises me. What did you do?"

Slowly, Jake reached into his jacket pocket and pulled out Sonja's badge and gun. "I believe these belong to you."

"Thanks." Sonja stared at her belongings, feeling like her chest would burst with gratitude, but she couldn't show it. Not with how tense she still felt.

"You know, Pennington had that look of disbelief on his face, too, when I eagerly persuaded him to reinstate you."

"How did you convince him?" she asked.

"I told him I'd go to Internal Affairs with everything," Jake reported.

"I would have liked to see that." She paused for a moment, then looked back up at Jake. "You don't know what this means to me."

"I think I do. You're a good cop and you deserve the badge," Jake said. "And you can repay me by helping me bring down Pritchard."

Something in the man's eyes mirrored vengeance, and Sonja knew more than anyone how personal vengeance could be. "This a personal case for you?" she asked.

Jake took a long drink of orange juice. "Of course. I take every assignment personally, and the Bureau has been after these bastards for a long time." Then he glanced at Derek, who had been completely silent.

"Hey, what's going on in here?" Christie entered the dining room, and as soon as she saw Derek, the mug of coffee slipped from her hand and onto the hardwood floor.

Rosita rushed through the door from the kitchen. "What on earth happened here?"

"Cassandra?" Derek asked, not taking his eyes off her. He rose from his seat in one smooth move and wrapped Christie in his arms. "It's been so long."

The tears rolled down Christie's cheeks. "Derek…we all thought you were dead. I don't understand."

He pulled a handkerchief from his pocket and wiped her eyes. Then, in a soft voice, he told her, "It's a long, awful story, but my brother Dillon was the one who… I didn't find out he'd pretended to be me until it was too late."

"I'm so sorry," Christie whispered. "This is unbelievable."

"Thank you." Nodding, Derek ushered Christie into a seat at the table, and she stared at him like there was no one else in the room.

"Derek," Sonja started, "why did you decide to come back here?"

"It's simple," he said, staring back at Christie. "I'm Lydia's father."

Chapter Thirty

"WHAT?" CHRISTIE SHRIEKED. "YOU can't be serious."

"I'm quite serious."

Christie stood from the table in one swift movement and glared at Derek. "Just how is that possible? Don't you think I would remember? Besides that, you're...you are..." She tried to blurt it out but couldn't quite make it.

"Gay is the word I think you're looking for, Cassandra. And yes, that's true, but there are things you don't know," Derek told her sympathetically.

Sonja shook her head, not quite believing this whole tale. Lydia was right—it was a soap opera.

"Would you like to do the honors, Jake?" Derek asked with determination in his eyes.

Jake nodded, then reached into his jacket pocket and pulled out his miniature tape recorder. "Whenever you're ready, Derek."

Sonja glanced at her watch. "And since we have an emergency on our hands, could you please have the ending come as close to the beginning as possible?"

"Of course. After all, I'm here to help get Lydia back home." Derek then turned to Christie. "You know the kind of man Brenton was, Cassandra, and I know the torture you went through in being with him. I was sort of a "gopher" for Brenton. Whatever he asked me to do, I was there to do it. I made quite a bit of money, which made it a trade-off. One night, after he'd beaten and drugged Cassandra, Brenton had a little get-together with his cronies. He forced me to attend this get-together, basically to be a waiter.

"He asked me questions regarding how I felt about Cassandra. I told him I liked her very much and we'd become close friends." Derek's voice shook then, and he paused to take a sip of his coffee. "He grabbed my arm and took me to the master bedroom where Cassandra lay on the bed, unconscious from the beatings and the drug he'd slipped in her drink. He told me to prove how much I liked her by having sex with her. I, of course, hesitated, and Brenton picked up on that..." Derek's voice trailed off into silence and his hands trembled.

Tears streamed down Christie's cheeks as she touched his hand gently. "Are you okay, Derek?" she asked softly.

He nodded and went on with his story. "He told me to take off my clothes, and when I hesitated again, it annoyed him. He said, 'You're not a queer, are you?' I knew by his tone that if I didn't do what he wanted, I could be dead. I remember wishing I was. Reluctantly, I took off my clothes and then Brenton pushed me onto the bed with Cassandra. He ripped off her clothes, and when I didn't make a move toward her, he pulled out a gun. So, I did what he wanted…and he watched." Derek then looked somberly at Christie. "Cassandra, I'm so sorry."

Christie reached out and embraced him, wiping the tears from his eyes. "Shh. It's not your fault. He was a horrible man, and you had no choice. It also means he wasn't Lydia's father, and that makes me incredibly happy," she told him.

Sonja attempted to keep from being sick, and she barely managed. There were too many questions in her mind. "Derek, how can you be sure you're Lydia's father? I mean, Christie...Cassandra has told us herself she'd been sexually abused several times," Sonja offered.

Jake looked at Sonja and stopped his tape recorder. "Sonja, the DNA matches up. It's true."

"When did you suspect you might be Lydia's father?" Sonja asked Derek.

"To tell you the truth, I never gave it a second thought. About three years ago, I had some blood work done at William's insistence. I found out my blood type." Derek then looked at Christie. "Cassandra, if you don't mind, could I ask you your blood type?"

"It's A," Christie answered quickly.

"Mine is B and Lydia's is—"

"AB positive, I remember," Christie interjected. "Oh my God. Brenton's blood type was O, so he couldn't possibly have been Lydia's father. That never occurred to me."

"So then, the birth certificate isn't an issue with Joel," Sonja offered. "This puts a new spin on things."

"But he thinks it is, and that makes it dangerous for Lydia," Christie said, looking right at Sonja.

"Christie's right. The deadline's coming up," Sonja said, studying her watch again and unable to sit still.

"If I might intercede here," Jake said, "let's not panic. I have some men placed outside the warehouse where we believe Pritchard's holding Lydia."

"I don't like this, Jake. Not at all," Sonja said, finally pushing her chair back and getting up from the sanctity of the table. She stood behind her chair and glared at Jake.

"We're not going to help Lydia by rushing in there," he replied. "This is not some two-bit operation. We've got to have a clear head and knowledge of the facts."

Sonja let out a long sigh. "Okay, okay." She reached down and took a sip of her newly refilled coffee. "As long as we're reviewing the facts, let's go over them again." She still couldn't believe most of them. It was too unreal. "It was 1963 when you were nineteen, Cassandra, and you moved in with Brenton. Is that correct?" It was strange, trying to remember to call her Cassandra, since she'd only known her as Christie Stoddard.

"Yes," Christie acknowledged.

"Now," Sonja continued, "in 1964, when you were twenty, you met both William and Derek, though not together. William was a business associate of Brenton's and Derek worked for Brenton in a private capacity." After seeing Christie nod, Sonja continued as she looked back at Jake, making sure his recorder was on. "During the course of your time with Brenton, you endured many beatings and were coerced to perform sexual acts for Brenton and his associates. After one such session in the late summer of 1964, you made a cassette tape of a business meeting with Brenton and his associates and placed it in a silver, beaded, antique purse. You then put it away in a safe deposit box in a secret destination. A few months later, when you left Brenton, you went to the safe deposit box only to discover it was missing. In late October of 1964, you realized you were pregnant and left Brenton with William's help."

"That's right," Christie agreed.

"When was the fight again, Derek?" Sonja asked.

"I believe it was that same month in 1964. It was in December that William told me he was going to marry Cassandra," Derek said sadly.

"Do you know anything about the cassette tape, Derek?" Sonja questioned.

"I didn't know it existed. I never really saw the purse after the night of the fight."

"Okay. I remember Lydia telling me that you, Derek, were in William's room the day he died, because she said you passed her in the hallway. Are you telling me that was Dillon who impersonated you on that day?" Sonja's mind raced, and hearing all the facts again in line like this greatly helped her to work it out.

"Yes. I know it seems far-fetched, but Dillon and I always had a sort of rivalry, and he was envious of my relationship with William. I really think he would have done anything, including playing at being me, to get whatever it was he was after. Being my twin, Dillon was the person I confided in, and I suppose he learned a lot about William that way," Derek said. "He fooled a lot of people. I just wish Lydia hadn't been one of them."

"Is it possible that Dillon found the cassette tape in the purse and disposed of it?" Sonja asked, trying to think of everything.

Derek got up from the table and paced around the dining room.

"I don't believe he'd do that, no. I can't believe he would do something so foolish. God, what am I saying? He's already gone and gotten himself killed."

Sonja's mind scattered with thoughts, and in one instant, it all seemed suddenly clear. "Derek," she asked, "do you have a copy of the birth certificate?"

"No, I don't," Derek said, shaking his head.

"You all stay here," Sonja said, glancing around the table. "Finish your breakfast. I'm going to head upstairs just for a minute." She got up from the table and stepped into the kitchen. "Rosita?"

Rosita stood in the kitchen with Jackson, making another pot of coffee. She turned around with wide eyes. "Yes?"

"Something just occurred to me. Have you cleaned out Mr. Blackwell's room since he died?"

"Not thoroughly, dear," Rosita answered.

"Do you think you'd like to start?" she asked, giving Rosita a look she hoped would inspire the woman.

Getting the hint, Rosita told her, "Sure. I've got nothing better to do right this minute."

They ventured up the spiral staircase to William Blackwell's room, and Rosita slowly opened the door—the same room where William Blackwell had finally succumbed to his disease. After a long sigh, Rosita softly said, "Lydia asked that we wait for a bit before going through his things."

"Well, I'll try not to make a big mess," Sonja said, determined to find something to lead her in the right direction. She studiously searched every nook and cranny of the gigantic room—inside every closet, underneath every piece of furniture—until finally she explored the bedside table. Perusing through the drawer, she glanced over papers but found nothing that would lead to a clue. Stumped for a moment, she leaned over the open drawer in front of her.

"Sonja?" Rosita called.

Startled, Sonja jumped and upset the artificial potted plant sitting on the bedside table. "Dammit. Sorry, I'll pick this up so you don't have to—" She stopped when her eyes caught on a white piece of paper buried in the artificial moss and pebbles on the floor. She bent down, pulled out the folded paper, and carefully unfolded it. Her heart pounded so loudly she was sure Rosita would tell her to calm down. At last, the paper was its appropriate size, and Sonja felt her eyes widen on their own accord as she read the document.

"What is it?" Rosita asked, her eyes wide with anticipation.

Sonja got up quickly from the floor and made her way past Rosita to the door. "Lydia's ticket home."

"Oh, no you don't, Missy. You are not leaving this room until you let me in on it."

Sonja knew by the woman's tone that she'd better oblige her. If not, she may never recover. "Your insistence is terrifying," she said, but couldn't help a small smile as Rosita stood beside her. "Here." Sonja showed her the document and watched her reaction.

"Oh," Rosita let fly from her lips, then put a hand up to her mouth. "Does this mean what I think it means?"

"I sure hope so." Sonja just prayed it was enough.

Chapter Thirty-One

JAKE'S FACE LIT UP as Sonja reappeared in the dining room. "You look like a dog who's found his long-lost bone."

Sonja nodded. "Thank you, I think. It's a bone we never knew was buried." She took a deep breath and asked Jake if he was ready to go.

"I think it's important to have all the players in this production." Jake peered across the table. "Derek, I need you to go with us. I think you could help save your daughter's life. I will have other agents there to protect you until the time is right to show yourself. What do you think? Are you willing?"

Without hesitation, Derek nodded. "Of course. Let's go."

Knowing that Christie would want to go, Sonja tried to head her off at the pass. "Christie, I know you want to be there, but please just stay here by the phone. The less people who come, the safer it will be for Lydia."

"Uh, Sonja? May I speak with you for a moment, privately?" Jake interrupted.

Sonja turned to frown at him, then nodded and followed him into the kitchen. "What is it?"

"I think it's imperative that Christie...Cassandra goes with us. She's a key element in this whole thing. I want no stone unturned, nothing left to chance. The Pritchard family, especially Joel, will pay for—" Jake stopped himself in mid-sentence.

Sonja sensed something else in his voice and caught his gaze, holding it intently. "This is more than just another assignment, isn't it?"

"What do you mean by that?" Jake asked. The blush rising up his neck gave him away.

"Don't give me that. You can fool a lot of people, but not me," Sonja told him, looking right into his eyes.

Jake was clearly nervous and began sweating. "You have no idea, Sonja, the people I've fooled..." His voice trailed off into a mere whisper.

Confused, Sonja shook her head. "What are you talking about?" She was determined to get the whole story, if indeed there was one. And she wasn't about to take more secrets from an FBI agent.

"This operation has been underway for years. It's both professional and personal."

"I thought the first rule of police work was to never make it personal," Sonja offered.

"In almost all cases, that's true. But this has to be personal. It's the only way." Jake let out a deep sigh. "Joel Pritchard is my brother."

All the blood seemed to drain from Sonja's face. "Then you're—"

"Michael Pritchard, at your service. I left the family years ago. They sickened me. One might say I lacked that 'killer instinct'," he joked, but his attempt at a smile was deceivingly grim.

Only a faint smile crossed Sonja's lips. "So, you've been undercover all these years?"

"Yes, and I am more than willing to shed the persona and take my so-called family down," he stated emphatically. "I am the only one who can do it, the only one who must do it. I appreciate your involvement in this, and no matter what happens, it's been an honor and privilege working with you." Michael held out his hand to Sonja and she shook it diplomatically.

"The honor has been mine." Sonja looked into Michael's eyes. "Are you ready?"

"I've been ready for a lifetime. Let's go."

During the drive to where they believed Lydia was being held,

Sonja tried desperately to let it all sink in. Michael's confession was an incredible tale, though not terribly surprising given all that had taken place. She wondered how it would all end, or if it ever would.

While Sonja was lost in her thoughts, Michael gave explicit instructions to Christie and Derek, who were still amazed they shared a daughter. He explained that they were to stay completely out of sight and sound while he and Sonja entered Joel's territory. They would, however, be given a two-way radio in order to listen for the exact moment they were to appear, if it came to that.

The abandoned, dilapidated gray warehouse lay somewhere off Interstate 94 outside of Wheeling, as per Joel's directions. Three unmarked police cars, conspicuously hidden some thirty feet away, greeted the group as they arrived. There were little signs of life now, but obviously there had been at one time. Trees and bushes, once lively and green, were now brown and dead, surrounding a run-down parking lot overgrown with weeds and grass. In essence, it was a good place to hide someone away and not be found.

Not far from the warehouse stood Michael's supervisor, two other agents, and a SWAT team. Michael, Sonja, Christie, and Derek quietly stepped out of the car. Michael asked Derek and Christie to follow him to a secluded spot ten feet away from the unmarked police cars. Varying sizes of shrubbery and thick foliage still managing to cling to life would hide them well enough there, and they would still be within range of the two-way radio.

"Okay," Michael whispered to them, "this is it. You have your instructions, and if you follow them to the letter, we will all come out of this safe and sound, especially Lydia. I realize this is difficult for the both of you, and you will want to race in there and save your daughter, but you have to trust me. I've waited too long to have this backfire. Got it?" Both Christie and Derek nodded. Michael left them with the radio and informed them that if he needed their intervention, Sonja would give them the word.

He briskly walked back to the car where Sonja waited with the Police and SWAT team. Michael's supervisor, Captain Wade Vincent, approached him. He was tall and reminiscent of a cowboy, wearing tight jeans, a checkered shirt, and a black blazer. His dark, curly hair waved in what little breeze existed in the desolate area in the middle of nowhere.

"Mornin', Jake. How are your nerves?" he asked Michael after shaking his hand. Wade Vincent was one of the few in the Bureau who knew of Jake's true identity, but he couldn't very well blow the man's cover so close to their victory.

"Morning, Captain. Right now, my nerves are what's keeping me sane," Michael replied with half a grin.

"Good. That will keep you on your toes." After a deep sigh, Captain Vincent said, "It's all yours, Jake. I don't have to tell you to be careful, but I will anyway. Be careful. We want you back in one piece."

"I don't have to tell you not to worry, but I will. Don't worry, boss," Michael told him. "I'm ready. Let's go." The Captain nodded and took his place among the unmarked cars and SWAT team.

Sonja stepped up to Michael once she saw his conversation with the Captain had ended. "Jake?" She didn't want to give him away, either.

Michael turned around, somewhat startled. "Oh. Yeah, Sonja, what is it?"

"How confident are you about this? The last time I spoke to Joel, he specifically said not to bring in law enforcement. I'm just worried he'll take it out on Lydia, if he hasn't already." Getting Lydia home remained Sonja's top priority.

Michael gave her shoulder a squeeze. "Believe me, I know how important Lydia is to you."

Sonja took notice of the knowledge behind his eyes. "You couldn't possibly know," she uttered, almost under her breath.

"I do know, and might I be so bold as to say it? She's one lucky woman," Michael said.

"Well," she said as her fists tightened, fighting the urge to run into the warehouse, guns blazing, to save Lydia, "I'm only lucky if we get her the hell out of there." She fell silent, staring at the old, cracked concrete of the warehouse walls.

Clearing his throat, Michael redirected the conversation. "To answer your question, I have to be honest with you. I'm only partially confident this will work, but we have to take a chance. And believe me, if Joel was going to kill Lydia, he'd have done it already. Pritchards are not known for sitting on the fence."

Sonja nodded. She'd figured Michael would answer her like that, but she agreed with him. They didn't have any other choices.

"There's something else, isn't there?" Michael asked.

Sonja's mouth set in grim determination. "I really think I should be the one going in. I know you're against it, but I'm the one Joel called. He gave me that ultimatum—no one else," she stated, her voice focused as she caught the man in her stare.

"I realize that, and that would seem to be the logical choice. But if I don't do this by the book, nothing I ever get on the Pritchards will stick. I'm sorry, Sonja, but I can't take that chance," Michael told her.

"That's such bullshit, and you know it. I'm not concerned about my safety," Sonja told him, nearly shouting and losing her cool. After a few seconds, she realized yelling at Michael wasn't going to get her anywhere. "Look, I dealt with Joel in Wyoming. He kidnapped me, for God's sake, and forced me to go against all I believed in, but then I stood up to him. I can use that to my advantage. Please, Jake. At least let me go in first," Sonja said, taking a step inward, invading his personal space so he had to listen to her.

Michael couldn't make an argument with anything she said, and she saw that realization dawn across his face. After a long sigh, he nodded. "All right. Let me talk to Captain Vincent and get the okay first. I'm pulling you out at the first sign of trouble, do you hear me?"

Sonja smiled quickly and nodded. "Of course. I wouldn't expect anything less."

Michael strolled toward Captain Wade Vincent, who had just finished briefing his other agents and the SWAT team. "Captain, may I have a word with you?"

The Captain excused himself and stepped aside with Michael.

Sonja couldn't hear what they said, but she noted the scowl on Captain Vincent's face and her heart fluttered. His eyes flickered toward her. She stared back at him, unwilling to back down. Michael's determination to convince his Captain showed through small but poignant gestures and the confidence in his approach. Sonja felt like the whole world held its breath.

Finally, Michael turned toward Sonja and gave her the thumbs up. Walking quickly toward her, he said, "Put on a vest and get to it, MacIntosh."

Sonja did as instructed, more relief filling her in that moment than she'd experienced in the last few days put together. They went over a rough sketch of the changed plan together, which was more than she'd expected. She really had not worked out a specific plan yet, because that would mean she would have to second-guess Joel, and that was one thing she didn't dare do.

Chapter Thirty-Two

AS LYDIA SAT ON the luxurious cot Joel had so willingly provided for her, she had to wonder how this mess would resolve itself, or even if it would at all. Through their discussions, Lydia had planted the seed in Joel's head that she could very well be his half-sister. She didn't want it to be true any more than he did, but she couldn't deny it. It was quite possibly the only reason she was still alive. Joel hadn't harmed her—at least, not yet.

She gazed at her surroundings and let out a deep sigh. She longed to tell Sonja how sorry she was for arguing that night, and how she ached to wake up in her arms instead of on the flimsy, ratty mattress to which she was now attached. How could finding her mother have led to all of this? People looked for their parents every day without getting kidnapped. She shook the cobwebs from her head, knowing in her heart that Sonja was doing all she could to find her. Lydia had to believe that. She didn't have much of a choice.

The ring of Joel's cell phone broke Lydia away from her thoughts. She tried to listen in as much as she could when she heard the name MacIntosh. Her heart beat faster just hearing the name, and she knew it had to be Sonja calling. She couldn't keep the smile off of her face, though she still knew a lot was at stake until this whole nightmare could be over.

Then she heard Joel's heavy footsteps approaching from the concrete hallway. Her smile disappeared when she saw him. "What is it?" she asked.

"Just some business I need to take care of. Nothing for you to worry about. You keep quiet, and I mean not one word passes your lips unless I say so. Understand?"

Lydia knew by his tone not to push her luck. She nodded but didn't say anything.

"Very good. One way or another, this will all be over soon," Joel said, glancing at his gold watch. "Yes, very soon."

As he walked away from her, Lydia knew it wasn't just anyone coming to see Joel. His last statement told her more than anything else he could have said. She'd had enough time to gauge his reactions to information, and had practiced certain skills of observation to find any detail she could about what was happening. After all, this was her life they were negotiating.

They held her in an old office supply room in the warehouse. It was a modest-sized room, split down the middle by a row of lockers. There were no windows, no chance for any air to come through except for the times Joel briefly left the door open for her. The air was musty, but it was air just the same. The lock on the door had been changed, of course, and an intercom system had been installed for the solitary purpose of dealing with a person trapped in the repulsive room. Debris littered the corners of the room—old pieces of wood, a couple lead pipes, and boxes of nails. Lydia's mind went to work on her own plan; she didn't want to take the chance in leaving her rescue to fate. She knew the men Joel entrusted to look after her were just that—men. And they were men no other woman really wanted. Lydia was not one to miss an opportunity when it presented itself.

Once Joel was safely away conducting his 'business', Lydia took a deep breath and pressed the red button on the intercom. "Boys?"

"Yeah, what is it?" Gus, head of the other two men, answered. The man weighed in at three hundred and twenty pounds, with greasy black hair and Elvis sideburns.

A true advertisement for becoming a lesbian, Lydia thought. She took a deep breath to prepare for her performance. "I'm really not feeling very well," she reported in a soft whisper, adding a tiny whine to her voice.

"What do you think's wrong?" Gus asked.

"I must be coming down with something. I'm all feverish and I feel sick. I really think I need some help."

"Well, okay. I'll be right there."

***

Gus made his way down the main hallway and turned right down another short corridor to find the storeroom. His mind wandered, thinking about this woman Joel had entrusted to him. He remembered his instructions as he searched his pockets for the keys. The woman should be "kept alive and relatively well." Gus also remembered all the time he'd put in, sometimes without sleep or a good meal, and never received his due. Lydia was a good-looking woman, no doubt about it. It was nice just to see a woman around. A smile crossed his face as he knocked on the door and nervously slipped his key in the lock.

He opened the door to find Lydia lying on the cot, dressed in only her bra and panties. He moved in further, taking note of the sweat on her forehead. "What seems to be the problem?"

"I really do feel ill," she said. "I think it's because I'm just so upset and lonely. I can't help thinking that maybe it wouldn't be so bad having a man around to handle these situations. I would feel safer. I've never known that before." She gazed up at him with her big eyes, looking almost completely pitiful if it weren't for her lack of clothing.

Gus watched, listening to her carefully. He thought maybe it couldn't hurt to just comfort her. He would consider it a bonus. When he reached down to touch her arm, he felt a sharp pain on the side of his neck, and everything went black.

***

Lydia drew back the lead pipe she held in her hand as she looked at Gus' massive, unconscious body laying at her feet. She shook her head, thinking for a moment how someone could work for a man like Joel. Pushing that from her mind, she knew she had more important matters to attend to than Gus' job qualifications. Then came the sound of footsteps out in the hallway—Wiley, the other man on babysitting duty. As soon as she headed for the door, it opened in one swift, announcing movement.

"What's going on here, woman? Where's Gus?"

Lydia answered him with a strong knee to his midsection. She watched him double over in pain. Moving quicker than she thought she could, she grabbed the lead pipe and bashed him on the back of the head. He fell to the floor, unconscious, and she dropped the pipe. Shaking the pain of impact out of her hand, she took stock of her handiwork. "I am *way* too gay for either of you," she whispered, trying to catch her breath.

She quickly searched both men's pockets for the keys to the storeroom. Then she hastily pulled on her clothes and let herself out, scanning the area to make sure no one else was around. Locking the door behind her, she took a deep breath, then searched for a good hiding place. The pile of stacked lumber near the center of the warehouse would work well enough.

Lydia had the distinct feeling that Joel's meeting involved Sonja. At least, she prayed it did. Carefully, she climbed up the mountainous pile and situated herself so she could see enough of the meeting and hopefully hear every word. There had to be an end to this, somehow, someway.

She had a moment to realize how her life since her father's death had turned into something out of *The Godfather*. How could William Blackwell have left such a trail of unanswered questions? But with all the questions, she'd at least found her mother after a lifetime of wondering and wishing. It truly had been a miracle amidst all the chaos. She thought about her mother now, what she must be going through, thinking her newfound daughter might be dead. But her mother couldn't have known how much of a survivor Lydia actually was, and that she refused to go down without a struggle—without knowing the truth.

Chapter Thirty-Three

SONJA HAD TO CLEAR her mind of everything except getting Lydia the hell out of there. Bringing down the Pritchard family empire was Michael's job. With one last check of her wire equipment, she nodded to Michael, took a deep breath, and knocked on the steel door.

A man she didn't recognize opened the door, but behind him she saw Joel Pritchard standing there and watching her. "Ah, MacIntosh," he said. "How wonderful that you made it home from Wyoming safely. By all means, do come in."

"Joel," Sonja acknowledged as she stepped inside. She knew man would have her patted down, but just in case, Michael had informed her there were other listening devices throughout the warehouse. He wasn't taking chances.

"You don't mind if Toby here checks you out, do you?" Joel asked as he made eye contact with Toby.

Toby made a move towards Sonja as she put up her hand. "As a matter of fact, yes, I do mind. He will not put one hand on me, Joel. I'm not really in any position to cause trouble."

"Quite brave of you, MacIntosh. You realize, of course, that I could kill you right this very minute," he said, glancing at Toby.

"Of course. But I don't think you will, at least until this matter between us is settled." Sonja had to call his bluff. It was the only way.

"Very well," Joel said. "You're right. This has gone on too long. It's time to end it."

There was no point in asking Joel to release Lydia, so she thought better of it and kept her silence for a moment.

"So, Lieutenant...or are you a lowly officer now?" Joel's eyebrows raised in anticipation.

"If anyone knows, you do," Sonja answered with a brave glare.

"Smart, MacIntosh. Very smart. I've underestimated you." He paused and rubbed his chin slightly with an index finger. Watching his guest silently for a moment, he stepped a little closer. "I trust you have brought with you what I asked for?"

"That depends." Sonja moved further from the door and into the middle of the room.

"I suppose you want me to let your little girlfriend go first, is that it?"

"Yes. She has nothing to do with this."

"That's where you're wrong, Lieutenant. She has everything to do with this. Your lover and I have had, well, let's just call it a meeting of the minds. It's become clear to me that she's more closely involved than I once thought."

Sonja took a moment to process what she'd just heard. Lydia must have shared with Joel the possibility that they were siblings. "I see," she said softly.

"I have to say, MacIntosh, you have excellent taste in women, or at least this woman."

"Enough. Tell me what has to happen in order for Lydia to go free," Sonja said. She imagined her eyes as daggers of cold, hard steel, piercing his gaze just enough to show him she wasn't playing.

A deep, hearty laugh came from Joel. "Too early in the game for negotiations. I have certain matters to discuss first." He walked around the metal chair he'd been sitting in, slowly and methodically.

"Such as?" Sonja just wanted to race through the place, find Lydia, and get the hell out of there, but clearly, Joel wanted to have his fun.

He whipped around suddenly and snapped, "Such as this nonsense about Lydia being my half-sister. Maybe you can tell me where this load of bullshit came from."

Lydia had indeed made him think, Sonja realized. "I do know

something about that, as a matter of fact."

"Well, let's talk about it. Then I'll decide what we do from there." Joel let his jacket fall back enough to purposely show the pistol strapped in a holster around his waist.

Sonja took notice carefully. She quickly surveyed the room, looking for signs of an exit or something plausible to memorize the room. Her eyes fell gingerly on a pair of eyes watching her from a lumber pile not more than fifty yards away. A smile seemed to capture Sonja's heart, though she couldn't let it show on her face, not even for an instant. It had to be Lydia. "Sure, let's talk," she said to Joel. "I did come prepared for anything, in fact. I've also brought reinforcements. Not the kind you think, but the perfect kind to answer your questions."

Joel reached for his weapon. "Really? How thoughtful of you, Lieutenant. You'll excuse me if I bring out my own reinforcement, just in case."

"Of course. Allow me to bring in mine. It will only take a minute." Sonja tread this ground as delicately as she could.

Joel eyed Toby and nodded. "You don't mind if Toby accompanies you, do you?"

"By all means." Sonja had known Joel would insist upon it. As she opened the steel door to the outside, she waited for Christie and Derek, who had been listening in just around the corner but out of Toby's sight. They now walked briskly toward the front door. "Could you two come inside for a minute? Joel has been gracious enough to invite you in for a chat." Both Christie and Derek smiled nervously and nodded.

Joel didn't speak as his eyes perused up and down Derek's physique. Then he looked at Christie. "MacIntosh," he started, "perhaps you can explain to me why this man and this tramp over here are your reinforcements. You really need to get out more."

"This is Christie Stoddard," Sonja began, "whom I believe you know as Cassandra Lexington, and this is Derek Meade."

"That's impossible," Joel stammered. "I—"

Sonja felt herself almost smile at hearing Joel sputter around his words. "You what, Joel?"

Regaining his composure, Joel cleared his throat. "Nothing." He took a long time in taking in the sight of the two new arrivals before him. "What's this all about? I don't have time to play these little cop games," he said, clearly agitated.

"It's no cop game. This is Lydia's life. Right here," Sonja said, pointing in Christie and Derek's direction.

"What are you babbling about, MacIntosh?" Joel said, seemingly disinterested at this point.

"Derek, would you like to tell the tale?" Sonja offered.

Nervously and quickly, Derek cleared his throat. "Well, Mr. Pritchard, as it turns out, I'm Lydia's father."

A quirky smile covered Joel's face. "Well that would be just peachy, wouldn't it? But you're supposed to be—" Joel stopped himself, seemingly processing the information.

"Dead? Is that the word you're looking for?"

Joel's hand tightly gripped his pistol. "Yes. Dead is where you should be, old man."

"I believe you're referring to my twin brother, Dillon. He was the one who crossed your path," Derek told him.

"You stupid, stupid man. You have no way of proving anything of that nature. My hands are clean." Joel dismissed the topic quickly and moved on. "And I do not believe you're Lydia's father. Weren't you William Blackwell's lover? Do you know what being gay means?" Joel laughed. "Or maybe you haven't quite grasped the concept yet."

"Yes," Derek said. "I was William's lover, and I'm quite proud of it."

"All right, all right," Joel said, putting up his hands in protest, "enough with the gay pride speech. I'm only concerned with how you could possibly be Lydia's father. Believe me, I could care less. The last thing I would want is for her to be a Pritchard, but I still require proof."

Derek gave Christie a warm glance, and she nodded for him to continue.

Joel signaled Toby. "Toby, please bring chairs for our guests. I want them to be comfortable, just in case we're the last people they see."

Chapter Thirty-Four

DEREK TOLD THE SORDID story of how Joel's father had forced him into sexual relations with the drugged-up, beaten Cassandra all those years ago. Joel knew his father was no angel, but the story itself was unbelievable. Once again, there was no proof. "Tell me, Derek, why on earth I would believe something so ludicrous."

"All I know is the truth," Derek said. "It's up to you whether or not to believe it."

"Fine." He rubbed his face and scratched his head, suddenly unclear as to how this would all turn out. He certainly hadn't planned any of *this*. Taking a deep breath and letting out an annoyed sigh, he looked right at Christie. "I don't know if I believe you, though. My father used to talk about all the men you slept with and how you deserved all you had coming to you. Maybe everyone else buys this victim routine of yours, but I certainly don't."

"I wouldn't expect you to," Christie replied bluntly. "To be honest, I always believed your father was also Lydia's. I only recently discovered otherwise."

Joel glanced in Toby's direction. "Toby?"

"Yeah, boss?"

"It's time for you to take a break with the boys. I would like to deal with my guests alone," Joel instructed. Toby nodded and cautiously walked out of the spacious area towards the back of the warehouse.

"So," Sonja said, "you see now that the birth certificate is of no interest to you. Lydia is not your half-sister, or any relation of yours, for that matter."

Grinning, Joel looked right at Sonja. "Nice try, MacIntosh. But no go. I've invested too much time and effort into this, and I'm not about to let it go just yet."

"What is it you want?" Sonja asked without hesitation.

"You know what I want, MacIntosh. I want the birth certificate and all that accompanies it, or your pretty girlfriend will suffer the consequences. I can't make it any clearer than that." Nothing had changed in Joel's eyes. So what? His father had charged him with this mission. Details really didn't matter.

A loud noise came from the wood pile, pieces of lumber tumbling to the floor. Joel squeezed his pistol tighter, pulling it from the holster and thrusting it into the air as he ran to the pile and saw, to his surprise, Lydia sprawled out at his feet. The woman attempted to rise from the floor.

"Oh, no you don't! You're coming with me, little darlin'," he grunted, grabbing her arm and pulling her to her feet. As he dragged her to the middle of the warehouse, the huge steel door burst open.

"Hold it, Pritchard! Stop right there. Let her go," the new man ordered.

"Who the hell are you?" Joel barked.

"Jake Ashton, FBI. You're surrounded, Pritchard. The game is over." The newcomer had his gun firmly trained on Joel and Lydia.

Joel noticed something familiar in the man's eyes but he couldn't place it—so familiar, in fact, that he momentarily lost his focus. Suddenly remembering the situation, he grabbed Lydia around the neck with his left arm, tightly holding her against him. "What makes you think I won't do it?"

"Okay, Joel. How about putting the gun down? We'll talk this out."

Joel's face bloomed with a rage he hadn't known before. "This has to do with family honor. What the fuck would you know about that?" Every second he felt more and more out of control, and he despised it.

"I know plenty about you, Joel," the man said calmly.

Lydia's breathing came rapid and erratic as Joel's hold on her grew stronger. "Really?" Joel said. "So what? Many people know of the Pritchard family. That's no surprise, especially if you're FBI"

"No, Joel, that's not why I know so much about you and your family," the man added.

"Suppose you tell me before the sand in Ms. Blackwell's hourglass runs out," Joel told him, pushing the barrel of his gun even harder into Lydia's side.

"Very well." The FBI agent slightly lowered his stance. "There was a time when I, too, was part of a family, until honor became my priority. Not family honor, mind you. Just honor. My own honor."

All at once it came back to Joel why the man's eyes were so familiar. "Michael..."

The man who used to be his brother nodded in heavy certainty. "I've come to stop you from this madness. Its time has passed now," he said.

"Family honor is not madness, Michael. It's something you never learned." Joel couldn't take his eyes off his brother, shaking his head in disbelief of what he saw before him.

"If that's family honor, then it's a lesson I'm grateful I never learned."

"Unbelievable," Joel said, pacing in front of the man.

"What is? Did you think I was dead?"

"You were dead to him and you were dead to me. Now you come back as FBI?" Joel was incensed. Who the hell did he think he was coming back now to take *him* down?

"Joel, this is no good. Let Lydia go," Michael repeated.

"If you know me so well," Joel spat, "you'd know I can't possibly do that. I want what's coming to me and the Pritchard family. Our father entrusted that mission to me, and I cannot, *will not*, let him down. I am a Pritchard!"

"I wouldn't bank on that," Sonja piped up suddenly. Both Michael and Joel shot her a surprised glance as she pulled a piece of paper from her pocket. It was tattered, yellow from age, and slightly torn.

"Is that the birth certificate, MacIntosh?" Joel asked eagerly.

"Actually, no, but it's still quite fascinating," Sonja stated. "A legal document stating, among other things, the nature of your own origins."

"*What*?" Joel exclaimed in a disconcerting, booming voice. "Let me see that," he yelled as he pulled Lydia, still under his grasp, with him to yank the paper out of Sonja's hand. Joel read in haste, the silence of the warehouse spurring him faster until it ached to breathe and tears filled his eyes. "No!" he screamed. It felt as if he'd been stabbed in the heart.

As Sonja watched the words on a piece of paper tormenting him, she said softly, "It's a notarized letter from one Brenton Pritchard, stating Joel Pritchard is not the son of Brenton and Anna Pritchard. Not by blood, anyway."

"Then who—" Michael asked.

"Antonio Delgado," Sonja said. "This paper signifies a private adoption to which William Blackwell was a witness. The document has been signed by all three parties. Brenton, William, and Antonio," Sonja explained carefully.

"How is that possible?" Michael asked.

In one swift move, Joel dropped Lydia to the ground but kept his gun on her. "Don't even think of moving," he ordered. Turning his attention to the chaos in his mind, he uttered, "Jesus." His voice left him in a soft, distraught whine. "I remember father talking about Antonio, how years before the man had betrayed him and Antonio's wife had just died in childbirth. He'd mentioned the child lived, that it had been adopted…that child...that child was me." The handwriting was distinctly his father's; there could be no mistake.

The tears spilled down his cheeks openly now, and the reserve that had been so much a part of him was suddenly erased from memory. Being a Pritchard was everything. Nothing else mattered. Not women, not friends...no one had entered his soul. Just the knowledge of being a Pritchard. But now... How could he look anyone in the face? He couldn't live this kind of lie.

Watching Michael's reaction, Joel reached into his jacket and pulled out the silver purse, the instrument of ruin in so many people's lives, and threw it across the floor in Michael's direction. The purse slid on the slick warehouse floor until it hit the tip of Michael's shoes. Michael did not move to pick it up; he just studied Joel with guarded eyes.

Joel lowered his gun from where he'd had it aimed at Lydia's head, clutching the paper tight. "Get up," he said. The woman stood and walked, slowly and nervously, toward the two people who had effectively destroyed him. She was too slow, and he shoved her on her way. As soon as she stumbled forward, he brought the gun up to his own temple. "Goodbye, Michael." He pulled the trigger.

Chapter Thirty-Five

JOEL'S MOTIONLESS BODY LAY on the cold, blood-soaked floor, and after the screams subsided Sonja wrapped her arms tightly around Lydia, not caring about the tears flowing from her own eyes. Derek and Christie ran to Lydia and embraced the daughter they'd just discovered.

Michael slowly approached the wounded man on the floor. As he bent down to check Joel's pulse, Toby and the newly conscious Wiley and Gus came running, only to observe their slain boss on the floor. The three men watched Michael and then reached for their guns.

Quickly, Michael raised his own on them. "I suggest you boys disarm yourselves," he said. "You're already in deep enough, don't you think?"

Just as Toby cocked the hammer of his gun, the S.W.A.T team stormed through the steel door, aiming a dozen rifles at them. Obviously realizing the game was up, the man glanced at his compatriots, and they nodded without a word. They slid their guns to the middle of the floor, where FBI Captain Wade Vincent stood. He instructed his team to take the men outside, read them their rights, and take them in for questioning. The SWAT team vacated the warehouse and the medical examiner was on his way to pick up Joel's mangled body.

"Not so fast, Lieutenant," a voice bellowed from the dark shadows of the warehouse.

Sonja turned her head. "Who's there?" she asked as she lifted her shirt slightly to put a hand on her gun.

Out of the darkness came Bradley Pennington, pointing his gun squarely at Sonja. "You should have taken me up on that offer,

MacIntosh. Things are quite unpleasant now."

She didn't say a word.

"What? You have nothing to say?" he asked with a sneer, approaching them.

"I'm not surprised," Sonja finally acknowledged. "Just disgusted."

"No, what you two do together is disgusting," Bradley said, nodding at Lydia in her arms. "Toss me your gun, MacIntosh."

Sonja carefully let her eyes search the area for any sign of Michael, but saw nothing. She shoved Lydia behind her, where Derek and Christie wrapped her in their arms and stepped back. Pennington didn't even know Lydia. His beef was with Sonja. She knew he'd been working with Joel, and it really didn't surprise her to see him here, now.

As she tossed her gun across the floor, she realized the wire she wore must still be functional. "Why are you doing this, Captain?"

"Just business, MacIntosh. That's all. You're out of commission."

"Really?" Sonja stuttered, unable to comprehend what he was implying. What was the point now? Joel was dead. "We're done here."

"Not by a long shot."

"Is it because I wouldn't sleep with you?" Sonja cringed at the thought.

"Hardly. This is about—" Pennington froze when the click of a pistol sounded behind him.

"I suggest you drop it, Pennington, and save us all the trouble," the voice behind him ordered.

A smile crossed Sonja's lips as she saw the face behind the gun. Without turning around, Pennington smiled and let slip a sarcastic chuckle. "Or what? You'll shoot? What a joke, Kovacs. I'm your Captain, remember?"

"I think when you hold a gun on one of your Lieutenants and innocent civilians, you give up the title," Hank told him. "It's over."

Sonja then realized she still had a small pistol strapped on her leg, the weight of it heavy as she anticipated Pennington's next move. In all the confusion, she'd forgotten about Hank. Luckily, he hadn't pushed Sonja from his mind. One wrong move now could cost them all.

"Put down the gun," Hank repeated.

A gunshot rang out abruptly from somewhere above them. Pennington fell to the ground, clutching his leg. In that instant, Sonja leapt on top of him to hold him face-down. She kicked the gun that fell from Pennington's hand toward Hank, who tossed Sonja his handcuffs. Carefully, she read Captain Bradley Pennington his rights as he grimaced in pain.

Sonja paused for a moment after she finished and couldn't stop herself from grinning as she whispered to her former Captain, "You know, I might have reconsidered, but in this light, you're kinda ugly." As she stood, she glanced up to see who the shooter had been, but she saw no one behind the railings overlooking the room.

"Sonja?" She turned to see Lydia staring at her, and she couldn't get to her fast enough. The women wrapped themselves in each other's arms and didn't notice the police taking the limping Pennington outside.

"I'm okay, I'm okay. Really, let's get out of here," Sonja said as she broke away from Lydia's embrace.

Derek and Christie joined them from the shadows of the warehouse. "Are you okay?" Derek asked. Sonja nodded. "What was that all about?"

"Long story. Maybe I'll tell you sometime," Sonja said. They walked out of the dungy building together, finally free.

Chapter Thirty-Six

HANK REMAINED INSIDE, WORKING with forensics and taking care of the formalities with Pennington. Sonja stepped out of the warehouse with Lydia and her parents. She thought it had to be Michael who had shot Pennington and saved them all.

Then there he was, walking briskly toward them. "Michael Pritchard, Ms. Blackwell," he said to Lydia. "Sorry to have to meet you under these circumstances." He extended a hand toward her.

Lydia politely shook his hand. "I am too. It seems a bit inadequate to say thank you for saving my life."

Michael smiled warmly, though his brows furrowed in concern. "You're most welcome, though I didn't do it alone." He glanced at Sonja and gave her a nod. "You're a lucky woman to have this one fighting for you."

Lydia looked up at Sonja with wide eyes. "I know."

"MacIntosh, sorry I couldn't be in there to deal with Pennington. I wasn't aware right away," Michael added.

"What?" Sonja wrapped an arm tighter around Lydia. "You weren't inside?"

"I was dealing with phone calls and handling the squads." He seemed to catch the confusion in Sonja's voice. "Wasn't Kovacs in there?"

Sonja nodded. "Yeah, Hank was there. But he didn't shoot Pennington. I thought you did."

Michael carefully scanned the officers in the area, seemingly looking for anything out of place. "It definitely wasn't me," he said.

"I'm going to have somebody dust up on the balcony for prints, see if we can figure that one out."

"Any ideas?" Sonja asked.

Michael scratched his forehead. "Oh, Pennington had several enemies. It was someone who knew what was going down today, maybe someone in the Pritchard family circle. Whoever it was must have also known the layout of the warehouse and figured out a plan to get past us."

"Makes sense," Sonja said, though her mind still revolved around Lydia and the fact that they'd actually gotten her out alive.

"Take that beautiful woman home, will you?" Michael said, nodding at Lydia. "Put this chaos aside for a day."

Sonja nodded. "I can do that. Thanks for everything." They shook hands, and Sonja turned in relief, ready to be anywhere else.

***

It was nearly evening by the time Sonja, Lydia, Christie, and Derek arrived back at the Blackwell Estates. When Lydia walked through the door, Rosita barreled toward her, tears streaming down her face, and held her tighter than she ever had before. "Oh, my sweet angel. You came home safely."

Lydia's eyes filled with tears instantly, and she only hugged Rosita tighter, burying her face into the woman's hair. Jackson appeared from further down the hall, and he too raced down the hallway when he saw Lydia. He wrapped his arms around both Lydia and Rosita, then kissed Lydia on the cheek. "Thank God you came back to us."

Rosita pulled back and held Lydia's face in her hands, wiping away the tears with her thumbs. "You look like you haven't slept in a week. Go on upstairs and rest a while. I'll bring you something to eat later."

"That sounds perfect," Lydia said with a tired, weak smile.

"Good." Rosita caught Sonja's eye and nodded to her. "You go with her."

Sonja grabbed Lydia's hand, and they ventured upstairs to Lydia's bedroom where they both could find some sanctity from the outside world. Rosita must have known they would need it. Lydia's eyes scanned the room carefully, taking in every detail. She'd never have thought her father's mansion could offer such welcome relief and security.

After the first hot shower in what seemed like days, Lydia threw herself on the big bed. She let out a deep sigh as her body sunk into the mattress.

"How are you feeling?" Sonja asked carefully.

"Better," Lydia said, then motioned for Sonja to join her on the bed. When she did, Lydia quickly sat upright and searched Sonja's eyes. "Sonja...I—I'm so sorry I ran out last night. So sorry. I could have…could have not made it back, could have never seen your beautiful eyes again."

Sonja reached out to gently stroke Lydia's face, smiling with both warmth and concern. "I'm sorry too, for the things I said. Neither of us could have known what was going to happen, and you can't blame yourself for any of it. The only thing that matters is that you're home, where you belong, and I can hold you. I love you more than anything on this earth." She gathered Lydia in her arms and held her tight, almost as if it would keep her from ever losing her again.

***

Lydia really took advantage of the peace and comfort of her father's home, having slept late into the next morning and then retiring to her room again a few hours before dinner for another nap. It surprised her how exhausted she was, but she welcomed the chance to rest.

Sonja came up just before dinner, which Rosita had spent most of the day preparing, to wake Lydia and sit with her as she tidied herself. Lydia stared at her reflection in the mirror. "Do you think we will ever get back to our normal lives?" she asked Sonja with a heavy sigh.

"Sure we will, babe," Sonja said, her voice compassionate and carrying just a hint of concern. "Whatever normal means. Your life has changed so much in just a few short weeks, but that doesn't last forever. Things will settle down."

Saying it and believing it were two entirely different worlds, but Lydia managed a smile anyways. "Think the talk show circuit would have me?"

Sonja let out a little chuckle, then looked lovingly into the other woman's eyes. "Well, I have to say my life will never be the same because of you."

Lydia nodded, not taking her eyes off the woman before her. "Good. When I think about it, after all the chaos of the last few days, I have the answers I wanted and people in my life I never dreamed I'd have. Like you. Have I told you how much I love you?"

Sonja looked at her and winked. "Say it again."

"I love you, Sonja MacIntosh." Lydia leaned in and kissed her.

"I love you, Lydia Blackwell. You know how hard it is for me to admit how scared I was. I'm so grateful to have you back." Sonja's words came out in no more than a whisper.

Lydia grabbed her and pulled her toward the door. "Let's go get dinner."

Chapter Thirty-Seven

AFTER ROSITA'S GLORIOUS DINNER, Lydia walked to the dining room window and gazed out upon the night. William Blackwell could have never known the torment he'd caused. Then Lydia thought of her mother. Christie was just as guilty, though it would be pointless to blame her for mistakes she'd made so many years before.

She turned around and watched her mother with Martin, who'd arrived during the chaotic rescue and had awaited his wife's return to the mansion. Martin was a genuinely caring man, and Lydia could tell he really loved her mother. As if she felt her daughter's eyes studying her carefully, Christie turned her head and gave Lydia a knowing smile.

"Rosita?" Lydia asked. "Can you bring some coffee into the den and come relax with us a bit?" Everyone expressed their consent for coffee and Rosita went to prepare it.

They all made their way down the long hallway three doors down, and Jackson worked on getting a fire going. Lydia put her arm around Jackson in a side-hug. "You've read my mind, Jackson. A fire sounds like the best thing right now." Lydia couldn't help from reaching back into the memory of that musty warehouse. Never would she forget the smell of it, the feel of the dirty air. Now, the warmth of the fire and the people around her made her feel like a person again.

Christie sat down on one of the plush, dark burgundy couches in the den between Martin and Derek. She pulled out the silver purse Michael had given back to her after all these years and gazed lovingly at it while Martin watched her. "It's a beautiful purse, Christie. It tells a story of love, loss, torment, and undying devotion."

"Yes, it certainly does. This purse also helped a daughter find the parents who had almost been ripped from her existence," Christie acknowledged and glanced again at Lydia.

Lydia's eyes surveyed Christie and Derek, wondering if this were just another fantasy of hers. How else could it be that she only found her true parents through William's death? He would always be her father in her heart, her mind, and her soul. But had William Blackwell really had enough faith in Lydia to trust she'd find her own way? She had to believe that was what he'd intended; it was the only way to make sense out of the madness she currently called her life.

Martin stood and stared out of the den window overlooking the grounds. "This is a beautiful place, Lydia. Thanks for inviting me for such a magnificent view," he said.

"Of course," Lydia replied. "You belong here with your wife, too. I'm only sorry it was under these strange circumstances. I can only imagine how unbelievable this must seem to you."

"No more than it must be for you, dear," Martin noted as he took a sip of his coffee.

Lydia could not respond. She wasn't even sure how she was having conversations and going on with life right now after being taken hostage. Broken out of her trance, she slowly looked around for the absent Sonja. "What happened to Sonja?"

"She said she had to take a phone call just after dinner. She'll be right out, don't worry," Derek told her, finally breaking the silence he'd held for a few minutes.

Lydia gazed gently at the man she'd just learned made up half of who she was. "Derek, may I ask you something?"

"Anything," he answered politely.

"How long have you known you were my father?"

"I guess it was about three years ago, when William wanted me to take those blood tests. You know, it was a routine thing. At least, I'd thought it was," Derek explained carefully.

"Do you feel differently now?" Lydia felt the uncertainty within her gaining ground.

"Lydia," he said as he motioned her to sit next to him. "I know it's a lot to take in right now. Thinking about losing you before we've had a real chance to know each other was torture. I am grateful for you." He touched the top of her hand.

"That's a great place to start. Thank you, Derek." Lydia felt strangely comfortable sitting next to him and she couldn't quite explain why.

Sonja entered the room, wide-eyed and looking like she'd just received a surprise gift. "I just had a phone call from Clayton Hughes," she said.

Lydia raised an eyebrow. "Police Chief Clayton Hughes?"

"That's the one," Sonja acknowledged, seemingly unable to say anything else.

"Well?" Derek prodded.

"It seems I'm being promoted to Captain," Sonja announced. A smile, so wide it barely fit her face, finally bloomed from behind the disbelief.

"That's fantastic," Lydia said, standing and almost skipping to the woman to wrap her in an excited embrace. "I'm so proud of you!"

They all congratulated Sonja and hugged her, the support from this unlikely but loving family difficult to ignore. Even Christie, with whom Sonja had been at odds so many times in the past, embraced her with genuine emotion. "It's a wonderful thing, Sonja, and so well deserved. Especially since you never gave up on our girl."

"That means a lot to me, Christie. So does Lydia." Sonja briefly lay a hand on Christie's shoulder.

"I couldn't agree with you more," Derek added, and gave Sonja another pat on the back.

Rosita tugged Jackson on the sleeve and the two excused themselves for a few moments. A few minutes later, they returned with a bottle of champagne and a tray full of glasses. "I think this is the perfect occasion for some bubbly," Rosita offered.

"Absolutely, Rosie," Lydia agreed and helped them pass the champagne around until everyone held a glass.

Derek lifted his glass into the air. "As the last lucky person to enter this diverse tribe of wonderful people, I'd like you all to allow me to make a toast." Everyone nodded and Lydia shot him a warm glance, giving him the go-ahead. Derek gently cleared his throat and took in a deep breath. "Many men who just discover they have a daughter after so many years are not as lucky as I am. They have not been able to witness firsthand an adorable, dark-haired little girl grow up and blossom into such a beautiful, loving, intelligent woman. Though I wish I could have known all those years I was your father, Lydia, I wouldn't trade a minute of watching you grow up. Even from a distance, it was a privilege I won't soon forget."

Derek stepped toward his daughter, whose eyes filled with tears, put his arm around her, and raised his glass. The others echoed his sentiments and raised their glasses, drinking to the woman who'd brought them all together through impossible odds.

Lydia cleared her throat. "Let's not forget about our newly appointed Captain over here." Though she was proud to highlight Sonja's accomplishments as well, she really wanted to take the attention away from herself. After drinking a second round of champagne, they all decided to call it a night.

***

Christie was relieved to have Martin by her side again, but she couldn't help but notice how nervous he'd been when she'd filled him in on the whole sordid series of events. Undressing for bed, their slightly tense silence didn't last very long.

"Marty?" Christie asked, noticing his mood.

"Hm?" Martin sat on the bed, pulling on his pajama bottoms.

"What are you thinking? You've been awfully quiet."

Taking in a deep sigh, Martin climbed onto the bed where Christie sat and spoke softly. "Honey, I'm worried about you, about everything that's happened since you took off with Lydia."

"I know. It's been crazy and more than a little terrible, but everything worked out. Lydia's home now, and it's all behind us. I don't want you to worry anymore, okay?" Christie patted his hand softly, then started to get up off the bed until Martin grabbed her arm.

"No, Christie, I can't stop worrying. Just how long do you plan on putting our lives on hold? You can't live in this fantasy land forever," Martin told her.

Christie glared at her husband, noting the strength of his grip on her arm. "What on earth do you mean by that?"

"I'm just concerned that the longer you stay here, the more time you spend with these people, the less likely it is you'll ever come back home."

Christie pulled away from Martin's hold on her. "Martin, one of 'those people' happens to be my daughter...a daughter who's been out of my life for almost forty years. I walked out on *her*. I cannot and *will not* make that mistake again. There's nothing more to discuss!"

"Christie! You don't realize what you've been doing here. I don't hear from you for days, then when I do, your life is in danger from some mob guy. What the hell is going on? Christ, look at what finding your daughter has already cost you!"

Christie could not believe her own husband spoke this way. "I don't understand you at all. You were so supportive about Lydia when she found me, and now all of a sudden you want me to abandon her. Again!"

"That's not what I'm saying. I just want you to think about me, us, what this is doing to our marriage. I want you home," Martin pleaded.

"It's not up for discussion, Martin. My place is here with my daughter. You could not possibly comprehend what having her back in my life means to me. I won't let anyone or anything get in the way of that. Not even you," she told him, her eyes matching her fiery tone.

Martin's jaw dropped slightly. "What are you saying?"

"I'm saying either you support my choices and my relationship with my child or you don't support me at all. I'll leave that decision up to you." Christie put on her white lace-and-silk robe and left Martin alone in the room.

She needed some air, and even though it was November, it was an unusually warm night. She grabbed a heavy blanket, wrapped it around her shoulders, and took a stroll out by the gazebo. Even covered in the light snow, it was so beautiful there. It had always been her favorite place because of its tranquility.

Looking down at the single rose bush near the top of the steps, she found the snow hadn't covered it and she smiled. William had loved his roses with a passion she'd rarely seen him exhibit in anything else. Christie sat next to the once flowery bush, staring at it closely. She gently brushed the snow away around the stem and reached out to feel the cold dirt beneath her hands. She wanted to touch something real, something full of life.

With her fingers in the dirt, she felt something hard graze the tip of her fingers. Puzzled, she dug deeper, then deeper still. Finally latching onto the object, she pulled it out carefully. When she brushed off the dirt, she recognized it instantly. "I'll be goddamned."

Chapter Thirty-Eight

CHRISTIE LEFT THE GAZEBO and went back into the house, running upstairs to her room and momentarily forgetting her recent argument with her husband. Then, as she burst through the door, it all came back to her.

Her eyes perused the room, but she didn't see Martin—or any of his things. The only proof he'd been there was a note on her pillow. Christie's heart sank. Slowly, she walked over to the pillow and picked up the note. As she read it, she knew the words couldn't be right.

She'd expected her husband to stand by her and support her through this madness. Martin had forced her to choose, and in that instant Christie was thrust back in time all those years before to the last choice she'd been forced to make. And she'd chosen wrong.

Wiping the tears from her eyes, she took a deep breath and concentrated on the object from the garden in her hand. Then she raced back out of the room and down the hall to Lydia's bedroom. It was almost two in the morning, but she couldn't wait a second longer. She lightly tapped on the door.

"What is it, Christie?" Sonja asked as she opened the door, then yawned sleepily.

Holding the object in the air, Christie grinned. "I believe you police folk call this evidence."

Sonja's eyes grew wide with realization and her jaw dropped miles to the floor. "Is that the—"

"That's right. It's the tape I made all those years ago. I recognized it instantly," Christie said, crossing her arms in victory.

Sonja closed the door softly behind her and whispered, "Let's go down to the library and figure this out so we don't disturb anyone. I don't want to wake Lydia. She's finally asleep, and it's not necessary to worry her with this right now."

Christie nodded and they tiptoed down the spiral staircase and into the library. Sonja looked just about to ask Christie questions when the door creaked slightly. Sonja stared at the door for a few seconds. "I should have known. Rosita, get in here."

"It's a good thing I'm a light sleeper," Rosita said, peeking her head through the doorway. "Lord knows what kind of trouble you all could get into without me." The woman checked her pocket watch and stepped in to join them. "What's going on here, anyway?"

"We're going over some evidence," Sonja reported.

Rosita shot a glance at Christie. "Is Martin back?"

"What do you mean?" Christie really didn't want to be reminded that her husband was gone and she wondered how Rosita knew at all about Martin's departure.

"I heard a car earlier, so I went out front and saw a taxi leaving. Where did he go?" Rosita prodded.

"Actually, he's gone," Christie answered.

"Gone?" Sonja asked, her obvious excitement over Christie's find replaced now by concern.

Tears came back to Christie's eyes. "Yes. Gone. He went back home. We had an argument..."

Rosita put her arm around Christie's shoulders. "It's all right, honey. I'm sure he'll be back."

"I'm not so sure. He wanted to know when I was coming home for good. I told him I wasn't leaving Lydia again and that he should understand."

"I'm proud of you, Miss Cassandra. You did the right thing. Lydia needs you now. Not many people get a second chance," Rosita said, wiping the tears from Christie's cheeks.

Christie took a haggard, uneasy breath. "Thank you, Rosie."

Sonja gave a stern nod. "I'm proud of you, too, Christie. I know we've had our differences in the past, but I really do admire you. Now I know where Lydia gets her determination." She broke away from Christie's teary gaze and asked, "So, what about this tape? Are you certain this is *the* tape?"

"Yes, it is. I remember the label specifically," Christie acknowledged.

"I'm going to go get some coffee. This could be a long night," Rosita announced and swiftly left the room.

"Thank you," Sonja called after her. Then she looked at Christie. "Where did you find it?"

After just a moment's hesitation, Christie relayed her argument with Martin and how she'd then walked outside by the gazebo to get some much-needed fresh air. "...and I came across something hard and plastic beneath the dirt. So I dug deeper and there it was."

Sonja blinked, the wheels in her mind obviously turning. "It was here all the time. My old tape recorder is in the trunk of my car. I'll be right back. Thank you, Christie, for bringing this to me so quickly." Sonja quickly exited the room and stepped outside to her car.

Rosita came in with the coffee seconds later. "Thank you," Christie, watching the woman carefully pour two cups and hand one to her.

"Miss Cassandra?" Rosita asked, looking her in the eye. "Have you given any thought to where you want to go from here?"

"Hm?" Christie was puzzled by the question. She hadn't had much time to consider anything past being here with her daughter.

"What I mean is...do you have any thoughts about the future? You know, when this is done with and everyone gets back to their own lives."

"Oh. Rosie, I don't know. I guess that's what Martin wanted to know, too. I couldn't bear to leave Lydia again. So much time has been wasted already, and I want to get to know my daughter. The thought of going back to Wyoming just breaks my heart," Christie confided.

"Then why leave?" Rosita asked. "Have you thought of moving in here?"

"Well...I don't..." She didn't even know if she should say anything at all.

"Cassandra, don't you know this is where you belong?" Rosita touched her hand.

Christie fell quiet at Rosita's sentiment; the thought of it made her heart race. She fidgeted with the sleeve on her sweater, her mind dueling with itself over not having her husband but having her daughter. Not long ago, she'd been unsure of Rosita's feelings toward her. Now, maybe, the housekeeper trusted her—or at the very least, that trust was growing. "You really do look out for Lydia, don't you?"

"Naturally. She's been my heart and soul. It's a job I recommend highly."

"Do you think Lydia would want me here?"

"Where do you think I got the idea? Besides, now that Mr. William is gone, I'm not sure what will happen to this place. This is your home." Rosita paused, pursing her lips, then added, "Don't worry too much about Martin. If he truly loves you, he'll be back."

"She's right," Sonja interjected carefully as she entered the room. "How about we all give this little number a listen?"

Such kind words from these women suddenly made Christie feel better about her future. She had their support, at least, and that made a world of difference even when it came to Martin.

Sonja set her somewhat ancient tape recorder on the coffee table, checked the batteries, and slipped the tape inside. As they listened to the voices filling the room, Christie shivered on the inside at the eerie sound of the man's voice—the man who had caused her so much pain. The grave didn't even seem to stop him from hurting her. The dialogue clearly implied that these men were planning to kill someone, and whether or not it actually happened didn't much matter. They'd been orchestrating murder.

"This is amazing," Sonja whispered. "Not only are there names, they give locations and a step-by-step agenda. I can't believe—"

A new voice appeared on the recording, interrupting her. "This is for my brother Derek. Derek, if you've found this tape, it means I'm dead. I've played the game until the end, and now my time has run out. I am so sorry for all I've done, most of which will become apparent to you in the days to come, if it hasn't already. It's only now, as I sit here, searching my soul for some peace, that I realize what it must have been like for you. You were the truly great one, my brother. The Pritchards are after you, and I must make the sacrifice to pay for my actions. Please use this tape as you wish, but above everything else, bring them down. I never told you, but I did always love you. Goodbye, brother." The tape ended with a click.

All three women lost their speech after hearing the voice of Dillon Meade. Sonja nervously cleared her throat. "He knew he was going to die. He planned it."

"He said he had to make sacrifices to pay for his actions. What did that mean?" Christie asked.

"Damned if I know," Sonja answered with a frown. "But I'm going to find out."

"Mr. Derek should know about this, shouldn't he?" Rosita added.

Sonja nodded. "Yes, and he will. First thing in the morning. I'll have him come down to the station."

"For your first day as Captain."

"Yes!" a voice shouted from the other side of the door.

"Lydia, what are you doing out of bed?" Sonja approached her when she stepped into the library and kissed her on the cheek.

"I might ask you all the same question. No one invited me." Lydia shot glances toward everyone in the room.

"We just didn't want to wake you," Christie said after motioning for her daughter to sit next to her on the sofa.

"You didn't wake me. Sonja did, when I turned over and she was gone," Lydia stated with a wry smile.

"If we want to blame someone, your mother was the one who woke me," Sonja said. "Go ahead and tell her what you found."

"Well," Christie started, "I stumbled upon the infamous tape everyone's been looking for. Quite by accident, too."

Lydia held out her hands and asked, "Does it answer any of our questions?" A deafening silence overtook the room, and Lydia frowned at them. "What, exactly, is on that tape?"

"Well, just listen," Sonja said, settling into the recliner and playing the tape again.

Lydia joined her mother and Rosita on the overstuffed sofa, grasping her mother's hand as she heard the voices of the Pritchard family mob make plans for murder. And just when she thought the tape was over, she heard Dillon's voice come to life. "Oh, Jesus," Lydia whispered before she could stop herself. "What has he done that's so awful?"

"We don't know that yet, but we will," Sonja said quietly. "And I'm going to start tom—well, later today, apparently." She glanced at her watch. "It's after three in the morning. How about we all try to get some sleep?"

They all headed up the stairs to get back to bed, and Lydia leaned toward Christie. "Does Martin know about all this yet?"

Christie paused. "Uh…no, dear. Not yet. He had to leave for Wyoming. I'll tell you about it in the morning. I promise."

"Are you sure you're all right?" Lydia said, putting a hand on her shoulder and stopping her in the hallway.

"I'll be just fine. I'm here with you." She searched her daughter's eyes, knowing she'd made the right decision. "Goodnight, darling." Whatever remained of Christie's hesitation and her concern over Martin's choice to leave disappeared completely as she watched Sonja and Lydia walking off to their room together, hand in hand.

Chapter Thirty-Nine

A FEW HOURS LATER, Sonja was up and showered, ready to go to work and thrilled to have Pennington's job. They'd have a small induction ceremony in a few days, but she had work to do in the meantime. She kissed Lydia goodbye for the day, who whispered, "I love you, Captain MacIntosh," before rolling over and going back to sleep.

Rosita waited for her by the kitchen. "Would you like some breakfast on your way out?"

"Are you telling me you haven't already prepared something?" Sonja laughed, knowing full well Rosita had been up early, fussing in the kitchen. The woman was unfailingly dependable.

"No, I'm not saying that at all." They chatted shortly while Rosita prepared Sonja's breakfast to go—a couple homemade biscuits with sausage and egg, fruit salad, orange juice, and a thermos of coffee.

"Rosita, you don't know what you're doing," Sonja said, a bit overwhelmed by the treatment but feeling her stomach growling anyway. "I could very well get used to this, and then you'll never be rid of me."

"That's the plan, Madam Captain," Rosita said with a smile as she handed over the small package. "I know you'll do good things, Sonja."

"Thank you. I hope so."

In her car and heading down the driveway, Sonja smiled at the receding image of the mansion in her rearview mirror. Though things were going really well with Lydia, she would never let herself believe she'd fully earned back her trust. Maybe she never would, but Sonja knew Lydia still loved her. If nothing else changed, she decided, she could live with that.

The drive into Highland Park was somewhat refreshing, seeing the frost cover the trees and the first signs of the approaching holiday. With Thanksgiving drawing near, Sonja was more thankful than ever before. She was in love and had just been handed her dream job. Even though she wouldn't officially be Captain for a few more days, she was still anxious to get started. Since Pennington was in jail, Sonja would be "acting" Captain until everything was official.

When she got to the precinct, she was greeted by well-wishers from different departments. She was grateful and more than a little relieved that the decision was a popular one. The first order of business was a meeting with Clayton Hughes, which entailed some training and tying up a few loose ends in regards to Pennington's dealings.

Clayton Hughes was an honest man, if nothing else, and he knew a good cop when he saw one. A dapper, sophisticated man of fifty-eight and bald by choice, Clayton Hughes seemed to feel responsible for Bradley Pennington. Though the decision to hire the man had not rested on Clayton's shoulders, it still looked bad for the department. Dressed in a three-piece, dark blue pinstriped suit, Clayton Hughes opened his office door to let Sonja inside. "Good morning, Sonja." He greeted her with a smile and a firm handshake. "Please, have a seat." He pointed at one of the expensive leather chairs positioned in front of his desk.

"Good morning, Mr. Hughes," Sonja said as she sat down. "Thank you."

"Call me Clayton," he said, sitting in the vacant chair behind his desk. "No sense in being so formal." He reached over and pressed a button on his phone.

"Yes?" a voice answered through the speaker.

"Could you please bring in some coffee for the Captain and me?"

"Certainly, sir."

"Thank you, Margie," Clayton called back. "Now then, Sonja

MacIntosh. I've heard quite a lot about you."

"I'm sure you have." Sonja smiled politely. "But I guess it depends on what you've heard and where it came from."

"Fair enough. I want you to know that I don't take anything from that son of a bitch Pennington seriously. Uh...I'm sorry. This whole thing disgusts me. You're a good cop, Sonja. One of the best I've seen. I know your work. I've been a witness to it and I also have a glowing report from Michael Pritchard and the FBI."

"Thank you, Clayton." She still felt strange calling him by his first name, but the man had told her to use it.

Clayton rose in response to the knock at the door and opened it. "Thank you, Margie," he said, taking the tray from his assistant. "May I pour you a cup, Sonja?"

"Yes, thank you." She gingerly took the porcelain cup once he'd filled it and offered it to her.

Clayton sat back in his chair and studied her. "And as for the trouble you got involved in while you were in Wyoming...well, let's just say it's taken care of. Upon some investigation, it appears the whole thing was a setup between Pennington and Joel Pritchard. I believe that, deep down, you felt you had no choice. You wouldn't have compromised the badge in such a manner otherwise. I have to say, Sonja, that besides being a good, decent cop, you are one hell of a brave woman."

"I'm not sure what to say. Thank you. And I promise to do my best as Captain," Sonja told him sincerely.

"I know you will." Clayton Hughes sipped more of his coffee. "One more thing. It's a touchy subject, and I apologize for bringing this up, but I want you to know my view on this...for future reference."

Sonja nodded, having a distinct feeling she knew what was coming. "No apologies necessary, Clayton. Please, feel free to ask me anything."

"I appreciate your candor." Clayton smiled. "Let me just say that your personal life is your own, but sometimes it does affect your work environment. I want you to know that I do understand. I believe that you find in life the people who will stick by you and love you, no matter what you do. Whether it's a man or a woman makes no difference. I say this to you, Sonja, because many years ago I had a daughter, and I imagine, if she were here today, she would be something very much like you."

Sonja stared at him for a few seconds, convinced his words were genuine and noting distinctly the fact that he'd said he *had* a daughter. "Thank you," she said.

"Of course." He seemed only a bit uncomfortable with his vague confession, but a smile twitched at the corner of his mouth and he glanced down at his desk. "Now, for the business at hand."

Clayton explained to her where the investigation into Pennington's activities was headed. Sonja found the right time to show Clayton the infamous tape unearthed at the Blackwell Estates. He slipped the tape into his player and listened diligently, his eyes growing wide with each passing second. Afterwards, Sonja shared with him everything else she knew, leaving nothing out in her story up to the moment Pennington had held them at gunpoint.

"Speaking of Pennington, his arraignment is in a couple weeks, but I've got other people working on that case. For now, I want you to concentrate on closing this Pritchard case and—"

"Mr. Hughes?" Margie's voice came through the speaker on his desk once again.

"Yes, what is it?" Clayton answered.

"There's an urgent phone call for you on line one from Hank Kovacs."

"Thanks, Margie. I'll take it." Clayton picked up the phone. "Yes, this is Clayton Hughes. Yes, that's correct." He paused to listen, and Sonja wondered why Hank would be calling the man now, of all times. "I'll send her down there at once. Thank you, Hank." Clayton hung up the phone, folded his hands on his desk, and looked at Sonja with bright eyes. "Well, Captain," he said with a slight smile, "here's your chance. Antonio Delgado is downstairs in interrogation ready to turn state's evidence. Since you are so heavily involved, I want you to continue your investigation there. You deserve this one."

Sonja rose from her chair and smiled. "Thank you so much, Clayton."

"My pleasure. Good luck." He stood to open the door for her and ushered her out after another brief handshake.

Sonja smiled to herself as she left Clayton's office, grateful for the opportunity to have met with the man before anything else happened today. As she made her way down to the interrogation rooms in the basement, she wondered what secrets Delgado, a known enemy of the Pritchard family mob, would divulge to the police. Hank waited for her when she walked down the hall. "Hey, Hank. What do we know?"

"Not sure. He hasn't said anything, except…"

"Except what?" Sonja prodded.

"Except that he's refused a lawyer or any legal aid. He only wants to talk to you." After a short pause, Hank leaned in close, put his arm on Sonja's shoulder, and told her, "By the way, good job on the promotion, Captain."

Sonja grinned. "Thanks. Let's do this." She grabbed her notebook and pen, then knocked on the door before entering the stale room.

"Ah, the illustrious Sonja MacIntosh. Thank you for seeing me," Antonio said. "Congratulations on your promotion, Captain."

Sonja studied the man carefully. She couldn't yet tell if his words were graciously intended or some form of forced politeness. "Thank you." She sat in front of the portly man.

His hair had once been black but was now gray and disappearing. With his round, unshaven face and stout belly, he looked like any other man's feeble grandfather. His aged brown eyes told Sonja the exhausting life he'd lived had already taken its toll. Antonio wore blue jeans and a white t-shirt—not the attire Sonja expected to see.

"I'm a bit surprised to hear you're turning state's evidence," she said. "Wouldn't that be considered a betrayal of family loyalty?"

"Under normal circumstances, yes. But there's nothing left of the family now," Antonio stated.

"I have to inform you I'll be taping this conversation so we can be clear on your statement. You understand." Sonja placed a new tape into the tape recorder on the table.

"Of course, Captain." Antonio nodded respectfully, as though this was the most natural conversation for him.

"Why don't you begin by telling your story? And then I'll tell you what I know," Sonja suggested.

"Fine," Antonio agreed. "I'd just married my wife Deidre, and at the time Brenton was actually my chauffeur, believe it or not. He was tired and hungry for something bigger than life. Since I was now a married man, I really didn't want to jeopardize my new family by remaining so involved in the...business. I didn't like the direction things were going. I made Brenton a proposition and spent the next couple of years showing him the ropes, so to speak.

"About five years down the road, he took over the business in a big way. His ego was gigantic, and it made him absolutely horrible to be around. Oh, Brenton would consult me about projects and people, but I was basically pushed aside until he needed me for something. Please understand, I'm not complaining. The choices I made then were of my own volition. That is, except for one. And that regards my son."

"I assume you mean Joel Pritchard," Sonja interjected.

"Yes." Antonio nodded. "Deidre and I were unable to have children for so long. Once we quit trying, she finally got pregnant. I was elated and, of course, had been secretly hoping for a son. When the time came, there were complications. My sweet Deidre died giving birth to our son. He was such a beautiful boy, my Joey. The devastation of losing my wife battled the sense of responsibility and obligation I felt for our son, knowing I still had a part of her in little Joey. This was my sense of family.

"By this time, Brenton and his wife Anna had three-year-old Michael, but when he was born, the doctors had told them it was medically impossible for Anna to bear any more children. Brenton took this as a sign of weakness on her part. He wanted another son.

"Back then, I was involved in sort of a subsidiary of one of the major businesses. Brenton wanted non-stop profits and would hear of nothing less. A man named Jordan Hicks was a long-time friend of mine who'd provided the family with thousands of dollars of profit from his chain of sporting goods stores. Times were hard then, and profits fell drastically. I attempted to explain to Brenton the reasons for this, and the importance of holding on and waiting for things to improve. He wouldn't hear of it and ordered Hicks killed. I was the man to do it. I've done many things, Captain, but that I could not do. Even if it cost me my life."

Sonja quietly jotted down notes and kept an eye on the recorder, practicing what she'd been taught in her career and emotionally removing herself from anything she might hear now. "Brenton obviously spared your life for a reason."

"Yes. When I refused to do this deed, he exploded. In fact, he had not planned to spare my life. But I had something he wanted," Antonio stated.

"A son," Sonja answered.

"Exactly. I was shocked that Brenton could be so selfish as to take my son from me. He arranged for an adoption through an associate, William Blackwell. My punishment for refusing to kill Jordan Hicks was to watch my son, my only child, be raised as a Pritchard. And I was to never mention it again."

"What was it about William Blackwell that made Brenton seek him out for this adoption?" Sonja asked.

"William was sort of underground and fresh. One of Brenton's lawyers knew about him through various contacts. The man had a reputation for doing these private adoptions, and Brenton basically bullied him into it. He knew William was gay and used it as leverage. Back then, a man's reputation and career was affected as much by his actions in public as in the bedroom. He had no choice. I would rather have had Brenton kill me."

"And the document from this adoption through William Blackwell was the same found at Blackwell's home."

"Yes, and now my son is dead. You can't know the pain of

hearing your own son killed himself after discovering he wasn't a Pritchard. Joel's death would of course have already created a vacuum, and there's no shortage of men aching for the throne of the Pritchard empire. Pennington was one of those men, and I was left with no choice but to shoot him."

"*You* shot Pennington." Sonja tried as hard as she could not to make it sound like a question, but she hadn't expected that confession at all.

"Yes. I'm here because this empire needs to be taken down. Now that Joel and Pritchard are dead, it's time. My boy could have been so much more."

Sonja took a deep breath. "How about some more coffee and a break?"

"Sure, Captain."

Sonja excused herself to get the coffee, glad for the few moments of relief. It gave her a chance to comprehend what Delgado had revealed. She took a few minutes to phone Clayton about the Pennington shooting, who seemed just as surprised at the news but grateful for a swiftly forthcoming confession.

She returned to the interrogation room and handed Antonio his coffee.

"Thank you, Captain," he said. "May I ask you something?"

"Go ahead," Sonja answered, looking him in the eye.

"Do you know about the tape?"

"I know about it. And I have it in my possession. It leads to some interesting questions. The tape clearly states details, names, and locations of a planned mob hit. We got a lot of crucial information listening to it. We also know this tape has changed hands several times. Did you know anyone by the name of Dillon Meade?" Sonja asked.

"Of course. Well, I knew *of* him through various employees of mine. Most of them helped me keep an eye on Joel's dealings as much as possible," Antonio stated, offering the information freely.

"Tell me more," Sonja prodded. She realized now that it didn't take much to get the man talking—just the right questions.

"Dillon Meade worked for Joel and was instrumental in the Blackwell murder."

Chapter Forty

SONJA COULD HAVE PICKED her jaw up off the floor if she hadn't been in such a state of shock. But she pulled herself together quickly and forced herself to remain calm. "Are you talking about William Blackwell?"

"One and the same," Antonio answered.

"William Blackwell died of cancer," she said, wondering what other revelations this man had stored up his sleeve.

Antonio smiled and leaned across the table, bringing them face to face. "You can believe whatever you like, Captain. I'm just telling you what I know."

Sonja had to do something, so she rose from the table and paced around the room. Only now did she start to doubt Antonio's intentions; after all, he was a known member of a mob family—a criminal and a gangster. No matter the outcome, she had to hear all of it and keep her cool before she drew any conclusions. "All right, Delgado. Suppose you tell me what you know about that, too," she said, placing her hands strategically on the table in front of him.

"Dillon Meade was apparently down on his luck and had a real nasty hatred for his twin brother, Derek. He came across Joel in Vegas when he'd lost big at one of the casinos. Joel struck him a deal. Dillon would work for Joel, anonymously of course, and they would wash Dillon's debt. I'm sure Dillon couldn't believe his luck, but nothing with Joel was ever left to chance. Nothing."

"Had Joel planned that meeting with Dillon?" Sonja asked.

"Yes. He knew who Dillon was but was aware of the man's

connection to Blackwell through his brother. Joel wanted the purse because Brenton asked him to retrieve it. He considered achieving that goal the highest honor—to fulfil the wishes of a dying man, not to mention the only man he idolized. Brenton's men had apparently lost the purse in a struggle some years before and, of course, those men were abruptly…thrown aside. Brenton had also known about that tape, but never divulged to me who'd made it. It was only after Dillon started working for Joel that we found out Blackwell had the purse."

"Where do you think Dillon got that information?" Sonja pushed.

"I assume from his brother Derek, perhaps in what was intended to be confidential conversation. Most likely, Joel decided shortly after that Dillon was invaluable to him, and he devised more plans," Antonio revealed.

"What plans are those?" Sonja bit the bullet, hating to have to goad the man, but she had no idea where this would lead and she needed the information.

"The plan was for Dillon to masquerade as his brother in an attempt to get William Blackwell to tell him everything Joel wanted to know," Antonio stated, finished his coffee, then set down his cup.

Sonja's mind instantly went back to what Lydia had told her about the first time she'd seen Dillon, whom she'd thought was Derek at the time. "God," Sonja whispered. That had been the day William Blackwell died.

"What is it, Captain?" Antonio asked.

Sonja turned back to him and frowned, shaking off her surprise. "You said Dillon hated his brother. Any idea why?"

"Not really. Guess that wasn't Joel's concern at the time, either."

The tape recorder clicked off and Sonja leaned over the table to change the tape. "Okay," she said when it was back in place and recording once again. "Let's go back to when you said William Blackwell was murdered."

"First, do you have a coke around here, or am I supposed to just deal with this sludge you call coffee?" Antonio grunted.

Sonja smirked. "Sure." She shut off the tape and stepped out of the room to search for Hank. He stood at the end of the hall. "Hey, Hank, wanna get me a couple of cokes?"

Surprised, Hank nodded. "You bet. Be right back."

Sonja watched him walk down the hall, and she was grateful for his patience. She knew the other detectives down here were more than curious, waiting around the room and watching through the two-way mirror but unable to hear a single word. She couldn't tell anybody what she knew until she'd gotten enough out of Delgado to satisfy herself. The tension from the other curious detectives hung thick in the hallway, but Sonja was grateful none of them approached her to ask questions. They knew they'd hear it all when she felt the time was right.

"Here you go, boss," Hank said, reappearing around the corner and handing over two cokes.

"Thanks, Hank," she told him, searching his eyes and wanting to tell him all she'd learned. Hank held her gaze, seeming to understand, then he smiled and nodded, wordlessly giving his support.

Sonja stepped back into the grungy room filled with the smell of old cigarettes and bad coffee. "Here's your coke, Antonio. Cheers," she told him, raising her can in the air.

"Salut," Antonio echoed.

"Now, where were we?" She felt her head could barely hold all the new information, and part of her wanted to see just how much Antonio had been paying attention.

"William Blackwell's murder," he replied without hesitation.

"Yes." Sonja started the tape again. Still standing at the table in front of Antonio, she looked squarely into his dark eyes, then walked around the room. "Tell me more about the plan."

"I must say, Dillon improvised most of it himself," Antonio said.

"Such as?"

"Such as the intricate details of impersonating his twin brother," Antonio stated. "Many of these details I could have no way of knowing."

"Why would there even be a plan to murder William Blackwell

when he was already dying of cancer? Why not just let nature take its course?" Sonja put forth the question carefully.

"Not fast enough for Joel, most likely. I think he felt he was doing Brenton a favor. You know, an added bonus. Plus, Dillon intended to pin the murder on his brother if anybody asked any questions. Joel backed him completely." Antonio took another sip of his coke.

"How did Dillon do it, then? How did he kill William Blackwell?"

"Cyanide," Antonio replied without batting an eye.

Sonja gave a pert smile. "I'm going to need you to explain this, Antonio, because Blackwell's autopsy didn't mention poison in the least."

Antonio chuckled and shook his head. "Captain, you should have already pinned down how a Pritchard would handle that kind of situation by now."

"Educate me," Sonja stated firmly.

Antonio smiled as he took yet another sip of his drink. "Pritchards have always had officials on the payroll. Money dirties many hands, Captain, as your predecessor discovered."

"I need you to tell me more, Delgado. For the record," Sonja said, careful not to put words in the man's mouth.

"Certainly. The medical examiner, coroner, and a good deal of both paramedics and triage nurses were on Joel's payroll. Sometimes, autopsies were skipped altogether and documents presented were falsified."

"Here's a pen and paper," Sonja said, sliding them toward him on the table. "I want you to write out all the names of the individuals involved." Antonio nodded, and she waited a few minutes for him to finish. When he set down his pen, Sonja gently retrieved the paper, folded it, and placed it in her pocket. "Now tell me about the murder." By now, she already expected an immediate answer.

"I don't know exact details, you understand, just that it was done. Dillon spent some time with William, convincing William he was Derek and getting him to share the purse's location. The plan was that, once he got the purse, Dillon would inject William with the cyanide, tying up that loose end, then bring the purse and its contents back to Joel."

"But something went wrong," Sonja added.

"Yes. Dillon apparently turned against Joel at the last moment, and that's something you just don't do to a Pritchard," Antonio emphasized.

"Evidently," Sonja quipped. "So, what about Dillon's murder?"

"What about it?" Antonio asked flippantly. It was the first hint of attitude he'd given her, and Sonja didn't know what had caused it.

She paced again, having to stretch a bit after standing in one spot. Stopping next to Delgado, she stood over him and watched him carefully. "Look, Delgado, don't fuck with me. Now's not the time to stop answering my questions. I suggest you make it your business to tell me what you know."

"Nice set of balls you got there, Captain." Antonio smiled. "Honestly, I think that, in my son's mind, Dillon's death was accidental."

"But?" Sonja pushed with necessary swiftness.

"From what my sources reported to me, it seemed entirely too contrived to be an accident," he confessed. "Dillon had told Joel his brother had the purse and its contents, then specifically told him when Derek would be home."

"How does any of that seem contrived to you?" Sonja asked.

"My men told me Dillon had seemed off in those last few hours, especially when called Joel to report to him. That's their job, Captain, to notice something that doesn't feel right."

"All right, Delgado. You've been here for over three hours. I'm going to take a longer break, and I'm going to check your story," Sonja stated honestly. She didn't know what to make of the information, and she needed time to figure out exactly how to treat the man's confession.

"Then you'll find, Captain, that everything I've told you is true," he told her without a hint of doubt.

"Why should I believe a man who's made his living running with the mob?" Despite the information Delgado had given her with seemingly little difficulty, Sonja wasn't so sure he was being completely forthcoming with her. How could he be?

Antonio rose to his feet slowly, leaned toward Sonja, and looked her in the eye. "Right now, Captain, what other choice do you have?"

Chapter Forty-One

SONJA LEFT THE INTERROGATION room and made the walk upstairs to her new office. Her life since the moment she'd met Lydia flashed through her mind like movie scenes. As she opened the door, she saw the reception area, complete with a desk, chair, and an empty filing cabinet. There were no signs of anyone in the office; everything had been moved out, repainted, redone, and cleaned, possibly in an attempt to erase the stench of Bradley Pennington.

The smell of new leather overtook her senses, and Sonja smiled at the chair behind her desk. It had a majestic appearance, as if she would be overseeing a kingdom instead of a precinct. She sat in the luxurious, black leather chair and turned to her left to witness the view through the large window.

Life had changed so much in just twenty-four hours. Lydia had returned home, Joel was dead, and long-buried secrets had been revealed. And Sonja was Captain. Then she replayed the past three hours and her time with Antonio Delgado. As she stared out toward the Midwestern skyline, she remembered Delgado's last words and realized he had, in fact, been right. She had no choice but to believe him. Believing Delgado was one thing, but giving the news to Lydia that her father had really been murdered was yet another.

After sifting through some paperwork, Sonja glanced at the clock on the wall—six forty-five. She sighed, knowing it was time to head to the mansion where Lydia would be waiting, wanting news of Sonja's first day as Captain. She knew Lydia would be far less excited to hear just what that first day had entailed. Even still, not one to avoid a situation, she packed up her things and left the comfort and security of her office.

In her car, she got a call on her cell phone. "Yeah, MacIntosh here."

"Hello, Captain," the voice said with a slight giggle.

A broad smile came across Sonja's face. "Well, hello there, sweets. I was just thinking about you. Are you my psychic girlfriend?" Just hearing Lydia's voice seemed to interrupt the madness in her head.

"I don't know, could be. Tell me what you're wearing and I'll let you know if you're right." Lydia laughed.

"You always brighten my day, Lydia. I'm on my way to you now, as a matter of fact. About another ten minutes."

"Good. I missed you today." Lydia said it gently, in a soft voice.

"Me too. I'll see you in a few." Sonja smiled through the phone.

"Wait," Lydia added, her voice tinged with a hint of desperation. "There's something else."

"What is it?" Sonja asked, suddenly a bit worried.

"I love you."

Sonja sighed, feeling her heart flutter. "I love you."

She spent the remainder of their conversation listening to Lydia describe her day. She knew she had to tell her the news about her father, but she still didn't know if she believed it herself.

When Sonja turned into the long, winding driveway, she smiled to see Lydia sitting on the front steps and waving. The rest of her day seemed to melt away into oblivion as she got out of the car and wrapped her arms around Lydia tightly. Wordlessly, they walked arm-in-arm through the huge front doors of the mansion, then strolled into the den and sat together on the sofa to relax.

Even with the relief she felt in Lydia's presence and within the cozy den, Sonja couldn't keep herself from fidgeting for very long. She was sure she was transparent and she hated it.

"Give it up, Captain," Lydia said, staring her squarely in the eye. "Something's on your mind. No more secrets, remember? Even if there are good intentions."

Sonja sighed, the burden of all she knew resting on her shoulders. She'd known she wouldn't be able to hide her feelings from this woman for long. "I need a drink first. You?"

"Good idea," Lydia agreed.

"How does a beer sound?" Sonja asked. Lydia gave her a thumbs up. "I'll be back in a flash," Sonja added and left the room in search of their drinks.

***

Lydia wandered toward the desk with the intention of taking in the spectacular early-winter view from the den's window. The ringing phone interrupted her plans. She grabbed the receiver. "Hello?"

"Is this Lydia Blackwell?"

Not recognizing the voice on the other end, Lydia asked, "May I ask who's calling?"

"That's not important," the voice stated firmly. "I need to speak with Lydia Blackwell."

"Speaking. What can I do for you?"

"I am calling on behalf of Dillon Meade."

"I see. You have my attention. What exactly do you want?" Lydia felt the distinct need to choose her words carefully.

"I don't want anything other than to make good on my promise to Dillon. I am an associate of Dillon's, Ms. Blackwell. Should anyone find out I made this call, my life could be in danger. Dillon told me that if anything happened to him, I was to contact you and tell you how sorry he was about the way your father died and that he regretted it all until the end." Nothing but silence and a click followed.

"What do you mean—hello? Hello?" Lydia yelled into the phone. When she heard the dial tone, she knew the conversation was over. "Damn!" she shouted just as Sonja entered the room with their drinks.

"Who in the world is making you curse on the phone? I guess you're not the delicate flower I thought you were," Sonja said, attempting a joke to lighten her own mood more than Lydia's. Then she seemed to take another look and noticed Lydia's discomfort. "What is it?"

"I'd tell you if I knew. I don't even know who the hell I was talking to. Someone just called, saying he was an associate of Dillon's and he was to call me if anything happened to Dillon. He delivered a message," Lydia said. She couldn't quite yet extract herself from the phone call and the haunting voice attached to it.

"What was the message?" Sonja asked.

"The man told me that Dillon was sorry for the way my father died and he regretted it 'til the very end…" Lydia's voice turned into a mere whisper.

Sonja's face blanched. "Jesus."

Lydia noticed, and something about it didn't seem right. She walked away from the desk and the phone. "Sonja, do you know something about this? What did he mean, 'the way my father died'?"

"I found out some things today, and I was about to tell you after these beers. I'm not sure I believe it myself," Sonja said. She popped the top off both the beers and handed one to Lydia.

Lydia took a long sip and sat back down on the sofa. She watched Sonja pace in agitation, back and forth, in front of her.

"What I have to tell you," Sonja started, "is somewhat related to that phone call. A surprise visitor came to the station today to turn state's evidence."

Had Lydia's mind been clearer, she might have guessed, but her brain wasn't quite working correctly at the moment. "Anyone we know?"

"Antonio Delgado. Lydia, what I'm about to tell you came straight from him. I shouldn't be telling you, but you need to know. No secrets, as you said." Sonja stopped and looked down at her with a mixture of fear and confusion.

"So, tell me." Lydia took a sip of her beer and then another to prepare herself.

"Delgado shot Pennington. Apparently, Pennington was out to take over where Joel left off in the family business. I questioned him about Dillon, and that's when Delgado said he knew him because Dillon was involved in the 'Blackwell murder'." Sonja paced around the sofa where Lydia sat.

Lydia's eyes grew wider by the minute. "Murder? What—how can—" She couldn't even finish her thoughts.

Sonja finally joined her on the sofa in what seemed an attempt to comfort her. "I know. I had the same reaction, but then he told me the whole story and it's starting to make terrible sense." She reached out to hold Lydia's hand. Then she relayed the entire story of Delgado's confession in interrogation.

Lydia barely moved for what felt like a very long time after Sonja finished speaking. "My poor father," she whispered. She felt her eyes glistening wet as she remembered her father's last breath. The sadness bloomed into anger when she realized that breath had been taken from him. And Dillon had been the one to take it. She gasped.

"What is it?" Sonja asked.

"I must have passed Dillon in the hall right before my father died. It was probably right after he…" Lydia couldn't deal with the knowledge she'd just acquired. It was too much. She rose from the sofa and paced the length of the den. Then she walked slowly to the window, more than willing to lose herself in the dark sky outside.

"That's the same thing I thought earlier today. I'm so sorry. There are still so many pieces we have yet to fit together," Sonja told her as she fiddled with the label on her beer bottle.

"Why is Delgado turning state's evidence now?" Lydia asked. "It seems a little odd at this point in the game."

Taking another long sip of her beer and rising from the sofa, Sonja walked toward Lydia. "I guess Delgado figures that, with Joel killing himself the way he did and for the reasons he did it, he doesn't have anything else to lose. I think he only stayed in the business to keep an eye on his son."

"It's so hard to understand." Lydia turned away from Sonja and went back to the window, gazing out upon the night, searching for answers or some kind of explanation. She felt Sonja touch her shoulder.

"What are you thinking?"

"Nothing is clear. And maybe nothing ever will be again," Lydia said somberly. She felt a chill run down her spine. "I'd really thought that maybe, just maybe, this chaos I call my life would settle down...especially with Joel out of the picture. It's never going to end, is it?"

Sonja turned Lydia around to face her. She leaned in and gently wiped away the tears. Lydia fell into Sonja's arms, clutching onto her shirt. She couldn't hold on tight enough, but the feeling of Sonja's body against her, at least, felt real.

Sonja whispered, "Yes, baby, it *will* end. When it's supposed to. There's a reason for all of this, even if we never know what it is." Then she pulled Lydia away and held her face in her hands. "And your life is not just chaos, not by a long shot. Look at all the people you've brought into your world. Think of the good things that came from bad things. Look at the people you can depend on, always."

"You're one of those people," Lydia said as she nuzzled herself closer.

Sonja rested her head on Lydia's shoulder as they embraced. "Yes, I am. Don't ever forget."

Lydia regained her composure and whispered in Sonja's ear, "Not a chance." She let Sonja lead her back to the sofa so they could try to piece things together. Lydia drank some more beer. "I wonder why Dillon had such a violent hatred for Derek. He's such a beautiful person. I just don't understand."

Derek's voice startled them. "I think I do."

Chapter Forty-Two

"DEREK, WE DIDN'T EVEN hear you come in," Lydia said as she stood to embrace him.

"Hi, Derek."

"Sonja," Derek said. Rosita followed in seconds later with more beer. "Thank you, Rosita. You think of everything. Cheers." He raised his fresh bottle in the air and clicked it against theirs.

"So," Sonja prodded, "you think you know why Dillon had such strong feelings against you?"

"Strong feelings? Hell, he hated me with a passion," Derek stated, then almost drained his whole drink.

Sonja smirked at his forwardness. "Did you happen to hear the tape with Dillon's voice on it?"

"Yes. I went down to the station today. Clayton called and asked me to stop by. It seems Dillon's conscience got the better of him in those final hours. Amazing, the clarity that comes with impending death. But he did save my life, and I'm certain he meant to." Derek nodded. "Most twins are very close, but that didn't happen with Dillon and me. I think it was the path he chose for himself that drove us apart. Dillon hated me for so long for only one reason." He caught Lydia's gaze, and she nodded for him to continue. "It was all about money—everything."

"Extortion? Blackmail? What was it?" Sonja asked eagerly. If Derek held some answers to Dillon's existence, she was willing to push a little harder to uncover them.

"Inheritance, actually, from our parents. They were wonderful people, and quite wealthy. They'd gotten into real estate, played the market, and invested wisely. Of course, it was extremely lucrative for them and, ultimately, for us. We traveled constantly and always had a big house. Nice childhood, I must say. You don't appreciate those things until you're older.

"But Dillon never appreciated them, even after we grew up. He always wanted more. I know many wealthy people hire nannies and butlers to raise their children, but our parents refused to take that route. I can't recall a single moment they weren't there for me. I don't know. Maybe Dillon was born that way and couldn't help himself." Derek shook his head and took another long drink.

"What happened with your inheritance, then?" Sonja asked.

"My parents boarded a plane to London—Lord, so many years ago. Dillon and I were only eighteen when we heard the plane had crashed into the ocean. A few years before that, I'd become aware of Dillon's contempt for me. By that time, he had been drinking heavily and using drugs, practically living on the street. My father had kicked him out of the house until he could get his life together. So when our parents passed away, Dillon's hatred rose to a whole new level, and he became a different person altogether."

"I'm so sorry," Lydia said.

Derek nestled himself next to her on the sofa. "Lydia, I wish your grandparents could have known you. They would have adored you." He gently touched her shoulder, then looked up to meet Lydia's gaze. "My God, girl, you have my mother's eyes."

Lydia tilted her head in surprise. "Really? I can be proud of that."

Sonja loved to see Lydia's blooming connection with Derek, and she couldn't help thinking there was something more. "What did the Will state?"

"A lot of complicated things," Derek said, looking up at Sonja. "Dillon and I were old enough to handle being thrust out into the world, but Delia…" He seemed unable to even finish the sentence.

"Delia?" Lydia asked.

"We never discussed her, unfortunately, but Delia is our sister,"

Derek revealed quietly. "And now, sweet Lydia, only three of us remain. You, Delia, and yours truly."

Sonja studied Derek's demeanor, searching for more clues about this man. "Does she know any more about Dillon?"

"No, she has nothing to do with this, or with Dillon. I just returned from seeing her. That's where I'd been before I came back to town." Derek's eyes seemed lost in another time, another place. "My sister," he continued after taking a few deep breaths, "is ten years younger. She was born with Down Syndrome and has the most beautiful soul of anyone I've ever met. Delia stole my heart from the minute my parents brought her home. Of course, my parents were devastated, but only for a short while. Sadly, my brother never bothered to get to know her. He felt she was just another obstacle in the way of what he felt my parents owed him, even when he was a child. Delia was a source of shame for him. But then, I guess, we all were."

"Where is she?" Lydia asked.

"Upstate New York. She lives in a facility, a grand house with thirty other, beautiful souls. This was what my parents wanted for her, somewhere she could be the person only she knows how to be without complete dependence on someone else."

"That someone being you, I presume," Sonja interjected. She felt a deeper admiration for Derek and would have never guessed he'd been through so much.

"Yes. My mother didn't want me giving up my life to care for Delia, though I was prepared to do so. I'd still do anything for her. She deserves it. My parents stipulated in their Will that Delia go to a facility where she would thrive. I was put in charge of all the details. There was a lot of money set aside for her. She hasn't and will never want for anything the rest of her life. I'm grateful every day to have had such wise parents."

Derek took a deep breath and then another swig of his beer. "My parents' Will was extremely specific in Dillon's case, as well as my own. They left us our inheritance, but the Will stated both Dillon and I would have to wait until we were twenty-one in order to access it. More specifically, Dillon was not to be allowed access to his own money until I felt he was responsible enough to handle it."

"That's a lot of pressure," Lydia acknowledged.

"Yes, and Dillon resented me for it. He did until the end, because I never thought he was ready. With what I've invested over the years, the money's about double now what our parents initially left us. I did allow him a portion of his inheritance a few years ago, when he was doing well and making good choices. But it didn't last very long."

"You're an extraordinary man, Derek Meade," Lydia said, reaching out to touch his hand.

"Oh, I don't know about all that. I could have easily taken the same path Dillon chose, but I always felt I had to be the strong one. It's been both a blessing and a curse. Dillon's hatred for me was a combination of his greed and my refusal to let him ruin his life. Ever since our parents passed away, he'd attempted to get the money in a variety of ways. He threatened me, my friends, and even William. After a while, I think it became more about revenge for him than getting the money. I can only hope he found peace in his final hours," Derek said grimly.

Lydia exchanged glances with Sonja, who knew they were thinking the same thing. Derek still had no idea that his brother had played a role in William's death. He had a right to know. "Sonja found out more about that today," Lydia said carefully.

"For God's sake, what?" Derek asked, his eyes widening in the slow fashion of all his movements. "How in the world can there be more to tell?"

Lydia elaborated for Derek on all the mysteries Antonio Delgado had unraveled through Sonja's interrogation. The words seemed to slip out when she said, "William was murdered."

"Murdered?" Derek exclaimed. "But...I don't understand. How can it be murder? He died of cancer."

"Apparently," Sonja added delicately, "Dillon poisoned him, a plan Joel had approved. There were no autopsies, no investigations performed, and all the documents were falsified to cover it up."

Derek's face flushed a deep shade of red. "I swear, that brother of mine is damn lucky he's dead!" He rose from the sofa and paced around the room. Upon finishing his beer, he took a huge breath, closed his eyes, and stood up straight. "So, Captain, where do we go from here?"

"I'm not sure, exactly," Sonja said. "Most of it will probably involve checking out Delgado's story and confirming it. I don't know what else we can do, seeing as the two major suspects are both dead. Delgado did give us a list of people working the family business, from doctors and lawyers down to people like those buffoons with Joel in the warehouse. I don't think there's anywhere to go beyond that." She shook her head in disgust.

"Well, that's something, I guess," Derek confessed. "Maybe this is the beginning of the end."

"One can only hope," Lydia said.

Chapter Forty-Three

THE NEXT MORNING PRESENTED a list of tasks for Sonja to tackle. After leaving the Blackwell Estates at promptly seven-fifteen, she reached the precinct without any major distractions by eight. With all Derek's new information, endless questions flooded her mind. It seemed no matter how much she learned, nothing was ever fully resolved. She did know, however, that some of these questions might finally have some real answers.

The reception room outside her office door now house a large desk, furnished with a computer, phone system, and various personal pictures, coffee cups, and papers Sonja didn't recognize. On the far wall sat two more filing cabinets, and built into the wall next to them was a sink and small countertop with storage underneath. It must have taken a lot of work to complete the room like this when it had been completely empty the night before.

Sonja entered her office slowly, closing the door behind her and smiling as she inspected every inch of her office. Some things seemed to be working themselves out. Sitting at her desk, she jotted some notes concerning the information Derek had shared with her. There had to be a way for her to see all the information in one place and perhaps make a new connection.

Some twenty minutes later, a buzzing noise broke her concentration. After discovering it came from her phone, Sonja realized she knew nothing of the complex phone system others took for granted. A process of elimination guided her in rushed frustration toward the correct button. Then she cleared her throat. "Yes?"

"Well, it's about time, Captain. You have a call on line two," the voice instructed. "It's the second button on the left." The direction was followed by an only mildly stifled giggle.

"Thanks," Sonja said gruffly. "Who are you, by the way?"

"Marcella Whittaker, your personal assistant."

"Good morning, Marcella. Nice to meet you. I'm Son—"

"I know, Captain Sonja MacIntosh. Would the Captain like to take her phone call now?" she teased.

Sonja threw her hands in the air and chuckled at herself for getting so distracted. "Yes, thank you." She quickly punched the blinking red light. "Hello, this is Captain MacIntosh. What can I help you with?"

"Sonja, it's Martin Stoddard."

Sonja felt herself freeze for just a moment. "Uh…Martin. I'm surprised to hear from you. What can I do for you?"

"I'd like to meet up with you and discuss some things."

"What about your wife?" Sonja said flatly. "Have you contacted her?"

A long sigh came through the phone. "No, I haven't, and I'd prefer you didn't mention this call to her, either."

"I don't know if I can do that, Martin. Christie and I have come to an understanding, and for Lydia's sake, I can't risk messing that up," she told him.

"Look, Sonja, all I am asking is for a few minutes of your time. Please."

"Where are you, anyway?" She got out her notepad from a desk drawer. She didn't have a good feeling about Martin or anything he'd have to share with her.

"Highland Park," he admitted.

"Christ, Martin," Sonja grunted, but she realized yelling at him over the phone would be a waste of both their time. "All right, all right. I'll meet you. Where?"

"At my hotel, room 402. Does around five work for you?"

"That should be fine," Sonja agreed, and she jotted down the name and location of Martin's hotel. She thought the whole situation odd and wasn't sure she trusted it. Why hadn't the man actually gone home? But there was no sense in mulling it over until she met with him.

She decided what she needed to round out her morning was a giant dose of caffeine. Remembering the coffeemaker in the reception room, she opened her office door to find a stunning woman sitting at the desk, typing diligently at the keyboard. The woman obviously had some African-American roots, mixed with something else Sonja couldn't quite place. She was older, possibly in her mid-forties, and quite sophisticated with a rare air of confidence. Sonja couldn't help but take in everything about the woman, frozen in her doorway and smiling at the sight.

Without taking her eyes off her work, the woman said, "Coffee's over there," and pointed at the back wall. "Help yourself, since it's the only way you'll get any."

"Thanks." Sonja appreciated the woman's straightforward attitude. After pouring a steaming mug of fresh coffee, she turned her attention back to the woman. "It's nice to see you in person, Marcella. I think I'll enjoy working with you. Would you care to join me for a cup?"

Marcella suddenly turned away from the computer and looked at Sonja for the first time. "Why on earth would I do that?"

"So I can get to know my personal assistant. I can guarantee you know more about me than I could even guess about you," Sonja taunted.

Marcella stopped typing and pointed her finger at Sonja. "Well, that's the nicest offer I've had in the hour I've been here."

"No other offers in an hour? I find that hard to believe."

Marcella winked. "Slow day." Then she turned back to the computer and continued her work.

Sonja returned to her office and tried not to inhale the coffee. Her mind traveled back to Martin's phone call and Christie's state of mind when he'd left suddenly. She didn't understand what he would want in a meeting with her, though. Interrupted by the now familiar buzz on her phone, Sonja jumped at Marcella's voice through the speaker.

"Drinkin' coffee all day or going to answer the call on line one?"

"Drinkin' coffee sounds more appealing," Sonja said, "but I guess I have to get the phone. Thanks." She definitely enjoyed the light-hearted communication with Marcella. It already made her day more bearable. After pressing the appropriate button, she answered, "This is Captain MacIntosh and how may I help you?"

"My, aren't we just the picture of politeness?" The voice on the other end chuckled.

"Hank, you buzzard. I've told you not to call me here!" She laughed as she sat back in her chair. She missed working with him; Hank kept her well-balanced and grounded. Now, she needed it more than ever.

"I couldn't resist you, Captain. Listen, I'm calling because someone is asking for you," Hank said.

"Who?"

"Delgado. You're the only one he'll speak to."

Sonja sighed. "Yeah, all right. Bring him to interrogation and tell him I'll be there at noon. With lunch."

"Okay, you're the boss."

Sonja quickly glanced at her watch. Ten. That gave her some time to finish up some files and make a few phone calls before she left to pick up lunch from the bistro around the corner. After pouring herself yet another cup of coffee, she settled into her comfy chair and dug into her work. The first call she made was to Clayton Hughes, updating him on the case and discussing some options.

When she prepared to step out for lunch, she found herself still thinking of Martin and where their meeting would lead. The world made it clear to her more and more that fate had dealt her a pretty good hand, and chance meetings had brought her positive things before. Take Lydia, for example—Sonja knew she wouldn't be sitting here in this chair if it hadn't been for her chance meeting with that woman.

Chapter Forty-Four

SONJA TOOK DELGADO FOR a roast beef man, so she picked up a couple roast beef and Swiss sandwiches, complete with chips and a big dill pickle from her favorite bistro. She returned to interrogation at noon, stopping briefly to snatch a couple cokes. Hank waited in the colorless, stuffy room with Delgado, who appeared tired but not visibly shaken. Sonja had to admit he had balls, considering he most likely would spend the rest of his life in prison.

"Captain," Delgado acknowledged upon Sonja's arrival. "Smells like roast beef. You go to Gordo's?"

"Good nose." She unpacked their lunch and asked, "How was your night?"

"A moving experience, I must say," he told her with a slight chuckle. Then he took a bite of his sandwich and his eyes grew wide. "Damn, that's good, Captain. Thanks."

"No problem." Sonja couldn't help but flash a tiny smile as she watched the man enjoying his lunch like he'd never had a sandwich before. "What did you want to discuss with me, specifically?"

"I'd thought of something I missed the other day. Dillon seemed to spend a lot of time with some drug dealer friend of his. From what I hear, he was a horrible man. When I remembered having heard about him, I realized it would be out of character for him not to be involved in Blackwell's murder."

"Do you have a name for this guy?" Sonja watched him with guarded eyes as she stood and put her hands in her pockets.

Delgado's face scrunched with concentration. "I think his last name was Parker…somewhere out of Reno. You might ask Derek Meade."

Sonja's eyebrows raised at the mention of the name. "Why Derek?"

"You know, I have to admit to doing my own investigating after Dillon's death. I had a couple of my men sniff around to see what they could find out. Derek had to deal with the repercussions. This dealer guy was probably behind several scams to get a hold of the money Dillon felt he was owed," Antonio stated matter-of-factly as he munched on a pickle.

"What were you trying to find out?"

"I really was looking to find out what happened to Derek. That's when one of my men told me about Parker."

"What about him?" Sonja asked, adding some extra notes on paper.

"He was seen by people hanging around Dillon quite a bit. One of my guys overheard him talking about how he wanted to get his hands on the money owed to him. As greedy as I heard Parker was, I'm sure he took over for Dillon after his death."

Sonja's mind worked overtime to remember Derek's story about his brother. "What does this have to do with Derek Meade?"

Antonio took a long swig from his coke. "Just saying you should ask him about Parker. He might know more."

The new information intrigued her, but Sonja wasn't foolish enough to believe Delgado had given it just to play nice. He fed her only bits and pieces. She knew the game, but she wasn't about to reveal what she knew of Dillon and his voice on the tape. Experience had taught her that less was more. She smirked. Just when she thought she knew all the players in the production, here came another one. Still, it was her job to figure out how it was all connected.

Antonio looked up from his lunch, staring Sonja down and smiling. "You know, Captain, your eyes give you away. I understand your silence and I trust it. All you can do is check it out and see if I'm right."

"I will. Any other tidbits you care to share with me?" Sonja asked, briefly glancing over her notes.

"Not at the moment, Captain," Antonio said, flashing a politely contrite grin. "Thanks for the lunch date." He reached his hand out toward her and Sonja shook it with a steadfast determination. She didn't altogether trust the man, but in an odd way she did have some respect for him. Like everyone else, he too had to live with the choices he'd made in his past.

"It's been interesting, to say the least. Thank you, Antonio. I'll be seeing you soon," Sonja promised. She then motioned to Hank outside the interrogation room; Delgado was ready to go back to the holding cell.

As she walked down the corridor, she glanced at her watch. Almost two. Delgado had been right; she needed to talk to Derek. Making her way back to reception, she smiled at Marcella and entered the sanctuary of her office. Sitting at her desk, she looked up Derek's number in her book and made a phone call.

"H-hello?" The voice sounded out of breath.

"Derek?"

"Yes. Sonja?"

"Yeah. Why are you breathing so hard? Everything okay?" She made her voice sound just a little teasing, but another part of her prepared for something she'd need to worry about and check.

"I'm unpacking in my new house and had to run to get the phone," he said, laughing.

"Oh, you must have found a place then?"

"Actually, yes. It's a great little place. Needed a new start. Don't worry, I'm not going anywhere out of town."

"That's good." Sonja felt a sudden, empathetic sadness for the man. He'd gone back to the house in which his own brother had been murdered, and she was amazed he'd put up with it this long before finding a new home. "Where's your new place?" she asked, almost forgetting why she'd called him in the first place.

"I found a great four-bedroom ranch house a few blocks away."

"That's great. Listen, could you come down to my office? I have some follow-up questions and I need your help," Sonja said.

"Really? I was hoping we'd reached the end to all this mayhem." Derek paused and took a deep breath. "All right. When?"

"As soon as you can. I have an appointment at five, so anytime between now and, let's see… Yeah, now would be best."

Derek laughed into the phone. "Well, at least you're consistent. Let me get cleaned up and I'll be over as soon as I can."

"Great. Thanks, Derek." She hung up and busied herself with rehashing her notes from the discussions with Delgado. Her concentration was short-lived, broken by her cell phone ringing. "Well, hello there, gorgeous."

Lydia's laughter came through the phone. "I guess I should call you more often. How's your day?"

"Better now. Your voice is just the pick-me-up I needed," Sonja replied. "How about you?"

"It's okay. I've made some calls to my answering service and have patients I need to contact. I think it's time to get back to reality," Lydia admitted.

"I think it's a great idea, if you're sure it's the right time. Work is therapeutic, and I think we all could use a little therapy." Sonja herself would be lost without her work; it was in her blood.

"That's for sure. Just wanted to tell you I love you."

"I love you, too, Lydia. I'll see you tonight. I have an appointment late this afternoon." She'd added that quickly, almost as an afterthought. She hated keeping this meeting from Lydia, but she thought it was best not to make Lydia worry over a meeting with Martin until she'd heard what the man had to say.

"All right, babe. I have some errands to run later, too. See you tonight."

As soon as she hung up, Sonja's intercom buzzed. "Haven't you had enough fun for today, Marcella?" she joked.

"Actually, no, I haven't. It takes a lot. You have a visitor. A Mr. Derek Meade."

"Great. Send him in. And Marcella, if you wouldn't mind, Mr. Meade and I shouldn't be disturbed."

"Of course, Captain."

Derek smiled at her as he opened Sonja's office door and poked his head inside. "Hey there, Captain." He closed the door behind him and inspected Sonja's new office. "Wow. This is some setup, here. You deserve it."

"Thanks, Derek." She stood to give him a short hug. "Have a seat," she said, gesturing toward one of the chairs. "You don't mind if I record our conversation, do you?"

"Not unless I need a lawyer," Derek answered. His brow creased in concern.

"Oh, not at all. I just don't want to miss anything." She hoped that would relieve his obvious stress.

"All right, then. Record away," Derek said, settling into the chair.

Sonja rummaged through her drawer and found the recorder and a fresh tape, then placed it in the tiny machine. "Okay, here we go. Could you state your name, please?"

"Derek Meade."

"Okay, Derek. I spoke with Antonio Delgado earlier today, and he mentioned that Dillon, your twin brother, had dealings with someone named Parker. This man may have assisted in William Blackwell's murder," Sonja stated. She hated having to be so coldly professional with Derek; he felt like family to her, but she wanted to cover every square inch of this thing.

"Oh. I didn't even think of that. Frank Parker…that bastard," Derek grumbled, seemingly unconcerned that his outburst would be on the record.

"Can you tell me more about him?" Sonja gently prodded.

"Sure," Derek agreed. "My brother met Frank Parker almost forty years ago in a seedy bar in Milwaukee, I believe. Parker was ten years older than Dillon and was always on the lookout for the next big scam. More than the thrill of stealing from people, Dillon was more interested in the man's drug connections. Always drugs. The news of our parents' death was a topic of conversation for some time in certain circles, and I'm sure Parker already knew who Dillon was when they met. Parker made all manner of promises to him, among them giving him a fancy home and an endless supply of drugs and alcohol to keep him satisfied. In return, Dillon would share his wealth by investing in some of Parker's overseas endeavors.

"I couldn't seem to make Dillon understand that our parents had set things up this way, not me. But I had to respect their wishes. Parker was despicable. He knew what a junkie Dillon was and used it all to his advantage. Dillon was also an incredibly gifted liar, so I have no idea what kind of creative story he concocted to keep Parker on his side. He probably didn't even know half of what the dealer did behind his back."

"What did Parker do?" Sonja stood from behind her desk, walked across the room to the coffee table, and poured Derek a glass of water from the pitcher. Then she returned and handed it to him.

"Thanks." He took a sip and sighed. "Parker played his part well in getting Dillon to entrust everything to him. I tried so many times, in so many ways, to get Dillon the help he needed, including getting him away from Parker. When the man realized smooth talking and flattery wouldn't get him Dillon's money, he jumped right to threats and scare tactics."

"He made a threat on your life?"

"Dillon had told Parker about Delia, who had already been living in the facility upstate for a while. He had also obviously expressed his anger over what he felt was an unjust distribution of our parents' money. Parker must have agreed with my brother, and they attempted to kidnap Delia and hold her for ransom.

"The men Parker had hired for the job were caught on the grounds by the facility's security, and the police got involved. Parker, of course, wasn't smart enough to hire decent criminals, and his men spilled everything. Then Parker and Dillon disappeared for a while.

"I don't know for sure if Parker had anything to do with William's death, but he had a hold on Dillon for a long time. I'm not sure Dillon would have had the determination to pull it off on his own," Derek stated, shaking his head in disbelief.

Sonja held a new respect for Derek, now having had a glimpse into the depth of pain he must have experienced. She pressed the stop button on her recorder. "Thank you, Derek. I admire your strength."

Derek smiled. "I hold that in the highest regard, Sonja. I fear I may have given you more questions than I answered."

"Not at all. Can you remember the last time you or Dillon had any contact with Frank Parker?"

"I don't know. I'm sorry I can't be more helpful. I hadn't even spoken with Dillon for over a year. Our conversations were limited and usually ended in pointless arguments," Derek explained.

They spoke casually for the next few minutes and then Derek left the office. After closing the door behind him, Sonja glanced again at her watch. Four. It was time to leave for her meeting with Martin; if she left now and got through the worst of the traffic, she'd just make it by five. She still felt a little anxious in anticipation of what Martin intended for this meeting, and then an idea struck her.

Stepping out of the door, she sighed and glanced at her assistant. "Marcella, how'd you like to get in some overtime tonight?"

Chapter Forty-Five

"ARE YOU SURE, HONEY?" Christie asked with a frown.

Lydia stared her mother down carefully. "Quite sure. My patients need me and I've let things go long enough. Going back to work will be the best thing. You know, a strong dose of reality."

Thanksgiving had come and gone. It had been a beautiful holiday with Sonja by her side. But now it was time to get on with life. It didn't take Lydia long to notice that her mother's thoughts weren't entirely with their conversation. She touched Christie's hand gently. "Mom, you look far away. What's going on?"

Christie let out a long sigh that seemed to last forever. "It's Martin. I've been calling him for days and he won't answer. Not even on Thanksgiving. I've called the office and they keep telling me he's out of town."

"Maybe he is," Lydia said, attempting to sound reassuring.

"I feel so lost, Lydia. I don't know where to turn. Martin and I have been through so much, and I don't think I could handle life without him."

Lydia reached out to embrace her mother. "Martin would be a fool to live without you, and I don't think he's a fool." After a few moments, she pulled away. "Have you thought about calling this place your home again?"

"I have, but I really don't know what to do. I have to talk to Martin at least once before I make any decision." Christie's voice trailed off into parts unknown.

Lydia gave her arm a squeeze, fully aware of all the torment her mother had had to endure for moments like this. Then she glanced at her watch. "Mom, I have some errands to do, especially if I'm going back to work soon. We can talk about this more at dinner, if you want," Lydia promised, then she kissed her mother's forehead.

Christie smiled. "Okay."

Lydia walked out the front door and made her way to her car. She had to admit, the excitement of going back to work overwhelmed her, especially the notion of reclaiming her real life and leaving the crazy version of the past few months behind. As she drove onto the highway, she mentally went over her list of errands, including stopping at the bank, the office supply store, and paying a few bills. She decided to make the trip to Highland Park, where she could stop by the bank and maybe surprise Sonja between meetings. It was only twenty minutes from Kenilworth to Highland Park, and she loved the drive down Green Bay Road.

It didn't take her very long to get all her errands done, and she knew immediately she was ready to be back in the trenches of other people's problems. Then, as an afterthought, she stopped by her favorite flower shop to pick up a surprise for Sonja.

***

As Sonja drove them to Martin's hotel, Marcella studied her meticulously, then said, "So, tell me about your girlfriend." Sonja's eyes widened and she was sure her mouth would gather dust on the floor mats of her car if she didn't shut it. Marcella could only laugh at her boss's reaction. "Please, how could I not know?"

"Is it that obvious?" Sonja tried to laugh, but it came out as nervous hesitation.

"Oh, don't worry, Captain. What you and I talk about is between us. You'll learn that about me," Marcella reassured her.

"Thanks. It's actually a relief to know I don't have to always sweep certain things under the rug. Her name's Lydia, and she's the best thing that's ever happened to me. Do you believe in fate?"

"Of course. I believe there's a rhyme and reason to life we may never understand. All we can do sometimes is blindly believe that everything will work out the way it's supposed to," Marcella told her, nodding.

Sonja smiled as she pulled into the hotel parking lot. "You're a wise woman, Marcella. Thanks for agreeing to come with me."

"Speaking of which," Marcella asked, "why exactly are we here?"

"I'm not exactly sure how this conversation will go. I asked you here to be a witness, and I thought you'd be able to take some notes for me if it's needed. This meeting is with Martin Stoddard, Lydia's step-father, if one wants to get technical," Sonja explained carefully.

"What are you expecting to happen?" Marcella prodded.

"I'm not sure. Martin called this meeting, but I have some apprehensions about it." Sonja then briefly explained to Marcella as much of the story as she could.

"I see. That's some life you lead, Captain. You and Lydia are lucky to have each other."

"I think so." Sonja took a breath and then glanced at her watch. "It's five now. Room 402, he said. Ready, partner?"

"Let's go." Marcella opened the car door and swung her long legs around to step out. Sonja joined her, and they walked together into the hotel, taking the stairs to the fourth floor.

***

Lydia sat in her car in the hotel parking lot. She had driven down the street on her way back from the florist when she'd seen what looked like Sonja's car. When she caught a glimpse of the license plate, though, she knew. So she'd pulled behind Sonja's car into the parking lot, hoping to be able to surprise her there.

Her heart pounded in her throat when she saw a tall, beautiful older woman step out of the car and into the hotel with Sonja. Lydia shook her head in disbelief. It really couldn't be happening. Her mind told her it had only *looked* like something impossible. Sonja wasn't a cheater. But her heart didn't listen to her mind, and it only kept sinking slowly into a world all its own. She lay her head on the steering wheel and tried to breathe.

***

As they approached room 402, Sonja couldn't imagine what Martin would possibly have to tell her that she didn't already know. But when she knocked on the door, she knew she'd have an answer to at least that question in the next few minutes.

Martin nervously opened the door and stopped, his dark eyes traveling carefully back and forth between Sonja and Marcella. "Sonja, hello. I guess I thought you'd come alone. But come in."

"Thank you," Sonja said. Martin offered them seats at the table in the corner, and after Sonja took her place, she took a moment to survey the room. "Martin," she said, gesturing to Marcella, "this is Marcella. She's my personal assistant, and I've asked her to be here as a witness and to take notes, though I'm not quite sure where this meeting is headed."

Martin smiled at Marcella. "Nice to meet you." He then turned to Sonja. "I understand completely."

"What did you want to talk about?" she asked. If Martin was, in fact, wanting to talk about his relationship with Christie, Sonja knew she may have gone a bit overboard bringing Marcella along. But the Police Captain side of her didn't want to risk anything.

"I have some information," Martin said carefully.

"Let's hear it, then," Sonja said, nodding to Marcella to begin taking notes.

"To be honest, I never left town. Everything had me a little rattled, and Christie had only recently revealed *some* of her past to me. She wouldn't come home with me, so I decided to do some more research on Brenton Pritchard and my wife's past. I have since discovered her connections to Dillon and Derek Meade and William Blackwell. And most importantly, Frank Parker."

"You know Frank Parker?" Sonja couldn't believe the name had come up three times now in the same day.

"Yes," Martin confessed. "We have a history. But, more to the point, Christie has a history with him. It's not a pleasant one."

"You definitely have my attention, Martin. Go on," Sonja stated, baffled by the ever-changing direction of this saga.

"I can only imagine how rough life had been for Christie when she left Chicago all those years ago. I never really knew anything of the life she appeared to have escaped. I worked on the Reno police force back in those days," he said, his eyes glazed over as he traveled back in time. "I was a detective with the vice squad. That was when I met Christie. I caught her working the streets and rounded her up with a few of the other girls to take into the precinct."

Sonja scratched her head in disbelief. She wondered how Lydia would react to that news.

"I know. When I had Christie in custody, she told me her pimp's name was Frank Parker. I spoke with her a lot, and she told me she feared for her life and had been trying to plan a way to get out from under Frank's control and leave the entire lifestyle." Martin shuddered.

"Did she tell you how she'd started that work?" Sonja asked, cautious of her words.

"She'd only told me at the time that she felt she had no other choice. Maybe she'd left even worse things behind, and I think it was what she thought to be her only option in a new city, with no friends and nowhere to go. I'm sure some part of it just came from complete despair. It wasn't until recently that I learned exactly what she'd left behind," Martin said, hanging his head and staring at the floor.

"That's how you met Christie?" Sonja asked.

"Yes," Martin continued. "I spent a lot of time speaking with her when she was in holding. Something clicked, then, just getting to know her, and I knew she'd only taken up that profession because she didn't have any other choice. Frank Parker had stopped by once to try to see her, but she refused visitation. As far as I know, he never came back, and the fact that she wanted nothing more to do with him convinced me enough that she did really want to turn her life around. We kept her there for a few days until the judge gave her a suspended sentence for her first-time offense. Then she was free to go.

"I had no desire to see her go back to the cruelty of the life she'd led for over a year, so I offered to let her stay with me. It was against my better judgement as an officer, but I couldn't help the way I felt for her. Thank God she took me up on my offer, and the rest is history.

"Having found Frank Parker's name come up again in relation to all this recent chaos in Chicago, though, worried me more than I can say. I had to tell you."

Sonja closed her eyes and slowly shook her head. She hadn't thought it possible to be surprised by anything else today. "I'm glad it worked out that way. Any idea how the man got to Chicago?"

"Not really, but Parker has been in and out of jail for years. Nothing seemed to stick for long, somehow, but I assume he felt the need to move his dirty business somewhere else after a while," Martin reported.

"Interesting." Sonja rubbed a hand down her cheek. "God, I don't know how to tell Lydia about this part of her mother's—"

The door to Martin's room must have not been latched completely closed, because it burst open. "Maybe now's a good time to tell her. Everything."

Chapter Forty-Six

"LYDIA, I—DID YOU follow me?" Sonja stuttered, standing abruptly.

"I wasn't following you, Sonja. I found you by accident. That seems to be the only way you ever tell me anything!" Lydia shouted.

Martin stepped between them in an attempt to calm her. "Lydia, Sonja's done nothing wrong. I promise."

Lydia shot Martin an angry look. "Martin, after what you did to my mother, I really don't care to hear anything you have to say." She then took a deep breath and glared at Sonja.

Sonja cleared her throat. "Marcella, Martin, would you mind leaving us alone for a minute?"

Marcella smiled nervously and glanced at Martin. He nodded, then led Marcella out of the room. "How about some coffee down in the lobby?" he asked, closing the door behind them.

Upon hearing the door close, Sonja glanced at Lydia with uneasy apprehension. "Why didn't you call me? You had to have seen Marcella and I walk in if you knew where we were. What did you think was going on?" It never occurred to her that anyone, let alone Lydia would think she'd cheated. The thought of it made her heart sink to the floor. Ever since Wyoming, she'd worked so hard to do the right thing, and now, she'd hurt Lydia one more time.

"I don't know what I think about anything anymore…especially you," Lydia answered, fists clenched, her face radiating anger.

Sonja felt a stabbing at her heart. "What on earth does that mean?"

"It means that when you do things behind my back, it makes me distrust you all over again."

Sonja's immediate reaction was to defend herself, but then the anger hit her even harder. "You're jumping to conclusions without knowing anything."

"Then make me understand," Lydia demanded, looking her square in the eye.

"No," Sonja said flatly, though inside she was fuming. She was so tired—tired of explaining herself, tired of trying to prove her worth to the woman she loved. No more.

"No?" Lydia scoffed. "What do you mean, no?"

"No. Lydia, I don't know what it is you think I've done, but really, it doesn't matter. If you trusted me and how much I love you, you wouldn't be here now accusing me of God knows what. I understand where that mistrust comes from, honey, I do. You've been lied to your whole life, and I know I've made my own mistakes, but I refuse to let you thrust the anger of your entire past on me. I love you like I've loved no one else in my life and I've spent my time trying to earn your trust back, but if you never let me, there's no point to this anymore." Sonja forced herself to hold back the tears as she stepped past Lydia and walked out the door.

***

Dumbfounded, Lydia sat on the edge of the bed, placed her head in her hands, and wept like she'd wanted to when she first saw Sonja step into the motel with another woman. So involved in her own misery, she didn't hear Martin come back into his room.

"Lydia?" Slowly, he sat down on the bed next to her and put his arm around her.

She let Martin console her, realizing she'd spoken harsh words to him just a moment before but too much in pain to let that push him away. After pulling herself together, she finally broke away from his embrace, and Martin stood to bring her some tissues. He gently and briefly wiped her face. Lydia gave a weak smile. "Thank you, Martin."

"Sure," he acknowledged.

"Martin, I…" She wanted to apologize, but she couldn't even look him in the eye. She wanted to be as mad at him as she'd been a few moments before, but the misery of how Sonja had left their argument overshadowed her anger.

Martin patted her thigh. "Shh. Never mind that, now. I want you to listen to me, and you can be mad later, okay?" Lydia nodded.

Martin slowly rose from the bed and walked to the dresser, where he started a fresh pot of coffee. "I made it stronger than usual," he said. "Come sit with me." He took a chair at the table on the other side of the room, and Lydia joined him while he poured them both steaming mugs of coffee. "The first thing I want you to know," he continued, "is that Sonja didn't have anything to do with setting up this meeting. I'm the one who called her. I had some information no one else knew, and I felt Sonja was the only person I could trust with it. So please don't blame her. Marcella is her new assistant from the office, and she was only here to take notes."

"I see," Lydia acknowledged, then quietly took a sip of her coffee. Sonja's words pierced her memory like a bad dream. She couldn't understand how Sonja could really have walked out on her, but she was sure that hadn't been the end. Lydia shook it from her mind and focused her attention once again on the man sitting across from her. "This has to do with my mother, doesn't it?"

"Yes, it does. I want to tell you these things even though I know your mother should be the one to do it."

"Why hasn't she told me herself?" Lydia asked, realizing there was so much more to her mother's life than even the incredible things she'd already discovered in so little time.

"I'm sure she never wanted to relive that part of her life ever again," Martin told her solemnly.

"I need to know, Martin. Please tell me. It won't make me think less of my mother. I love her, and nothing will change that. I've spent too long without her."

"Okay," Martin said as he took a deep breath. Slowly, methodically, he shared the rather shortened version of the story he'd just finished telling Sonja. "That was twenty-seven years ago. I have to tell you, I love that woman more today than I ever have. Just knowing the hell she went through before I even met her is staggering."

Lydia placed her hands over her face, closing her eyes to everything. After a few moments of silence, she asked, "Why did you leave her, then?"

"When I left, I was so sure of the answer to that question."

"But now?"

"Now, I don't know why I ever left," he said. "I think I wanted her to choose."

Lydia watched him closely. His face was sullen and looked like he hadn't slept in days. She could see the struggle he endured just telling her about her mother. "Between her husband and her daughter," Lydia stated, appreciating Martin's honesty more than ever.

"Yes. Now, of course, I realize how incredibly unfair that was, especially after everything we've been through."

His words hit her hard, and Lydia gasped for air. "Oh, God. What have I done?"

Hearing the shrill sound of Sonja's voice in her head over and over, she felt like she was breaking in half. Since Wyoming, Lydia had kept her guard up, and she still wouldn't let the woman in—truly let her in. She'd gone through the motions, but she'd never actually given Sonja the chance to get any closer. As the tears fell, she realized everything Sonja had said was the truth. "Sonja will never forgive me this time."

"I wouldn't say that," Martin said with a calm, concerned smile. "You may just have to try harder, that's all."

"Maybe," Lydia said in a raspy, tear-soaked whisper, and she stared at her mug of coffee. "What's next for you?"

"To go find my wife and tell her how much I love her. Tell her that I don't want to be anywhere she's not," Martin said. Lydia stared at him, locked in his gaze, and the visible glint in his eye told her there was more. She raised her brows at him, urging him to continue. "I've been offered a transfer. I need to tell my wife we're moving to Chicago." His eyes lit up, sparkling as he clapped his hands together one, showing his excitement for the opportunity.

Lydia raised her mug in the air and Martin did the same. They clinked their mugs together. "Cheers," she said. "I think it's wonderful." She tried to smile, though her face felt tight and the background thoughts of Sonja made her stomach drop.

"Everyone deserves a new beginning," he said, pulling her in for a hug. When he drew back, he grabbed Lydia's hand and added, "Even if it's more than one."

Chapter Forty-Seven

MARTIN AND LYDIA DROVE their own cars up the long, winding driveway to the house, and Christie, Jackson, and Rosita came through the front door. Christie wasn't sure whether to move toward her husband and hug him or turn and run in the opposite direction.

Once Lydia got out of the car, she stepped up close for a tight embrace and whispered, "It's okay, mom. He's here for you." She motioned for Rosita and Jackson to follow her back inside.

Tears filled Christie's eyes. "I don't under—"

Martin silenced her with a kiss. "I am so sorry I left like that, honey. You deserve better than that from me." His voice was soft as he leaned in closer. "I love you, Christie. I really do. And if you'll have me back, I'll always be by your side, no matter where that happens to be."

Christie pulled away from her husband to study his shining eyes. "What are you trying to say?"

"I'm saying I love you, Christie Stoddard, and since you've given me the best twenty-six years of my life, let's spend the next twenty-six right here. What do you think?" he asked, looking deep into her eyes as if locked in their trance forever.

"What do I think? What do I think?" Christie exclaimed. "Martin, I love you, too!"

He held her close for another long-overdue kiss, then linked her arm in his and walked inside the mansion with her, finally able to tell his wife about his transfer and moving plans. They joined Lydia in the parlor, who sat watching the fire Jackson had started just an hour before. She seemed completely lost in thought and didn't acknowledge having heard them come inside to join her.

Christie walked up behind her daughter and gently touched her shoulder. Lydia jumped. "Sorry to startle you," Christie said. "I wanted to make sure you're all right. You seem so far away."

Lydia's eyes flooded with tears as she turned toward her mother and fell into her arms. "I think I really messed things up this time."

Christie held her daughter even tighter and gently stroked her hair. "I'm sure it just seems that way right now. Why don't you tell me what happened?"

"It's Sonja. She walked right out of my life, and I don't know if she'll ever come back. The worst part is that she had every right to leave. Maybe she's better off without me. If we'd never met, she'd be in a different place altogether. Most likely a lot saner, too," Lydia said through muddled tears.

"She'd be miserable," a voice called from across the room.

"Derek," Lydia said, smiling as she looked up to see him enter.

He walked toward them and grabbed a tissue from the coffee table to wipe at Lydia's cheeks. "What's with the tears?" he asked.

"I don't know what to do," Lydia said. "I feel like my whole world is crumbling beneath me, and I've got no one to blame but myself. I'm a therapist, for God's sake. Shouldn't I know better?"

Derek wrapped her in a warm hug. "It's always different when it's you, my dear. Things will work out when they're meant to." After a moment's pause, his eyes lit up and he grabbed Lydia's hand in his own. "I just received a call from New York."

"About Delia?" Lydia guessed.

"Correct. Since I'm on the board of directors there, they call me whenever a staff member leaves or is hired. It's mostly administrative personnel. They've hired a new director for the facility, and she wants to meet with me to go over plans for the next fiscal year, bounce ideas off me, yadda, yadda, yadda. The thought occurred to me that you could really use a break from all this drama. I would love for you to meet Delia. Would you like to come with me?" Derek stared Lydia down until her eyes met his.

"I would love to, really, but I'm not sure now is the right time."

"Nonsense. An hour ago wouldn't have been the right time, but now is perfect. You said yourself you're at a crossroads. Sometimes, getting away from the source for even a little while can help bring the two roads together."

"Okay then, I guess. I don't know that I'll be very good company," Lydia said with a shrug.

"Thanks for the warning. It'll be good for you, you'll see. Plus, we can get to know each other better."

Christie stepped up to Lydia and took her hand. "Derek's right. It's a good idea." Derek looked up at Christie and locked his eyes on hers. Christie found herself more grateful than ever that this man was still in her life, even after acknowledging all the violent circumstances which had brought them together.

Lydia threw up her hands. "I guess that settles it, then," she said. The hesitation in her voice was obvious, but it was tinged with excitement and the possibility of something different.

"Is tonight too soon?" Derek asked.

"Not at all. Now that we've decided, I'm anxious to go," Lydia said.

Derek smiled and kissed his daughter on the cheek. "I'm going to arrange the flight. I'll be right back." Then he stepped out of the room, almost seeming to skip through the doorway.

"His excitement is so cute to watch," Christie observed. It was especially warming to see Derek so excited about the trip after everything he'd lost—first William, then Dillon, and not being able to say his goodbyes to either one had to have been devastating. She often thought about William herself, and it made her happy to know he'd found love, after all.

"I'm going to go pack my things," Lydia said.

"It'll be good, you'll see," Christie told her with a nod.

Lydia kissed her mother on the cheek. "I hope so." She then left the warm, spacious parlor and ventured up the spiral staircase toward her room.

Christie let the smile fade from her face as she watched Lydia walk up the stairs. So many unsettling events had taken place since she'd made this trip with her daughter, and she only hoped there could be a way to balance them out soon.

"Hi, Miss Cassandra."

"Oh! You scared me, Rosie," Christie said, turning on the couch and placing a hand over her heart.

"Sorry about that. I learned a long time ago how to be quiet. Sometimes it looks like I'm sneaking up on people, but I'm really just spying." Rosita's eyes sparkled, but Christie found herself biting her lip instead of smiling in response. "What's going on, dear?"

"Lydia's taking a trip to New York with Derek to meet his sister," Christie reported, hearing the flattened tone in her own voice. She stood and walked to the fireplace, enjoying the warmth.

Rosita followed her. "No, I mean what's going on with *you*?" she repeated. "You seem a little down to me." The woman grabbed a poker, removed the cage, and stoked the fire.

Christie let out a frustrated sigh. "Oh, I don't know. Things *appear* to be working out here."

Rosita returned all the tools to their proper place, years of practice having formed the habit. "But?"

"But why do I always feel like the other shoe's going to drop?" Christie folded her arms and stared into the orange and blue flames.

"Because, dear Cassandra, it always does. You've spent so many years running, always fearing the past. You have your husband, your daughter, and this glorious place to live. Enjoy life. No more running. We're not getting any younger, now, are we?"

Christie turned from the fire and studied Rosita's face. "You're right. Everything could have turned out much differently. I can't tell you how grateful I am that Lydia's car broke down on the highway that day. It's turned my life around in ways I could have never imagined."

"Lydia has that effect on people," Rosita replied. "I told you, it's a good job to have." She looked at Christie, then added, "Don't squander it." Then she turned and left the room just as quietly as she'd appeared.

Before Christie had a chance to reflect further on Rosita's advice, Lydia came downstairs and set her bags outside the parlor. "Well, I think I'm ready to go. It's just for a few days, anyway."

Christie walked toward her daughter, opening her arms to embrace her. "You two just make sure you have a good time. Enjoy it. Let yourself relax, and you can work things out when you return. Time will take care of everything."

Lydia pulled back and looked at her mother. "That sounds like something Rosita would say."

Christie tilted her head back and laughed more freely than she had in a long time. "She definitely makes you listen to her."

"Yes, she does. I'm so glad you're here." Lydia gave her one last, quick hug. "Well, here we go."

"Where's Derek?" Christie asked.

"Right here," he said, popping his head around the corner. "We're off and running. Don't worry, I'll bring our girl back home safely, ready to take on the world again." He stepped around the corner to give Christie's hands a brief squeeze. "No worries."

"Yeah." She walked them to the front door and watched them load their luggage. "Be safe, you two," she called and waved them goodbye as they drove off in Derek's car.

She went back inside and went straight to the small bar against the wall to mix herself a drink. Only then did she notice that Martin had left without saying a word, and this time she thanked his subtlety in giving her a bit more time alone with her daughter. They'd needed it.

She set her drink down and stepped out into the hallway, looking for Martin to come join her. Instead, she found a figure from much further back in her past.

"Jesus."

Chapter Forty-Eight

"WELL, I'LL BE DAMNED. If it ain't little miss thing! What the hell. Looks like it's my lucky day, after all." Frank Parker pushed Christie back into the parlor and closed the door behind him.

"Frank," was all Christie could muster.

"That's good, sweetheart. All these years and your memory's still pretty good."

"My memory is just fine, unfortunately. Why are you here?"

"That's no way to be, woman," Frank said, stepping forward to stand just inches away from her. "Here." He pushed her to the sofa with a sneer. "Have a seat and we'll chat, just like old times."

"Any old times we've had I've erased from my memory," Christie said, glaring at him.

"Your sarcasm shocks me. Though I have to say I'm surprised to find you here, you'll do just as well to help me get what's mine." Christie had all but forgotten the vicious grin spreading across his face.

"I don't have anything of yours."

"Ah, not so fast, my sweet. You may not have it yourself, but it seems you know the man who can get me the money Dillon Meade promised me," Frank informed her. "I was actually looking for Derek, and now I'm here, looking at you, sweetheart. Why on earth did they let you through the front door?"

"I live here now. Derek and I had a child together."

Frank looked around the massive room, running his bony, dirty fingers across the end tables as he explored. "My, oh my, what a nice setup you've got, sugar. Very nice."

Christie felt her blood pressure rise the longer she sat on the sofa. "Again, Frank. What the hell do you want with Derek?"

"We got some business to discuss regarding his brother."

"You mean Dillon? How in the world do you know Dillon?" Christie leaned toward the edge of the sofa, watching him, and her fingers tapped nervously on her thigh.

Frank eyed the mini bar at the other end of the room. "Well, let me tell you a story, sugar." He found a glass and some bourbon, pouring himself a distastefully large amount. After the first sip, he said, "Oh, that's beautiful. Dillon Meade. Yeah, we knew each other real well. I met the man in Woodstock—Illinois, that is. We were cellmates there. I'd moved from that shithole, Reno, you know, finding myself on the wrong end of a business deal. And Dillon and I were buddies. He promised me some money, and I intend to get it."

"You know Dillon's dead, right?" Christie folded her arms, thinking the statement sounded harsh, but her disgust with the man trumped any remorse.

"Yeah, the poor slob. I guess he got himself tangled up in some shit. But that's not my deal. Just looking for Derek. I went to the old house and saw a sold sign in the front yard. But Dillon had told me about his brother and William Blackwell. So, I figured I'd look here, too."

"Isn't that brilliant? Except for Derek's not here," Christie spat. She despised this man and she wasn't afraid to show him the door.

Frank sat close to her on the couch—too close. He reached behind his back and pulled out his silver pistol. "I guess you can be of some use to me, finally. He'll give me what I want. I'll wait right here."

Chapter Forty-Nine

AS SONJA STARTED THE car with Marcella in the passenger seat, she wondered what she'd done, and more specifically what it meant. She still wasn't sure how she could go on living a life without Lydia, but the woman's last words ate at her soul. For once, it felt like something she couldn't fix.

"Are you sure you're all right?"

"No," Sonja said, pulling out of the parking lot.

"No, you're not sure? Or no, you're not all right?"

"Both, I think," Sonja said. "Wanna stop for a drink? It's time to be off the clock now, anyway."

"Sure. Looks like you could use one," Marcella said. "And a friend."

"You're right on both accounts."

She drove them to a lounge she enjoyed called JoJo's. It was off the beaten path but not far from the Police Station. The place had soft lighting with small, round tables, dark red table clothes, and candles in round crystal holders. The chairs were made of dark brown leather and swiveled comfortably. A fire crackled in the fireplace in the center of the room. It was quiet and relaxing, and that was something Sonja badly needed.

She was glad Marcella had come with her. Of course, the woman had been right; she did need a drink and a friendly ear. She also needed to push thoughts of Lydia out of her mind, though she wasn't so sure that was exactly what she wanted.

Marcella followed her to a corner table by the back wall. "This place ain't bad," she said. "I've been here a few times." When the waitress came around, she ordered a whiskey sour, and Sonja asked for her usual rum and coke. The drinks arrived a few moments later and, after the stress of the day, nothing else could have soothed the ache in Sonja's heart. "Good," Marcella said, nodding. "Now, tell me what happened."

A smile came to Sonja's lips for an instant. "I'm having a battle between my heart and my head. It's murderous."

"I know it is. You've told me about your relationship with Lydia. Tell me more," Marcella prodded.

"Basically, I just walked out on my life today. Ever since what happened in Wyoming, all I can think about is earning back her trust. That means everything to me. I still feel completely terrible about it, and I've never loved anyone in my life as much as I love Lydia. She's been through so much, and our entire relationship is the product of her chaotic life and my role in it. But she walked into that hotel room and just assumed I'd done something wrong. She thought I'd kept something from her, or...God knows what. I lost it. I thought in that moment that there was no chance of ever making up that trust. Especially if she never gives me a chance. I told her that if she actually believed in what we had together, she wouldn't ask me any questions." Sonja took several more sips of her drink and finally let it all sink in for the first time.

Marcella listened intently and sipped her drink. She nodded and motioned for Sonja to continue.

"So then I walked out, and I still haven't figured out what to do." She picked up her glass and swirled the drink around with her straw, feeling more lost than she had in years.

"I think you did what you had to do," Marcella said. "Sometimes, you have to take a hard stand to make someone you love see what they can't on their own."

"Maybe. If it's such a noble thing to do, how come I feel so shitty?" A tiny voice told her Marcella was right, and she knew it, but it didn't make her feel any better. She couldn't help but wonder what

Lydia would do if the tables were turned.

Almost like she read Sonja's thoughts, Marcella patted her hand. "She'll be back. People don't share what you two have shared and then just walk away. If she does, she's foolish. That much I *can* tell you."

Sonja shook her head. "Lydia's not foolish. She's been through too much, and really, even attempting a relationship in all this drama is beyond crazy. I just couldn't help myself." Sonja gave a half-hearted shrug, followed by a deep sigh. "Dammit, it's hard leaving things up to someone else!"

"Here, here," Marcella said as she raised her glass to Sonja's. "I'll drink to that." Then she glanced at her watch. "Wow, it's almost eight. I have to get home to catch a phone call from my grandkids. I can't miss that. Do you mind driving me back to my car?"

"Not at all."

They talked shop on the way back to the station, and when Sonja pulled up next to Marcella's car, she paused for a moment in the silence. "Marcella, I can't thank you enough for tonight. You helped clear my head. It's good to have a friend. Thank you."

"Of course. Hey, I may need you one of these days in return," Marcella said with a wink.

Sonja gave her the thumbs up. "That's a deal. You've got some lucky grandkids."

With a wave goodbye, Marcella hollered, "I'll tell them you said so!"

Sonja waved back and felt herself relaxing even through the tension of her body. Being a cop didn't give her the opportunity to have too many female acquaintances, and she appreciated Marcella as both an assistant and a friend. Lost in thought for a moment, the familiar ring of her cell phone caught her by surprise. "Yeah. MacIntosh here. Who's this?"

"Sonja? It's Rosita." The woman's voice came across in a frightened whisper.

"Rosita? What's going on?" Sonja asked, suddenly worried.

"There's trouble here. I don't know what it is, but I feel it,"

Rosita whispered.

"Rosie, don't be so damn cryptic. Just tell me. Is Lydia okay?"

"She's not here. She took off with Mr. Derek to New York. They just left for the airport."

"New York? Wha—never mind." Sonja squeezed the bridge of her nose. "What's going on at the house?"

"It's Miss Cassandra. She's inside the parlor with some man that's not Mr. Martin." The woman's normal resolve had fallen to an unusual tremble in her voice.

"Where's Martin? I thought he'd gone back to the house."

"He did, but then he told me he was leaving to get a surprise for Miss Cassandra and would be back in about an hour. This man came to the door asking for Derek, and I explained he wasn't here. I left to grab a pen and paper so he could leave a message, but when I got back he was gone. But I heard him talking to Miss Cassandra in the parlor. I have a really bad feeling about it. Miss Cassandra sounds angry." A hushed sigh came through the phone. "I know you had a disagreement with Lydia, but please come right away."

"I'll be right there," Sonja said, then hung up and threw her phone down on the passenger seat. She started her engine and left the precinct parking lot, then grabbed her phone again, calling the person she thought could help the most. "Michael? I need you. Blackwell Estates, please. I'll fill you in then!"

Chapter Fifty

BUCKLING HER SEATBELT ON the plane and preparing for the flight next to Derek, Lydia smiled at him. "I'm glad you overpowered my weak defenses to make me come with you." She already felt her some of her tension relax a little, and maybe, after all, this would be a good time to learn more about the father she'd never known.

Derek looked at her with mock pity. "You poor, poor thing. Who knew I could overpower anyone?" He made some adjustments to his seatbelt. "I'm glad, too. By the way, I happened to get us adjoining rooms. It'll be late by the time we get in, so we could order up some room service and call it a night, if you'd like."

"That sounds wonderful. I think this will be fun, and if Delia is anything like you, I know I'll love her. All these years, I thought I didn't have much family at all. Now look at me."

"Darling, you always had family," Derek said. "You just didn't know who they were yet."

They happened to get a direct flight right into White Plains, which was unusual but fortunate. The flight was so short, neither of them realized it when the plane prepared to land. They had chatted away the entire two hours without a moment's thought. If Lydia had ever doubted the fact that this man sitting next to her was her father, that doubt had now vanished. They connected far more easily than she'd anticipated.

Though she loved William Blackwell for the man he was and for raising her, she had never been able to confide in him or even sit and talk with him for hours about nothing and everything. It was easy to see why William Blackwell had been so in love with Derek Meade.

After collecting their luggage from baggage claim, they retrieved their rental car and drove to the hotel just a few miles away from the facility where Delia lived. Years before, Lydia had visited White Plains during a psychiatric convention, but had since forgotten how much she'd enjoyed the city. "It's beautiful here, Derek. Thank you for the invitation. I think this is just what I needed."

"Good. I had a feeling now was a good time for both of us," he told her.

Lydia smiled and studied his profile as he drove. "Your feeling was right."

Derek turned briefly to wink at her, and she caught the shimmer of dampness in the corner of his eye.

It was close to midnight by the time they checked into their hotel rooms and got settled. The rooms were clean and Derek had obviously spared no expense on Lydia's behalf.

An arrangement of brightly colored lilies decorated her room, astonishing her and rendering her almost speechless. "You couldn't have known ahead of time that I would actually agree to come with you."

"Amazing what one can do with a phone call, isn't it?" Derek held out his arms for a hug, and Lydia didn't hesitate to embrace him. "I want you to remember this trip with me for the rest of your life, Lydia. You've made an old man very happy."

"And who would that be? I don't see an old man here." She pulled away slowly, hoping to lighten the mood. She felt really good about this trip, and the uneasiness was melting away.

"Are you hungry?" he asked.

"I am, actually," Lydia admitted. "Won't the kitchen be closed this late?"

Derek held up his index finger. "One can never tell. We got flowers, didn't we?" He dialed room service and discovered the kitchen was, in fact, still open for late-night food. "What's your pleasure, darling?"

"How about a Chef's salad, French dressing on the side, heavy on the croutons?" She hadn't realized just how hungry she was.

"Diet coke, I suppose?" Derek suggested, fluttering his eyelashes.

"Of course." Watching Derek talk and move about, taking in his personality, amused her. In some ways, this man was the polar opposite of William, and Lydia couldn't help wanting to learn more about him.

"Anything else, crouton girl?" Derek joked.

"That'll do it." She stuck her tongue out at him.

Derek tried not to laugh into the phone as he ordered a cheeseburger, fries, and a diet coke for himself. "I ought to take you away more often. You make me laugh." Then he nodded to himself. "Yes. I think I *will* take you away more often."

"I love that idea," Lydia replied. "I can't tell you how much I needed this. Things seem to come along at just the right time, and for just the right reason."

"So true. Sometimes you don't even know what the reason is and, more often than not, it doesn't matter in the least."

They sat at the table in Derek's room and ate their late dinner, continuing their conversations from the plane ride with the same ease. "Do you think you'll ever fall in love again?" Lydia asked.

He seemed stunned by the question. "I don't know. William was the greatest part of my life for so many years. I'm not sure where I even would begin, honestly. On the other hand, you never know where love is going to hit you. Or when."

"That's true. When you're in love, you always think its forever..." Lydia hadn't quite realized she'd voiced the thought aloud.

"True love *is* forever, my dear," Derek said. Lydia looked up to meet his gaze, realizing he knew exactly what she was talking about. "It's a part of your heart you just can't recapture in quite the same way. As for Sonja, I know she loves you, and I think that, for her, that's the largest undertaking ever. Even harder than loving someone is trusting them. Especially for you, my girl. You've spent your whole life not knowing who the hell you are or whom to trust. You may think Sonja isn't trustworthy, but let me tell you, she's put her life and her career on the line *because* she loves you.

"What happened in Wyoming was all about Joel. You have to understand that. He was a powerful man, just like his father. That kind of power isn't easily overcome, if at all. Just remember how much that woman loves you." He watched her for a few seconds, then reached over the table and dabbed the tears on her cheek with his napkin. "Now eat, will you? You're watering down your diet coke."

Lydia laughed through her tears and tore into her salad again. When they finished their meal, she hugged him tightly before telling him goodnight and heading off to her room.

The next morning, the sun shone brightly through the windows, assisting Lydia in the task of opening her eyes. A smile spread across her face when she recalled where she was and how relaxed she felt for the first time in months. She turned in bed to glance at the clock. Eight-fifteen.

As she sat up on the edge of the bed, she heard a gentle tap at the door from Derek's side. "Yes?"

"I have breakfast in here, if you're ready," he called through the wall.

Lydia threw on her robe and opened the door. "Coffee?"

"I made that myself. And I ordered fresh croissants and juice, too."

Lydia laughed. "Excellent. You sure know how to treat a girl. Are you sure you're gay?"

"That's *why* I'm gay, my dear." Derek laughed so much, he could barely stop.

It didn't take them long to finish their breakfast and coffee before they prepared for the day. They each were showered and ready to go by nine-thirty. Derek's appointment with the new director was scheduled for ten.

After a ten-minute drive to the facility, past rolling hills and beautiful scenery, they arrived at the home resembling a Georgia plantation, complete with tall white pillars and a gorgeous brick foundation.

"Wow, Derek. This is spectacular. I never imagined a building like this." Lydia gasped as she examined the gigantic structure.

"It's not well-known, and I'm actually grateful for that. Delia seems quite happy here," he said as they stepped out of the car. "Shall we?"

"Certainly." Lydia smiled as she walked with Derek through the giant, solid-oak front door with the brass-colored handle.

Walking down the marble hallway, Lydia was stunned by how pristinely the staff maintained the building. Pristine, yet it looked like a comfortable home in which anyone might live. Derek explained the activities available for the residents, such as the bowling alley, pool and ping-pong tables, and an Olympic-sized swimming pool for both leisure and therapeutic swimming. Derek said he loved the facility especially because Delia and her peers went out into town every now and then to spend time among the community.

Lydia knew most special facilities were nothing like this one, and Delia was absolutely fortunate to be able to afford it. She followed Derek through the building and had to smile when so many of the residents shook his hand and called him by name. High fives and hugs were passed all around as they made their way toward Delia's room. She found herself feeling nervous about making a good impression with her newfound aunt.

They stopped outside the door to Delia's room and Derek turned to fix Lydia with a warm gaze. "She'll love you as much as I do, I promise." He gave her hand a squeeze, knocked softly on the door, then walked inside.

Delia sat in a rocking chair, watching television, and she turned to see who had entered. Her eyes lit up and she jumped to her feet. *"Derek!"* she shouted, running toward him and jumping into his arms. "You here now!" She clapped her hands together vigorously, shouting, "Yay! Derek is here!"

Lydia smiled and felt a foreign warmth spreading through her heart upon seeing something so simple. Delia showed nothing but pure joy in seeing her brother.

Derek gently touched his sister's shoulder. "It's okay, Delia. Let's be calm now and have a good visit. Remember what we talked about?"

Delia dropped her head, as though ashamed of her behavior. "I sorry, Derek. Better now."

"It's all right, sweetheart. I'm not upset with you at all. I want you to meet someone very special." He turned toward Lydia. "Delia, this is Lydia, your niece. Remember, we talked about Lydia the last time I was here?"

Delia shook her head. Then, hit by a sudden revelation, her eyes grew wide. *"Lydia!* Yes! Yes, Delia 'members. Lydie, Derek's baby, right?"

"That's right, Delia. I'm so proud of you for remembering," he said, patting her hand.

After watching their exchange, Lydia was even more nervous as to what she should say. "Hello, Delia. It's wonderful to meet you. I know we'll be great fri—" Delia grabbed Lydia and hugged her tight, cutting off Lydia's nervous introduction. She laughed in surprise and returned the hug.

Derek watched them with a huge grin, then glanced at his watch. "Delia, I have to go meet your new boss," he said. "We'll come back to see you afterward."

"Lydie stay with me, Derek? Please?" Delia begged, jumping up and down.

"What do you think?" he asked Lydia.

She glanced at Delia, who looked about to explode with excitement. "I'd love to stay here with you, Delia."

"That's great, if you're sure," Derek said.

"Shoo, Derek!" Delia shouted. "I want to be with Lydie!" She swatted her hand at him like he was a fly.

"See?" Lydia said, holding out both hands. "What can I say?" She shrugged, beaming.

"Okay, okay. I'm going."

***

Derek laughed as he closed the door behind him and left the girls to themselves. He knew they'd be just fine. As he walked briskly down the hallway and through the twists and turns leading to the Director's office, he thought of their last director. He'd been sad to see her go, but apparently she'd gotten a better offer out-of-state. Derek could only hope this new one was just as good.

"Hello, Mr. Meade." Sarah, the receptionist, greeted him when he stepped into the office. "Good to see you again."

"Good morning, Sarah. Good to see you, too." Sarah Jenkins was probably in her mid-thirties, not much younger than Lydia, slender, petite, with long, flowing blonde hair and blue eyes. "How's the hubby and kids?"

"Just great, thanks. Charlie just got promoted. Matthew and Jenny are doing very well at their new school. I bet Delia was excited to see you," Sarah stated, shuffling some papers on her desk.

"I'm sure you heard her screaming. I brought my daughter Lydia with me to meet her, and it turned out better than expected," Derek offered.

"How wonderful. I'll announce you, if you're ready," Sarah said.

"Ready as I'll ever be. Go ahead and buzz me," he joked.

Sarah pressed the intercom button on her phone. "Ms. McAllister, Mr. Derek Meade is here for his appointment. Shall I send him in?"

"Sure, Sarah. Thanks."

Sarah smiled and started to rise from her chair, but Derek held up his hand to stop her. "No need for that, Sarah. I know the way." He winked as he slipped past her and slowly opened the door.

Lillyann McAllister rose from behind her desk to greet him. She was tall, her blonde hair pulled back from her face. "Hello, Mr. Meade. It's a pleasure to meet you," she said, extending her hand.

"My pleasure."

The woman gestured to the leather chair in front of her desk.

"Please, have a seat. Thanks for traveling all the way from Chicago to meet with me."

"That's not a problem. I was due for a vacation, believe me."

They discussed the plans for the fiscal year and talked about the building itself and ongoing repairs they needed. After twenty minutes listening to problems with the building and talking about Delia's continual care, Derek stopped the conversation. "If I may interrupt, I've just made a decision about something that's been on my mind for some time. You've given me the justification I needed."

"Oh, really?" Lillyann's eyelashes fluttered as though he'd really caught her off guard, and then she chuckled. "I'm glad I could help. Can I ask what decision that is, if it's not too personal to share?"

Derek folded his hands in in his lap, shaking his head briefly while watching her reaction. "It's purely financial. I have some money sitting around, just collecting dust. It's my brother's inheritance, but, sadly, he passed away recently. I've been in charge of it for quite some time, and I had no idea what to do with it until just this conversation." The director regarded him with wide eyes, and he leaned forward ever so slightly. "I'd like to donate the remainder of that money to this facility. Use it for whatever you need here, and I will continue to contribute for Delia's care. It's the perfect solution for all of us."

Chapter Fifty-One

ON THE OPPOSITE SIDE of the house, donning binoculars, Michael Pritchard and Sonja staked out the parlor room from across the patio. The window into the parlor was small but gave all the view they needed. Sonja filled Michael in on everything since the warehouse and Lydia's kidnapping. There wasn't much he didn't know, as it turned out; he had followed the case diligently, thrilled now that Frank Parker had been stupid enough to show himself at the Blackwell Estates—or anywhere, for that matter.

They carefully plotted out the plan to move in on Parker, but it had to be synchronized in just the right way to ensure Christie's safety. Michael had called for backup, and they'd just arrived, remaining out of sight for the time being. Once Michael and Sonja agreed on the details, they entered the house through the patio door and made their way through the kitchen as gingerly as possible.

Creeping down the hall toward the parlor room, they heard voices on the other side of the door. "Dammit. It sounds like Rosita's in there, now," Sonja whispered. Frank's voice escalated, then Christie screamed.

Sonja nodded at Michael and they burst the door wide open to find Frank Parker towering over Christie. He jumped at the noise and whirled to face them. Sonja's eyes flickered sideways to catch Rosita standing around the corner, a silver serving tray of cookies in her hands. The instant their eyes met, Rosita hurled the tray at Parker, cookies flying everywhere, and it hit him on the side of the head.

"What the—" Frank shouted, ducking too late and scrambling to get a better grip on his gun.

"Chicago Police!" Sonja yelled. She and Michael had their weapons trained on the man. "Drop the weapon and put your hands behind your head, Parker." She hoped he would, having never wanted to put her training to use when it came to bullets.

Parker cocked his pistol and pointed it at Christie's head. "I don't think so!"

"Drop it!" Sonja ordered, tightening her grip.

"*No!*" Parker yelled. He only took a second for himself before pivoting to bring the gun in Sonja's direction.

She took the shot. A red stain bloomed on his chest and he fell to the wood floor. The only sound was the ringing of the silver tray as Parker's limp arm shoved it toward the wall.

Sonja caught her breath, then remembered what she was doing there. She rushed to Christie, who now sat on the floor in front of the fireplace, obviously in shock. "Christie?" She snapped her fingers in front of Christie's face. "Christie, answer me. Do you know where you are?"

The woman blinked rapidly a few times. "Yes. Blackwell Estates. I'm fine, Sonja."

She helped Christie up from the floor, and the woman immediately threw her arms around her and sobbed into her shoulder. "Thank you!"

Sonja tightened her embrace of the trembling woman. "No thanks necessary. I'm just glad Rosita called me."

After kicking away Parker's pistol and kneeling by the body, Michael radioed the backup team outside and instructed them to call an ambulance and the medical examiner. Sonja sat Christie down on the couch and asked her to explain what happened.

Christie wrapped her arms around herself and swallowed. "Frank wanted the money he said Dillon Meade had promised him. He came here looking for Derek, but he found me instead."

The paramedics and medical examiner came through just as Martin rushed into the parlor. He stopped, dropped the bouquet of flowers in his hand, and put the bottle of champagne on the table. "What the hell?" he uttered, then caught sight of Frank Parker's body being removed on a stretcher. He ran to Christie and grabbed her for a tight embrace. "God, I could have lost you. Again," he cried.

Christie kissed her husband several times. "But you didn't. Sonja got here in time, and I can't ever begin to repay her. I've never been so scared in my life." She gasped in relief, clutching his shirt. "When will it just be over, Marty?"

Martin stroked his wife's hair and dried the tears from her face. "I don't know, love. I don't know."

Chapter Fifty-Two

DELIA BROKE THE SILENCE in the hallways when she caught sight of Derek standing just outside her room. *"Derek!"*

"Hey there, sweetness. How was your visit with Lydia?" he asked, throwing a wink Lydia's way.

"It was *great*! I love Lydie! Can she come back, Derek?" Delia shot up from her chair next to Lydia, jumping up and down. When Lydia rose from her seat by the television, Delia grabbed her hands and held them, bringing them into her chest. "I love her! *Please, Derek!*"

"Well, Lydia, looks like you're trapped." Derek grinned, throwing his hands in the air.

Lydia squeezed Delia's hands. "Good. I'd love to come back and visit you, Delia. Thank you for such a wonderful time." She gave the woman one last, tight hug before heading towards the door. They definitely had a great time, watching television and talking about Delia's favorite movie characters, books, and her most favorite foods. Lydia had felt surprisingly at ease with the woman. She was so full of life and so instantly accepting of her new niece. There were no judgments of Lydia for haven't existed in Delia's life for thirty-eight years, just a genuine love for who she was.

"We'll see you soon, Delia. I promise. I'll be back in just a few weeks," Derek said, hugging his sister and gently tucking her hair back behind her ears. "I love you, Delie girl."

"Love you, Derek boy, and Lydie, *too*." Delia waved goodbye from her room as they traveled down the corridor.

"She's wonderful," Lydia said. "What a beautiful spirit."

"She is. She lives a great life here, and it does my heart a lot of good to see her so happy," Derek said. He took Lydia's hand and linked her arm in his as they made their way out of the building.

"Let's go get some lunch, and I'll tell you all about my meeting," Derek suggested. He started the car and they pulled out of the parking lot.

Derek wanted to go to the Italian eatery, which served a great buffet lunch. A waiter seated them in a quiet booth with a great view, and they made their way to the buffet. Everything in the quaint restaurant definitely looked like something straight out of Italy. The smell of garlic permeated the air, and old tables with checkerboard tablecloths and waxy, drippy candles made it seem like the real thing. As the Italian music played softly through the ceiling speakers, they both found themselves trying out the vegetable lasagna with cheesy garlic toast and salad. When they returned from piling the food on their plates, the wine had been poured and sat waiting for them at their table.

"Ah, wonderful," Derek said, then took a long sip of the burgundy wine. "Excellent."

After sipping the wine, Lydia nodded. "Definitely."

Derek tipped his glass for another gulp of wine, then took a deep breath. "You know, I was just thinking of William and how he loved New York. We used to make these trips together to see Delia. He adored her."

"I miss him so much," Lydia said, swirling the wine in her glass. "I'm sure he loved this place." She couldn't think of William without also thinking of the chaos which followed his death. "Do you think he was proud of me?"

"I know he was," Derek replied. "He told me many times, and I always saw it in his eyes. William adored you so." He reached out and touched Lydia's hand.

"I'm glad. He had his faults, like anyone, but I'm grateful for him." She lifted her glass in the air and she said, "To William." Derek raised his glass, echoed the toast, and tapped it against hers.

Laughter came easily as they chatted for another hour, eating their food and even sharing a dessert. After the decadent slice of Tiramisu, Derek told her about his decision with his brother's inheritance. Then he took her on a tour of the city, all the places he'd seen which always gave him that sense of tranquility when he looked for it. They even managed to squeeze in an afternoon matinee and a trip to the mall. The scenery was breathtaking, and Lydia enjoyed the town, and her company, more than she'd anticipated.

Chapter Fifty-Three

WHEN THEY RETURNED TO the hotel and stepped into Derek's room, a light flashed on the phone by the bed. He listened to the message for a few moments, then yelled, *"Oh my God!"*

"What is it?" Lydia asked.

"It's your mother. She's okay, but apparently there was some confrontation with Frank Parker. *Damnit*!"

"What?" Lydia shouted. "Who left the message?"

"Michael Pritchard. Everything's fine, I guess." Derek shook his head. Just as he sat on the edge of the bed to ponder the news, his cell phone rang. He glanced at his watch. It was after midnight and he wondered who would be calling. "Hello?"

"Derek? It's Christie. Sorry for calling you so late, but I need to talk to you."

"Honey, are you okay? Michael left me this message about Frank," Derek said.

"Yeah, I'm fine. It's a long story, and I *will* tell you, but I just thought you should know that Frank was here looking for you."

"Of course he was," Derek said, not shocked at all. He'd almost expected the man to show up sooner after Dillon's death. "He wanted money, I'm sure."

"Yes. You aren't surprised, are you?" Christie asked.

"Not at all, but his timing is a bit ironic, to say the least. I just donated the rest of Dillon's inheritance to the facility where my sister lives. Obviously, Frank had tried to take over where Dillon left off, and I'm so tired of that old game. I'm just glad you're okay. Lydia and I will be back home tomorrow, and we can talk more then, okay?" When Christie agreed, they said goodnight and Derek put the phone down. He really didn't want to hear any more about Frank Parker. Michael had said the man was dead, and Derek was relieved. Enough was enough.

***

Lydia wished Derek goodnight, then stepped through the adjoining door and closed it behind her. She took a long, deep breath, wondering how it all could have happened so quickly—these revelations of her life. And there was still someone missing. God, she could think only about the one person who'd given her stability and love like she'd never known before. Sonja never left Lydia's mind, let alone her heart. She had to give in, and she reached for her cell phone nestled in her purse.

She didn't even care that it was one-thirty in the morning; she dialed Sonja's cell phone anyway. No answer. Thoughts filled Lydia's mind—thoughts of the dinners, the times at Allie's Coffeehouse, and, most of all, lying in Sonja's arms, safe from the world outside. Sonja had done that for her. She'd saved her life over and over again. Now, though, she seemed far too out of reach.

Sonja always answered her cell phone. Maybe it was truly over. Lydia placed the phone on the bedside table and threw herself on the queen-sized bed. She hadn't expected to, but she cried herself to sleep anyways.

***

"Lydia!"

The knock on the door seemed so loud, but Lydia didn't answer. She sat in the chair at the table, just staring out the sliding glass door to the balcony, and she didn't move when Derek opened the door. She wore the same clothes as the day before, her hair a mess, and she sat with her feet on the chair, hugging her knees to her chest.

Derek approached her and, touching her knee slightly, said, "Sweetie, what's the matter?"

Lydia saw Derek kneeling in front of her. She didn't say a word, just watched him.

"My dear, you've slept in your clothes and you have bags under your eyes. It's Sonja, isn't it?"

As soon as Lydia heard the name, her bouts of weeping started all over again, and she could barely speak. Derek reached out and held her as she cried. "Baby girl, it'll all work out. When we get back to Chicago today, you'll have the chance to find her and tell her what you need to tell her."

Finally, Lydia looked up and broke away from Derek's embrace. "What if she doesn't listen? What happens if she's gone for good?"

"Then it wasn't meant to be, darling. True, your life will never be the same, but it will go on. For the sake of your heart, you have to try to show her what's inside. Make her see how much you love her. If she doesn't see it, then she's not the woman I thought she was." He looked her up and down, then nodded once. "Come on, let's get you in the shower so we can get back home."

Lydia rubbed her eyes and rose from her chair to finally take a shower. She watched Derek carefully. "Derek?" she asked.

"Yes?"

"Thank you for this trip. You knew I needed it. Getting to know you is the best thing. I love what I see." She had a hard time denying the fact that Derek had a part of her. She hadn't remembered feeling so good about anyone before.

His eyes sparkled as he reached out and embraced her. "I love you, too."

Lydia emerged from her room a new woman. Derek grinned. "That's much better. Are you ready?"

Lydia nodded. "Let's go home." They grabbed their respective bags and left the hotel room. Derek had checked out a few minutes earlier, so they walked to the car, chatting and watching the strangers who crossed their path along the way. Lydia was reminded of when she'd traveled home that day with Christie. How could it all be true? Still, it felt right no matter how crazy it seemed. No matter what issues arose with Sonja when she returned, she had a complete family. For Lydia, that could be enough.

Chapter Fifty-Four

CHRISTY AWOKE EARLY AND witnessed the sun come up from her room. She looked over at Martin, still sleeping peacefully. She wanted to be angry with him for leaving and then again for spilling everything about her past to Sonja and Lydia. She'd wanted to keep that from people…especially Lydia. What would her daughter think of her now? She shook it from her mind, choosing to believe there was nothing that could make Lydia turn from her now.

So involved in the sunrise, she didn't hear Martin slip out of bed and come up behind her. She jumped a mile high when he wrapped his arms around her waist. "Hey...hey, it's only me. Your loving husband," he whispered.

Christie turned around and took his face in her hands. "Yes, you definitely are, my love."

Martin beamed at her. "You don't have any idea just how much I love you, do you?"

She gave him a soft kiss. "I'm not supposed to know. That's why you have to keep on telling me."

"Ah, so that's how it works! Well then, I plan to tell you several times a day for the rest of our lives. How's that?" Martin tenderly brought his lips to his wife's neck.

"I guess that'll do." She wrapped her arms tightly around him. "Now I know why I've kept you around for twenty-six years."

"I'm great under the sheets?" Martin whispered in her ear and nuzzled his face in her neck.

"Well, of course there's that," she replied, softly giggling at him, her head falling back as he trailed kisses down her neck. "You always know how to make me feel better. I love you, Mr. Stoddard." She brought her lips back to his again. "Now, about those sheets…" Raising her eyebrows and fluttering her lashes, she led her husband, the one truly good man she'd ever loved, back to the bed.

About two hours later, as Christie and Martin dressed after enjoying each other to the fullest extent, they heard Rosita's voice through the intercom. "Hey, you two, are you ever getting out of bed? Breakfast is cold."

Martin laughed and said, "Life here will be interesting, I have to say that."

"Be down in a minute, Rosie," Christie called back through the intercom system. Then she glanced at the clock on the wall; it was almost ten. "Won't be long now," she commented.

"Nope, not long now. It'll be fine, you'll see. I'm starving since you made me work so hard." Martin grinned sheepishly, obviously enjoying every minute with his wife.

"You didn't seem to mind, mister." She jabbed him playfully in the ribs. "But Rosita mentioned breakfast, and now I'm starving. Shall we?" she asked, grabbing Martin's hand leading him out of the room.

"But of course." He seemed only too eager for Rosita's famous breakfast.

Rosita met then in the dining room, where she'd decided to serve breakfast that morning. "It's family-style this morning," Rosita reported. "Welcome to the family!"

Christie watched the woman who, just the night before, had shown so much courage and resolve in the face of danger. "Why don't you and Jackson join us?" she asked.

"We ate early, but we'd love to join you for some coffee and chitchat. How's that?" Rosita offered.

"Perfect," Martin agreed.

Rosita left them to eat the biscuits and sausage gravy, hash browns, and fresh fruit. Within ten minutes, she and Jackson joined them with a pot of fresh coffee. The morning conversation was entertaining, and they allowed it to take its own course as it turned to the events of the previous evening and what had happened with Sonja and Lydia.

"Rosie, you seem to know everything around here. What do you think happened between them?" Christie asked.

Rosita let a small sip of coffee pass her lips. "I really don't know, other than Lydia's particularly distressed over it. I'm sure it'll work out however it's meant to be."

"True." Christie then remembered her conversation with Derek the night before. "You know there wouldn't have been money for Frank, anyway."

Rosita looked up from her mug of coffee. "Really?"

Christie nodded. "Derek told me last night that he'd just donated the rest of Dillon's share to their sister's facility." She stared at the biscuit crumbs on her plate for a moment. "I wonder what would have happened if Derek had been here."

Rosita stood to refill everyone's mug, including her own. "Miss Cassandra, you only invite trouble by searching for answers to the unknown."

Christie took a long drink of her coffee after taking her last bite of food. "I guess you're right."

The foursome continued their chat, which gave Rosita and Jackson the chance to get to know Martin a little better. The only thing to disrupt them at the table an hour later was the sound of Lydia's voice coming from the foyer. "Hello? Anyone here? Rosita?"

Rosita called back, "Dining room." For the first time, she didn't race to greet anyone at the door.

Christie stood and beamed from ear to ear at seeing Lydia again. Just the sight of her made her heart beat faster with love and almost unbearable pride. So much had happened to bring Cassandra Lexington Blackwell Stoddard here, and she knew, as she took Lydia in her arms, that she wouldn't squander the chance again.

THE PURSE

Chapter Fifty-Five

AS THE HOMECOMING SUBSIDED and Lydia's family wanted to hear about her short trip to New York, Lydia found she couldn't focus. She could only think of Sonja; she had to find her and tell her—tell her all she knew, all she learned about herself and the world around her.

She excused herself from the table, went upstairs to her room, and attempted to phone Sonja one more time. Still no answer. She even called the office and spoke to Marcella.

"No, dear," Marcella answered softly. "She took a leave of absence for a couple days. Personal reasons, she said."

"Did she say where she was going?" Lydia asked.

"No. I'm sorry, hon. She didn't. She could be at home, for all I know."

"Thanks, Marcella." For some reason, Lydia had the feeling that Marcella would know, of all people, but it occurred to her that the woman may have felt a professional obligation not to give anything away. She hung up the phone, feeling defeated and guilty.

Finally, she pulled herself together and resolved to take the initiative. She had to know—to at least try. Grabbing her purse and keys, she walked down the spiral staircase in a flash and popped into the dining room to tell her family she'd be back later. No one made any objection, and Lydia chose to ignore the few looks shot across the table.

As soon as she was safe inside her car, it suddenly occurred to her what Marcella had meant on the phone. She had a hunch the woman had actually told her Sonja was home. Frantically, she drove down the long, winding driveway of the Blackwell Estates and made the drive through town at a dangerous pace toward Highland Park. Twenty minutes later, she sat in her car in front of the building she knew only too well.

She glanced up to the second floor and felt her heart pounding to see the light on in the bedroom window. She'd memorized that window of the apartment building months ago, and she knew Sonja was home. Lydia nodded to herself, shrugged her shoulders, and figured that this was the last chance she'd get. She stepped out of her car, her heart racing faster than she had driven, and walked into the apartment building.

When she made her way up the stairs, she stood in front of Sonja's door and thought her legs might give way beneath her. Taking a deep breath, she knocked.

"Who is it?" came Sonja's voice. Lydia didn't say a word. Then the door opened abruptly. "I said—oh."

"Sonja—" Lydia got only that out of her mouth before the door shut in her face. A hot flush crept up her face and she felt nauseous. She could hardly take a breath to say anything else.

"Go away and leave me alone."

Sonja's voice was muffled through the door, and Lydia clenched her fists. "No. I can't do that. I love you." She waited, forcing the tears to stay. "Please."

"I'm done, Lydia." Sonja's voice cracked. "I am through saving you from yourself. You need to go. Let me live my life without you."

Lydia stared at the door, not knowing what she was going to say until it came out. "I don't want you to save me anymore," she said quietly. In that moment, she knew it was true, and she knew Sonja could still hear her. "It's my turn. Let me be the one you run to. Let me be the one who keeps you safe. Let me be the one in charge of your heart. You've had mine since the day we met. Let me in, Sonja."

Only silence met her on the other side of the door. Lydia sighed, closed her eyes, then said, "You might as well, because I'm staying in your hallway until you open this door and talk to me. I can't do this without you."

Lydia counted the seconds, and then she heard the latch turn. The door opened slowly, and her stomach turned over when she saw Sonja's face streaked with tears. They stood there staring at each other, and without a word, Sonja reached out, grabbed Lydia's arm, and pulled her inside. Wrapping her arms around Lydia's waist, she looked deep into her hazel eyes, smiled, and kicked the door shut

.

Rambunctious Ramblings Publishing Inc.
Norristown, Pennsylvania 19401, USA

www.ramrampublishing.com
ramrampublishing.tumblr.com
www.facebook.com/RamPubInc
twitter.com/RamPubInc

About The Author

Born in Marshalltown, Iowa, Julie Burns spent many of the in-between years of her life in that state. Then she lived in Wyoming for six years and fell in love with mountains. Her other identity is working with mentally challenged and/or mentally ill adults.

"I seem to fit in well!" Julie says. "I spend time with people who call me mom, Nana, and 'hey, you chick."

Contact Julie and learn more about her work at:

Facebook: www.facebook.com/JulieABurnsAuthor
Twitter: twitter.com/jadegally48

If you loved this book, don't forget to leave a review for The Purse on Amazon and Goodreads. Thank you!

Made in the USA
Middletown, DE
06 June 2016